DEVON LIB

Please return/renew this
Renew on tel. 0345
www.devonlibr

GU00838412

Prizm Books

Aisling: Book I Guardian by Carole Cummings
Aisling: Book II Dream by Carole Cummings
Aisling: Book III Beloved Son by Carole Cummings
Changing Jamie by Dakota Chase
City/Country by Nicky Gray
Climbing the Date Palm by Shira Glassman
Comfort Me by Louis Flint Ceci
Devilwood Lane by Lucia Moreno Velo
Don't Ask by Laura Hughes
The Dybbuk's Mirror by Alisse Lee Goldenberg
Echo by Amanda Clay
Foxhart by A.R. Jarvis
Heart Sense by KL Richardsson
Heart Song by KL Richardsson
I Kiss Girls by Gina Harris
Love of the Hunter by V.L. Locey
Josef Jaeger by Jere' M. Fishback
Just for Kicks by Racheal Renwick
The Next Competitor by K. P. Kincaid
Repeating History: The Eye of Ra by Dakota Chase
The Second Mango by Shira Glassman
A Strange Place in Time by Alyx J. Shaw
The Strings of the Violin by Alisse Lee Goldenberg
The Eye of Ra by Dakota Chase
Lunaside by J.L. Douglas
Tiffany and the Tiger's Eye by Foxglove Lee
Tyler Buckspan by Jere' M. Fishback
Under the Willow by Kari Jo Spear
Vampirism and You! by Missouri Dalton
The Water Seekers by Michelle Rode
Eagle Peak by Elizabeth Fontaine

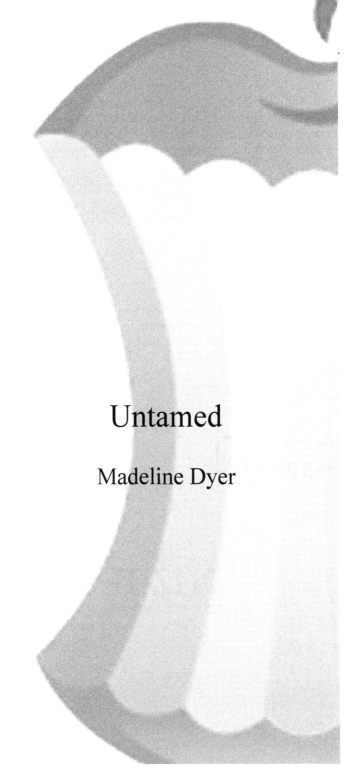

Untamed

Madeline Dyer

Prizm Press Publishers an Imprint of Torquere Press LLC
P.O. Box 37, Waldo, AR 71770.
Untamed Copyright 2015 Madeline Dyer
Cover illustration by BSClay
Published with permission
ISBN: 978-1-61040-917-9
PRINT ISBN: 978-1-61040-918-6
www.prizmbooks.com

prizm
there's room under the rainbow
www.prizmbooks.com

DEDICATION

For Mum, Dad, and Sam

UNTAMED
Book One in the Untamed Series
by Madeline Dyer

Chapter One

"Your mother's gone."

The leader grunts at me, then places his fuel can in the shade of the boulder, next to mine. He turns to where his nephew is shrugging the emergency packs onto the dry ground, and both men pant hard. Dust rises up.

I frown and my ears crackle. My legs feel too soft, insubstantial. My mother's gone?

Corin Eriksen—the leader's nephew—peels off his button-up shirt revealing a threadbare T-shirt. I watch him tie the damp material around his thick waist.

"You listenin' to me?" Rahn, the scrawnier of the two men, pushes his dark glasses back up his nose, and jabs a gnarled finger at me. He always wears those glasses. Well, he's got several pairs actually, different styles, but he always has to wear some sort of eye protection because he has weak retinas or something. The rest of us just wear our sunglasses when we're raiding. Mine are now folded over the neckline of my shirt. Corin's aren't visible, probably in his pocket.

I look at the two of them for a few seconds, then frown. Covered in beads of sweat, their hair hangs in sweaty clumps over their foreheads. Rahn's finger remains where it is—inches from my nose. It looks like the old tree root I tripped over earlier.

"She's gone, Seven," Rahn says. He withdraws his finger, and places his hands over his knees, leaning forward, still panting. "She ain't comin' back."

Gone…

I shake my head, and turn away. The city of New Kimearo

is down there in the distance, rising out of the sand. I fix my gaze on the stone buildings. Blocks. Dark masses. It's flatter down there: a sort of valley in the southern part of the Titian Mountains.

"Seven, did you hear me?"

My stomach rumbles loudly. I grab my survival bag from the desert ground and empty the contents at my feet. A compass, three squashed energy bars, a map, a pack of water purification tablets, some toilet bags, two boxes of waterproof matches and a wind-up torch. My foil jacket isn't there. I curse. I always keep it in my leather rucksack. Numbly, I pick up one of the bars, peel back the dry paper and take a bite of cardboard-tasting nothingness.

"Look at that." Rahn nods his head toward me, then turns to Corin.

"Eating is a method of distraction." Corin rubs at his nose, where the skin's crimson and flaking off.

"Or maybe she ain't that bothered, maybe she's goin' to choose them too. Like mother, like daughter."

My spine clicks. I glare at them and the remaining half of the bar drops from my hand. I focus on the tiny specs of sand coating it as it rolls down the slope, stopping at the boulder that shades the fuel cans.

Gone....

"This... this is your fault." The words are out of my mouth before I can stop them. "This—you did this. You hate us, you always have..." I clench my fists and stand up straighter. I'm the same height as Rahn. "I know you did it. This is your fault."

The muscles in Rahn's neck flinch twice, and his head snaps toward me. The sun glints off his dark glasses. "How—"

"Finn's driving the truck around the long path." Corin's voice is neutral as he pulls a water bottle from his pack. He's a few feet behind Rahn, still shielded from the town by the rock. "He shouldn't be long. We need to be ready to move fast."

Rahn nods twice, then turns back to me. "Seven, Katya's a lost cause. We had nothin' to do with her choosin' them, because that's what she did."

I stare at him, my eyes feel heavy. My mother wouldn't choose them. I know she wouldn't. Rahn's lying. They were getting food, Rahn, Corin and my mother. Now they've left her behind. They think it's some kind of joke, pretending she's chosen them. But she wouldn't, she'd never join the Enhanced. None of us would.

Nausea washes over me. My fingers burn with ice.

I look back down at New Kimearo, three miles away. The southern part of the town is there, those buildings... I can see them, there. Smaller ones, and bigger ones. Dark gray stone. Electricity wires stretch from one block to another.

My mother's down there. I breathe evenly through my nose. It wouldn't take me long to reach her. I'm the fastest runner we have—a long line of good genetics made me this way—and Corin and Rahn wouldn't be able to stop me from getting her. If I left my pack here and—

"She's with them, Sev." Corin's voice is lower, quieter. "She *chose* to join them. You can't go after her. We can't get her back—"

"We always try! No matter who it is—"

"Not when they choose it." Rahn's hands fly up in the air, as if tiny strings have jerked them up. He looks like one of those puppets from the shows Kayden and Faya performed when I was young. "There's no hope. Even if we go after her, she'd fight us. If we have to fight the Enhanced *and* Katya, to get her back, we have no chance at all. And you know it." His smile is triumphant.

I shake my head. Electrcity snaps through the left side of my body. We can't leave her. If it was me down there, I know my mother wouldn't give up. She always promised that if I got caught she'd rescue me before the Enhanced converted and replaced me with their artificiality. She promised it to all of us. My brother and my sister promised it too. Our whole group *always* promises. So why are Rahn and Corin saying this?

"Lookin' at it from a practical way, it could've been worse." Rahn brushes his hands on his shorts now, leaving behind huge smeary orange marks. "Someone else could've switched. At least she's not a big loss. She wasn't a great Seer anyway."

I gulp hard, tears blurring my vision. *Not a big loss?* I want to scream at him, shout at him, hit him—this is my *mother* we're talking about! And I know my mother—she wouldn't have given up. All her life, she's been drilling into me how bad the Enhanced Ones are. She would not join the people who ambushed our villages and forced everyone to convert themselves into pathetic excuses of humanity. Kidnapping children, forcing augmenters down their throats—stuffing them with so many artificial feelings that they no longer know who they are, only that they're with the 'good' people now. *No.* I shake my head. My mother wouldn't join them! She wouldn't join the people who killed her oldest child. The people who make us live like this, in fear, as they hunt us down, pretending what they're doing is for the greater good.

My mother would never volunatarily become an Enhanced. She raised me, and my siblings, to hate the Enhanced. I grew up attacking Enhanced bases, trying to save the freshly converted with her. It never worked—the addiction to the Enhanced Ones' life, and their augmenters, is too strong; a person can never go back to how they were before. But it was the attempt to save everyone, that proved who my mother was. She never gave up.

"Sev." Corin steps around Rahn, and looks down at me. I feel a jerk of something through my body, like a scalpel's running along my veins. Corin's eyes are dark and warm, like chocolate—the only part of him that isn't burnt and angry and raw. "It was what she chose." He shrugs, and the bands of muscle around his thick neck ripple. "We'll wait for Finn. Then we'll get back to Nbutai."

Behind him, Rahn nods, then sits down in the shade of the boulders, folding himself into a rangy knot of arms and legs. I stare at him. I don't understand. He shouldn't be sitting down. He's our leader; he should be making plans, discussing tactics of how we're going to rescue my mother.

Biting back tears, I melt against the edge of the huge boulder. I slide down, the clamminess of my skin pressing into the jagged surface, skin abrading, until I can feel the fine sand sticking to my legs. I sniff loudly, the tang of fuel tainting the air.

I'll cry later. Not in front of *them*. The traitors.

I glare at the side of Rahn's head. He's facing the grainy surface of the rock in front of us now, his huge nose jutting out in front of him from beneath his wrap-around sunglasses. His nose is massive. I narrow my eyes, until all I can see is that monstrous construction protruding out from under his sunglasses. I could easily hit that beak-like target if he were the mark during gun practice.

I watch as he flexes his fingers. They're resting on his knees now. I grit my teeth. He set her up, he must have. Any of them could have—Rahn, Corin or Finn.

"It'll be for the best." Rahn makes a sort of cackling noise under his breath. "You'll see." He turns toward me. The bright light flashes from his glasses and I flinch. "After all, what's the good of havin' a Seer who can't even warn us 'bout stuff?"

What's the point in having a prejudiced leader? I narrow my eyes at him, tasting bile at the back of my throat.

My fists burn as I watch the two men. I want to jump up, slam my fist into Rahn's face. But I can't. I know better than to attack our leader.

I wipe at my face angrily, but Corin notices.

"Save your tears for someone worth crying over."

My face burns—I can feel the color rushing to it like the heat of a fire pressing against tender skin. "But she didn't choose them!"

"She did," Rahn says. "You weren't there. Walked straight toward them, she did. No hesitation." He sighs heavily; I know he's lying. "We tried to stop her, but she was determined."

My knees sink even deeper into the hard ground. I clench my fingers tightly, dragging them across the rough stone. I watch three of my knuckles split open, like the old leather of a roadkill carcass. Redness oozes out.

"She chose them, Sev," Corin snaps at me. He sits down with a sigh, his legs wide, and his bare, muscular arms rest on his knees.

"She wouldn't."

No. If she's joined the Enhanced, it's because Rahn and Corin and Finn let her be caught. Or maybe they got her killed, and this story's a way of nursing their guilt.

I clench my jaw so tightly my gums throb. I think of my father, back at the village. I try not to think how he's going to react. Or my brother, Three. They'll be angry. Blame themselves. My sister will scream and scream and scream. We need to get back quickly. The sooner we're there, the sooner we can all set off, the whole group of us. We can storm into New Kimearo, we can get her out. I haven't got a chance on my own.

"Where's Finn? He should be here by now. It doesn't take long to fill up from the stone pool. And he's got the truck." Rahn's voice breaks the silence.

He pulls the radio from his pocket and clicks the button. No sound comes from it at all. He glares at me.

"And your brother needs to do better than this." The radio jerks in his hand. "How're we supposed to stay alive if we've got no communications? We need back-up ones too. The radio Finn's got is probably a dud. This ain't good enough, Seven. Tell Three that we ain't got time to play at this."

I look at the ground, refusing to rise to his bait. It isn't my brother's fault—Three had to improvise, making these foxhole radios after Corin smashed the decent ones in a fit of anger a few months ago. It had taken my brother two days to make each of them. I'd seen the blisters on my brother's hands from the coating that the Enhanced treat their copper wire with to stop us from using it, but Rahn didn't care then, and he wouldn't care now.

Corin stretches his arms out. "How long do we wait?"

"Bit longer."

Finn. Tall, lanky. Huge ears. The unsolicited image of him invades my mind. At eighteen—a year older than me—Finn thinks he's a man—that he can boss anyone around. I've hated him ever since he emptied a toilet pot over me when I was six.

Corin takes an unopened pack of cigarettes from the pocket of his khaki shorts, and pulls one out, along with a lighter. It's a new lighter—the fluid almost reaches the top.

I watch him, wrinkling my nostrils as the smoke curls around me. I taste it on the roof of my mouth and behind my front teeth, darkness and ash. It reminds me how useless I'm being. I should be doing something to save my mother, but I'm not. I'm just sitting here.

"Did you get any mouthwash?" I look over at Corin, but my eyes settle on the dusty ground in front of his feet.

Rahn snorts. "We ain't got time to get luxuries. We got to survive."

Corin purses his lips, blowing a thin line of smoke away from him, toward the city. I watch the smoke dissipate.

"Right," Rahn says a few minutes later. He stands up slowly, and I watch as he looks over the top of the rocks, down toward the rugged mountainside and New Kimearo. "We need to get back to Nbutai now—for the Gods' sake, Seven, stop snivellin'. We'll send a search party out for Finn later. Once we're safe."

"What about my mother?"

Corin turns away from me, and Rahn makes a grunting sound. I bite my lip, narrowing my eyes at the two men as I stand. Adrenaline races around my body. Yes. I need to run. I need to get back to the village before Rahn and Corin, and I need to tell our people what really happened back there, before they infect everyone with their malicious lies. Those two have always hated my family, because my mother's a Seer.

"Take the fuel," Corin barks at me, blocking the sun from his eyes with one stocky hand as he gets up.

I gather the small containers and packets from my bag, shove them back into the leather rucksack, then pick up the fuel cans. Rahn adds a shoulder bag to my load. Inside it, glass clinks against glass. I straighten up. I'm tall for my age—my body's a strange build: childlike, not in the least bit curvy, but I'm taller than my sister who's twenty-five. Out of all my siblings, I look the most like our mother. I gulp.

"Seven, you take the long route, past the black rocks— it's safer. Corin and I will go the direct path. We'll meet by Mountain Rock." The usual meeting point, two miles from the village. "Any trouble, you follow the lessons."

I nod. The heat of the sun feels strange on my wet face, like unwelcome fingers caressing my skin. I shudder. It'll be a long run, taking that detour, and the terrain will be mostly uphill. But Rahn's right—it is safer. I frown, instinctively.

"Take this." Rahn hands me a gun.

I stare at him, and my fingers wrap around it slowly. It's a Luger. My lips start to form a word, but Rahn shakes his head.

"We've all got them." His voice is flat.

I tuck it into the back of my waistband. It feels cold against my sweating skin.

"Go now. You'll need a head start."

Timing's important, as always. I scramble backward, turning and lunging over the sand and shingle. The sun leaps in my eyes.

Keep your breathing even. Don't overdo yourself before you're really going.

I speed up, my feet finding a regular rhythm. The fuel cans and shoulder bag are bulky, and the rucksack bruises my spine. Pain grips my shoulders. More tears blur my vision.

I will get you back, Mum. I will.

I punctuate each step, each slamming of the bags on my back, with a word. Over and over. *I. Will. Get. You. Back.* I'll get my brother and sister, my father and a truck. We will not give up.

Ahead, the horizon's rocky, rising above me.

A minute goes past. Two. Five. Ten. Dust kicks up under my feet. A few solitary trees rise above the hollow lava channels ahead of me. I jump over a small pit. Loose gravel and sand. Shards of rock, sharp.

I slow down, my lungs burn. I try to push the straps of the bags higher onto my shoulder with the momentum. Long strands of my hair flap into my eyes. I curse. Have I got time to stop? Sharp breaths. Yes, I can afford a ten second stop. There's a band on my wrist—I can feel it cutting into my skin. Five seconds at the most, that's all it would take.

Turning, I put the fuel cans down and ease the shoulder

bag off. I let out a short sigh. I cough as I tie my hair back, phlegm flying from my mouth onto the dry ground.

There. Five seconds. That allows another stop later on.

I stoop, scooping my fingers under the cans' handles and—

I whirl around as the flash of a mirror captures my eye.

That's when I see them: the figures rising out of the sand.

The people who kidnapped my mother.

Chapter Two

Lesson one: You can never outrun the Enhanced Ones. They are better, faster and stronger than you.

I drop the cans and the bags and I run. I know what the lesson says, but I have to try. I can't not. I force my body onward. They let me stay just ahead of them, for a minute. Two minutes. Five minutes. My legs are giving out, my chest throbs. They could catch me easily if they wanted. No, they're enjoying this: the chase. If they *were* running lean, they'd only need a top-up. It would take three seconds for them to guzzle another chemical augmenter, and get the speed they needed. No, they've got the capability all right— they're playing with me.

My head pounds. Another five minutes, and the heat's making me dizzy. My eyes are blurring. I flick my head around. There are four of them, men and women. Shouts like stone on tin fill the air.

"We won't harm you, poor Untamed creature, we want to help you."

The voice is full of kindness. Kindness I know isn't genuine.

The Luger rubs against my lower back with every bound. Breathing hard, I look ahead. To the right, behind the dunes is our village, out of sight at the moment. Nearer is the stone circle with Mountain Rock in the middle. I look toward it, squinting through streaming eyes to see Rahn or Corin. I look for the glint of sun on dark glasses, but it isn't there. Rahn's not standing against the orange rock. And he's not in the shadows. Am I too early? No. They were going the direct route; they'd get here before me, unless they've been caught.

"We are the Chosen. We command that you stop!"

Lesson two: Don't ever lead the Enhanced Ones toward the village, no matter how scared you are. Sacrifice yourself.

Rahn's words jolt through me. I snake off to the left, weaving between boulders, my lungs burning. Dust kicks up against my bare legs. I squint, trying to catch the outline of another human shape—or help—amongst the rocks. Looking for huddled figures, or the hidden barrel of a gun.

My feet pound the ground. My eyes search frantically. Are any Untamed there? Is there somewhere to hide?

Pain in my lungs. Can't go on for much longer.

There are four of them. Four to one. But I have a gun. They won't have guns. They never have guns or any weapons because they claim that murder—though it happens 'accidentally'—is never their intention. Conversion is.

I drag out the Luger. It feels good in my hand. I look ahead. The jagged darkness of a dead tree looms up, and just beyond is the old well. I skid, then change direction. There are black rocks to the right. The back of my neck smoulders.

Sudden pain—my knee buckles, but I regain my balance. I falter. The tips of their shadows touch me. I start to reach for my sunglasses, but there's no point. They know I'm Untamed.

The Luger raises my other hand up, almost as though the semi-automatic pistol is in control, not me.

"Surrender!" The Luger is slippery in my sweaty hand as I point it at them, flicking the safety off in an instant. I catch the face of the nearest woman—her reflective eyes steal light and fire it back at me. My breath catches, they keep coming at me.

Turn, Seven, run. Run now.

But my legs have gone soft. I look first at one then another. The man, the two women—I twist hard, jerking my neck painfully, but the fourth Enhanced being isn't to my left. Or my right. I step backward, the gun filling me with confidence. Then I turn toward the black rocks and—

I scream as the Enhanced man lunges at me. He gets to

me too soon. They're not running lean, after all. I pull the trigger, but it's a wide shot. The bullet explodes off a rock.

I thrust the gun between us. Its barrel nearly touches his chest. I want to ram it forward, but something stops me. This Enhanced man is young, but most of the Enhanced look young; appearance means nothing. His skin is as dark as mine is, and his eyes are the mirrors characteristic of the Enhanced. His face is deceptively kind. He can appear in any way he wants—or needs.

He smiles, and I see how the skin around his mouth is unbelievably smooth. "You're hungry, poor child. Let us feed you."

My hand shakes. My finger's on the trigger. Just one movement. That's all it would take. It's the only way.

I make eye contact; my stomach hardens. It's not natural looking at a human whose pupils, irises and sclera are all the same metallic surface—distinguished only by a thin line that separates the iris from the sclera. There's no definition for his pupil. I can just about make out my own distorted reflection in the convex mirrors. Nausea rises in me, and I look away.

The others are approaching. Slowly, almost cautiously, they walk up to us. They can see I have good line up, and I know I'm a good shot. I glance around, keeping them in my line of vision. The landscape is barren. Rahn is not here. No Untamed are here. Does that mean...?

"Join us, dear. You are not a person, as you are. We want to save you, make you whole." The female with the blond hair speaks. Her voice is brisk and I see her gaze drop back to my gun. "Don't worry, dear. We will save you from the evil temptation that lies within you, and you'll never have to feel negative emotions again. Lower your weapon."

My fingers tighten around the gun, my grip stronger. My intended victim's breathing is heavy and fast, coming in quick, distinctive bursts. In fact, I'd almost say he was shaking—though, no, he can't be. The Enhanced Ones won't feel fear. It's *me* who's shaking.

"Lower the gun." His voice is low. "You are bad. You need help. Let us save you."

His voice almost sounds genuine. Sincere. Human,

even. But he's not, I know that. All the Untamed know the Enhanced Ones are like robots. They may sound like they're still human, still us, but they're not. They're fake…imposters. *We* have the real emotions. We still feel pain, anger, hurt. We are the real people. Not them. How can they *really* be human when they let their drugs choose which emotions they feel? When part of being human is experiencing the pain, the anger, the loss?

Lesson three: They deserve to die. Each and every one of them.

Another of Rahn's survival lessons echoes in my head. These people took my mother. They won't get away with it. They *won't*.

For a second, I think I can still taste the smoke from Corin's cigarette on the back of my front teeth as I look at the man in front of me. He *does* deserve to die. This is our land. This has always been our land, until they converted our people, tried to take over.

Shoot them now. Whilst you have the chance. Do it!

I bite at my tongue, unable to stop myself from looking straight at the Enhanced man. His face is full of emotion, but it's not real emotion; it's all due to the augmenters. I *know* it is, because they're not real people. Three hundred years ago, the Enhanced Ones weren't like this: three hundred years ago, the first Untamed converted themselves into the Enhanced; they became robotic people. The only augmenters they'd made back then were the ones that gave them speed and strength and stamina. Made them inhuman at the expense of their humanity. But now they can create emotions too—so long as they're positive; the augmenters were created to make people *better*, to eradicate crime, violence and poverty.

Now they use their 'emotions' to their advantage, converting more and more of us into them; my father's told me countless stories about this, where they trick you, tell you you'll still be able to feel everything, and then before you know it, you've lost who you really are.

"We will save you." The Enhanced man's dark hair is styled flawlessly, and not a hair has moved in the pursuit. He's not even sweating; his skin is the smooth surface of a

19

lake, shimmering in the harsh sunlight. He looks perfect, like he's stepped off a catwalk. "You can join us, become a Chosen One too. Let us help you and you need never feel negative emotions again."

I flinch; the Luger also flinches. Its metal burns my fingers, just as the sunlight reflecting from their eyes burns my own.

"Put the gun down." It is the dark-haired female who speaks.

She exchanges glances with the other man, and their eyes bounce light from each other. He is tall, and also has the same coloring as me, but has a scar that falls from his right eye, down to the corner of his mouth in a jagged, fierce red line. I'm surprised he's kept it, the Enhanced rarely do.

My Luger remains where it is.

Then they grab me. They're strong. Of course they'd be strong! Arms snap around my waist and ankles, like bars of steel. I cry out as I fall, trying to turn. Fingers pull my hair, my scalp burns. I hit the ground heavily. My Luger's yanked away as I squeeze the trigger. My bullet hits the kind-eyed man in the foot. His scream is blood curdling, and, momentarily, I feel guilt.

Then I remember who they are. I can't afford to feel guilt. Not with them involved.

I struggle, trying to get free. I can't. The women lean over me, their hands force my back against the dry earth and loose rocks. It feels rough, scratching my skin through the thin cotton of my shirt.

The sun flashes in my eyes. I blink rapidly. One of the women produces a vial of liquid. My skin burns, yet my fingers are shards of ice. My chest hardens. Rushing fills my ears. It's too close. The augmenter is too close.

Lesson four: Never let yourself be Enhanced. Once it's done, there's no going back.

My mouth dries. An addiction to the augmenters, and the Enhanced Ones' lifestyle, is unbreakable. *Everyone* knows that. Oh Gods.

"No, please, no!" I try to roll over, try to escape, but my limbs won't work. They're too heavy, shaking too much. The vial containing the augmenter gets closer and closer. The liquid is as blue as the clear, shimmering sky.

"You have violent intentions. There is no other way," the first man says. His eyes flash, throwing light back at me. I squint, try to blink the sharp stings away. "You have to be saved. The hunger and fear is controlling you. It is not healthy."

"You *must* taste our way of life," the blond female says. "Then you will understand, and you will wonder why you ever resisted. Why feel fear if you can choose not to?"

I roll over, taste blood at the back of my mouth and scream as the dark-haired woman grabs me again. She forces me onto my back again as the other woman lunges for my hands. The uninjured man is a heavy weight on my legs. The one I shot is still standing; who knows what augmenters he's taken?

My heart pounds, I can hear it in my throat and my head, beating in time to my shaking, cold fingers. The vial's less than an inch from my mouth. The dark-haired woman flicks its lid off, whilst the other female crushes her nails into my shoulders. I try to break free, but she's too strong. I don't have the strength; everything but the augmenter is dimming, swirling away.

The augmenter gets brighter, steals color until it's too blue, too vibrant. My eyes burn.

"Not the augmenter! No!" I pull a hand through the air, trying to gouge chunks out of the nearest arm, but everything's blurry. I move, but they're too powerful. Sweat drips into my eyes. I know I can't escape, not without the Luger. Especially not once I've swallowed an augmenter. No, I need my gun. I have to fight them.

I turn my head as the dark-haired woman forces my mouth open, her fingers latching onto my lips like clamps. I struggle again. A few feet away, I see my Luger lying on the dusty ground. It's shimmering, smiling at me.

"Get it in her!"

Her grip on my jaw is tight, and she pulls at my lips roughly. I shriek, turn and try to strike out at the woman. Adrenaline suddenly pounds through me, getting stronger and stronger, pulsing, coursing, forcing its way through my body. I kick out.

"No—"

Air rushes through my ears. My stomach turns.

My mouth is forced open. The vial tips up. The blue color disappears. I choke, try to turn away, try to spit it out, but I can't. Everything moves, blurs, spins. Heat pours through my body, chased by blinding coldness. Pain shoots through my chest, holding me down like tiny stone arrows. I gasp, my body stiffening, as the world around me drains of color, until even the skeletal images fade entirely, merging into a spectrum of grays, whites and blacks that won't stop laughing at me as I'm crushed, choking and drowning.

Chapter Three

The coils of rope around my wrists and ankles are too tight. My hands and feet are numb, foreign. Stretched out on my back, each of my limbs is pulled in an opposite direction. My shorts and T-shirt are gone, replaced by a blue gown. Anger flares through me at the thought of them touching my body.

The mattress is hard and lumpy under my spine, but it smells of honey—something I've only tasted twice. I pull weakly on my arms. Pain snaps through my shoulders. For several seconds, I clench my eyes shut, trying to control my breathing. I will not cry.

I am in a small pale blue room. I turn my head, and the skin on the back of my neck sticks to the sheet for a second, then makes a wet, squelching sound. The light around me gets brighter, and my eyes sting. My mouth tastes dry and bitter, a strange aftertaste. My eyelids are heavy. Fear pulses through me. I remember the flash of the augmenter burning through my body and... and nothing else. It's just... just a blank.

Gone....

I gulp. The Untamed will come for me. We always come for each other. Always.

Except... Rahn... my mother....

My head hurts; there's a buzzing in my ears as I remember the chase on the sand. I see the augmenter dripping toward me in the back of my mind. Bile rises.

I look around again. That's when I see the woman. She's

standing at the back of the room, next to the door. Her skin is paler than can be natural, and her hair is a metallic red that hurts my eyes. Her lips part, revealing perfect white teeth that are too white as she moves toward me. Twin metallic pools glimmer for an instant before light refracts into my face, like laser beams. I wrench my gaze away, but the flashes from her eyes have left two circles of murky redness in my vision, as if I've been looking at the sun for too long.

I fight the restraints harder, until blood is drawn about my wrists. I jerk my head to the left, away from her hand. "Get away from me! Help!"

"We *are* helping you."

She turns away from me, and the door springs open. Bodies. People. Everything's a blur. Too much color. Too much movement. It's everywhere. I don't—can't—

There are too many of them. Too many for me to fight, especially restrained. I count ten of them, plus the woman who was here first.

She smiles at me. A man passes her a small box. A sharp needle's pulled from it. My heart palpitates. A needle?

"My name is Rosemary Webber," the woman says. Her red hair is too perfect, one solid mass that doesn't move as she leans over me. "It will be easier and less painful if you do not resist the conversion."

She smiles down at me, her demeanor soft, sympathetic and welcoming. Or, at least, it would be if they hadn't kidnapped me, and tied me to the bed.

More of them turn toward me. They are all dressed in pale blue. Huge grins plaster each face, their lips stretched to garish angles. Soft music plays from a nearby room. There's the sweet smell of honey floating around, curling toward me, stroking my skin, kissing my eyelids. The room is bright and airy. There's a slight breeze too. Not too hot. Not too cold. It is perfect.

"What is your name?" A small, dark-skinned woman smiles brightly.

My lips freeze.

"Your name?" The tone is harder, spoken with a bite.

I eye each of them carefully, lifting my head high, until my neck protests. Five men. Six women. All of them are tall. No scars here. And the eyes: Enhanced. It's not as bright in here as it is outside in the desert, so their eyes aren't truly blinding me, but it's still bright enough for them to throw light about and mark my vision. It's disorientating, and I try to look away.

"Your name?"

"Seven Sarr," I say.

"*Seven*?" Several people question me at once. Their voices are too sharp, too shrill.

I nod. My mother named me. She named all my siblings in the same way. I'm the seventh-born, and she said my name was important.

"*Seven* isn't a name. Only those Untamed creatures would use that. You don't want to be one of them any more, do you? No, I can see it now, your mind will awaken, with our help. Leaving your old wild life behind is the only way to become fully enlightened. I can tell that your memories disgust you."

Whatever powers Rosemary has are useless. She can't tell anything about me. None of them can.

"Embrace our life and it will be easier for you. Less painful. Full of delight."

Never let yourself be Enhanced. Once it's done, there's no going back.

Oh Gods—that augmenter out in the desert. They've started it, started the conversion. They're going to convert me.

My heart pounds as I drag my eyes around the room. There's only one door—the door through which the Enhanced came, and they're standing in front of it. There's a window. But it's small, too high up for me to get to, and I'm tied to the bed. Can't even sit up.

"You need a new name. You cannot be called *Seven*."

"I *am* Seven. That is my name," I speak through gritted teeth. I can hear my mother's voice now, her soft voice: *Don't ever forget who you are, Seven. Never forget. Your name will lead us through this age.*

"No." The woman steps nearer, bringing with her a blanket of artificial sympathy.

I try to recoil away from her, but there's nowhere I can go, only deeper into the mattress. I yank at the ropes around my wrists again, but they're too tight.

"My dear, *Seven* is a number. And, here, we are all people, unlike the Untamed. We are all the Chosen. We are all equal. And we are all perfect." She walks right up to my bed, resting her pristine hands with the immaculate nails in front of me. I can't help but stare at them. "We will give you a new name." She pauses, then smiles. "Welcome, Shania. Shania Sarr. Such a pretty name."

I flinch. *Shania*. The name tastes fake. I want to spit it out. My stomach feels uncomfortable, turning and churning.

"No. I am called Seven."

The woman laughs this time. "The name *Seven* belongs to a bad person, my dear. It belongs to a wild Untamed. And you're not that... thing any more, you're a person. A Chosen One who is valued and respected."

My head pounds. I jerk my arms toward me, but the bindings are unyielding. "But I—"

She shakes her head. "You were bad. The Untamed are ruthless murderers who spill blood for fun. You ran around with them, like scavengers, taking what you wanted. Stealing what you wanted. It breaks our hearts to see such savagery in this world. Yet we—the Chosen—still want to help you; we won't hold your past against you. We are fair people. We don't hold grudges."

Fair? I feel sick, still can't swallow properly. "You kidnapped me."

The woman—Rosemary—nods, then smiles—actually *smiles*. Her fingernails tap against some sort of radio attached to her belt. Its red light winks intermittently.

"We saved you. There's a difference. You have to understand, Shania, you have to realize this is necessary. You were bad, you *needed* saving, in order to become a truly perfect being now, a person who is not in denial about your previous self. Don't be embarrassed. We are here to help."

The corners of her mouth lift up, her face radiating a

strange sense of beauty and wisdom and knowledge. If it wasn't for her coruscating eyes, I'd almost believe it. She lifts her hand toward me, and her skin makes contact.

"Never!" I yank at the bindings again. But nothing's giving. Only my own body. My fingers tingle. Pins and needles weigh down my legs.

"Ooh, you *are* a fighter, how lovely."

I flinch. It's one of the Enhanced men who spoke. A deep voice. He's standing off to the left, and his face has that glassy, almost-bored look that a face has when it's been watching something for a long time. Now, the corners of his mouth lift up, and he steps toward me. His fingers are cold on my forehead. I try to look behind him, but I can't move my head. My neck creaks. Something pricks against my wrist.

"You cannot win at our game. You'll realize that soon, my dear butterfly."

Heat rushes through my veins. The room and their faces start to spin, swirling out toward me.

"Oh, I am sorry," he says. "I haven't introduced myself. How rude. I'm Raleigh." He smiles at me, but it makes my blood curdle. He turns away, toward Rosemary. "Take her to the chamber. A level four is necessary. She's strong." He turns back to me, grinning. "It won't take long. We'll break you into perfection."

***

The cloth is heavy over my face. Some light filters through it. I can see the flashing green and red lights of the box high up on the ceiling. It's some sort of power-base, I'm sure. Before they brought the cloth, I saw lots of metal components and wires hanging from it, stretching to the corners of the room. My brother, Three, would love to examine it.

The cloth over my face gets tighter. It presses against my nose, trying to force it down. I can feel their hands all over my body, pushing me onto the platform with cold fingers. I know better now than to resist. But they don't believe me.

They aren't taking chances, they say.

"Join us willingly." It's the same man. Always the same man who speaks. Raleigh. The one who called me a fighter. The one who promised he'd break me.

Katya's a lost cause. She went willingly.

"No," I gasp. My word tangles in the cloth. I blink and my lashes drag against the material.

"Very well." He's smiling. I know he is. His voice is always lighter and amused-sounding when he's smiling. "Very well, indeed."

The water slams against me.

My body's crushed deeper into the platform.

My throat constricts. I taste bile. I turn, trying to pull away. More water hits me.

Mumbled voices over me. A laugh?

Too much water.

I swallow hastily, my throat constricting again. The syrup in my mouth won't go away, won't dissolve.

I clench my fists. I tell myself I'm not drowning. I can't be. I'm not. I didn't before. I won't this time. I can't, can I?

I *am* drowning.

They are drowning me.

My mouth's forced open by vomit that squeezes through my teeth. The cloth doesn't move. My vomit sticks to my lips as I choke on the acid. And the water pounds.

My lungs burn.

For a second, I smell cigarette smoke... *Corin*. I look for him. But the swirling water gushes and gushes, never stopping for me to see. Just blurriness.

I scream. More bile. My throat constricts again. I gag, retching. Fingers press against my cheeks. The back of my head hits the platform again. Another wave hits me. I taste more syrup.

Pain rushes to my feet. I'm still screaming. I can't stop screaming. It's all I know, what I have to do.

Give up... don't fight... you can't win....

No...need to fight...have to...I can get away. My dad always says we can win...I mustn't forget...mustn't....

The cloth lifts up a few inches. My vomit drips onto my

face, stinky, smelly. Streams of air burst down my throat. I scream, trying to sit up, but they won't let me.

"You're not murderers!" I scream. "The Enhanced aren't murderers!" It's what we've been taught: the Enhanced don't believe they're murderers.

"We're not," the man, Raleigh, says. I still can't see him. It's just his voice, floating. "We wouldn't let you drown. This is all in your head, this pain. It's the evil in you fighting our goodness. It needs to be purged out of you. We have to save you. It would not be right if we didn't."

The cloth is lowered again.

Another wave pours down.

It's not worth it, they'll break you in the end.

"Join us and this will stop."

Save yourself. Give up now. You can't go back to being Untamed now anyway.

"I'll never join you voluntarily, I'll—"

"You're lying, your voice is too high-pitched."

I scream out in anguish. I can't feel my body. The water's still coming, still crashing onto my face. I gulp, swallowing more and more until my throat burns again.

"Join us now, and we'll stop this."

"No—" I choke, eyes streaming.

Water. Too much water.

"We can keep this up for as long as we need to. Surrender and make it easier for yourself. Limit the pain and join us now. Or suffer for days, months, years. The outcome will always be the same. If I want something. I get it. And my dear, Shania, I want *you*."

Chapter Four

"Life is like a clock, don't you think? Time always comes around. It was only a matter of time before we had both you and your mother to boost our power. And I'm so glad we've got you, Shania. Such a sensible little one, aren't you?"

The tingling peal of laughter drags me from the darkness. I force my eyes open, struggling to stay conscious. I'm lying on a bed, unrestrained for the first time. And it feels like an accomplishment, like I've achieved something.

For seconds, minutes even, I look around. The room's too bright; my head hurts.

There. He's there. On my left. By the door.

It's him. Raleigh. He thinks he's broken me.

He's got dark hair, dark skin—like me. But his eyes are mirrors, set under heavy, thick brows. Even the sclera, that should be white, are metallic. It's not right. He smiles at me, displaying perfect teeth, as he steps closer to my bed. He's a big man, powerfully built—as muscular as Corin—and he walks with the confidence only a hunter can have. My gaze drops to his hands. He's laden with tiny bottles, bulging with an array of chemicals: more augmenters.

I lift my head higher, eyeing those bottles.

Look away, Seven. Look away now.

But I can't... my neck hurts too much... the colors are too bright, too intriguing. My spine clicks, and the movement reminds me of something... something that's too far away.

"Hello, Shania." His voice is tender. He looks down at me. His short hair is black, thick and lustrous.

"How long have I been here?"

He grins. "Don't worry, Shania. You're safe now."

I shake my head and the bright light above me dances about. "How long?"

"Five days."

Five days. The light dims. Five days. How long is it before we give up on a person? A week? Or sooner? I can't remember. My head feels too heavy; I don't know how long I can fight the augmenters.

Are the Untamed still out there? My father, he'll be looking for me, won't he? Unless Rahn's forbidden it...but they'll be looking for my mother too. Two of us. They have to come for us. They *have* to. Don't they?

Katya's a lost cause. She went willingly.

Rahn and Corin didn't see the Enhanced steal me. What if…could they think I....

My mother. The Enhanced have her too. I look around, twisting my neck until black dots appear in front of my eyes.

"Don't worry, Shania. You were too recognizable before, too easy for others to spot you, but your new name will stop them. They won't find you." He smiles.

Raleigh sits down on my bed. He is systematic in his assessement of me. My gaze returns to the augmenters in his hands, held together by a thin wire contraption.

"Your Benevolence is fading," he says. "Rosemary says you're running lean again—it just shows how deprived you've been, my poor darling. That's how the Untamed part of you is still able to fight. It's a strong parasite, but every augmenter you have will weaken it. It's almost gone as it is; you can beat it. I know you can. One more drink would probably do it. And you have a choice for your next augmenter."

He smiles as if I should be grateful. But I don't feel grateful. I feel strange. Everything feels strange. Just strangeness, it's overwhelming.

Raleigh moves his hands and all the vials jump a little, each wanting me to pick them. Each one contains a different color liquid, and the full color spectrum—from the palest blue through to the deepest red, and back down to an almost-transparent yellow—smiles up at me.

"What would you like?" he asks. His breath is hot on the side of my face, and my skin tingles. The faint aroma of alcohol clings to me, as he reels off the names of the augmenters. He watches me the whole time. "I have Kindness, Benevolence, Happiness, Calmness, Prosperity, Courage, Compassion, Good Will and Selflessness."

His gaze gets sharper, like a needle, and my head feels heavier. He leans closer, his arm going around me and I shiver, despite his hot skin and the warmth radiating from his body. Raleigh nods and smiles again. His teeth seem to get even whiter, the longer he smiles. I blink, nausea rising in me. Maybe it's some sort of side effect... I shouldn't feel sick... I'm safe here...side effects; it has to be. Yes. I nod. Definitely the side effects.

"What would you like?" His words are repeated, only a little louder this time.

I shake my head. "I'm fine." I lift my head up higher. The aching's getting worse. I need to clear my head of the augmenters, not take more.

Raleigh laughs. "Nonsense, my dear butterfly. You need one of these to make you feel human, to help you overcome the evil that is inside you. How about this, Shania: I'll give you a shot of Calmness *and* if you're good, I'll enquire about boosting your beauty for you. We could even make your nose a little shorter," he whispers.

I hope it wasn't Raleigh who changed my clothes.

"No, I don't want any." I try to lean backward, but I'm eyeing the colorful liquids, unable to look away. He shouldn't waste them on me. Others are more deserving.

Raleigh's arm is around me and his fingers catch onto my shoulder, teasing my skin through the blue gown. I shiver.

"Come on, Shania," he croons. "It's the only way to make you a better person." I start to recoil away from him, but then stop. I frown. Then smile.

He stares at me intently, and I wonder how old he is. His perfect skin, and the light stubble with the youthful contours of his face, place him in his mid-twenties, earlier thirties at the most. But his eyes offset everything.

Raleigh smiles softly. He redirects my gaze to his hands,

Madeline Dyer

to the augmenters. "These are what you want. All these confused feelings within you, they're normal. But it's not nice. This uneasiness, the negative feelings—you won't ever feel them again, I promise. Let me free you from your chrysalis."

The waterboarding flashes through me—the waves pushing down at my soul, my burning lungs—but before I can move, Raleigh lifts two vials to my mouth. Cold glass presses against my sore lips.

Don't… he said one more drink would do it….

But the ache in my chest directs my hands to hold the vials, as if my body is under someone else's control, and almost before I've realized what I'm doing, the liquids have disappeared. For a second, my stomach tightens; then coolness screams through my body. Adrenaline and a dozen other hormones fire up. For a second, my whole body stiffens, and I can't breathe. Then the endorphins kick in. I sigh as I turn my head toward him. A smile dances across my lips.

Raleigh takes the empty vials from me. "Do you like being one of the Chosen?"

"I like being an Enhanced." My words slur into one long sound.

The corners of his lips twitch. "You like being one of the *Chosen*," he corrects. "We do not call ourselves the Enhanced here, that is the name the Untamed gave us. Tell me, Shania, do the Untamed have a secret name for themselves?" He raises his eyebrows, leaning forward, his index finger on the light stubble on his chin.

As I look at him, I can't tell whether he's amused or serious. He's the kind of mystery that can't be solved. I swallow, my throat feeling rough.

"They… no. Just the Untamed." I blink hard. Can't think properly. *Do* they have another name for themselves? A long, long time ago maybe… didn't my father say they'd embraced the name that the Enhanced had given them, becoming proud of it? I can't quite remember. Everything is too hazy.

After a few minutes, Raleigh gets up and leaves. Just

33

before he opens the door, he turns back. "You look better already, my butterfly. And, soon, you'll feel *perfect*. Welcome to the Chosen."

Chapter Five

It's almost funny. All my life, I was taught that being Untamed is the safest and best thing to be, yet I have never felt better than I do now. There's no worrying about safety or shelter. They feed me three times a day, and I'm allowed as much as I want. They've said if I'm good I can see my mother soon. I have my own room, with a bed and a wardrobe and a mirror. They've even given me a teddy bear. I've never had a teddy before. I think I will call him John.

I pick John up and head over to the mirror on the wall. My breath catches as I see myself and for a few seconds, I can't breathe.

"My eyes…"

I stare at my reflection. My heart rate speeds up. The eyes reflected are silver. There's no white at all. No colour in my iris, only the mirror-silver. I lean in closer, and can just about see a faint line around each iris that moves as I look at the different corners of the wall mirror. Then I look down at John, in my arms. I can see him perfectly. My vision's the same as it was when I was Untamed, despite my eyes being mirrors now. I'd thought that the Enhanced One's vision would be altered somehow, but mine's not.

Actually… I frown as I stare at my teddy. My vision *is* different: it's better. Sharper. I look around the room. My sight is perfect. A smile forms on my lips as I turn back to the wall mirror.

I look like an Enhanced.

We do not call ourselves the Enhanced here.

I flinch at Raleigh's sudden words in my mind.

"The Chosen," I say, but the word doesn't taste right. Still, I do try. Again and again. "I am one of the Chosen. The Chosen. I am one of them." I frown, then try the alternative. "I am one of the Enhanced." These words come out easier.

The *Chosen*. The *Enhanced*. I test the words out, over and over again, mumbling, hoping that the *Chosen* will sound better with use. But it doesn't. Not when I'm taking about myself.

I turn back to the mirror again. Look at my *Enhanced* eyes.

Other than that, I'm the same as before. Dark skin, black hair. Full lips and a fairly long nose. I am tall, very tall—or at least I was amongst the Untamed—but here, all the women have perfect bodies. Willowy, tall frames, the right amount of curves... everyone looks perfect. And I know I will soon.

This morning Raleigh said he'd book me in for some appearance-altering augmenters.

"We'll make your nose shorter, and your hair softer," he said.

I expected to feel self-conscious under his evaluation of my physical appearance, but I didn't. I felt calm.

"And once we've got your appearance exactly how you'd like it, it will be easy to maintain." He leaned closer, and the strong smell of liquor wrapped around me. "The first session's always harder with physical alterations... takes longer. But Dr Jade is excellent. And then it's just a matter of keeping it that way." He pointed at his own jawline, rubbed two fingers across it, emphasizing its strength. "I only need to take three augmenters a day to keep it this well defined."

After that, Raleigh told me more about how the appearance-altering augmenters worked, but I found it hard to concentrate. His voice isn't the nicest of tones, and he kept tapping his fingers on my shoulders. I didn't like that.

I sigh, still staring at the mirror.

"You will look perfect, Shania, with the right treatments and time."

I turn to find Rosemary standing in my doorway. She looks energetic and lively. Her pale skin is glowing, and her red hair is as shiny and neat as before. Perfect. Unreal.

"My eyes," I say. "They're mirrors... but I can see?"

Rosemary smiles. "Of course you can see normally. Our eyes are highly developed. They say eyes are the gateway to the soul, so we need to protect that entranceway. A one-way mirror is the ideal solution. We can see perfectly. And no one can see into us. Our souls need to be guarded. That's the problem with the Untamed, their eyes are too expressive, and that's a weakness. You don't want everyone who meets you knowing your secrets, do you? This—" She indicates her own eye-mirrors, "is the perfect solution."

"But how?" I ask. My fingers pinch at the fluffy texture of John's back. "The mirrors? Is it… an operation? Bio-molecular?" I struggle to think of the words.

"Our augmenters contain the ingredient. You have looked like us for a while, Shania. It only takes ten to fifteen seconds for your eyes to change after an augmenter has entered your system. And the effect, from just one augmenter can last for days, although we all try to top-up at least twice a day."

It's then, as she's talking, that I notice the tray she's holding. Or, more specifically, the contents: augmenters, and food. In the center of the tray is some sort of cake. A soft, airy looking cake. Light. It's a pale beige color, with darker specks in it. I can smell the cinnamon and ginger from here. Honey's been drizzled all over it, glistening. It's a huge cake, already cut into twelve slices.

I look at the woman's face, then back at the cake. Six slices each, if she's hungry... my stomach rumbles, feeling uncomfortable. I've only had cake a handful of times before, at celebrations. Normally we just have semolina pudding or baked sweets or dried mangoes... but here, they've got actual cake. And I could have it whenever I wanted, I'm sure. I start to smile.

"So, how does it feel to be civilized?" she asks as she crosses the room toward me. "How does it feel to be safe?"

Nowhere is ever safe—that was one of the first things my father drilled into my head, after making sure I could recite Rahn's survival lessons, of course. *It's when you believe that you're safe, that you're at your most vulnerable.* But my father's not here, he's one of the wild ones. He lies and commits acts of violence against the Enhanced Ones who never lay a finger on him.

It's my father who lies. Of course some places are safe!
They have to be. And this place—I look around again—is
safe. The colors are happy, and the air pulses with calmness.
Of course this is a safe place.

"It's good," I say.

My hand stretches forward, and before I can help myself,
I'm scooping up a slice of the cake from the tray. My fingers
shake as I pull it toward me. I take a big mouthful as the
woman laughs. And it's bliss. Sweetness and softness and
spice explode in my mouth. I inhale the aromas and lick
honey from my fingers and lips.

Rosemary smiles and sets the tray down on the little table
by my bed. She brushes down her silk dress, even though it's
not dirty in the slightest. None of the cake got on her.

"We have not had any violence within our own society for
over two hundred years." She beams at me widely. Her lips
are scarlet. "You need not fear that any of us will harm you.
We all work together in harmony to ensure that we are living
in the perfect world. No violence. No crime. No poverty.
Everyone is equal. I am sure you can see already how much
better it is to be civilized and safe and in control, rather than
wild and angry and living in fear?" She does not wait for my
answer, but continues. "We are free of negative emotions."

I squint at her groggily. There's something, a memory
somewhere that contradicts this.

"Everyone is entitled to this life. It is our job, as the
Chosen, to help the poor Untamed creatures into this way
of life—to rid them of the evil that possesses them—for
everyone can be saved, making this world a better place. We
will help everyone; we have no prejudices. And it will help
us lead a better, more prosperous life where violence and
evil intentions will soon be forgotten, completely eradicated.
I am so glad we've enlightened you. Now, which augmenter
would you like?" she asks, still smiling. Always smiling.

"Calmness." I say the word automatically. I eye the cake,
but she doesn't offer me another slice, and it would be rude
to help myself again, wouldn't it? Even if there are enough
slices for both of us to gorge ourselves with. Never again

would I have to be so hungry I couldn't sleep.

"Calmness. Good choice," she says, then leaves the room, humming under her breath.

A few minutes later, she returns with a bottle full of the familiar blue liquid. I close my eyes as I drink it. It feels wonderful. Sublime. Worries flee. This life is perfect. This is the life everyone should have. Why was I ever trying to avoid it? Why would *anyone* try to avoid it?

The woman looks down at me, the usual smile plastered on her face. Maybe it's a permanent feature. "You agree that this is better than being an Untamed creature who only knows how to be wild and unruly?"

I nod and my neck cricks slightly. I feel pain, but only for a second. I look back over at the cake again.

"There's more to our food than just the cake," she says. "We've got every food that you could ever want. Doughnuts, cookies, baked sweets, honey, oranges, mangoes. Antelope, couscous, meat pies, stews, beef, fish, lamb, goat, maïs grillé, beans, rice. The list is endless. And that's just our food. You needn't worry about a lack of food or shelter, or warmth or security, or stability with us." Still smiling. "So, you think that your Untamed friends should experience this too?"

I nod. There's no comparison between the two lifestyles.

The smile gets even wider. "And you remember where they live?"

I nod. Just the thought of seeing my family and friends again fills me with warmth.

"Good. Shania, will you lead them to us?"

There's something about her voice. Something irresistible. Something beautiful. There's no way I can refuse. Not when this will help my friends. I think of Rahn. He'll be an even better leader when he's Enhanced. And my brother, Three—he'd be even faster at thinking and making radios. And Rahn's nephew and niece—they'd be even stronger and faster. Not that Corin needs to be any stronger or faster; he's strong and fast enough already. But Esther could be.

They all *need* to be.

They don't know the danger they're in, the evil that's controlling them. I clench my fists, trying to block out the way the room is moving around me. I squint.

"Will you lead them to us?" the woman asks again. "We'll be able to save them sooner if you're able to help us."

Don't ever lead the Enhanced toward the village, no matter how scared you are. Sacrifice yourself.

But I'm not scared, and this isn't a sacrifice. This will help them. Rahn doesn't know what he's missing. None of them do. I have to help them. I have to show them. They'll be thanking me in the end.

"Yes," I say. "I will lead you to them. We will civilize them. It is for their own good."

And that's when the first gunshot goes off.

Chapter Six

"Give Shania to me!" Raleigh appears in the room in an instant. His face floats for a few seconds. But then I see his body, joined to his head, and it makes me feel strange. "We need to get her out. Her system won't handle sudden stress yet."

Another gun goes off. My body freezes, and I drop my teddy. I'm passed from Rosemary to Raleigh.

"Come on, Shania. Walk," he barks at me, his hands on my shoulders, pushing my body in front of his. "Rosemary, get some teams out there. We're under attack."

Then Rosemary's gone. She left her cake behind, as if it wasn't the most amazing food in the world. I can still smell the soft spiciness and taste the sweet tanginess of the honey.

Under attack. I rub at my arm. The skin feels strange, tiny raised bumps. *Under attack*... the Untamed? They're here... they can't be... they wouldn't come for me now, after so long... and I don't need to be rescued, they don't understand.

As Raleigh leads me out into the corridor, I try to look around. Try to see something. But it's just the corridor. The normal corridor. There's no one there. No Enhanced, and no Untamed.

"Come on, you need to be faster." Raleigh pushes at me. He's speeding up, behind me, his feet catching mine.

I stumble forward, my legs aching. I turn again, but all I see is Raleigh. I feel exposed, vulnerable. The flimsy gown I'm wearing isn't enough. It's too revealing, too....

Nearby, someone shrieks. Shards of icy sleet burrow into my skin.

Raleigh's hands get harder around my waist, squeezing me slightly. "Turn left." He steers me into another corridor, and I feel him falter for a few seconds, then we continue again.

Another gunshot. But it's farther away. Raleigh curses.

"Hurry up. It's that way."

Right. We turn right. And then right again. My legs ache too much, my feet hurt. I slow down, unable to—

I see the fight.

It is horrible.

It is violence.

It is evil.

Six people, no seven—all wearing dark glasses—wave guns about. They're shouting, and, as I look at the nearest man, I think—

"That way!" Raleigh shouts, pushing me forward. I catch a glimpse of him pulling a radio from his belt. He shouts into it as another bullet fires.

Figures fall. More screams. A body flies across the room. Blood sprays everywhere.

The Untamed are *ruthless*.

My eyes widen. Nausea rises. It's horrible.

I need more Calmness.

My feet test the floor behind me. I step back, and press myself against the wall. Raleigh's to my left, and I watch as he throws something at the dark figures. A flash of white burns my eyes. I scream, turning away. My hands slap against my face.

"Shania, move, that way!"

Raleigh's right; I need to get out of here. There's too much blood. It is wrong. I turn and I sprint away. My lungs burn, trying to stop me. My legs are wobbly, too wobbly, and I can't stop shaking. Can't see properly. Need more augmenters.

My feet pound against the white floor, sounding like a countdown to my death. I've always wondered what my death would look like, and for a split second, I see myself lying on the cold tiles, my skin lusterless, lifeless. I shake my head, jerking my body as I force one foot in front of the other, as fast as I can. I push my head up. Adrenaline rushes to my head.

"Keep going! Get out of here!"

Raleigh's voice pulls me back slightly. I hesitate, my fingers lingering on the white walls. Someone screams behind me.

I keep running. Ahead, there are two smaller doors, and a thick, heavy wooden box against the wall. A cupboard. A *glowing* cupboard.

It is straight ahead of me. It's glowing, like it's lit from within. It looks *perfect*. I didn't think I could get any faster, but suddenly I am, and it's like the cupboard's also moving toward me. My fingers tease the handle, but then I can't stand it. I pull open the door, savoring this moment. The jewels spread out before me. Thousands of them; thousands of beautiful colors, teasing me with their sparkling, flirtatious glances.

Walk away, Seven.

I reach out and pluck out the brightest yellow one. I don't know what it is, but that doesn't matter. It's an *augmenter*. Made to be good, a delicious chemical that will help me. In my hands, it feels beautiful. It is the most precious thing in the world.

I unscrew the lid. I smell the liquid, letting the honey and beauty and love fill my nostrils, my head, my mind. Saliva pools under my tongue. My teeth taste stale.

Bringing the vial to my lips, I tease myself with the faintest of tastes. I shut my eyes, breathing deeply. Faintness and darkness wash over me. I'm sure I'm falling, but I know the rows of augmenters haven't moved. They're smiling at me. Congratulating me.

I take a gulp of the sweet liquid, feeling the wonderful way it beads on my tongue, how it slips down my throat, how it—

How it's *gone*.

Knocked clean from my hand.

Glass shatters. My ears cry.

I scream. My eyes spring open. Light darts toward me, as I turn away from the man—the *horrible* man—in front of me. Doesn't he know what he's done? I drop to the floor, my bare shins hitting the glass-laced tiles heavily. A whimpering sound escapes my lips. The liquid's running away from me.

"No," I cry, the sound drawing out, on and on and on and on.

My fingers dabble at the beautiful liquid. Shards of glass stick into my skin, but I don't care. It's not significant; nothing is... just the augmenters.

I get a bit on my finger—it's all gloopy, and I'm licking my finger, hyperventilating and delirious—when a hand clamps around my wrist. The person's fingers are strong and firm. My hand's yanked down.

"Get off!" I cry, but my voice is weak with the effects of the last augmenter. I try to force my hand to my mouth, but I can't. I lunge forward, reaching for more with my other hand, but the man stops me again. I cry out.

"Sev, stop it! Come on." His voice is dark and dangerous. *Dangerous.* He is dangerous. He has not been saved yet. He needs to be saved. The evil's still inside him. He'll hurt me. I need to save him quickly, before he hurts me.

I look up into Corin's warm face. His dark glasses have gone. His eyes are Untamed. Fire leaps through my veins, my blood's alight. I *will* save him. I have to save him, then we can save everyone.

"*Seven!*" He shakes me. He has a gun in his hand. It's a semi-automatic 17C Glock pistol, and it's pointing at me.

I choke, my throat burning. I look up at him, and all I can think is how he looks a lot older than his twenty years. His skin is lined, coated in grime that covers his peeling sunburn and light scars. But we could sort that out, if he became one of the Enhanced, if I saved him. I can see him now: beautiful skin that longs to be touched, eyes that dance and exhilarate me until I want to—

"Rahn!" Corin yells, his face contorting.

His eyes are wide, the pupils so dilated that I can barely see the warm chocolate color. A muscle in his jaw twitches in time to his shaking hands.

I smile. They came for me. Now I must help them.

"It's all right," I whisper to him. "I'll help you."

I turn back to the sticky, wet mess, trying to gather up more of the liquid. He just has to taste it, then he'll know, then he'll understand. He'll taste the security this life can offer him, the stability, the safety, and the food. None of us need ever be hungry again!

Corin's stone arm suddenly locks around my waist, hauling me back. He smells of sweat and dirt and musk and smoke and fear and—

"Rahn!" Corin shouts. His face is red, on fire. "They've converted her!"

"It's all right." I look up at him, furrowing my brows softly. And it really is all right. He's here, they all are. I can save them, we can all be together.

I need to save us all.

I push my hand upward, aiming for his mouth. The liquid drips from my fingers; need to move quicker. I try to press my sticky fingers against Corin's bruised, ripped lips, but hands seize me. Pain shoots through my shoulders. My head jars as I'm ripped backward. Corin's arms disappear. Coldness replaces his warmth, like a serpent around my waist.

Arms wrap around my torso. I should fight them, but I can't; fighting is bad. I'd be intending to hurt them, if I fought them. I am a good person. The Enhanced Ones said I would be a good person, if I embraced this life. And I am, that's what I'm doing!

"Please get off me," I whisper. My voice is calm. Wonderfully calm.

"Get out of here now!"

That's Rahn's voice—I recognize it immediately—and I turn to see the leader of my old pack. He looks even older. The lines around his mouth are deep and make tracks in his leathery skin, running under the rims of his black glasses. He doesn't look much like Corin, his nephew. Rahn's hair is darker, his skin tougher, his frame smaller.

Whoever is holding me starts to force me backward. I should fight him. But I can't. I'm a good person. I'm a perfect being. I should not fight.

Fight him!

My head hurts. A gun goes off a few feet away and I scream as a figure at the end of the corridor falls down, limp.

"Smash the augmenters!" someone shouts. I recognize the voice, but can't think whose it is.

To my left, Corin steps toward the cupboard. His shoulders are broad, and his upper arms ripple with bands of muscle. I watch as, almost in slow motion, he sweeps his bulky arm across the first shelf, pushing the vials to the edge of the shelf and—

I scream as the glass shatters all over the floor, as the liquid pours out. I try to lunge forward, but the arms of my captor stop me. I scream again. I cry. I shout. But no one listens to me, least of all Corin. He continues until every vial is lying in a sticky mess on the floor.

"No! No! Please, no!"

"They're comin'," Rahn shouts. I see more Untamed figures behind him, ones I recognize: Esther and Yani. Behind them, are the Enhanced. I breathe a sigh of relief.

Gunshots go off. I cry out. The sounds are too much.

In one swift motion, arms haul me against another body. I don't know who it is, only that it's not an Enhanced One. My stomach turns. Then the Untamed are running, taking me with them. Out of the corner of my eye, I see Corin turn and shoot behind us. I catch a glimpse of the Glock. I flinch at the sounds of death. *Of course* Corin wouldn't miss.

"Have we got everyone?" Esther shouts. She's a few years older than Corin, but she shares the same sturdy build and warm coloring.

"Keelie's dead," a low voice says.

My head burns, there's too much color. Nausea grabs hold of me, refusing to let go.

"That way!" Rahn shouts. I see him pointing toward a door to the left. Corin reaches it first and yanks it open.

Outside it's dark and cold. I scream as the coldness hits me. Unease erupts in my chest, along with a throbbing pain. My whole body shudders and convulses. I can't see. My eyes—everything's dark. My fingers burn with iciness, the fire spreading, spreading, spreading….

"What's happening to her? What've they done?"

"You should've left her. It's too late."

Everything is black. Everything is dark. Everything has gone. The air is too thick and far too clammy. It is poison, and it's seeping into my body. My skin soaks it up. This is wrong; I should feel fear. These people have guns. They've taken me from the Enhanced Ones. They've stolen me—catapulted me back into my life of fear, danger and instability.

I retch as my vision bursts back. I can feel tears welling up. I don't know what to do. I don't know how to stop them. How do I stop them?

"Where's the truck?" Rahn shouts, just as Esther pushes past him.

"Give her to me," Corin snaps, turning toward myself and the man who's holding me.

"I don't—"

I break free. One fist, that's all it took.

Immediately, hands grapple at my shoulders. My legs start moving, almost mechanically, though my knees shake. Corin's right behind me. But I'm faster. I jerk my head up. I can see the Enhanced Ones' compound there, we're not far away. Corin's hot breath is on the back of my neck.

I scream for help.

A hand slams down onto my left shoulder, fingers digging in painfully. I shriek as I'm whirled around.

Corin dives at me, his arms fighting their way around my waist. More figures appear behind him.

"Get off!" I shout. I try to turn my head backward, toward the building, but I can't. "Help me!"

Corin's grip tightens. His hands are warm. I don't know what he's done with the Glock.

Glock... clock….

Life is like a clock, don't you think? Time always comes around. It was only a matter of time before we had both you and your mother to boost our power.

"Let me go!" Huge tears plaster my face. I need to stay where my mother is; Raleigh said I'd get to see her soon.

But these people don't obey orders. They're wild. They need civilizing, the Enhanced are right! They need help.

"You've got to come with us," Corin snaps. I flinch. He pulls my trembling body against him, until there's no room between us, and I can feel his heartbeat, like an eerie countdown. Then he drags me backward, his arms locking under my ribs.

I throw my weight downward, trying to make it harder for him—trying to stop him—but he barely stumbles. His arms thrust me up higher.

"Leave her!" Rahn shouts. I turn, and catch a glimpse of the leader pulling on Corin's shoulder, right behind me. "They'll be comin' out after her any second, we need to go! Cut our losses! It was stupid comin' anyway, we knew she'd be converted—"

"*No!*" Corin's word rings through my head for several seconds. "We're not leaving you, Sev. We're not letting them get another one of our people!" I can feel him shaking as he looks at me. "You *are* coming back with us, whether you like it or not."

Nearby, an engine starts up. More angry voices. My head snaps toward the building, toward the open door. But there are no Enhanced there. Raleigh's not there. He's not going to save me. He promised I was safe with the Enhanced....

"Leave her!" Rahn waves a Glock about and its metal flashes somehow in the darkness. "She's gone."

"Come on, Sev!" Corin's fingers get tangled in my hair as his expression contorts with anger and frustration, his face burning. He's the only one who's lost his dark glasses; they always wear glasses when they're in the presence of the Enhanced, trying to hide who they are. "You are not one of them. You're one of us—"

"No, you've got it wrong!"

Our faces are only inches apart. The vein in his neck throbs in time with his flaring nostrils.

I shake my head. Blood pounds in my ears. "I'm not going with you."

Somehow, his arms just drop away from around me, *plummeting* down, as if he was shot.

But he hasn't been. He's still standing, like a menacing figure of darkness and strength. His feet are shoulder-width apart. His hands, clenched into loose fists by his sides, each hooked onto his belt loops by his thumb. His head is at an angle, and after three painful seconds, our eyes meet. His are imploring, begging me as the lost emotions surface within them.

I see the scars on his face, his sunburnt skin. I cringe. How can he want to keep living like that? How can any of them? Rahn's always drilling it into them that the most important resources are shelter, food, water and warmth. And aren't those just the things that the Enhanced Ones are offering us, offering us all?

I take a step backward, forcing myself to look away from him. "Leave me behind. Or join us."

Chapter Seven

Corin and Rahn stare at me.

I stare back. No one's moving. I should be running. I should be getting back to the building. I should be saving myself—that's *exactly* what I should be doing.

But I'm not.

I breathe hard. Why the hell did I give them a choice? I should just make them stay... they need help. Giving them a choice makes it seem like this life isn't as good, like they have the chance of escaping it, with little effort....

"Look, Sev," Corin steps closer. He raises a hand, pointing at me with a shaking finger. His finger is stronger than Rahn's. "You are *not* an Enhanced. *You* are Seven. You hate the Enhanced. We all do. They're freaks, unnatural, they've got no humanity. You do not want to be one of them." It sounds like a warning.

"She's a lost cause," Rahn hisses at his nephew. The familiar truck pulls into view behind him, its brakes squealing. "We need to go now."

Corin shoots him a dirty look, and, still, I haven't moved. *A lost cause*... and he's talking about me? I snort. The Enhanced Ones know I'm not a lost cause; they saved me. *No one* is a lost cause.

"Remember your old life? Our people went missing because of them. They've killed our families. They killed my parents." Corin's voice has a hard edge to it. A sharp edge. A dangerous edge. An edge that makes it impossible to look away from him again.

I shake my head, but my gaze doesn't leave his. He's

wrong. The Enhanced aren't murderers. They don't intend to kill people. His parents' deaths, like all the Untamed deaths during conversion attacks, *must* have been accidents; the Enhanced wanted to convert them. I look at Corin, my bottom lip quivering. He doesn't understand. None of them do. I need to help them. It's what Rosemary says we have to do. Our duty. I have to help them.

"We need to go, *now*."

The Untamed start to retreat toward the truck, all except one. My chest hitches. I shouldn't let them go. I need to help them. It is my job to help them all.

"Corin, leave her. She's been converted. There's nothin' left in her. We have to go *now*."

Corin's watching me carefully. His face is softer now. Despite the darkness, I can see the contours of his face clearly. My vision really is great. I can see the patches of ragged sunburn, the ugly, red raw skin, and the faint scars along the left side of his face that he got when a wildcat attacked him as a child. I saw the whole thing. The way the claws ripped mercilessly through his skin, dragging the blood out.

I ran straight for him then, even though the cat was there. Somehow, I frightened it away, before it pulled his muscles out. I saved him. I was scared, and my terror made me protect him.

And I don't know why but it's all I can think about now. And Corin's all I can see. His Untamed face. Something pulls through me, but I don't understand it. I should be trying to get Corin to Raleigh, but I'm not. I don't know why. I'm selfish, I don't want to help the Untamed, even though it is my job, my duty.

I don't understand. I can't think properly. I know what I should be doing, yet I'm not doing it because it doesn't feel right. Nothing feels right. There's nothing to feel at all. The augmenters are blocking it, and there's nothing there. I'm not in control. I'm not in control at all. I should be scared—I need to be scared—but I'm not. I *should* be shaking, but I'm not. It feels horrible.

Horrible. A negative emotion. I latch onto it, and I know I shouldn't, because feeling horror is an Untamed way of life. I shouldn't be able to feel it. But I can. It's strong now. It's all I can feel. And feeling it—feeling something that's raw and true—is good, even when I know it shouldn't feel good to feel something so bad.

"Sev, you don't belong with the Enhanced," Corin says. "You're one of us." He steps up to me and puts his arm around me. His body is sweaty. "Let's go." But he doesn't move.

I frown. I *don't* belong with the Enhanced? I'm not a perfect person?

"You're *Seven*," Corin says. "You're an Untamed."

Part of me screams to fight him, to protest, to do something. And the other part just doesn't understand. I'm lost. I'm lost because of the Enhanced. And they're not out here. Raleigh's not here. He's not trying to save me. There's only one person who's trying to save me, even if he has it wrong.

I gulp, and suddenly my eyes are watering. The sensation burns me, and I know it's not right. I shouldn't be able to cry. I shouldn't be able to feel sorrow or loss or anything that would make me cry. But I am. I'm crying. And I'm shaking now. Stress pours through me, and I remember something… something Raleigh said about my system not coping with stress.

I wrap my arms around myself, moaning.

"Come on," Corin says.

I let him lead me away.

***

After throwing up six times, my head is a little clearer. I can still taste the spicy cake, rippled with grains of disgust, on my tongue and it won't go away.

Never let yourself be Enhanced. Once it's done, there's no going back.

I gulp, feeling like I'm going to gag. *There's no going back…* it's always going to be a part of me, I know it is. Can feel it. My heart pounds heavily, and clammy sweat dribbles down my spine; the Enhanced part of my subconscious isn't going to die quickly. If at all.

And the worst part is that I don't know if I made the right choice. I can't tell. No. Of course I did. I can breathe now, I can think.

Half a minute later, I pull myself back into the truck— it's one of the old Mitsubishi L200 pickups that Kayden, Finn and Three stole six months ago. I tell Rahn that he can continue driving—the nausea's gone, for now. Rahn gives me a look—a cross between dubiousness, irritation and annoyance that makes his eyebrows almost disappear under his dark glasses—but he starts the engine. Esther and Kayden—a red-haired, thirty-two year old man who's the most skilled hunter in our group—are also hunched together in the front of the truck, and they both turn to look at me. Then they glance away in unison.

I lean back against the inside of the truck's wall. I want to close my eyes, to block all this out, but something's stopping me.

"Do you want to lie down?" Corin's voice is as cold as a dead snake.

Rahn steers the truck back out onto the dusty road as I shake my head. Corin just nods, his eyes unfocussed and looks behind us. I turn and look at the backs of Esther and Kayden's heads in the truck's cabin. Neither turn to look at me; I can't blame them, if it was the other way round, would I want to look at them? I know the answer instantly. I'd thought about it enough times, what I'd do if my brother or sister, or any of us, became Enhanced and we managed to rescue them.

I never thought *I* would need rescuing.

Never let yourself be Enhanced. Once it's done, there's no going back.

A few minutes later, I follow Corin's gaze. The track we're leaving behind is dusty and dark, a blanket over the scarred earth. No one follows us.

I frown, feeling tears well up. I sniff loudly. I don't belong with the Enhanced. Yet now I don't belong with the Untamed.

I'm in between, lost in the dark void where neither world will acknowledge me. Corin won't even look at me. I swallow hard. How long's it going to take, until the augmenters are completely out of my system? A couple of days? A week? Longer? I shudder. My mother once told me a story about a woman her father rescued from an Enhanced Ones' compound; the woman never was the same—a shell of her former self. I can hear my mother's voice now: *Once your humanity's been siphoned out, you can't get it back, even if you're removed from that environment.*

Is that what I'm going to be like? Did I make the right choice in leaving the Enhanced? I'm not sure. I'm going to be hungry again. Thirsty. In danger. Yet it feels right, and I don't know why. My head's still too fuzzy.

My lips taste rubbery and I'm starting to sweat. I can feel the blue gown sticking to me. I pull at the fabric. The Enhanced Ones' fabric. I clench it in my fist.

I look around at my rescue party. Rahn, Esther and Kayden in the front of the truck, Corin, Elf and Yani are seated in the truck bed with me. I try not to think of Keelie. Seven people came to rescue me. And only seven of us are returning. I look at Corin, then at Elf. I think they both saw Keelie's death. Elf sits in a heap in the corner. His huge hands cover his face. His shoulders shake. Corin is still staring back out at the dark landscape we are leaving behind. It's full of doom, evil, and artificiality. But it's spreading.

And soon, we're not going to be able to outrun it. We all know it.

The Enhanced will take over. It's inevitable. It always has been.

Lesson five: Don't ignore the facts. Ignorance is not bliss. Ignorance is death.

***

The rest of the Untamed are waiting as we get back to Nbutai—our village. They're all standing outside their huts, watching with narrowed eyes—eyes that have coloured irises and white scleras, eyes that look so different from mine.

We all get out of the truck in silence. Esther jumped out first, and now she helps me walk, though the look of disgust on her face doesn't evade me. Weakness grabs me and my knees feel almost acidic; her arms are probably the only things that stop my face smashing into the ground.

It's then that I see my father: a tall, broad frame. Dark coloring, like me. Heavy eyebrows emphasize his brow, make his eyes look darker. He's watching me, his body rigid. My brother and sister, Three and Five, stand either side of him, their hands on my father's arms for support. As I make eye contact, Three looks away, his gaze dropping to the ground.

The silence speaks for itself. Marouska, a rather round woman, steps forward. She has a bowl of soup in her hands, which she hands to Rahn. He takes it, pushes at his dark glasses, and nods his thanks at her, then disappears into the nearest hut. The biggest hut.

"Come an' eat," Marouska says to the rest of us. She has a strange accent. She's not from these lands, but she's been here longer than I have.

I shake my head. Elf also declines the invitation. Shrugging, Finn tells everyone he'll have our food. My eyes narrow. So he survived that raid then.

Slowly, I make my way over to the shack I share with my father, brother, and sister. It is tidy inside; Five must've spent her afternoon tidying it again. She's always doing that. Or she's tidying her own appearance. One or the other. Very proud, my sister is. Vain, my brother calls her.

I change into my own clothes, feeling both glad and anxious as I discard the blue gown. It falls onto the floor. I kick at it for good measure, then pause, half expecting it to kick back. Except the Enhanced aren't violent, are they? They're good people... no. They're unnatural people. They're not even *people*. I shake my head in desperation.

Sighing, I sink onto the three-legged stool. It belongs to my father. I let my head fall into my hands, my arms struggling to support it. I can't stop shaking. I just want to sleep. Sleeping sounds like a good idea… if I had the energy to move.

A few minutes later, there's a knock on the side of the shack, then Esther pulls back the door cover. I peer at her through my bleary vision. She's holding a torch, and the bright light highlights the way her face is furrowed, and how she's biting her lip. I beckon her in.

"You sure you can't eat?" she asks. She squints at me, frowning. She's been sent here, probably by Marouska—it's obvious.

"I'm sure."

My hands shake in my lap. I try not to think of Raleigh and what he's doing; whether he's coming up with a plan to rescue me. I don't know whether I want to be rescued. Not again.

I watch as Esther crosses the shack. She stands in front of me. Her build is sturdy—like Corin's—and her short, cropped hair makes her look fierce. But she's a genuine, real person, I remind myself, the Enhanced Ones aren't. I'm not. Not at the moment. The augmenters are still in my system, controlling me. The thought doesn't make me feel any better.

Neither of us speaks for a few moments. Maybe she doesn't know what to say. Maybe I don't. Or maybe we both know that silence is healing. Neither of us wants to talk about what has happened. Just thinking about it makes me squirm. I can feel my face reddening.

The augmenters were controlling me. It wasn't really *me* they saw. It was the *Enhanced* me. But, still, I can't shake away the memory of my greed; how I was scrambling about trying to gather the sweet, beautiful liquid. And Corin saw me like that. Shame clouds my vision, and I blink rapidly. I don't want to give anyone an extra reason to think I'm weak.

And Keelie's death, it's my fault. If I'd run faster and hadn't been caught by the Enhanced, there'd have been no reason for the Untamed to break into the compound, seeing as Rahn wasn't going to rescue my mother.

I close my eyes for a second, trying to block out everything. But I can still taste the augmenters. The slight spiciness of the Benevolence, the sweetness of the Calmness.

And the cake. I'm craving it like I used to crave the small pieces of sugar cane my father occasionally gave me when I was little.

Never let yourself be Enhanced. Once it's done, there's no going back.

"They're going to be after us even more now," I whisper to Esther. I don't know why I'm telling her—giving her another reason to hate me, just like the rest of her family. I think of her brother, Corin, and wince.

Esther's still standing by the wall, her shadow falling over me. The torch is dimming, like everything in this world— like the chances of the Untamed surviving.

"Did you tell them where we live?" Her voice is already accusatory.

It's the first time any of them have asked me that. I'd thought the question would've come from Corin or Rahn as soon as I got in the truck, but no. Not Rahn, the suspicious leader who holds prejudices like they're his knives. Not Corin, the arrogant young man who thinks he's important, and exploits his connections to the leader.

I shake my head, and turn towards the window. "But I said I'd lead them to you." I blink hard, trying to clear my head. "But I didn't tell them where you live."

You... I should've said *we*. Why didn't I say *we*? I pinch the bridge of my nose with my thumb and forefinger.

"Well," Esther says, "that wasn't the best of raids." She laughs sarcastically, but it sounds as fake as the Enhanced Ones' feelings—as my feelings?

I just nod. My memories of the actual raid have paled and faded until they're practically non-existent. I barely even remember leaving for Nbutai with my load.

I fix my eyes on the blackness outside, trying to picture the landscape, the lie of the desert, the contours of the mountains. But my vision isn't as sharp now. The Enhanced, they could be out there. They could be hiding. They could be waiting. They could set our houses on fire.... except murder is not their intention. Conversion is.

I look at Esther. She squeezes her lips together. At this angle, she looks more like Corin. She nods once.

"They're always going to be after us." Her voice is crisp. "We just have to remain strong. We can survive this. Our families have survived over two hundred years of this already. We are not going to be the last. We can't let the whole of humanity become robotic machines. We *will* survive this."

Madeline Dyer

Chapter Eight

Hands shake me, jerking me from my sleep.
I blink into the harsh light. "Wha—"
"Get out!"
Three's face looms in front of me, but only for a second.
Then he's turning away from me. A blinding flash of light
illuminates his back. I hear a scraping sound as my brother
grabs at a half-made radio with spider-wire legs.

"Seven! Hide! They're coming! Get to the rocks in the
south!"

My feet trip as I jump up. Bedclothes are everywhere.
Three's gone, leaving me on my own. My father? Five? Not
here. For a second, I don't know what to do. My stomach
hardens and my chest tightens. Who's coming? The
Enhanced? My chest hitches. I don't know whether I should
be scared or pleased.

I head for the doorway. The sky's a pale peachy color
with a golden hue and hints of soft blue. What time it is? It
can't be that early already. It can't.

I skid to a stop, in front of the other huts. I taste dirt in my
mouth; my teeth feel heavy.

"Run, Seven, hide!" Three's shout is near, but I can't
see him, no matter where I look. I can hear movement, all
around me. Rustling and steps and things being dragged...
but no one's here. It's deserted. I can't see them, but I can
hear them? The effects of the augmenters? I don't know. All I
know is something bad's happening, and I can't see a thing.
I can't make sense of anything.

Keep running, Seven. Keep running.

My breath catches in my throat. Tension runs down my spine as I force one foot in front of the other. I speed up, my knees jerking as I gag on the night air. I keep going. I don't have a weapon. My hands feel empty. They're aching.

They're coming.

I choke and tears stream down my face. My heart pounds, blood races around my body. I clench my shaking hands to me, trying to see the others, but whenever I focus on something, it becomes a swirling haze.

The roof of my mouth feels too dry, sandy almost. I turn; the ground gets grittier beneath my bare feet. Bare feet? I baulk. My shoes? But the hut's too far away... they all are... I'm still running, my feet are still pounding the ground, and I can't stop. Dust is everywhere; I can feel it on my skin. Like the darkness around me — a blanket of nothingness.

It's just sand, and rocks. The shacks have disappeared. Have I run that fast? *That* far? I am the fastest, but I was *barely* running.

But there's no one here. I turn, looking around. The horizon's uncut, everything's okay, but the huts have gone and —

"Hello?"

I keep running, screaming and screaming, but no matter how loud I shout, my voice is like a lost whisper, buried within the world that's trying to engulf me. Tears pour down my face. It's cold, too cold here, too dark. And I'm alone. All alone.

What the hell? I clench my icy fists tightly. My eyes sting. All around me, the air is like pinpricks of glass, cutting into the tiny pores of my skin.

"Dad? Three? Help! Help me, please!" My voice sounds odd, strained, too quiet, yet it echoes.

I rake a hand through my sweaty hair. My fingers catch on a tangle. I tear it out. I falter, turn, look back. Icy winds wrap around me. My skin burns. All I can see is the sand and the rocks. Figures? No. I squint harder, my heart racing. Pain shoots through my chest, tugging at my heart. I swallow hard, trying to remember, trying to remember anything. I can feel bile rising in my throat. I gag, my cold hands gripping my even colder bare knees for support. Can't stop shaking. Can't see properly.

I swallow sand, feel it grate against my throat on its way down. There's a rushing sound in my ears as I steady myself, trying to see, trying to see anything.

I look down at my hands, at the broken skin of my fingers. Blood. Dried blood. What the hell?

I listen hard, trying to ignore my racing heart and the sand that's moving all around me. I step forward slowly, one foot, then the other, but still I'm panting, panting hard. My skin tingles.

Murky shapes rise out of the darkness. Dark silhouettes. Several of them. Moving, swaying slightly. I clench my fists and my teeth graze my bottom lip. I taste blood. More blood.

Run, Seven. Run now. The voice is loud. Too loud.

I flinch, frozen for too many seconds. My collarbones ache, unease rips through me. My head's jarring, everything hurts. What's happened? I can't remember… can't think… the Untamed rescued me, and—and they drugged me? Abandoned me here because I'm a liability? No, I saw Three… we were in our hut….

I cough up some sort of sour, foul-smelling liquid. The wind chaps my lips, drying them in an instant.

"A liability," I whisper. *Me*? I gulp.

To my left, the black rocks stand there. I look ahead. And the shacks are there: their irregular structures standing up on the horizon, like soldiers. I take a step backward, even though those people are coming. I freeze. I stare at the shacks… I frown.

We…we relocated our village? In the middle of the night? In, what, half a minute? A minute? Two minutes? Without me noticing, and without me helping?

I shake my head, gripping the side of my face with my cold, cold fingers. I look straight ahead, trying to blink everything into sense. But it doesn't help. The shacks are there. *Our* shacks. There are six of them. But there should be seven; Rahn lives on his own. He hates being with other people. Even when we went on a weeklong raid a few years ago, and had to set up camp in the bleakest part of the mountains, he'd insisted on his own abode.

Rahn always lives on his own.

But there are six shacks ahead. Only six. My skin crawls.

"Dad?" I start running toward the rough buildings, stumbling over the ground. "Three?"

But everything's dark, and it's getting darker. I can't see. It's too—

I shriek, throwing myself to the left. Land hard on my shoulder, roll over, the flames catching at my feet. I smell burnt flesh as I stagger up, wiping sand from my face.

Fire? I narrow my eyes at the flames in front of me—walls of reds and oranges. The heat's burning. I can feel the skin of my face smoldering, can taste more bile.

I scream, choking on the sooty air. I force myself to move, to get away. Need to get away. Far away. Quickly. Smoke billows toward me. I shriek.

And—

It's gone.

I freeze. Completely. Until all I can hear is the dying wind as it caresses my crying skin. I turn, wary, my body pumping with adrenaline. I can still smell burning, but the fire's gone. Darkness swims around me, but the darkness is lighter than before. I can see more clearly. The sky's purple. Dark purple. I feel even sicker. This... this isn't right... this can't be real... it doesn't feel real... I don't like this. I don't like this at all.

Run, Seven!

I run.

Far too soon, I reach the shacks. Everything inside me squirms as I drag open the drape to my family's shack. It is dark inside. There's a strange smell, like honey and mint, and rotting flesh and—

I scream.

Dark skin. Dark eyes. Dark hair. Blood glistens from his ear, pouring out, pooling onto the dry floor. Only it's wet now. Wet and sticky.

Blood.

Bodies.

I clamp a hand to my chest. My fingers zap any warmth

from my frame. With my other hand, I push my hair out of my eyes, lift my head up straighter, force myself to look behind my brother's body.

For minutes—or maybe hours, I don't know—the world stops.

Dead. They... they can't be. This, this isn't real... can't be real. But dreams aren't *this* vivid. And bad dreams never go on for *this* long. I pull at my hair, scrunching it up on the crown of my head, pulling so hard it hurts, each follicle burning. Still, I don't wake up.

I retch, coughing and spluttering, bending down so close that I see the bullet in Three's head. Weakness fills me, I try to move, try to get away, but I can't... can't do anything... nothing will work.

Somehow, I turn my head. I catch a glimpse of the purple sky: new orange streaks pull through it. I turn back; something catches my eye. It's a Luger. On the floor by my sister's head. A Luger... *my* Luger, the one Rahn lent to me. It's definitely the same gun: the one the Enhanced now have, because they must have picked it up when they took me.

I should run. I *know* I should run. Need to get out of here. But I can't.

I look back at Three's body. He can't be dead. He *can't*. Neither can my dad. Or Five. But they're here. Their bodies....

I feel numb.

"This isn't happening," I whisper, and my words echo all around me. "This can't be happening."

Dizzily, I back out, a strangled cry escaping my lips. I clamp a hand over my mouth, and then I'm running. Running toward the next shack. It's taller than ours, and a little more sturdily built. I start to lift the thick cover over the doorway, but then I stop.

I know what's inside there.

I don't want to see Corin's body. Or Esther's.

I crash to the floor. Mud covers me in an instant, smothering my skin. It's cold, sticky and—

Mud. I stare at it. Mud... in the desert? But this *is* mud. I dig my fingers into it, feeling the way it sticks to my nails, to my bloody skin. It's sloppy, gloopy and—

"They've killed themselves," an unknown voice shouts.

I jump, then cower in the mud, letting it plaster my body. It's glowing now, the mud, slightly purple too. I taste grit at the back of my mouth.

"These ones have as well."

The Enhanced. I *know* it's the Enhanced. They're here.

Killed themselves...the Untamed wouldn't do such a thing… unless it was to escape the Enhanced. *Being dead is better than being unnatural robotic machines fueled by artificial feelings*. At the sound of my father's voice, I bite my cheeks until I taste more blood. Too much blood. Everywhere, I see blood.

Breathing hard, I look around. It's almost light now. Another Enhanced shouts something, but I can't make it out. I need to get out of here, before they find me....

"Go now," I whisper the words. But my body doesn't move. I clench my fingers into tight fists. My bones crack.

The sky is changing color again. Dark swirls of navy blue appear and mix with the oranges and purples. I blink several times, like I'm seeing it for the first time.

"No.... no.... no!"

The Turning. The seasons are changing. *It's the Turning.*

My throat squeezes. Need to get under cover. Can't be outside. Not in the Turning. Need to find cover.

I clench my fists to me, squeezing mud from my palms. It sprays out like jets. I turn my head toward the nearest shack. It's Corin's. I can't go in there.

"Shania's body hasn't been accounted for. She's still out here."

Dark spots swarm around me. Oh Gods, they're going to find me. And I don't know whether that would really be a bad thing or not....

Hide, Seven. Hide now.

I push myself up, but my legs are too soft, too sticky... can't stand... I fall, crashing back into the mud, swallowing several gulps of it. I try to spit it out, gagging more. Can't breathe.

"Did she definitely escape with *these* Untamed?"

"Yes." There's a pause and I hear labored breathing. "I remember the red-haired man."

The red-haired man. *Kayden*. I haven't seen his body yet.

His body. I nearly choke. The other bodies. They've killed themselves. My vision darkens. They've killed themselves because of the Enhanced.

"Keep looking for her."

"She could have killed herself too."

There's a slight pause, then I hear footsteps. I look up toward the sky and—

What. The. Hell?

A bison stares back at me. His eyes are dark—two bottomless pits in the sky, waiting to swallow me up—and he's watching me. Never looking away.

The footsteps are getting nearer still. I should move. Need to move. Move now! But I can't. The mud is holding onto me. It's trying to protect me. I lie down in it. Mud slides over me.

"She won't. Not now she's tasted our life. It's too sweet a reminder for her. She will come back to us. She'll give in to temptation. They always do. Whether it's now or later, Shania will be ours again."

"No!" The scream escapes my lips before I even realize I'm going to speak. The mud disappears. My body powers up. I scrabble forward.

The men come. Four of them—why are there always four? Raleigh beams at me.

"My dear, Shania, darling." He kneels next to me, and I feel the cold touch of his hand on my forearm. But it doesn't stay cold. Heat sears between us, and his eyes arrest mine in blinding flashes. "Do not fear. We never leave one of our own."

I want to scream, but screaming doesn't feel right... it's Raleigh. He... he'll help me. He will. He knows me. He wouldn't leave me... he came for me.

You're not one of them. Remember what Corin said. You don't belong with the Enhanced. You're an Untamed.

I sit up straighter, push myself backward. Something sharp digs into my back. Pointy and hard.

"Do not fear, Shania," Raleigh whispers. His voice is dangerously soft.

My foot twitches, jittering up and down. He produces a tiny bottle from his pocket. I lean back farther, my back pressing into the sharpness. I feel pain, delirium. My heart races. My ears buzz.

"No..." I mutter. But my voice is weak. Too weak.

"This will calm you." He lowers the bottle toward me. The liquid is black. As black as the night should be... except the sky's not black. It's purple and orange and cream and blue and mauve and peach and a thousand other swirling colors. "It will help you a lot."

I scream, pulling my elbow back in one swift move. Then I punch Raleigh in the nose.

And I don't care. He hurt me. I remember the torture and pain—the waterboarding—and I suddenly don't know how I could've forgotten what he did. How could I believe the Enhanced were good people, when they tortured me into thinking that?

Raleigh shouts something, and spits blood at me. I crawl sideways, find my feet, and leap at him, hands out and ready. I'm like a cat. My nails are claws and they rip at his skin. He screams, his face contorting. Blood spurts over us both. Flaps of his skin hang from my nails.

I lunge for him, but the other three Enhanced are on me. Why did they wait so long? I cry and I shriek. I kick and I punch and—

"Seven! It's okay! Stop it! You're safe!"

I jerk awake, breathing hard. My eyes sting. The sharp rocks are still around me, I can feel them abrading my hands. I blink into the darkness, willing the burn beneath my eyelids to subside, and to bring reality into a clearer focus. The Enhanced are not here. Yet, I *know* it wasn't simply a dream. It wasn't... wasn't... couldn't have been... felt too real.

My father stares down at me, and Five's arms are around me. I cry and cling to her. My fingers curl into her dark hair. Three stands behind her.

"It was just a dream," Five whispers.

I shake my head. "It wasn't—"

"Go back to sleep," Three grunts.

I glimpse his face in the half-light. Deep bags under his eyes, accentuated by the shadows, hang from his sockets like meat hanging off a bone. But they're here. They're all here, safe. My family. But my mother isn't here….

"No," my father says. "Don't go to sleep."

I look toward him, and in the dim light there is a strange look in his eyes. A look I cannot quite fathom. A look that suggests something hugely important. His eyes are narrowed, but wide at the same time. His head's at a slight angle, tilted toward me, but he's leaning away from me at the same time.

"Tell us about it," he says. It is a command, not an option. Three looks annoyed. Five looks like she thinks talking about it is a very bad idea.

I tell them. They listen, although Three looks like he's half asleep. Five shakes her head as I finish. My father's expression is stern and hard.

"The sky? What was it like?"

Three groans. "Does it really matter what the sky looked like?" He throws his hands in the air. "You're not going to paint a picture of it."

"Seven, what was the sky like?" This time, my father's voice has a different edge to it. An edge that makes my stomach roll.

I look at him; his eyes are lighter than usual. They make me squirm, and I wonder whether my own eyes look Enhanced or Untamed. I think about what Rosemary told me, how the mirrors can last for days.

"It was the Turning. It was dark purple, and then there were streaks of navy too. And orange. And other colors. They were all mixing together."

"Only the Turning?" my father questions. I nod and he looks relieved. "Good."

"Good?" Five repeats. She doesn't look as though she thinks it is good. "Seven was outside, unprotected during the Turning." Her eyes get wider and her mouth drops into an O shape.

"For the Gods' sake!" my brother growls. "It was a *dream*. It wasn't real. Seven wasn't really outside in the Turning. Now, can we go back to sleep?"

Ignoring Three, my father turns toward Five, then back to me. "It wasn't real," he echoes my brother's words, as though he is the first to think of it. "Let's go back to sleep. We'll think about what this dream could mean in the morning—"

"It's obvious what it means," Three says. "Seven's scared they're going to come after her. We don't need to have a whole I-wonder-what-this-could-possibly-mean session." He makes an exasperated noise. "It's not surprising she's having bad dreams."

My father doesn't say anything. There's a movement to the side of our shack, and the small terrier that our family has had for years, nears me. He noses my feet then whines. I pick him up and cuddle him. He's shaking. His eyes are dark—but not as dark as the bison's eyes were.

"There was a bison," I say as I stroke the terrier. I don't know why I say it.

My father's head snaps toward me. He breathes heavily. "A bison?"

"This is *ridiculous*," Three moans. He's already getting back into his bed, pulling the blanket up around him and over his head.

"A bison is most definitely *not* ridiculous." My father looks at me sternly. "Where was this bison?"

"In the sky."

"Most *definitely* ridiculous."

"Shut up, Three." My father grips my shoulders. He wrinkles his nose and there's a long pause before he says anything to me. "It was the time of the Turning and you saw a bison in the sky, in this vision?" There is something strange, something odd, about his voice, as though this is the most important question he has ever asked.

I nod.

My father looks at me for a few seconds, his whole expression narrowing, as if someone is pinching the center of his face, drawing everything together, twisting it all into one fine point. He starts to open his mouth, but pauses. Then he looks at me severely.

"The Gods and the spirits have forgiven you."

A strange kind of relief floods through me. I'm not lost, not stuck in the middle of the void any more. And it's good. It's what I want. I think. I try not to picture my room at the Enhanced Ones' compound. The bed, and the wardrobe. My teddy bear, John.

My father turns toward Five and Three. "Go and wake everyone. She's a *Seer*." He looks back at me. "And we're about to be attacked."

Chapter Nine

"Let's hope that's the only way you're like your mother."

"What?" I look at my father, and I can't believe what he's implying. "You—you can't believe—"

"Rahn told me the facts. I can forgive you because you were kidnapped, but she chose them."

I throw my hands in the air. "That can't be what happened. Rahn and Corin and Finn, they planned it. She wouldn't—"

"Don't talk against out leader," my father snaps. "Help me with this. We ain't got time for this talking."

He holds out a big sack with the neck open and I squash another blanket and a bowl into it. I can hear more sounds now, from outside. Raised voices, and scraping noises. It won't take long for Three and Five to wake everyone else, and prepare for our departure—we've had enough practice, over the years.

The terrier whines at my feet.

I let out a long sigh. A Seer. Me? It felt wrong, especially when I can still feel how desperate I was for those augmenters... the two feelings shouldn't go together. But if I am a Seer, if my father's right... have the Gods really forgiven me that quickly? And the spirits, too?

My mother often talked to me about her being a Seer. She told me all about their powers, how she could distinguish normal dreams from Seeing ones. She told me about the Dream Land, an altered state of spiritual reality, that gives warnings of conversion attacks to Untamed Seers through revealing potential versions of the future. Seers reach the Dream Land through sleep, but sometimes traumatic accidents can throw a Seer into the Dream Land, to show them something when they wouldn't normally be sleeping. That had happened to my mother once. We were ambushed, and the spirits made her faint so they could take her to the Dream Land. She'd awoken with the knowledge that had saved us that day.

I swallow hard. I'd never really paid attention to my mother's talk of the Dream Land. Well, I had, but not to the extent that I'd listened to Rahn's survival lessons. I'd known his information would apply to me, and I'd thought my mother's wouldn't.

I close my eyes for a second, trying to remember her voice, her words, anything that could help me. I know Seer dreams are linear, and vivid, usually starting from the current position that the Seer's in. They're different to normal dreams, which are more fragmentary, weird and... dreamy. I frown. My mother had said something about it being difficult to distinguish the Dream Land from real life, when you're having a Seeing dream—and that made sense, didn't it? It *had* felt realistic.

"She was a good Seer, your mother." My father looks at me sternly, his whole face pinching slightly. His eyebrows are beginning to gray, and his dark hair looks even more wiry than usual in the strange light. "This is a gift from her," he says. "I never thought more than one of you would inherit the gift..." My father's expression darkens. "Two was a good man. He only got the vision five minutes before the attack—we weren't hasty enough. You were young. You won't remember."

He's right, I don't. I was five years old. But I've been told countless times how Two had been drinking, that the liquor had clouded his mind, limiting his Seer powers in the time they were needed most. My mother's powers were clouded by grief; Four and Six had just died from the fever. Although I can't remember that particular attack, I can still picture how weak Four had been at the end, how he'd been foaming at the mouth, glassy eyes rolling back in his head, delirious. It's just a snippet of a memory, but it's all I have of him.

And it's the only way I can remember him. It's weird how memories work. But at least I *can* remember Four. When I try to picture Six, my mind's just blank. No particular face comes to mind, just a generic, sick nine year old who splutters into the New World.

It's the same with One. He was killed during an attack before I was even born; he's a faceless older brother who I'll never meet.

"We have to be quick," my father says. "The Turning is in a few hours' time. We have to leave here and find shelter before it strikes."

"Yes."

"Seven." My father stops me as I pick up the last bowl from the floor. He looks at me carefully, evenly. We're the same height—or maybe I'm a little taller now—but his frame is wider and more worn. "Whenever the bison speaks to you, you pay attention," he says. "You've been chosen as a Seer for a reason. The future speaks to you. You must not ignore it."

It sounds like another lesson. Another rule.

One that I can't afford to ignore.

***

"I don't believe this." Rahn folds his arms over his chest and glares across at me. He jabs the usual finger toward me, but my father intersects it.

"We ain't got time for this! Everyone, get in the trucks now!"

Rahn tenses. "*I* am the leader. I say if we go or not, and this sounds like a trap."

"Yeah." Corin steps forward from the crowd around us. His eyes find mine. "I saw what you were like. You're barely Untamed now, as it is. There's no way you're a real Seer."

"She saw the bison."

"So she *says*." Rahn coughs. Behind him, Marouska jerks one of the dogs back to her.

"I did see it!" I cry, but my voice isn't strong. What if it *was* just a dream—that happened to have a bison in it?

My brother appears by my side. "She saw the Turning too. Look at the sky now. See, purple's creeping into it already."

"If there's a Turnin' comin' then we need to stay here, in the huts, under cover."

"And let the Enhanced come and get us?" My father snorts. "Look, my daughter's the only Seer we've got. I'm listening to her. Three, get the keys for the red L200 from Corin. We're leaving, whether you give us permission or not."

Three pushes past Rahn toward Corin. "Give them over, Eriksen."

Corin doesn't move.

"If we split up, survival will be harder. Safety in numbers," Rahn growls. "You know that. And I ain't havin' a mutiny here."

I pull my shawl tighter around my shoulders. "We all need to leave," I whisper. Then I say it louder. "We need to leave now. They're coming for us."

It's almost like I can hear a thousand tiny footsteps pounding the ground, coming for us now. I squint, focusing on the horizon behind the huts. It's still darkish, but I can distinguish the land from the sky, just about. Can't see anything else though.

"You could be workin' with them," Rahn says.

"She's not! The Gods have forgiven her—"

"If this is true, yeah. But I still think it's a trap. Can't trust her, she could be one of them."

I shake my head. The pounding's getting louder. "I'm not one of them!" And it's true, isn't it? "If I was, I'd tell you where I want us all to go, wouldn't I? But I'm not! I don't care where we go, that's up to you, Rahn. *You're* the leader."

"Yeah, you'd still be in charge of us all. It's not like you'd be taking orders from a seventeen year old girl. Just taking Seer advice." My father's voice is odd.

Rahn shakes his head. He presses his lips into a fine line.

"This is stupid. We're going now." My brother steps forward, and plucks the keys straight from Corin's clenched hand. "Rahn, if it was anyone else who was a Seer, you wouldn't be questioning what we should do. You'd have made sure we all left as soon as we knew about it. No, it's because it's one of us, one of the Sarrs, and it's because Seven was Enhanced. But she isn't any more, is she? And the Gods have forgiven her if they've made her a Seer. She's obviously Untamed again, on our side, and I'm not risking my life because of your petty little grudge."

Behind us, the others talk in quiet murmurs. I catch some words: "Maybe she's right," and "Better to be safe than sorry."

"Fine," Rahn snaps. "Everyone, get in the trucks." He nods briefly, but I see the look he shoots me, and the way his teeth flash in the cold light.

As soon as he's said the words, everyone starts moving. Sacks are hauled into the L200s, blankets are piled in, along with food and water.

Esther's in front of me, carrying tins of dog food, when I notice something in her hand. My blood goes cold. It's my mother's pendent. The one that stops her from getting stuck in the Dream Land. Every Seer needs one. My mother told me that only a few weeks ago; told me that if a Seer didn't have one on at all times the malignant spirits could trap them.

"Why've you got it?" I shout.

Esther turns back and I snatch it from her, clenching the crystal to my chest. It feels cold and lost in my hands.

"She gave it to me for safe-keeping. For you." Esther's whole face pinches inward.

"No." I shake my head. "You stole it." My lip curls with disgust. "She'd never give it away."

Esther's eyes narrow. "She gave it to me before she left to join the Enhanced."

Everyone around us has stopped moving. I know they're watching us, and a few feet away, I'm sure my father's giving me a warning look.

Esther looks at me. I can't see much of her face in the dim light, only her sharp angles, and the slight glint of her eyes as she turns on me. "Believe what you want, but I didn't steal her stupid pendant. And the fact that she gave it to me shows she planned to leave us, okay? You can take your mother off that pedestal you've got her on because she isn't all good. She wanted to join the Enhanced."

I clench my jaws together. Esther moves away. I stare at my mother's crystal in my hand. It feels strange, odd, wrong. I shouldn't have it, she should.

"Put it on," Corin hisses as he walks past me. "If you're a Seer, we don't want you getting stuck in the Dream Land." But his voice says the opposite.

I gulp, then lift the old sinew around my neck, testing the strength. The crystal feels heavy as I tie it securely.

"We're low on fuel." Rahn looks at me accusingly. Above his dark glasses, his brows dip.

I try not to show any emotion, but it's impossible.

Corin and Kayden climb into the bed of the second truck, the red one, just as Rahn jumps down. The two younger men exchange a few words, their figures silhouetted. Corin's broader, but Kayden's taller. Then they look down at me; I think they're frowning.

"Right, everyone in! I want the usual drivers and formations, radios in each cab." Rahn pushes his dark glasses higher up his nose, even though I'm sure they hadn't slipped down at all. He's always doing that. "I want a dog in each truck too. Everyone, get your weapons ready."

My father passes me a leather rucksack, similar to my old black one. "Survival kit," he says as I take hold of it.

I nod. It feels light. We're running low on resources.

"We'll drive out toward the Waters on the south road." Rahn looks at Finn's dad, Sajo. "If we encounter the Enhanced, we divide up. Usual plan. You all know the lessons. We'll meet in an hour's time and prepare a large shack to cover us all durin' the Turnin'. After that, we continue toward High Crag Rock. If one of our trucks does not make it by midday tomorrow, the other truck continues alone. Got it?"

We all nod. I hug my jacket closer, my arms prickling and tingling. It's still dark and cold, but the sky's getting lighter.

"If you encounter other vehicles, do what's necessary."

I shudder. We had to do that before—what was necessary.

There were only three of them. All quite young. Rahn and Elf hadn't hesitated. They'd just shot them all, even before they could be certain the people were Enhanced. It isn't one of my best memories.

I take a deep breath, trying to steady myself. But my head's starting to pound. I look into the distance. The horizon looks murky, and ahead, everything's shimmering slightly. The sky's still swirling and the pounding in my head—it must be in my head—is getting louder. My fingers twitch. We need to get going.

Three looks across at me, frowning. "Seven, are you okay?"

I shoulder the survival bag, and look toward my brother. He's standing near Marouska and Esther. His eyes are on me and—

I see them before anyone else does.

My breath catches. The land tilts up around me. I step back, heavily, into one of the men. I feel his rough hands on my back for an instant as he pushes me forward. His annoyed voice fogs my ears, but I can't understand the words.

I can't even look at him, can't say sorry.

Because they're coming. And... and they don't look like how I'd expected. I thought they'd look like the people who I saw, who I was with, but they don't.

Like ghosts rising up before us, they appear, an unbeatable army. They are silent—too silent—and far too stealthy. But their stealthiness is exquisite. They're our predators, yet they are also beautiful, elegant creatures. They move as one being, perfectly attuned to each other.

Hundreds of flashes erupt across the night, capturing what little light the stars have and reflecting it toward us.

"Enhanced!"

A gun goes off. One of them falls. Esther leaps toward me, grabs my hand, and drags me down. A bullet whizzes past my ear. I scream, my head spins, then I see Finn fall. Even on the brink of death, he is not majestic. He falls like a dead elephant, and dust flies up around him in a huge cloud that blurs everything. And that's it. That's all that happens. But what had I expected? To see a shadowy figure appear and collect him? No, that's stupid. Death isn't a person. Death is all around us.

I turn sharply, dragging Esther with me.

They're here. Too soon. How? But they are. The Enhanced are around us. Each stands with their feet shoulder-width apart, dressed in combat gear. They're all pointing guns at us.

The perfect beings are using guns.

Most of the weapons are handguns—revolvers and Lugers—but I notice several grenade launcher pistols. And some M79s. A few rifles too.

I freeze. Oh Gods.

We all stop, like the ground has got hold of our feet and we can't move. To my far right, Marouska gulps. Corin moves closer to her, but there's still a significant space in between them. I turn slowly, trying to see everyone. Elf's disappeared, and now Marouska's on the outskirts of our group. She's easy picking.

Corin draws his own Glock out from his waistband, takes another step toward her. Three does the same, and Marouska steps back in toward us.

"Stay where you are," the nearest Enhanced One snarls. He lines his rifle up with Marouska.

"We will not be joining you." Rahn's voice shakes slightly. The leader's stance is defensive, and his Glock is on a man with a rifle.

"You have no choice."

There's a deathly silence, so quiet that I'm sure everyone must be able to hear my frantic heart, and I look up at the sky. There's more purple now. I glance at Esther. *They have guns*, she mouths at me. I nod. She's shaking.

We've spread out too far, and with five Enhanced Ones staring at each of us, things aren't looking great. No one's moving. A stand off. A stand off between the Untamed and the Enhanced.

We do not call ourselves the Enhanced.

I look at them. The *Chosen*. No. Still doesn't sound right. I swallow hard. Should I want to join them? I was like them...

and everyone says the addiction's strong... but I can't feel anything now. There's no voice compelling me to join them. Still, it feels like a test of my strength. And I know I have to be Untamed. The spirits made me a Seer. I have to listen to them. The spirits want the Untamed to survive, that's why they warned me. It was a message, clarification in case I needed it any clearer: I have to be Untamed.

"You don't believe in murder," Rahn says slowly. It's one of the only things we can be sure about regarding their intentions. Except in this instance, because why else would they carry guns?

Their answer is immediate and it comes from every single one of them, at the same time.

"For the greater good, we do. We'll kill to save our own people. It is a last resort."

Rahn's voice is steady, and his Glock jerks slightly. "We are not threatenin' your people."

"All Untamed creatures are a threat. And you've stolen one of ours. We will do anything to get her back."

I can hardly breathe. My chest feels all jittery. They want me. Raleigh—is he here? Has he come for me? Oh Gods... I can't go—I can't, I have to—Oh Gods!

Finn's dead. They've killed him. *Dead.*

There's a click of a gun from an Enhanced woman near me, and I turn my head. She's loading ammunition into her revolver with such expertise and quickness that she has to have done it before. I gulp. I need a weapon. There's a knife in the new survival kit my father gave me, but it's on my back, and no Untamed are moving. If I move, they'll all look at me. If Raleigh's here, he'll see me and—

More Enhanced Ones load their rifles.

"We will not hurt you if you join us willingly." It's the same Enhanced man who speaks, he seems to be the leader, and his mirror eyes lock onto Rahn. He raises the barrel of the revolver up slightly.

Still, Rahn does not flinch. "You do not use violence," he says, and it sounds like he's instructing them. But it is lesson six, after all: *The Enhanced don't believe in violence. Use that to your advantage.* "The Enhanced never purposefully use violence. You say it is a weakness. Violence is an evil temptation."

"We will kill you if it means saving our people from your murderous intentions."

I can't help myself from looking over at Finn's lifeless body. He's lying at an angle, his head bent too far back. Blood covers his head. My chest stiffens and my right arm twitches. My bag feels damp against my back.

"And we will use violence to get Shania back."

I gulp hard and swallow with difficulty, nearly gagging, but the golf ball-sized lump in my throat won't go down. My vision blurs slightly. I breathe out of my mouth as evenly as I can. I can see my breath in the air. I can taste blood and rust around my teeth... and the memory of Calmness... and Benevolence... I can taste them *still*... the good way of life. My heart speeds up. We have to join them, if we want to live. The Enhanced are just misunderstood... the Untamed don't share their ways. That's all.

"This is your last chance to come with us freely." It's the same Enhanced man—the apparent leader—who says the words. The words that change everything.

Rahn raises his pistol. My father does the same. Corin, Kayden and Elf follow suit.

I flinch as the Enhanced Ones raise their barrels; I can't look anywhere but at the guns.

The barrage of firing begins.

Chapter Ten

The *Enhanced* are shooting us.

My eardrums are going to explode. Esther grabs my hand. Hers is wet. My terrier appears and snarls at an Enhanced man in front of us. He lowers his gun, and I scream, diving forward. I scoop up the dog. A bullet flies past me. More clicks, more shrieks. More blood. I taste bitterness.

A man falls. I can't tell whether it's one of them or one of us. It's just a body. A body that falls and no longer moves.

My name's shouted. I scramble about, and slip. My mother's pendant slams against my skin, like the pounding in my head. The terrier's protesting in my arms but there's no way I'm letting him go. Esther's hand has gone.

"Get back!"

Something wet and sticky splashes over the side of my face, clings to my skin. I recoil back, hardly able to breathe. Dust kicks up over me. I choke, eyes streaming. I scramble forward, barely able to see as a heavy shadow falls across me. A flash of metal, and something with a small, circular end hovers in front of my face.

I freeze. The dog whimpers. My heart pounds. I look up into his face. Coldness washes over me, freezing my blood. The faint aroma of alcohol ripples toward me. My nostrils flare. I try to duck my head, try not to look at him—or the gun—but I can't.

Raleigh laughs.

"Shania." Nausea grips me as his lips twist into a smile.

"Not the dog," I whisper. The sky's more purple,

throwing horrible light everywhere. The Turning's closer.

Raleigh grins. I feel smaller than ever. "I don't want the dog." He sounds amused. "Shania. You know you want to join us again. You remember what the augmenters tasted like. The buzz they gave you. The feelings of pure joy. The adrenaline. It's brilliant. Isn't it?" His tone is severe. "And the safety, the security, not having to live in fear, being free to do what you want. You know I can offer you all that. And you know you're one of us."

I don't trust myself to speak. *Shoot me now. But not the dog. Let the dog go.*

"Answer me!" The light glints off his mirrors, adding a demonic element to his countenance. The revolver presses closer to me, so close that the smell of burning fills my nose. "Join us again. What they tell you is lies. You know that. You're not a real person, if you're with them."

My hands are trembling uncontrollably. I'm going to drop the dog. I will anyway, when Raleigh shoots me, and my body joins Finn's. I squeeze the dog tighter. His fur is wet and he's shaking, whining in a low tone.

More gunshots go off, but not from Raleigh's gun. Ahead, more people fall.

"Get back!" someone screams.

Raleigh grabs me.

I shriek. His fingers burn my neck, sliding across my collarbone. The dog slides down, away from me. Raleigh's arms snap around me, pulling me to him. I struggle, and manage to kick him, but pain shoots through my chest. My numb arms flail about. He grunts, breathing hard, his mouth near my ear. I get another whiff of alcohol from him and feel the muscles in his arms ripple as my own body lurches upward. I gag, retching as he jerks me forward. The gun's barrel crushes into my side and I flinch.

I get a kick in at his shin, but he doesn't react. Something wet hits my back. I feel pain and more pain. My fists pound against Raleigh's shoulder and his side. But his body's like steel, too hard.

Another gunshot nearby. A strangled scream. The dogs howl. The sky's too purple. The temperature's dropping too quickly.

"I know you want to, Shania. You do, you can't leave the cherry now you've tasted it. Just surrender, my butterfly. If you surrender, I'll call my people off. And it's not really surrendering is it, when you want it?"

"Okay!" I scream, my lungs about to explode. "I—argh!"

Raleigh's body crumples under me. We both fall and he lets out a guttural scream, his body shuddering. His arms slacken from around me, dropping away from my chest. I pull myself off him, slipping in blood.

I scramble about, trying to find Raleigh's gun—or any weapon—and then there's a figure in front of me, blocking out the purple sky.

Corin looks down at me. The Glock in his hand is smoking. He throws it down to me, and somehow I catch it without firing a round—he left the safety off. Stupid.

I stand shakily, and my dog rushes to me, howling.

"Go! Don't just stand there. You've got a weapon now. Go!" Corin pushes his dark hair from his grimy face. I see his shoulder is bloody as he leans over the still-alive Raleigh and wrenches the revolver from him.

I turn away, and go. But where am I supposed to go? The landscape is full of gunshots and death. I see Esther stumble as she's hit. I race toward her, dodging another Enhanced. But Esther's getting back up, and I can't see any blood at all. Maybe she dodged it? She has one of the Enhanced Ones' revolvers too—a Colt M1892—and turning, she shoots an Enhanced woman at almost point-blank range.

I squeeze my eyes shut as the blood splatters over me. Nearby, Rahn shouts. Someone else screams.

I hear a clicking sound. And then a *bang*. I fall. My legs shake as I collapse. My bag slams back into my spine. The gun, I've still got it. The landscape flashes white as I pull myself up, and freeze.

Flames engulf the sky, leaping everywhere. Debris and heat soar over me, with dark smoke that billows, diving up my nostrils. My throat's closing in, I can't—

"The trucks!"

I cough, clasping a hand to my mouth, eyes streaming. I

can barely see. An Enhanced man looms toward me, but I duck out the way, the Glock a dead weight by my side.

"Get the trucks away!" Rahn's lips contort as he screams. I see him silhouetted in front of flames for a few seconds. Then he's running, firing at more of the Enhanced Ones. Someone near him falls. "The trucks!"

I turn. I can see them. Two blue ones and a red one. The red one's closest. It's the only one that the Enhanced aren't standing next to, the only one that they're not slashing the tires of. It's the one closest to the flames.

"Get the truck!"

But no one, Enhanced or Untamed, is near the red L200. I'm the closest. I look behind me. Kayden is fighting unarmed. So is Elf. Marouska's on the ground—unconscious? I can't see my brother or sister or father. I gulp.

Something hits me in the shoulder. Stumbling, hand clasped to my skin, I cry out. But there's no blood. Turning again, I—

"Get the other truck away!" Rahn's voice is strained.

He's struggling with his ammunition belt. Someone—my father—races past him, throwing an Enhanced One's gun at him.

"The *truck*."

I run for the pickup, clasping the Glock to me. But it's covered in blood and my fingers slide. My feet pound, I jump over a patch of bloody desert ground, turn and shoot at an Enhanced man before he's even seen me.

I reach the truck in good time. My terrier follows, and, as I throw the door open, he jumps in first. I climb into the seat, trying not to look over at the other truck. But it's impossible. The orange flames are a blinding point in the landscape. Heat pulses over me. I can smell fumes everywhere.

The keys are already in the ignition. I turn them, pumping on the accelerator. It doesn't start right away, but when it does, it splutters, choking. Putting the truck in gear, I pull away. I put my foot down, getting faster and faster until I'm away from the fire. Is it far enough? I squint into the dirty mirrors.

Behind me, death takes over the landscape, fighting

moving figures. My hands are still on the wheel, my foot on the accelerator. I pause, my whole body shaking. I'm the only one in the truck. Me and the dog. Everyone else is still fighting. But I'm safe.

It would be easy to drive away... so easy....

Lesson seven: If attacked by the Enhanced, save as many people as you can, and get as far away as possible.

I duck, looking into the mirror. Bodies. Figures hurtling toward me. Streaks of darkness. Guns shooting. Fires. *Save as many people as you can.* But they're far away...*get as far away as possible.* I flex my fingers slightly, look in the mirror again.

If I go back, we could all die. If I drive away, I know I'll survive... for now.

On the double seat next to me, the terrier sprawls out. He whines at me once, his eyes full of trust. His nose drips blood.

"Stay here," I tell him firmly, slamming on the brakes. "I'm coming back for you." I push the door open, swinging my body out. I gasp as I land, pain shooting through my legs. Can't breathe for a few seconds—

"Get back in! Need to get away now!"

Suddenly Corin's in front of me, followed by several other Untamed. I freeze, startled.

"Back in, Sev!"

Quickly, I pull my body back into the driver's seat. Corin slides into the middle front seat, pushing the squealing terrier into the footwell. Rahn appears next to him. I feel the weight of the truck's bed increase as several people jump aboard. Another person's half-pulled in. I look in the mirror, but I can't see who's there. Tears come to my eyes; the air's heavy with death.

Someone in the truck bed fires their gun.

"Drive away now," Rahn shouts at me. "Drive."

I hesitate, looking in the mirror. There are more people running toward us and I *think* they're Untamed. No, I'm certain of it. They *are*. I know they are. They'll be here in a few minutes. A few seconds... a few....

"*Now*, Seven!"

"They're still coming!" I twist in my seat. "They're almost

here."

Rahn thumps the leather seat with his fist. "We're cuttin' our losses, Seven. I'm the leader, I command you to drive." For a second, I think he's going to hit me, but he doesn't. "Drive, *now*!"

I gulp, taking in far too much air, and choke. I put my foot down on the accelerator, and trying not to look in the mirrors or see those who we're leaving behind, I drive away.

Chapter Eleven

I left my father and my sister behind.

Those are the only words I can comprehend. They run over and over in my mind. I can hardly breathe, but that could be because it's the Turning and the evil spirits are trying to hurt us. Or maybe it's because I'm such a bad person.

I left my father and my sister behind.

Six of us got away.

We're not driving any more. We made it about forty miles south of Nbutai, making our own road in the dusty mountainous region, before we had to stop. All six of us— Corin, Rahn, Kayden, Three, Esther and I—are huddled under the tarpaulin in the truck bed.

"It's safety in numbers against the evil spirits," Rahn had said.

I thought that it would have made more sense if we'd all squashed into the cabin, but Rahn didn't think so. We just counted our resources, then pooled together under the tarpaulin.

We've got a lot of weapons: a Colt M1892, an HS2000, two revolvers, two grenade launcher pistols, a rifle, three Glock 17Cs and two Lugers. I'm cradling the Glock that Corin gave me close to my chest—the safety's on. Corin checked all the guns' safety catches before we hid under the tarpaulin.

My other hand is on top of my terrier's back, keeping him still, and Three's holding onto my elbow. I can feel him shaking. I'm lying on one of the three survival kits we still have—none of which have any water purification tablets in them—and a wooden box with lots of carvings on it digs into my shoulder. I can't move and I dare not make a sound. No one's making any sound at all, save for our breathing. We're all listening.

Above us, the spirits are gathering. I can't see them, but I know the sky will be a rich purple with dark black holes in it that grow bigger and bigger as they fight the purple masses. There might be a few other colorful streaks in there too. We have to remain as still as possible. The spirits cannot know we're here. I imagine their shapes; wispy tendrils clinging to skeletal figures, but it is my imagination. People rarely see an evil spirit *and* live.

My mind whirs and I find myself thinking of Raleigh. Did he survive? Is he still going to come after me? I swallow hard. I can hear my pulse in my ear. Three's grip on my elbow tightens. If Raleigh's alive, he won't be cowering under a tarpaulin. He'll be in a building, safe. All the Enhanced will be safe. They won't be relying on a flimsy tarpaulin and the pegs holding it down.

I try not to think of my room at the Enhanced compound. I'm Untamed. The benevolent spirits made me a Seer because they need me to be Untamed, to be their messenger, to carry their warnings. I have to be Untamed.

And I am, I've just proved that. I fought against the Enhanced, helped the Untamed get away.

You were going to join Raleigh.

I flinch. No. It was a surrender. I was going to surrender to him save my people. That was the deal Raleigh had offered. But it doesn't even matter now. It didn't happen. Corin saved me. But what if he hadn't? If I'd gone with Raleigh, then our group wouldn't have been cut down to six; sure they'd have had to move to a new village where the Enhanced couldn't find them, but they could've taken more people, more supplies with them. The Untamed would be stronger. And I'd be Enhanced; I don't know how to feel about that possibility. Nothing's clear any more. Sure, I no longer have the burning desire for augmenters, and I know that my emotions are my own—that I'm in control—but I do want to be safe. I don't like hiding under tarpaulins from supernatural danger.

I press my lips together and listen to the raging spirits.

It'll be better in the morning, it'll be warmer then. The other trucks had most of the foil blankets in them, but we have three between us. Esther, Corin and Rahn are using them. I brace myself. My mother's pendant presses against the side of my neck. It feels cold, but alive; I can't feel the sharp edge any more. I want to reach up and touch it, but I dare not let go of the dog. Or the Glock.

***

Eventually, the evil spirits leave and Rahn pulls back the tarpaulin. His face is shadowed with dust and his arms hang by his side as he stares at us. I get up, and the terrier jumps down out the truck bed. Looking amongst us again, I try not to notice just how many people we left behind. My father and Five's empty spaces haunt me.

I look at the terrier. He's looking for Esther's dog. Her dog isn't here. My terrier turns toward Three and me. He whines at us, his face full of sadness. I have to look away.

Rahn decides it's best if we get going again soon, so, after relieving ourselves and doing our best to wash the dried blood from our bodies in a small half-dried-out stream, we pile back into the truck. This time Corin's driving, with Rahn and Kayden in the front. Which suits me fine. Esther and Three are good company, normally.

The terrier's sitting between my legs. He whines. He *knows*. I try not to cry, because once I do, the dam will be broken.

We're heading southwest. Now that we have no other trucks to meet up with, the idea is to skirt around New Azhalda—an Enhanced city—and keep going until we find a smaller town we can raid. Corin reckons New Zsai will be the closest after the city, and a lot safer for us to raid. Less of a chance of them having scanners in the shops.

I twist around so I can see Corin in the cabin. He's deep in conversation with Rahn and Kayden; I can just about hear their voices over the engine.

My stomach rumbles and I try not to think about how delicious that cake was.

The dog shifts over a bit.

"I still can't believe they had guns... they *shot* at us," Three says at last, shaking his head. A line appears in between his eyebrows. He's sitting opposite me, his elbows resting on his knees. "They say the Enhanced are perfect. No crime or violence in their society, no murders, that their guns are only for shooting sports, but it's all lies. They don't believe in that. Lesson six is wrong." He sounds upset.

"Just proves it. No one can be perfect." Esther coughs. "The danger is when someone tries to be perfect, and convinces themselves that they are. It's like a disease." She's leaning against my body slightly; I think she's hurt her side. "They think what they're doing is right."

"Their goals are messed up."

Just saying the words makes me feel strange, as if I'm betraying a small part of me. But I'm not. I'm Untamed now. I look at Three. He seems surprised that I've spoken. So does Esther. Maybe they both expect me to be Enhanced-loving still.

"Yeah," Three says after a minute.

He fixes his eyes on me, and I find myself comparing his eyes with Raleigh's. Three's are human; the sclera's the colour it's supposed to be: white. And his irises are dark, but the pupils are darker still. Raleigh's are just metallic.

I think of my own eyes. I hope they're completely normal now, but I don't want to ask.

Esther sits up a little straighter, one hand pressed against her side. "They're definitely messed up." She looks at me. "They're even going against their own values to get you back. They must really want you."

"Or it's just an excuse to kill us. Eliminate the threat if they can't convert us," Three says.

I press my lips together. Either way, I don't want to think about it.

***

A couple of hours later, Corin and Rahn swap seats. Wordlessly, Corin climbs into the other side of the cabin, and slams the door. Then the engine rumbles up, and we're on our way again. Esther sighs at some point, and I notice my brother giving her a concerned look. I raise my eyebrows, mainly to myself. Esther shuts her eyes, leaning back against the shaking wall of the truck bed. At least she hasn't lost any of her family; Rahn and Corin are both here. My father and sister aren't.

I struggle not to cry as I think of Five. Out of seven siblings, we're the only girls. We were close. I can picture her perfectly. Her skin's the same mahogany shade as mine, but her bone structure is sharper and more elegant. Her eyes are brown, like mine—at least when I'm not Enhanced—but her nose is smaller and slightly arched. Her figure's always been better. She's curvy and feminine. I look down at my own slouched body and try not to feel resentment. That emotion isn't appropriate, especially when she's either dead or Enhanced because of me.

For a second, I feel a glimmer of hope. If she's Enhanced, she'll be safe. Alive, at least. Maybe we could rescue them all. But no one's the same after they've been Enhanced. The addiction doesn't go away. I bite down on my bottom lip, and stroke the dog.

Corin got me back, yet will I ever be the same person again? None of the people my mother rescued were. They screamed for augmenters at every second. They were desperate. Still, I'm not like that. It must be my genes. Maybe Five and my father could be converted back, like I was. We'd just need to find them... and my mother too. But I can't see Rahn agreeing to march us back into danger now.

I blink back tears. I know it's unlikely Five and my father are Enhanced. They'd have shot themselves, rather than risk that. The Dream Land showed me their bodies. The thought leaves a bitter taste in my mouth.

"We should be parallel with New Azhalda now," Three says some time later. He has a map in his hands. It was in my survival kit, along with a compass. "Fifty miles away."

I nod because I don't know what to say. Only fifty miles separates us from their artificiality. Only fifty miles separates us from safety, security, and stability.

The truck takes a sharp turn to the left, brakes squealing. I hurtle into the corner and fall heavily, gasping. Three falls onto me, his elbow digging into my stomach sharply. I pull my Glock out of his way, making sure the safety's still on. It is. Then Esther lands on top of us, and the terrier cowers under my bent legs. The luggage moves, and the truck's wheels skid.

It doesn't stop.

"Argh..." Esther's hand reaches out toward my head.

I try to say something, but there's an elbow in my stomach.

"Slow down!" Three yells.

We're skidding to the left. Three and Esther crash further into me. I struggle to breathe, can't see the terrier. The butt of a gun presses into my thigh, along with something else. Huge boxes fall onto us. I scream, trying to bring my arms up to shield my head, but I can't move them; Three's lying against them. He's trying to move so his body shields Esther and me, but the gravity's too strong.

For a horrible second, I'm sure the truck will turn over. Momentum's building. We're skidding too fast. Metal scrapes metal. Something hits my back. I scream and cold air blasts over me. Three cries out. The terrier whines.

I'm falling, slipping down, falling, falling. Somehow, I'm now on Three's other side. I can't see the terrain outside, but something's not right. The ground itself is *moving*.

The luggage takes a sharp turn, the ties snap, and packages hurtle toward the tailgate. The three of us start to slide with them. I scream. Limbs flail about. Three's arms clasp at the side, and he grabs out at Esther who's nearest.

I'm still sliding. The wind rakes through my hair.

I turn back, looking at the luggage, but I can't see all of it. It's shrinking, getting farther away. Falling away. It's falling out. *I'm* going to fall out. We're going fast. Too fast. I try to turn. Try to find something to hold onto, but my fingers just scrape at the rough wooden bed. Splinters dig into my fingers, diving underneath my nails.

"*Seven,*" Three shouts, and his arm's stretching out to me, but I can't quite reach. Our fingertips touch, and then the gap's growing.

Something makes a loud noise right next to me and I scream. The wooden bed snags against my shirt. More splinters. Sharp pain. I twist around. Nearly all the luggage has gone. And the truck's still speeding up. Still taking crazy turns.

"Rahn! Slow down, stop!"

Three dives toward me. His arms stretch out. I feel the warmth of his hands around my wrists. He pulls me back sharply, my shoulders protest. Pain engulfs me, strangling me. But I go with him. And somehow, seconds later, we're clinging to the back of the cabin. The truck goes over a deep pothole and we fly into the air.

We land heavily in the truckbed. Three grunts loudly.

"What the hell are they doing?" Esther's breathing's too ragged.

I can barely shrug. We're still going fast. Too fast. Especially for this road… if it is a road. All I can see when I look over the truck's walls is dust in swirling shapes. If we've left the road, we should've let some pressure out the tires, given them a wider surface area, more grip.

"Stop!" Three climbs up slightly, one hand firmly on my arm, and pounds on the back of the cabin. "Rahn, stop! Eriksen!"

But Rahn doesn't stop. The parts of my skin I can still feel prickle—something is wrong.

Rahn would not do this. Rahn would not go *this* fast. Or maybe he would if he was having one of those competitions with Corin, but he wouldn't when the three of us, and all our stuff, is in the back.

"What the hell's happening?" Corin's voice. Distant, far away.

Three's grip on my arm tightens. "Move over to that side," he says. "There's a handle."

He guides me toward it and I latch on as we go over another bump.

At that second, I see the sky. It is dark red. Blood. The sky is bleeding all over us. A strange sound escapes my lips, kind of like a gasp and a shriek. I look at Three and Esther. They've seen it too.

One of the Gods is angry with us. Or an evil spirit is chasing us.

"I've lost control—"

"Slam the brakes!"

"We've lost everythin' in the back... the luggage... shit… the ammunition…."

"Are they still—"

"I can't see Sev!"

I hear Rahn and Corin and Kayden's voices, but they're distant. Too distant. But I can *hear* them over the roaring of the wind and the howling of the sky, and I shouldn't be able to.

Something crashes against the side of the truck by Esther. She screams and lets go of her handle. Three lunges for her, just as she's about to go over the side. He lets go of his handle. I reach for them and—

We're flying. The three of us. Esther screams. Three screams. I scream. The air soars under my arms. Stuff rushes past me. My hair wraps around my head wildly. I can't see a thing. We've left the truck bed.

Then we're falling.

Light floods my vision. There's a whistling sound, and a shriek.

I scream as the dusty ground jumps up to meet us.

Chapter Twelve

I land on my side. Something cracks. Pain snakes through my left hip, moves across to my lower back. I flex my arms, trying to push myself up. It takes many attempts. Breathing hard, and panting, I finally succeed, pulling my body into a sitting position. The pendant around my neck moves slightly.

I look around. The sky is blue again. The desert is still— eerily still. Too still. My mouth is dry. Coldness spreads through me. I spread my fingers out on the dry ground, pushing my hand down until sand covers them. I flick my head the other way. More sand.

Only sand. There's nothing here. *Nothing*. Nothing but me and the sand.

I twist around, one hand clamped over my left hip. My back feels greasy. I'm trembling. But I don't know whether that's because of the pain or because I'm alone. Maybe both.

They've all gone. Esther. Three. Corin. Rahn. Kayden. The terrier. No one is here. I frown, my heart racing. They've gone. Just gone. They're not even in the distance. And everything—the landscape—is still. Too still. Too normal.

I shield my eyes from the sun—it's high up in the sky. I gulp, rubbing at my sore head. Deep breaths. I have to remain in control. I need a clear head. But my head is far from clear. It feels groggy. Then I feel the most terrifying feeling.

It starts as a small kind of hunger. But it grows and it keeps growing, until my sides are aching so much that my hip feels numb in comparison. My arms and legs start to shake uncontrollably. Heat pours through me.

"No... no... no." My voice sounds strange. Too strange.

I press my hot fingers to my forehead. It's sticky, clammy. Cold? I can't think. I can only feel the panic rising within me, the panic that I struggle to push down.

Need to calm down. I have to calm down. Have to. My legs jerk out.

I need an augmenter. Calmness... I can taste it again, on the back of my teeth, like a sweet syrup that's stuck there. I run the tip of my tongue over my teeth, leaning back in the sand, savoring it and—

This isn't real.

I freeze. The taste of the Calmness is so strong, so evocative, but *I* know it isn't real. It can't be. The Calmness isn't real.

It's the memory. Just the memory.

I'm stronger than that.

I need to find the others. I take a deep breath, feeling my ribs shake with pain as my lungs fill up. I force myself to sit up again, my hands gripping my knees so hard my skin burns under my own touch. Deep breaths, more deep breaths.

Okay. Right. I take another deep breath. Esther and Three fell from the truck at the same time as me. I know that happened. We were all flying toward the ground together. They must have landed close to me. Only I'm the only person here. The landscape is flat and dusty and smooth. There are no other bulky shapes. And the sand around me is unblemished, as far as I can see—no tire marks. But I can't see much. I'm still sitting. I need to be taller if I'm going to see more.

Gritting my teeth, I somehow manage to stand. Biting the inside of my cheeks, I struggle not to throw up.

I can't see anything new. It really is just sand. There are no markers, no markers at all. But there are always landmarks, somewhere. Rocks, old trees, there's always something. But not here.

My head feels too heavy as I walk forward. Then I stop.

I am *walking*. Yet my hip *cracked*. It hurt. It hurt a lot. I look down at my left side. My hip no longer hurts.

I frown, pressing my lips together for courage, and I keep walking. My mother's pendant is bulky around my neck. It feels heavy, almost wrong. But it's not. It can't be wrong. I look down at the pendent. Then I freeze. It's not there. I put my hand to my neck. Definitely not there. The sinew's gone. The crystal's gone. I frown; I can still feel its weight. But it's not there.

I'm running. I have to find it. The sky darkens around me. It's turning Brunswick green. Swirling shapes. I turn frantically, looking for the bison. But he's not there.

Is this a dream? I pause. Am I in the Dream Land again? My hip...my mother's pendant...the sky *shouldn't* be green.

My breathing's getting faster. This is very wrong. I don't know where I am. But if this *is* the Dream Land then none of this is real—or at least, it's not real at the moment. I frown, what is this telling me? I press my fingers to my forehead, but it doesn't help me, doesn't clarify anything.

Now, the sky's shades of green are getting brighter and brighter. The desert is green. I'm in a land of greenness and nothing else. Everywhere I look, there is green. Foliage, leaves, trees, vines, grass—too green.

I walk forward again. I run. I run for hours. Or maybe I'm not running at all. The green around me closes in. The land gets smaller, smaller. I'm trapped. The sky's falling. Cobwebs press over me, blankets. I take a breath, but inhale fogginess. Fogginess that dives down my throat.

I fall down.

Everything's sticky around me, pressing against me, getting stuck. I can't move. Whatever it is that is solidifying pulls at the tiny hairs on my skin.

"Is she alive?"

The voice makes me jump. I try to turn my head, but can't. The green heavy stuff locks my neck into place. I can see it around the edges of my vision. A swirling, musty kind of green.

"Yes. Though she's struggling to breathe, looks bad."

The green's covering me, more slivers onto me, pulling at

my skin, pulling at everything.

"Put the pendant back on her!" That voice is more high-pitched. "Do it! She's a Seer. She needs it, Rahn! She could already be lost!"

My body's too stiff, too solid. I can't do a thing, I'm too heavy, I'm sinking, sinking deeper and deeper into the greenness.

"But *if* she's a Seer, she could be seein' valuable stuff. She could learn stuff that would help us... we need as many warnings as possible."

"She can see the stuff with the pendant on too—"

"Not as much though, we all know how one of those pendant works!"

"Without it she'll be trapped in the Dream Land! She needs the pendent to anchor her to this world. Put it back on her. Now."

I gasp and gasp and gasp as the greeness drags me under. The world disappears amongst the green. I'm disappearing. I look up at the sky—my last look at the world. The bison. Just a glimpse of him. The *bison*.

He's watching me, laughing as the walls of the Dream Land close in on me, until nothing's left.

Chapter Thirteen

I open my eyes, coughing and spluttering. Pain swarms my body, like water filling a container. I reach up to my throat. The pendent's there. Its beautiful weight rests against my skin. I clutch it so hard my knuckles crack.

I sit up slowly, with the help of Esther and Three either side of me. Three's arm supports my back. His skin feels like it burns through my shirt. I start to cry. This world feels more stable. It's real. It's true. And I'm not alone.

"What did you see?" Rahn demands.

He's crouching behind Esther and Three, cradling something on his lap—a wooden box with ornate carvings. Corin and Kayden are behind him. We're all together.

"She's weak," Three says. He glares at Rahn.

"We need to know what she saw. If she's a Seer, it's her duty to tell us." Rahn's voice is stern and commanding. But he won't look at me—he's looking anywhere but me: at the ground, the sky, Three, Corin, Esther, Kayden. Just not me.

Guilty. That's the face of guilt. I press my lips together. He got rid of my mother. Now he's trying to get rid of me too.

"What did you see?"

"Green," I mutter. "Everything was green. I was trapped... in the ground." I turn away, gagging.

Rahn wrinkles his nose. He folds his arms across his chest, and his index fingers tap at his armpits. "What does that mean?"

I shake my head, looking around. To my left I can see the Titian Mountains, but to my right the landscape is flatter, with less grooves and more vegetation.

"Anythin' else?"

Another shake of the head. I can't remember anything else. Just the overwhelming green. And the bison.

"You're hidin' somethin'," Rahn grunts, the sun flashing off his glasses. His arms fly out toward me and Three grabs me, yanking me back away from the leader. "What are you hidin'? You workin' against us?"

"Rahn!" Three glares at him. "Seven just got trapped in the Dream Land because of your idiocy—"

"No, I was tryin' to help her learn more."

"We nearly lost her in there." Esther's voice is quiet and subdued. Tears have streaked through the dirt on her cheeks, emphasizing the scarring below her left eye.

"What does green mean?" Corin snaps, turning on me as he pulls a rather soggy cigarette from his pocket.

I shrug as he taps at it, flicking water from it. The beads of water catch my skin and I shudder.

Rahn points his forefinger at me. "She knows."

I shake my head, even though it hurts. "I don't know what it means. Everything was green. The sky. The land. Everything."

Kayden steps forward, his red hair slicked back with grease. "Green can mean prosperity and life. It could be an omen for our survival."

Rahn does not look convinced. "Yes," he says, "because we can easily survive with no truck and supplies. With no nothin'." But he's still got that box with the strange carvings on it. I can't work out whether they're of animals, or just patterns.

There's a long silence. Eventually, I'm the one who breaks it.

"What happened?" I ask.

I no longer have the Glock Corin gave me, and I can't see the truck. Corin's still got a grenade launcher pistol and a rifle—he's balancing them expertly as he struggles to light the cigarette—and Rahn's got a Glock and a Luger, but they're the only weapons I can see. Four, between the six of us.

Corin answers. "We ran into a chivra. Didn't get a close look at it, mind you. But it got control of the truck, and then took it from us. And our stuff."

A chivra. One of the most evil spirits out there. Great.

"We need to keep moving," I say suddenly, the words spilling out.

"Why?" Rahn's voice is full of suspicion.

"She's a *Seer*," Esther says. "We shouldn't question—"

Corin and Rahn both snort.

"Seers aren't reliable," Corin says. "And they make mistakes. They can be stupid. Think what Two did."

I flinch.

"Seven's right though." Three stands up. "We should keep moving. If the Enhanced are after us, we need to be on the move. We can't just wait for them to find us."

Suddenly, I look around. "Where's the terrier?"

Three looks away and a tear falls from Esther's left eye.

"We don't know," she says at last.

Corin takes a long drag, then breathes out smoke.

I look at the ground, swallowing hard.

"Come on," Three says. "We're getting on the move again."

My brother is taking control and I can see neither Rahn nor Corin like this. Yet neither protest. At the moment.

***

Walking in the heat of the desert is never a good idea, especially with a badly bruised hip. We walk for a good few hours—Rahn, Kayden and Corin in front, Esther, Three and me behind them—until I think I am going to collapse from exhaustion or dehydration.

At last, Rahn calls a halt. He looks worn out and sweat patches cover his clothes. Somehow, even though I can't see his eyes, I know he's regarding me with the look a hunter sends his prey. I shudder. But Three's standing next to me, and I know he's on my side.

"Which way?" Rahn asks, he's carrying the wooden box. We are at a kind of junction in the dust road. "Left or right?"

"Right," Corin says, and my brother agrees.

Esther and Kayden both shrug. I go to voice my opinion, but Rahn doesn't even look at me, just nods and heads to the right. His pace is fast, and a part of me wonders if he's setting that pace to get at me. He knows I am hurt. But I won't protest. Not yet, anyway.

I look ahead, to the right. The desert spreads out, and although there is nothing obvious in that direction, a bad feeling sets into my gut. I shrug. I would've voted to go left.

No one speaks. All I can hear is a distant humming sound. No one else seems bothered by it. If the terrier were here, he'd be whining, or demanding to play. He'd make this journey lighter and less foreboding. But he's not here. It's unlikely he survived falling from the truck. Kayden said he looked for his body during the first few minutes when I was stuck in the Dream Land, but found nothing.

In front, Corin points ahead. His stocky arm is rigid as he indicates something ahead. I squint, peering into the distance. It's a rock. On the rock is a black dot. A black dot that is so black and glossy that it can only be an artificial marking. It's a marking I haven't seen for a long, long time. We had to get rid of all our signs around Nbutai as we feared the Enhanced would know what they meant. It was a precaution necessary for our own survival. Anyway, we'd thought there was little point in keeping them; we'd believed for a long time we were the last Untamed in this region. So there was no point signalling to anyone that our camp would be five miles directly behind a certain rock.

But this rock isn't one of ours that we'd forgotten to remove the black dot from. No, we're hundreds of miles away from the end of our territory.

This rock belongs to others. Other Untamed.

Rahn, Corin and Kayden have come to a stop now. Three, Esther and I catch them up in a matter of seconds. They're talking fast and quietly.

"They can help us replenish our supplies," Rahn says firmly. Corin agrees with a slight nod of his head. Rahn looks back me. "Did you foresee this?" he asks.

"No."

Rahn makes a sound close to a grunt. "What is the use of havin' a Seer, if she is not even gifted?"

"Seers only see stuff that is dangerous. They see stuff so they can warn us." Three folds his arms, then steps closer to me.

Now Corin looks at me, and for the first time, since he was trying to stop me from licking the augmenters from the floor back at the compound, our eyes meet properly. I see how dark his are, how they look deeper and more solid than usual. He looks away quickly. "So these people aren't a threat?"

I shrug. The movement hurts my back. "I don't know. I haven't seen anything about them."

But I haven't seen much. I wish he wouldn't ask such a stupid question, because now, if these people are hostile, they'll blame me for not warning them.

"It could be a trap," Esther says.

"No." Rahn shakes his head. "We have a Seer to warn us of traps. She does not think these people are dangerous."

That wasn't what I said and everyone knows it. I look toward the black-spotted rock. It is still a hundred or so feet away. I look at it hard. Something is wrong. Very wrong. I can feel it. We should have turned left. This is bad. We are on bad land.

I look up at Three, trying to tell him, but he's arguing with Rahn. And Corin and Esther and Kayden are all getting involved. No one's listening to me. So I walk over to the black-spotted rock. And with every step nearer, the unease within me grows.

At last, I reach the rock. Looking behind me, I see Rahn and Three are still arguing over whether I am a liability who's going to turn on them and lead them straight to the Enhanced, or a valuable asset.

I turn back to the rock. It's big. It reaches my knee and is a dark orange color. The black mark is perfect. Slowly, I walk around the rock. When I reach the back, I stop. My chest hitches. A red circle. It is bright, like a dying sun.

"Three!" I shout.

For a second, my brother looks surprised that I'm so far

away, but then he runs to me. His expression darkens when he sees the red circle. Then he grabs my arm, pulling me back.

Rahn blocks our way. "What the hell is happenin'?"

"A red circle," Three and I say in unison, and then we glance at each other. I'm shaking—can't stop shaking.

The corners of Rahn's mouth lift up slightly. "Then we *must* go there. They have no use for their resources."

"We can't!" I stare at him. "Are you mad?"

"You do *not* decide what we do or do not do," Rahn says. "Unless you have foreseen trouble. Which you haven't. And you *never* question my sanity."

Corin, Esther and Kayden now join us and Three tells them what's on the back of the rock. Corin goes and checks it for himself. When he returns, his face is grim.

"We must head in the opposite direction." He meets Rahn's stern glare with his own.

Rahn shakes his head and folds his arms. "They could have been dead for years," he reasons. He looks at me. "If there was a problem with us goin' there, Seven would know."

"Seers don't see everything, and even if they do, it's not always in time," Corin says. We all know he's referring to his parents' deaths. They were killed in the attack that my mother and Two failed to see in time. My brother was killed in that attack too but everyone seems to forget that. Corin folds his arms and looks down at Rahn. The couple of inches between their heights make all the difference. "We are not going there."

Rahn shakes his head vehemently. "We are." He stamps his foot, turning toward Esther and Three and myself, before looking back at Corin. "They might not even be dead yet. It would be stupid to not pay them a visit," he says. "They could have stuff that we need."

"We could be walking to our deaths," I say. "We've no idea how fresh or old the disease is. We could catch it." Now it's obvious what the green in the Dream Land stood for: illness.

Rahn points at his nephew. "You can see the sense in

goin', right?"

But Corin shakes his head. "Sev's right," he says and looks at me briefly, but his tone of voice suggests he's almost disgusted to find himself agreeing with me.

I sigh. Every time he looks at me, I'm sure he's seeing me how I was in the Enhanced compound. Maybe he still thinks I'm feeling like that inside.

Maybe I am.

"We'll vote on it," Rahn says at last. He's holding the box with the carving under his arm. "Yes. A vote." I'm surprised; he must be feeling confident enough to suggest a democratic vote. "Look at us. We only have the clothes we're wearin'. No food. No water. No medicine. Nothin'. Yes, these people are dead from a contagious disease, but we can use their stuff to aid our own survival—"

"We don't know that they're dead," Corin counters. "If there's just one still alive, we could get the disease too. We still could even if they are all dead. It's not worth the risk."

"Seven and Eriksen are right. It *isn't* worth the risk," Three says.

We look at Esther and Kayden.

Esther looks uncomfortable. "It may be our best shot though," she says at last. Rahn smiles at her widely, and I notice the sunburn around his lips for the first time. It's not as bad as Corin's, but it still looks painful.

Kayden nods. "We'll die without water anyway."

"We can find water somewhere else!" Corin shouts. And he actually looks toward Three and me for support. "Anyway, we're divided, we shouldn't go. Not without a clear-voted answer."

Rahn smiles, but it is not a kind smile. It's a smile that will haunt me. "I am the leader. My vote holds more weight in cases such as these. We are goin'. And, anyway, if it really *was* a bad idea, Seven would warn us."

He looks at me, waiting for me to speak. For a second I consider making something up. But I don't. I don't want to lie to them or abuse my powers as a Seer. Anyway, I'm an awful liar.

"There we go then," Rahn says. "We're goin'. *All* of us."

Chapter Fourteen

The five-mile walk is awful, and by the time we reach the buildings, I am breathing hard. I look around. These shacks are more sturdily built than ours. And there are more of them than we had. At least twenty. But they're old; fabric is rotting.

Something else is rotting too. I wrinkle my nose, trying not to gag. Flesh. Human flesh.

"I'm not going in," Corin says. He has stopped about two hundred feet from the nearest shack. "We'll stay out here."

It takes a second for me to register that he's including Three and me in the 'we', and it makes me feel strange. Triumphant? Scared? Nervous?

Rahn turns to the three of us, slamming his left fist into his right hand. "You'll do as your leader says. And you'll do it *now*. We're goin' in. We're salvagin' what we can."

I shake my head. "The disease is fresh. We can't go in there. We'll get it too. If it's airborne we could already have it."

"Then it won't make any difference, will it? We have to take what we can, whilst we can." Rahn steps right up into Corin's face and the two men attempt to stare each other down.

"I'm not sure about this any more," Esther says.

"We should go back," Corin adds.

Rahn swears loudly, and his fist leaps forward a few inches in a striking movement, but doesn't go any farther. "*I* am the leader," he says. "You obey me. You always obey me." He looks at Three, Corin, then me, then Esther and Kayden. "Do I make myself clear? Now, get in there."

For a long second, no one moves. Then Esther steps toward the abandoned Untamed village. Kayden follows her next, but there is a few seconds' delay. Rahn turns his heavy glare on me. I don't move.

But Three does. I stare at him, my mouth open, as he follows Esther and Kayden.

"Good man," Rahn says, but the way he says it is more like he's talking to a child, not a man who's only twenty years younger than he he himself is.

Rahn turns back to Corin and me. Then he moves his left arm slightly. I inhale sharply, my eyes widening as I see the Glock in Rahn's hand. He's concealing it slightly, behind his own body. You only see it when you're in the direct firing line. I gulp. Rahn wouldn't shoot us, would he? But I don't know the answer; that's what scares me.

"You're forcing us?" Corin's voice isn't as confident as before. I know he also has a gun in his belt, but he doesn't move to draw it out.

Rahn nods firmly. "I am. Leaders have to use whatever means necessary in order to protect their people. Now, go and collect what you can."

And, just like that, Corin walks off, his head held high in the air. I'm left standing with Rahn aiming a gun at my head. So I do what any sensible person would: I step forward into the village.

Rahn walks close behind me. Ahead, Corin's walking fast, going for the heart of the village. I can't see Esther or Three.

"You take these ones." Rahn indicates a row of shabby huts to the right. They're on the outskirts of the village.

I nod. Dividing up is always the quickest strategy—and the most productive.

Rahn grunts, and turns away. "I'll be nearby." The way he says it almost sounds like a warning; I shiver.

The first house I enter is the smelliest house I've ever been in. A pile of rotting flesh sits in the corner of the main room. I'm sure it's the remains of a person—or maybe two—so I refuse to let myself look at it.

Swarms of flies buzz and I can't even hear myself think. I step over something decomposing on the floor, and duck under a huge cobweb. I try to hold my breath, but I feel light-headed. I take a deeper gulp of the pungent air, and regret it. Coughing and choking and spluttering, I look around.

There's a bowl on the table, so I pick it up. There are a few fabric drapes folded over by one wall, but I'm sure there's something wrapped in them that's decaying as well. I've already looked for the obvious things like weapons and uncontaminated food, but there aren't any. There's just death, and I cannot wait to leave.

In the end, I grab another bowl, even though it's cracked, and duck under the drape by the entrance. Being outside, in the fresh air—even though it isn't that clean—is beautiful. I take a huge breath, revelling in it. Freedom, at last—

I hear the footsteps a fraction of a second before a hand clamps over my mouth.

Chapter Fifteen

I swear into the leathery skin, cursing Rahn over and over again as he drags me backward. Dust billows around me as I kick out. Rahn's stronger than I expected, and he tilts my head up, so all I can see is sky. The sun's bright and its flashes sting my eyes. I stumble, trip, but he doesn't let me fall. I smell a strong liquor, and feel metal against my head — his gun?

A drape slides over my arm. A new hut.

"There, there, my little one."

I'm forced to face him and —

It's not Rahn.

It's Raleigh. *Again.*

I turn, looking behind me, my eyes searching the darkest corners and the shadows. He's not going to be working alone. They always work in a pack. That's what Rahn's taught us all, and that's what I've found to be true. But I can't see any movement. No other Enhanced reveal themselves.

Raleigh smiles slowly. It's dark in the hut, but his eyes still manage to capture some light and throw it back at me.

"Get away from me," I say.

I raise my balled fist slightly. In my other hand, I still hold the bowls, but they won't be much use. Especially against a gun. I eye the firearm warily. A semi-automatic pistol, with a silencer attached.

"Shania, please, listen to me." The emotion in his face is deceptive.

"My name is *Seven*." I back away from him, deeper into

the hut, a hand over my mouth. This one smells worse than the last.

"You're hurt," he says, scanning my body. His gaze rests on my hip for a little too long. "I can fix that," he says, and he puts the gun into his belt. "I won't hurt you."

I flick my head back as I look around. The window is behind him, as is the door. He's backed me into a corner. I can't get out. Not easily. I need to swap positions with him, then run. But my hip... I swear under my breath.

Maybe I should just entertain him for as long as possible, until Three comes looking for me. Unless he's in a similar situation as well. No. I need to get out of here on my own.

"Join us, Shania. We won't let them take you from us again. You'll be my top priority. And I can tell you about your mother."

I flinch, and he smiles; he knows he has me, I'm sure.

"I can take you to her. A reunion. She asks about you all the time, Shania, she wants her baby back. All she talks about is you—"

"Stop it! You're lying." My voice wobbles.

"Am I?"

I nod, feeling a lump like coal slide down my throat. He has to be. It's a trick.

But he's talking about *my mother*.

And what if it's true? What if I could see her again? And I'd have food, and water, and shelter....

No. I need to stay Untamed. I take a deep breath. *I'm a Seer*. The spirits have chosen me. I can't let them down, the spirits are always right. If they've chosen me to be a Seer, it's because being Untamed is the right thing to be.

Raleigh smiles. "She always talks about you. *Where's my little Shania, Raleigh?* she says."

"No. She wouldn't. My name is Seven. She named me."

"All she wants is her baby girl."

For the first time he looks away from me and I take that moment to scream. I try to spin around, but my hip stops me.

Raleigh lunges for me; I knee him between the legs. He crumples up, moaning.

I jump over him, ignoring the pain in my hip, and I try to run. But his hand snakes around my ankle. I scream as I fall, landing heavily next to him, my shoulder crashing into his body. I roll over, trying to get away, but his hand is on me, and his fingers are strong.

"Be quiet, Shania," Raleigh hisses. His hand presses down on my mouth as he scrambles up, kneels over me. He moves forward, a knee either side of my body.

I'm not being quiet. I'm screaming as loudly as I can into his hand. Shouting for help. "Three!"

Raleigh holds me down. I scream and kick out at him. I miss. I fumble for something that I can use as a weapon, but there's nothing here. My blood rushes to my ears, my skin's clammy and my heart gets faster. He's going to get the pistol out, any second now.

"Stop it!" Raleigh screams. "Shania, I—"

He's cut off by a growl. A very loud and familiar growl.

"Dog!" I shout.

My terrier, my beautiful little terrier, appears. I watch, almost gleeful, as my dog tears a chunk out of Raleigh's arm. The man screams, showering me with spit, but his weight doesn't leave me.

I yell for my brother again, but Raleigh hits me hard across the chest. Fresh pain washes over me.

The dog barks at Raleigh, his teeth bared. Raleigh rolls himself off me, kneeing me hard in the stomach. I shriek. The dog growls and leaps at Raleigh, who's now standing.

"Get it away from me!" Raleigh tries to brush my dog off his ankle. But the terrier isn't giving up. Neither am I.

I try to get up, but Raleigh steps nearer. He plants his foot over my stomach, and blood drips from his arm onto me.

"I don't think so," he says. "This is your last chance, Shania. Your very last chance. Use it wisely."

"I am Untamed!" I shout, and the words reverberate within me, setting off a new type of power, of determination. My hands scramble about on the floor, looking for anything I can use as a weapon... a stone, anything! But there's nothing. His foot presses down harder. The dog's going crazy.

Then we hear footsteps. Raleigh looks pleased.

"They're here," he whispers, apparently now oblivious to my dog gnawing at his leg. "Come on, Shania. We'll get you home."

And the footsteps get nearer... nearer... nearer... the terrier goes quiet and I cannot see him.

Raleigh places a hand on my shoulder. "Come on. Stand up."

I do. I'm not stupid. I can't fight him and his men. Raleigh puts his uninjured arm around my shoulders, holding me close against his body. I try not to breathe.

An unknown hand moves the drape in front of the hut's entrance. I look away. I don't want to see them.

"Get your hands off her."

My gaze snaps upward. Corin and Three stand in the doorway. Rahn is behind them, with Kayden and Esther.

For a second, Raleigh freezes, then he pushes me forward. My body's his shield, and he presses me against him until I can feel every detail of his body.

"I said, get your hands off her. And I mean *now*." Corin steps forward, his gun in his hand.

"Let us out of here," Raleigh says. He presses a hand down on my shoulder and I feel blood trickle down my back. His blood. I hear a slight scraping noise, maybe his pistol? "I am taking with me what is mine."

"She is not yours," Rahn says. He points his Glock at us, its barrel is shiny. "She is part of *my* group."

Raleigh laughs and I feel his body shake. "I never knew the Untamed were so accommodating to ones we've *tainted* these days... well, I suppose you have to be, given how few your number is." He squeezes my shoulder, then lifts his gun up. I can see its barrel by the side of my face, too close. "Shania is one of us. She has developed a taste for the augmenters, and they are still in her system, even if her eyes say they are not. She needs augmenters to survive. Would you really want to cause her death simply by keeping her with you?"

"That is a lie," Rahn says, his voice deep. "Seven doesn't need them."

Raleigh pauses. "You're sure about that? Because I know

what she's feeling. She wants the augmenters. It's painful for her, the need to have them. She's trying to be strong, to prove she's still one of you. But she's not. She's one of us. You cannot change what has happened. I have been sent to claim back what belongs to—"

"She is not an object!" Three shouts, then he's right in front of us. He's got the rifle and it's level with Raleigh's eyes. "I will shoot you dead right now, right here. I mean it, old man. Let go of my sister."

Raleigh doesn't move.

They deserve to die. Each and every one of them.

I want to scream, but I can't... maybe because Raleigh doesn't deserve to die... but he's an Enhanced....

But no one deserves to die, do they?

"I mean it." Three positions the rifle by his shoulder. Behind him, Corin and Rahn step nearer, their weapons already raised.

"You don't," Raleigh says. He stoops. His mouth is behind my neck, and his breath is hot against my skin. "You won't shoot me, not when there's a chance of Shania being shot—"

Three pulls the trigger.

I shriek. Momentary darkness. Shouting. Blood splatters everywhere.

"Not a chance, eh?" Three laughs.

His gun is still pointed at Raleigh, whose hand has fallen from my shoulder. I turn and look at the Enhanced man, and, for a second, Raleigh doesn't move. He just stares at my brother. Then he falls, gasping. The bullet is in his leg. Not meant to kill, just in case Three's aim wasn't true. Then I see the blood. Red. Everywhere. There's too much of it.

I scream. I run.

"Seven!" Esther grabs me and pulls me out of the hut. She wraps me up in a hug. Raleigh's blood covers both of us. "Let's get you away from here," she says.

Esther leads me away. My terrier shadows us.

Another gunshot echoes through the landscape.

***

"He's not dead," is the first thing Three tells Esther and me when the others emerge from the hut. I can't see whether they've got Raleigh's gun with them, but I expect they must have. They're not stupid.

We're sitting not too far off, sorting through the items we scavenged from the dead village. It doesn't feel right, taking them, but Rahn's right—they have no other use.

Corin looks annoyed. He's lighting up, though he struggles with his lighter for a few seconds. There isn't much fluid left, but he'll probably have another one, even though we have practically no resources.

"Our bullets aren't enough to kill him. He's super-Enhanced. But he's not going to be moving from that hut for a long time." Corin glances at me, but doesn't say anything. Rahn is just behind him.

"And that is why we should have got Seven back through reasonin' with him. Our ammunition's goin' to run out, if we ain't careful. Violence is not always the answer, especially when we're against the *perfect* Enhanced."

I raise my eyebrows. *Violence is not always the answer.* Rahn sounds like the Enhanced.

Now, the leader turns on me. "And don't you go gettin' yourself into any more situations like that."

"Hey! That was *not* Seven's fault," Three says. He has a coil of wire hanging around his neck. "The fact is they're going to be after her. We already knew that. So we've got to protect her. Work together, not against each other."

"Protect her?" Rahn looks at me, then back at Three. "She's seventeen. Not a child. She doesn't need protectin'. She's practically an adult—"

"Then treat her like one," Three says. "I've seen the way you speak to her. You too, Eriksen. And, it is no different to how you treated our mother. Or how you treat the majority of my family. Just what the hell is your problem?"

There's a long pause.

"Problem?" Rahn says. He shakes his head. "I don't have a problem with you. But your sister? The fact is, she's a Seer. And my previous experiences with Seers ain't been good. Seers ain't trustworthy. They keep secrets." He looks down his hooked nose at me, his dark glasses glinting. "They deceive us. They pretend to be on our side. But they're not. So, yeah, actually I *do* have a problem with Seven. She's a Seer. Before her Seer powers were discovered, we had none of this. We still had our homes, our food, our resources, our people. This is her fault."

There's a startled silence. I gulp and look across at Corin. He's tapping the ash off the end of his cigarette, intent on it. Surely he can't blame me too? It's not my fault we had to leave people behind... but I *was* the one who drove the truck away from them all. I was the one who left my father and sister behind. My stomach twists into a tight knot. I was the one who left them to become Enhanced, or killed. I start to choke.

Three stands up and flicks his hands out. "You can't blame her for all that. If she hadn't seen it coming, we'd all be dead too. And you, Rahn, *you* were the one who told her to drive away."

"Well maybe dead is better than what we are now," Rahn says. He looks at me with such an expression of utter disgust that I can almost feel my blood curdling. "She's a liability. She's a Seer, she's not trustworthy. And, so long as she's with us, we've got the Enhanced after us."

"We are a group," Three says slowly. There's a warning note in his tone. "And we always have the Enhanced after us."

A long, long silence follows.

"Right, we need to get a move on." Rahn's voice is sharp as he turns away. "If one Enhanced is here, there'll be more on their way. We'll divide our salvage between us, and get goin'."

That's what we do. There's only one tarpaulin bag that's good enough to use, so all the little objects get piled into it until the seams are bursting. Corin—being the strongest—takes the bag, lugging it over his shoulder. Esther and I both have curtains and drapes over our arms, and Kayden has an old bow that he found. There are no arrows but he says he'll whittle them from the legs of a chair. Three and Rahn are carrying containers, skins, and buckets. They're empty at the moment, but when we find water we'll fill them up.

The six of us set off, and for a long time no one speaks. The terrier keeps close to my heels, and I keep having to look at him, just to check that he is still there—and that he is real and not a figment of my imagination. I can't believe he's here. It's almost like a dream. I never thought I'd see him again.

After a while, the six of us fall into our usual walking formation: Corin, Kayden and Rahn at the front, Esther, Three, and myself at the back. The sun is high in the sky: it's getting hotter. The dusty ground feels harder, my feet hurt. In the distance, some hyenas run away.

A couple of hours later we reach a spring, and we all greedily drink. For the first time in my life, I'm not excessively worried about the bacteria in the water, because it's *water*.

It won't do any harm, I tell myself over and over as I swallow. It's the only water available. I bite my lip, trying hard not to think of the Enhanced compound. There was water there: clean, fresh water. Would it really be so bad to live there and not be at risk of infection and disease, even if it meant losing our emotions, becoming Enhanced? I push that thought away quickly. I can't afford to think like that.

Rahn and Three fill up the containers, skins, and buckets, and we set off again. Three takes the tarpaulin bag, and Corin has one of the water containers. We walk in silence. I can't get rid of the feeling of Raleigh's hands on my shoulders or his hot breath on my neck, no matter how hard I try. Just thinking about it is enough to make me shudder.

And he's still out there. He's not dead. He's alive. He's after me. And something within me—that little voice of reason—tells me that he won't be giving up until he's got me.

Or until I'm dead.

Chapter Sixteen

The next day, by about noon—when heat pounds down the hardest, bathing us in sweat—we reach the outskirts of New Zsai, one of the Enhanced Ones' towns. Well, all towns nowadays are theirs.

For several seconds, the six of us stare at the buildings in the distance. They are big. Massive stone-colored blocks in the center. Flatter, squarer buildings on the outside. It's funny really, how they're all concentrated in one spot. Beyond the last buildings is just land, not a sign of the inhabitants in it. Few Enhanced—if any at all—live in the isolated, rural areas; if they did, all it would take would be for a group of Untamed to kidnap them, and starve them of the augmenters until they gained some of their humanity back. Or kill them.

My eyes fix on the town. Even from here, I can hear— or maybe, sense—the buzz of electricity that screams civilization.

Rahn frowns as he looks out toward the town. The outskirts, from what we can see, don't look as sophisticated as the skyscrapers peeking from the middle of the assembly.

"Right. We're goin' to raid for supplies," Rahn says after a few moments. He turns to Corin. "You're with me. And you." He nods at me, but the action is completely devoid of friendliness.

For a second, I'm too stunned to speak—*me*? He wants me? The liability, the one who's caused all this trouble? Sure, I may be the fastest runner, but he's sending me there? I don't know what to do, where to look or what to say at all.

In the end, I observe the distant city again.

The Enhanced will be in there. People... like me.

No. I push the thought away, feeling the muscles in my neck tense.

Oh Gods. I didn't mean to think that.

I look back up at Rahn. He's still looking toward the city. I take a deep breath, trying—and failing—to calm my nerves. Maybe this is a test. Maybe he wants to know whose side I'm really on.

"Kayden, you're in charge of Esther and Three."

Kayden nods. In this bright light, his red hair is blazing. The skin on his shoulders is starting to burn, emphasizing the ragged fire scars there. He got badly hurt in an attack seven years ago, when the Enhanced set fire to the house we were all in, to try to flush us out the front door. Kayden saved me—though I'm sure he mistook me for his girlfriend, seeing as I always was very tall for my age—throwing me out the window, but the walls of the house collapsed right after. A burning beam fell across him. My father and Sajo managed to get Kayden out, but no one thought he'd live more than a few days. Especially when we didn't find Faya's body, or his baby daughter.

"We'll take different ends of the town; I'll approach from the west, you the east," Rahn says. I nod to myself, just as I thought: Rahn, Corin and I have the furthest distance to cross. "We'll attract less attention in smaller groups." Rahn rolls up his sleeves and I see him looking at our meager belongings. "We'll hide these over yonder," he points at a group of rocks. "Kayden and Three, you concentrate on gettin' food. I'll get medicine. Corin and Seven, you look for clothes and better shoes. We're goin' to need more than just foot-wraps if we're walkin'. Esther, you get the girl stuff."

Esther nods. She looks somewhat like a warrior with her short, cropped hair, broad figure, and aggressive stance. The gun in her belt finishes the look. Next to her, I look like a tall, skinny, lanky girl. She looks like a woman.

We begin to move our supplies over to the rocks and after a few minutes, Rahn is satisfied that they are hidden well enough.

117

"Will your dog guard it?" Rahn asks Three and me.

Three nods, then tells the terrier to guard it. At first, he looks confused, but then he barks as though he has the idea.

"All got guns?" Rahn asks.

My words get stuck as I hold up empty hands. We only have five guns, including Raleigh's semi-automatic pistol.

"Just stick close to Corin," Rahn says, giving his nephew a meaningful look that I can't quite work out.

Then we're walking back out for the town.

"Act as normally as you can," Rahn says. "The Enhanced walk confidently with their heads held high. Mimic them. Don't do anythin' that will draw attention to yourself."

"What about our eyes?" Corin asks. He has a hand up over his, shading them from the sun. He's wearing a dark vest and lightweight shorts, and his skin is beginning to burn. It looks painful in places. "They'll notice right away what we are."

Rahn's quiet for a long moment. Back at our old village, we wouldn't have this problem. We had several sets of dark glasses for this purpose, but now Rahn is the only one with glasses—his retinas are too weak and he fears he will go blind without wearing them permanently; after all, his half-sister did. Then she got captured and converted.

"If you see any glasses, grab them," he says. "But we're goin' to have to risk it. Look down, avoid eye contact. If they do notice, use your gun and get the hell out of there." He looks across at me. "Put your hair down, it might help cover your eyes more."

I reach up, pull the piece of sinew from my hair, and shake the waves free. My hair's jet black, and hot to the touch.

"It's the hottest time of the day," Rahn says. "Most will be sleepin'. Just be careful. It doesn't matter if you come back empty-handed. So long as you come back."

After a few final words, we set off. Our trio is going first; Rahn's instructed Kayden to lead his team in once we're nearer the town.

Corin, Rahn, and I run in a wide arc toward the western side of the town. We set a good speed, and it feels nice to move without lugging drapes over my arms. My hip is still painful, but after a while, the pain numbs itself and the rhythmic beat of my feet becomes therapeutic. But I can't stop myself from shaking as we move. Even my fingers are twitching. I clamp them into tight fists. Corin's head turns toward me, but he doesn't say anything, just turns back again, his lips pressed together in a tight line.

Oh Gods. How am I going to manage this? Will the Enhanced recognize me as their own? I swallow hard. What if we all get captured? But the fear of capture is nothing compared to what it used to be like, because I know... the Enhanced... they're not all bad are they? They have food, shelter...they're just trying to survive. Like we are.

Then I think of Raleigh.

We slow down to a walk as we near the buildings. I'm trying not to look, but, try as I might, I can't keep my eyes off of the buildings. Will they recognize me? Will I recognize them?

We reach the first buildings—huge structures with ornate architecture and intricate decorations—in good time. There is no one else around, and I can't decide whether I'm pleased about that or not. Narrow roads weave between the buildings and Rahn leads us down one. Rahn goes first, then Corin, then me.

"We need to get closer to the center," Rahn says in a quiet voice. "It's just houses here." He looks up at the rooflines ahead. There's a tall steeple to the right and he points at it. "There's a square near. Shops should be there."

He's right. The steeple belongs to a church with amazing stained glass windows, and as we get nearer, shops begin to emerge from the unmarked buildings. The doors to most are open. There's a huge white building ahead with a green cross on it.

"I'll head in, and get medicine," Rahn says. "You take that road. Should be clothin' shops down there. If not, nearby." He hands Corin a small, blunt penknife, then gives him a handful of old receipts. "You know the plan."

Corin and I nod. We've done this countless times, though we've never done it together before. Normally, we go in same sex pairs as it's easier in the changing rooms then.

"We must have a hell of a lot of medicine by now," Corin mutters as we're walking through a side-street. It is deserted, and the air smells funny. His whole body is rigid, and the tension between us is thick enough to cut with the blunt penknife. "He's always getting it. And we never use it."

"I thought we lost it all, when we lost the truck." Wasn't that what Rahn had said?

Corin shrugs. "What's in that old box then? The one with the carvings? That's where he keeps it. Like I said, we must have a hell of a lot of medicine."

"Best to be prepared," I say.

He snorts as he increases his pace, then gestures for me to go first. I step in front of him and lead the way down the road. This one is narrower than the last and tiny tiles make up the path. Buildings press against each side of the road, and a few buildings down, I see one has lots of mobile phones in the window. The door is open and it looks dark inside.

Corin nudges me, then flicks his hand to where two Enhanced women walk together at the end of the road. My breath catches in my throat. They're in the distance, but I can't stop looking at them, checking to see if just one of them could be her....

I swallow hard again, feeling sick. The perfect beings aren't far away now. I gulp, trying to remain calm. Neither of them looks familiar.

Corin steps closer now, watching me. Although both our heads are bowed—and my dark hair's falling in front of my face—I know that his eyes are on me. I want to straighten up, to lift my head higher, to look at him and let him know that I know he's watching me, but I can't.

We keep walking. I think of Rahn. I know he set this up. He probably wants me to fail this, to go running to the Enhanced, begging for augmenters, so that he no longer has a liability in his group. He already got rid of my mother. But then, why's he put me with Corin? I glance over at him next to me. If I concentrate really hard, I can still remember the way Corin's arms wrapped around me as he tried to stop me from going back to the Enhanced Ones' compound.

Surely Corin would stop me now if I did lose it? I frown. If Rahn wanted rid of me, why didn't he pair me with himself and send Corin off on his own? He could've conveniently lost me to them without the others questioning or trying to stop him.

I scowl, but it doesn't help my feelings at all. Or the way my legs are shaking. I know without looking that the Enhanced women are closer.

Just act normally.

I try, I really do, as we walk down the cobbled street.

But they'll notice our eyes, of course they will. I look down.

The Enhanced pair walk right past us. Corin and I let out sighs of relief, and keep going.

I crane my neck as far as I can, searching every alleyway we pass, picking out the darkest of all the shadows. But there's never anyone there. Never a tall woman with my own eyes.

Only her eyes will be different now….

"Your mother's not going to be here." Corin touches my shoulder lightly and I flinch. "We're not going to bump into her."

I know he's right, but it doesn't make me feel any better. Worse, if anything.

We speed up. Corin steers me to the side. There's a doorway. I search for scanners, either side, but I can't see any. What if they've developed them since we last saw some? What if they're tiny or invisible?

Corin presses up behind me, and then I'm setting foot in a shop. No alarms go off.

It's cool inside and near the door, there are huge bottles of water. I'm drawn to them, and I linger slightly, but Corin urges me on.

I quickly pass the checkout counter. An Enhanced man sits behind it, but he doesn't look up. He mustn't be used to Untamed humans just walking into his shop in broad daylight.

I look around. There are racks and racks of clothes. Corin

has turned down an aisle and too soon, I lose sight of him. I take several jolty breaths. I see a rotating stand of sunglasses to my left and head for it. I grab a handful of pairs, then unhook a lightweight jacket and sling it over my arm. I see several pairs of heavy-duty shoes and pick up a big and small pair, for Corin and me.

Next, I get several shirts, then head for the changing rooms. Corin's already there, his back to me as he pretends to be engrossed in a leather jacket. He turns as I approach and nods at me. He has a pair of shoes, several shirts and pairs of shorts.

He holds open the door to the nearest changing room, and I duck under his arm. He closes the door. The cubicle itself is small, but even smaller with Corin's physique.

As quietly as I can, I pull the labels off the glasses, then hand him a pair, whilst I put one on. He takes two of the spare pairs from me, pocketing them. Then we both put on as many clothes as we can manage for a natural look. A couple of times, we bump into each other. It can't be helped. There isn't much room.

"Stand still," Corin says after I've dragged two shirts over my head. He cuts the labels off with the knife Rahn gave him.

I do the same for him. At one point, the back of my hand catches a bulky shape, just below his waist.

Gun, he mouths at me. I nod. Of course, he has a pistol with him, but it should be tucked in the *back* of his waistband, less damage in an accident there.

Rubbing at my head, I point at the floor. "Which shoes?"

He indicates the darkest pair with a flick of his fingers, and slides his own shoe-wraps off, stuffing them deep into the pockets of his new three-quarter length shorts. His old ones are still on underneath, but the new ones cover his belt and gun more effectively.

I put on my new shoes—white ones; wonder how long they'll stay that color—and wipe a thin layer of sweat from my forehead. My hair feels hot and sticky, and I can feel drops of perspiration forming down my spine. It's far too hot for this kind of work. I zip the lightweight jacket over the many shirts. It actually fits me well, when I'm wearing many layers underneath.

Corin raises his hand suddenly. We freeze, hear footsteps outside. Corin breathes heavily. Eventually, the footsteps pass.

"Quickly," he whispers as he pulls on a leather jacket. He bends down, picks up my old shoes—they're flimsy, but not as flimsy as his shoe-wraps—then lifts his shirts and jackets up, and squashes them under his waistband. I try not to notice how his stomach is predominantly smooth, less blemished and burnt than his face, neck, arms and lower legs, but I can't look away. He drops his shirt back down, oblivious.

We look around. There are only a few labels on the floor, along with the pair of shoes Corin chose but discarded—they're too flimsy.

"Ready?"

Corin nods. He gets out the receipts. After studying several, he hands me two. I nod. It'd be suspicious if we walked out without any transaction, because the Enhanced never just browse. We'll use one receipt to return an item that we'll claim we bought here a few days ago, and we'll get a refund or an exchange—whichever the shopkeeper offers us as we don't want to draw attention to ourselves by insisting on one or the other. The second receipt is there in case we need to produce one for the clothes we're wearing—after all, shop owners tend to know their stock pretty well.

"Remember to look cheerful," Corin says.

We leave the changing room, and Corin grabs a new pair of heavy-duty shoes from the rack—the ones we're going to 'return'. We approach the desk together. The gun under Corin's waistband is reassuring, even if it's in the wrong place.

The Enhanced man at the desk also wears sunglasses; we don't look out of place.

"Good afternoon," he says.

Corin nods at him. "We'd like to return these shoes," Corin says and smiles brightly as he places them on the counter. "My girlfriend got me the wrong size," he says, placing an arm around my shoulder.

Girlfriend?

Corin smiles down at me in a way that is warm and… sexy?

My eyes widen. My pulse quickens, and my fingers begin to shake. I'm going to drop the receipt. Corin's fingers begin to tap my shoulder.

"I've got the receipt here." I place the shorter one on the counter. It's one of the plain receipts that most of the Enhanced Ones' shops use. I pray that this one uses the same style too. I look at the till. It looks like one of the older, more simple ones.

The man nods, doesn't even look at the receipt. "Okay. Would you like another size, sir?"

Corin looks at me and I nod. I hope the owner doesn't notice how much I'm shaking.

"Yes. That would be great, thanks. Size nine."

I nearly raise my eyebrows. Corin actually has manners.

The Enhanced man moves off down the shop, soon coming back with another new pair. Corin's arm is still around my shoulders, but it feels heavy, not affectionate. He's probably forgotten about it.

The man then gives us a new receipt and the shoes in a plastic bag.

"Good day, sir."

It's always the leaving that I find the scariest. With every step, I expect someone to jump out on me, and call me out for what I've done. But that's only happened once. The majority of the Enhanced are very trusting of others, most likely because they're under the influence of Honesty. Besides, well, they live in a perfect society.

As soon as we're outside, I begin to sweat. I can feel my back getting moist, the many layers sticking together.

Corin steers me down an alleyway, his hand pushing my shoulder. We both look around, checking that no one else is here, hidden from obvious view. We appear to be on our own.

"The bag," he says, holding it open. He's already pulled out my old shoe-wraps from his waistband and put them in the flimsy white plastic bag along with some of the contents of his pockets.

I take off the jacket, then one of the shirts. Corin does the same, and we squash everything into the bag.

"Good work," he says, and nods at me. I make eye contact with him and nod back, but don't say anything. He turns away quickly. "We need to find Rahn," he says in a voice that sounds somewhat choked.

Chapter Seventeen

In the end, we go to the big white building with the green painted cross on it. It smells funny in here, like antiseptic wipes. Surprisingly, I've never been in a pharmacy before, and for a few seconds, I stare at all the tiny bottles and containers. Perfumes. Shampoos. Lotions. On a wall near me, there's a massive picture of an Enhanced woman's eye; the eyeball is a mirror, the eyelid has some bright purple paste on it, and the eyelashes are far too long to be natural. Underneath, there are hundreds of pots of powders, all in different colors.

"This way." Corin guides me down an aisle. He nods at a sign. "Medicine's upstairs."

I push my glasses higher up my nose; they're a little big for me. I read the sign, and freeze. The hairs on the back of my neck stand up. There's a rushing sound in my ears. My skin prickles. It's too hot in here. Yet my hands are freezing. I swallow down the strangest of feelings and glance at Corin, but he hasn't noticed. He's already plowing toward the stairs.

After a few seconds' delay, I chase after him. There are more people in here, all of them are Enhanced Ones, of course. I glance at one, and the feelings within me magnify. Oh Gods. *Just breathe.* I follow Corin up the stairs. I'm sure he's oblivious to what I'm going through. I gulp again. I can do this. I have to. I will. I won't give Rahn the satisfaction.

I'm breathing slowly and deeply as we reach the next floor; my heart pounds with anxiety. Corin keeps walking. It would be so easy to turn away, walk away from him. I force myself forward; my head feeling like it's going to explode. On the shelves all around us, are all sorts of small boxes. I recognize a few of them, but not many. And—

I see them.

My heart screams. My mouth dries. My fingers twitch.

Beautiful, mesmerizing colors. Sunny oranges. Aqua blues. Emerald greens. Rich, chocolate browns. Pure, innocent whites. A huge display of them, from floor to ceiling. There are even more augmenters here than there were in that cupboard.

Corin heads straight for them.

I freeze. Oh Gods. He's going to smash them. *He's going to smash them.* I start to race forward, not knowing whether I'm going for him or for them.

He walks right past them, as if he hasn't noticed them. Maybe he hasn't. They're insignificant to him.

But to *me...* I linger slightly, my eyes running over the colors again. Translucent greens, a liver color, deep silver... I look around, aware that I'm salivating.

Corin has almost disappeared from view.

An Enhanced female leans over me and plucks out a magenta augmenter. Sexiness. She smiles to herself, and her mirror eyes get bigger.

I take a small step to my right, moving down the aisle. The shelves of augmenters seem to go on forever. Kindness, Compassion and Calmness are in front of me. Benevolence, Good Will, Curiosity. They're beautiful. *I* felt beautiful when I was one of them. I was safe. I had a home, and food. Is that really too much to ask for? The desire to be safe?

The memory alone is enough to make me shiver and shake. It was lovely. Amazing. Beautiful.

Move away now, I tell myself.

No. Don't. Stay here. Feast on them....

Taking another deep breath, I look around. There's no one here now. My hand moves up toward a small bottle of Calmness. It would be easy just to pick it up and put it in my pocket. So easy.

My fingertips grace the bottle of Calmness and energy fizzes within me. It would be the most amazing thing to be permanently calm. No more worries. No more anger. Maybe the Enhanced life isn't so bad. It's better than ours. No more fear, no more worries. I inhale sharply as a new thought occurs: what if becoming Enhanced is the intended direction for humankind? The next step of evolution?

My hand closes around the tiny bottle. The weight of the augmenter is delicious. Already, I'm calmer. And the small bottle, the beautiful vial, is in my pocket.

Oh Gods. My stomach twists as horror fills me.

Step away, I tell myself. Corin will be looking for me soon. But I don't step away. I can't. My hand hovers again. A rich dark green bottle has captured my eye.

"Speed." I can barely breathe. I'm salivating. I'm fast, but I could be faster. If I'm faster, I could help the rest of my group more.... I'd be helping them.

It should be easier, this time. I've done it once. I glance around. No one else is here. My fingers touch the bottle. Adrenaline pumps through my veins. The sensation is so wonderful that—

"*Seven?*"

I turn, my heart slamming into my ribs, to see Corin standing behind me. My head pounds. How did he get here so quickly?

"Put it back."

But I can't. My fingers won't move. I don't want to let go.

Corin marches up and grabs the bottle from my hand. He chucks it onto the shelf, uncaring of how it hits others, causing at least six tiny exquisite bottles to fall over, then grabs me by the shoulders. He pushes me forward. Corin's tight grip on me doesn't slacken, and suddenly, I'm reminded of Raleigh. Corin is holding me in the same way, and the pressure of his fingers is just the same, enough to bruise.

Then I see Rahn. He's down the aisle slightly, carrying several bags of stuff and two small wooden boxes.

He's seen everything.

He knows I failed. He knows he was right. I am a liability.

Never let yourself be Enhanced. Once it's done, there's no going back.

"Let's get out of here." Rahn's voice is even, devoid of emotions.

I feel sick. But the weight of the Calmness in my shorts is comforting. I yearn to reach down and touch the little bottle, but I mustn't. I have to act normally.

Corin pushes me forward roughly. I stumble slightly, but he doesn't help me. Of course he wouldn't. I turn back to face him. But he won't look at me. He stares ahead, his lips pressed into a thin line.

Traitor, an unknown voice hisses at me.

Chapter Eighteen

"What the hell were you thinkin', takin' her in there?" Rahn jabs two gnarled roots of fingers into Corin's face.

We're on the outskirts of the town again now, and Rahn's the first to speak since we left the building.

Corin scrunches his nose up and bares his teeth. He still has his dark glasses on, and this makes me nervous. "How was I to know she'd act like one of them?"

"Do you know nothin'?" Rahn's fingers stay where they are. "It's far too soon, she probably won't even have the last dose completely out of her system yet. It would've acted like a magnet, drawin' her in. I'm surprised she didn't start guzzlin' the stuff there and then."

I keep walking, trailing behind them. Rahn's still yelling, and I don't understand why. He wanted me to fail; he wanted me to do that. Yet now he's angry at Corin, and not me?

The bottle of Calmness in my shorts gets heavier and heavier, dragging the garment down slightly, with every step. I should take it out and smash it. I should watch the pale blue liquid drain away. But I can't do it now. They'd see it. They'd know how desperate I am. Disgust fills me.

I'll dispose of it when I'm on my own. I'm strong—I can do it. It's what I *need* to do. I can't be like them, murdering innocent people... but with food and shelter....

"Let's just get back." Corin's voice is deeper, more dangerous, than usual. The muscles in his shoulders tense— my fault.

Rahn nods and then turns back to me. "Are you okay?"

I nod.

We walk back. Rahn decides it's best not to run. I don't know why he thinks that, but, nonetheless, I'm glad. My legs shake too much.

As we near the rocks, my eyes pick out Three and Esther. They are standing side by side. But there's definitely only two of them.

Kayden isn't there.

Rahn and Corin speed up, then they're running. I trail after them, my knees knocking against each other. As I near, I notice the bruise and cuts on Esther's face and the long scratch on Three's nose.

"What's happened?" Rahn throws his bag onto the floor.

My dog rushes up to me. He tries to push his nose into my hand, but suddenly, I don't know if I can pet him. It sounds silly, but if I stroke the little dog, I think he'll know what I did. And I need him to be on my side.

"Just a bit of trouble getting food," Three says. But there isn't any food around them.

"Where's Kayden?" Rahn asks the question that's burning me.

Three and Esther exchange a look. My heart drops. Suddenly, all I can think is that this is payment, my fault. If I hadn't stolen the Calmness, Kayden might be here. The universe works in strange ways.

"He's getting a car," Three says.

"What?" Rahn says. He waves his arms in the air, like a madman. "That was not part of the plan! Why didn't you stay with him? We never leave any member of our group on their own." As he says the words, he glares at Corin.

"He insisted," Esther says. "He took all the food with him."

Rahn makes a noise that suggests he is very angry. He turns back to look at the town in the distance. "Is he drivin' it up here?"

"Yes," Three says. "He said it could take him an hour to secure it and get it out of there."

"Is he stealing or buying the car?" Corin asks. He's standing about as far away from me as possible.

Three shrugs. "Anyone's guess." He wipes a layer of grime from his cheek and the scratch starts to bleed. My brother looks at me and I see his eyes widen. "What's happened?"

Corin looks like he's about to say something, but Rahn gets in first.

"Nothin'. It's just hot work, runnin'." Rahn turns toward the rocks where our stuff is. The dog moves away from him, growling. "We may as well sort out what we've got." He glances over at the clothing bag on the ground. The spare pairs of sunglasses are on top. "Excellent." He nods in approval.

***

About an hour later, a vehicle approaches—a Land Rover Discovery. Dust kicks up behind it from the tires. It's going fast.

"Get back," Rahn says. He has the Glock in his hand.

Corin, Three, and Esther draw their guns. Then Corin pushes Esther behind him. We all freeze. My hands are empty. Three hands me a knife.

We stand like this as the vehicle nears us. The dog cowers against my legs. At last, we make out Kayden's red hair behind the wheel. The guns disappear.

Kayden parks the vehicle a few feet from us, and throws the driver's door open. He jumps out, grinning. Like Corin, he's sunburnt, but his skin looks worse, angrier, redder. It's his red hair.

"What do you think?" Kayden looks wild and energized.

"I think you should've discussed it with me." Rahn's voice is tense. "But it'll do. Right. We'll load the stuff in now, and get on the road."

There isn't a lot of room in the four-by-four once we've packed everything in. And there are only five seats.

"Seven can sit in the boot," Kayden says. "There's still a little room in there."

I look at the boot. I'd be on my own in there. Almost automatically, I touch the small glass bottle through the fabric of my shorts.

"No," Rahn says. "We'll squeeze four into the back."

I end up wedged in between Three and Esther. Kayden—also in the back, much to his annoyance—has the dog sitting on his lap; Rahn had wanted the terrier in the front passenger's footwell, but the dog seemed to have a problem with Corin's feet. Kept trying to bite his toes.

Rahn's driving, and he goes faster than usual. The suspension's better than that in our old truck, but it's not great.

"Where are we going?" Corin asks, his voice level.

Rahn takes his time in replying. "I want to get as far south as possible. I looked at a map earlier in New Zsai. There's another town—New Sinyoh—a good way south from here, but after that the terrain looks rougher, more wooded, less built-up. I want to get as far on the other side of New Sinyoh as possible. We'll camp out there and the girls can sleep in here."

Esther grins, the bruise on her face stretching, as she turns to me.

I smile back, but I'd rather be outside. I need to dispose of the augmenter. It's still in my shorts pocket, feels bulky. Three's leg also presses against it, but he hasn't questioned what it is.

It smells fumy in the car; there are at least four cans of fuel in the back, along with the food—mainly canned stuff. No way near as good as that cake, with the cinnamon and the ginger and the honey.

A few hours later, Rahn pulls to a stop and Corin jumps out to get some food from the boot. I hear him rustle through the carrier bags, and then he returns to the front. He hands out several packages. The one he gives me is a small one in white paper. He doesn't even look at me when I thank him.

I eat my food—a chunk of beef and plain couscous—in silence, not joining in with the others' talk.

"Are you okay, Seven?" Three asks as Rahn starts the engine up again.

I nod and screw the white paper up into a tight ball. "Fine."

"You're a bit quiet," he says. He turns to face me, and I feel the bottle of Calmness move slightly between us.

"She's just tired," Rahn says. "We had a bit of trouble gettin' our stuff. Seven had to run farther than we did. And *I'm* exhausted."

I shoot a glance at him, frowning. Rahn's never on my side.

Corin snorts, hiding a laugh. Rahn gives him a sharp look, *tsking* under his breath.

We make it about twelve miles past the outskirts of New Sinyoh, half an hour before complete darkness. I help Three and Kayden get the tarpaulins out of the back of the car. We make two tents out of them. Rahn wants to sleep on his own, as usual. Three, Corin, and Kayden have no choice but to share.

The terrier has found an old stick and Esther throws it for him.

I make my way back to the car and climb in. My hands shake. Adrenaline pumps through my veins. I want to sprint, but know I can't. I drag a hand through my dark hair, then tie it up. It's been down for most of the day because of the raid, and it's tangled. Probably needs washing too. I'll sort it out in the morning. Too tired now.

My hand moves to the small bottle of Calmness in my pocket. I slide my fingers down it. It's cool and refreshing to the touch. I take a deep breath. I look out the window. Esther is still throwing the stick for the dog. Corin and Rahn are talking, heads bent close together. Kayden and Three are making a fire. The site they've chosen for the fire is closer to the car than I'd like, but I can't do anything about it at the moment; the keys aren't in the ignition.

That's when I realize it: no one's looking toward the car. I'm alone.

I take the bottle out of my pocket. My breath catches in my throat—makes a sort of raspy sound, like I'm choking and spluttering at the sight of the augmenter.

Dispose of it. That's what I need to do. What I should do, because I need to stay Untamed. I look around. I can't smash it in the car. There'd be too much glass. If I get out of the car, then they'll all look at me—it may be nearly dark, but there's a bright moon coming, and I know the others will see.

My fingers, around it, feel strange. Kind of heavy, but not that secure. I bite my lip.

Don't get rid of it yet. Not without a little taste. It would be such a waste.

My fingers tremble, as if little buds of electricity have grown and blossomed. I unscrew the tiny cap, savoring the tinkling sound the metal makes on the small glass rim.

I'm not in control. It's an automatic reaction. I turn my back to the window so no one can see what I'm doing.

I steady my shaking legs. I'm not doing anything bad by taking this. I'll be calmer. I'll be more use to my group if I can think straight.

The neck of the small, delicate bottle is by my lips. I can almost taste its beauty. What's the point in feeling fear if I have a chance to be calm?

Raleigh's right. There is no point in feeling scared. Not when—

Raleigh. I feel the warmth of his breath on the back of my neck and his grip on my shoulder. My eyes sting.

He is one of the Enhanced. I am not.

Disgust fills me. I screw the lid back on the bottle before I can change my mind, and put it back in my pocket. I am stronger than this. But I don't get out of the car and throw it away. I am not that strong, yet.

Chapter Nineteen

Corin nods at the pack of cigarettes in his hand. "Getting harder and harder to find these now." The flames of the campfire light up his face as he leans toward Esther, a look of contentment on his face.

"No wonder, is it?" Three grunts, and looks up from his work. I don't know how he can see properly in the firelight. He's acquired some untreated copper wire, a circuit board and some LED bulbs and is trying to fix them together into something useful, under the watchful gaze of Rahn. "The Enhanced Ones only use them for social purposes. They're not addicted."

Corin sticks his middle finger up at Three, who ignores him.

"It's true," Esther says. "You need to cut back."

"It's hard enough being hunted day and night without giving up this small luxury."

Three leans forward, toward the flames, the circuit board in his hand. He frowns, eyes dark. "Can't see a damn thing in this light."

"Want any help?" Esther says. Corin scowls at her as she moves to my brother's side.

The two of them work on the board for a few minutes, ignoring Corin's thunderous expression.

"I'll help Kayden check our resources," Rahn says after a few minutes. "We need to know what we've got. Need to be prepared for anythin' and everythin'."

He gets up and Corin follows him to the boot of the car.

Sounds of rustling follow, mingling with the crackling and hissing of the fire. Kayden's hooting laughter sounds a few moments later.

"Oi! Three! You got regular tea?" Rahn appears back at the fire in seconds, shoving the box of teabags into my brother's face. "Are you mad? It's got caffeine. It'll dehydrate us, do more damage than good."

"Hey!" Esther holds up her hands, complete with wires. "He's doing his best."

"Well it's not good enough! It never is." Rahn's gaze includes me in his accusation.

I try to ignore him. But it's hard, because he has every right to be angry with me. Furious, even. He could kick me out easily now, if he wanted.

I bite my bottom lip, thinking of my mother. I wonder which augmenters she's taken. She was always calm; she won't need Calmness. Maybe she'll have gone for one that improved her wisdom. Or beauty? No. My mother's not vain. Not like Five is—was. I gulp.

My mother... is she with Raleigh? Are the two of them together? Now? My skin crawls. I wonder if he's told her I was in his compound, near Nbutai. I wonder if he's told her about the waterboarding. I can imagine him telling people, laughing as he does. His lips would twitch.

Would my mother join in with his laughter? She wouldn't, no. But no one's the same after being Enhanced.

"They tortured you, didn't they?"

I jump, startled by Corin. He's sitting next to me, only a few feet away. I hadn't even noticed he'd returned from the car. Kayden's here too, on his other side, smoking one of Corin's cigarettes.

"Sev? They did, didn't they? Back at the compound." Corin pauses, and I keep staring at the fire. My hands feel like ice. "I can see that they did. You're different to how you used to be."

"I don't want to talk about it." My voice is small.

Corin nods. "I was just saying that I realized, that was all. It must have been horrible."

Horrible enough that you still want to be like them.

I stiffen.

"Was it physical? Was it that bloke? What's he called? Raleigh?"

"At least you're alive. Faya isn't. My daughter isn't." Kayden stands suddenly. His eyes narrow and his face flushes. I know he's thinking of the fire that killed his wife and child seven years ago. "Tortured or not, *you're* alive."

Darkness descends over us all like a foggy mist.

"I'm sorry," Kayden says a few minutes later. He stares at the fire, his eyes taking on a vacant look. "I shouldn't have said that. It's not your fault."

I nod. The wind's picking up now, sharp nails drive into my skin. I blink back stinging tears. I should've put on another jacket or—

I freeze.

Behind the fire, behind the flames. A shape. A head. Marred, by the wind. A figure. Tall, broad, strong, dark. Eyes that—

"What's wrong?" Corin's voice is sharp.

I start to point ahead, at the figure, but it's gone.

"Nothing."

I swallow hard. There's nothing out there. Just the Enhanced, somewhere, plotting to find me. And I know they will find me. I can feel it in the way my blood pumps around my body, like it's a magnetized pole, and the Enhanced are the iron filings. I know they're coming. It won't be long until they find me, or I find them.

Chapter Twenty

The moment I close my eyes, I see my father. He's standing in the same white land that I'm in. My heart jumps. He looks the same as he always has—tall, strong, and protective, not a hair grayer than before. He's facing me, but I know he can't *see* me. He's standing tall, with his feet shoulder-width apart, his arms by his sides.

I've walked closer to him before I even realize I'm moving.

The deep furrowed lines in his brow are there. But his expression is peaceful. His skin is as dark and as rich as mine, but on him, it seems to have a celestial quality. He is *glowing*.

As I stare into my father's dark, unseeing eyes, he blinks. I jump.

"Dad?" I reach out to touch his arm and am engulfed by his smell: the familiar combination of sweat, sand and campfire smoke.

But he doesn't acknowledge me. He doesn't move. His eyes are empty, glassy.

"Dad!" I throw myself at him and I'm crying. Emotion and feeling and guilt rip through me.

But still, he doesn't do anything. He stays still, like a statue, his body not even moving as I throw my whole weight against him. He's a solid pillar.

"Dad! It's me, Seven. It's me!" I fall back away from him, hitting the hard floor.

Like someone has pressed a switch, the whiteness around us disappears. There's a clap of what I can only describe as thunder all around me, echoing, and I stumble backward. Darkness falls with me, trying to suffocate me, and I scream, reaching out for him. Light flashes and my father moves. His eyes stare at me, seeing me for the first time, in that blink of light; his mouth turns down at the corners and his stare burns. I whimper.

Darkness again, but my father takes a step closer. "You are no daughter of mine." His powerful voice echoes in the empty space around me. "No child of mine turns their back on the Untamed."

My body stiffens. My veins burn. "I—I didn't—I'm sorry."

Something cracks behind him. I see a white fogginess with a dark shape. Arms, legs, long limbs. A new figure. A female figure. Tall, willowy: Five.

"You *betrayed* us, Seven."

"I'm sorry!" I choke as I try to swallow. Pain lashes across my throat.

I try to get up, but can't. I try to turn my head so I don't have to see them, but my neck's frozen. Icy needles drive into my skin. I can't move an inch. All I can do is watch as Five and my father loom over me.

"You left us, Seven." Five twists her hands together, like she's squeezing the water out of our clothes back at Nbutai. "You left us." She turns and I see the hollow of her cheek, as if the flesh has fallen in.

"You are no daughter of mine."

"You are no sister of mine."

"No child of mine leaves their family to die."

"And you're nothing better than one of them now."

Their clammy fingers reach out, touch me and I scream loudly. I scramble backward, but their fingers pull at my clothes as they grow bigger and bigger. I can't see anything but them now. Just them.

"Please! *Please*! Five, no!" I cower as she reaches for me.

Her skeletal fingers rip my jacket; darkness bites my skin, burning me. I shriek, get to my feet, my skin on fire. My father stands in front of me; now, I'm eight years old. I'm just a child. And Five is looking down her nose at me. Her eyes are dark, unseeing but all-knowing.

"You left us, Seven. You left us."

"You *betrayed* us, Seven."

"You still betray us all."

"You traitor."

"We were your family."

"Now you're on your own."

"No one will ever trust you."

"You'll be forever alone," Five says. Her hair plaits itself into braids in seconds and they fly at me like snakes that are forever elongating.

My skin stings as each one hits me. Her braids trap me, trap me in my guilt, trap me in my past. I can't get away. I open my mouth to drag air into my lungs, but it burns my throat. I can't see a thing... no, I *can* see: I see Five and my father's faces as they twist out of recognition. Their cheeks are sucked in, their glass eyes bulging out of their sockets. Veins and capillaries raise up, all over their skin, standing up, pulsing. I shriek.

That's what I did to them.

It's my fault.

"Seven!"

The world's shaking around me. An earthquake? I don't know. I'm falling. The floor's gone. There's just nothing... no, it's wet. Water. I'm drenched. It's pale blue, smells *too* nice. It's in my eyes, my ears, my nose. It's everywhere.

Calmness. No. No. *No.*

It slams against me.

It crushes my body.

My throat constricts. I taste bile. I turn, trying to pull away. More water hits me.

Mumbled voices over me. A laugh?

Too much of it. And I'm drinking it. I am. I can't help it. I'm gulping it down in huge greedy gulps. But I can't drink it quickly enough and I'm choking. It's over my head. I can't breathe. Going to be sick. Can feel the bile rising already.

"You traitor!"

I scream, fighting against the liquid, trying to cry out to tell them how sorry I am, but more Calmness invades me.

"You traitor!"

But I can't do a thing. I'm helpless. I can't see. I can't see anything but the blue of the Calmness. All I can do is drink it. Drink it before I drown in it. I'm trying to, really trying. But I can't swallow in time, choking... bile in my throat.

"No Enhanced is a daughter of mine!"

"You traitor! Death will get you."

***

Esther's hands clasp me, holding me upright. For several seconds, I can't do anything but swallow back tears. Exhaustion holds onto my body, like steel. Then I'm patting down my shorts. The tiny bottle of Calmness is still there and I let out a huge sigh of relief—they don't know about it. Then the sigh turns into a giggle. I feel funny, dizzy, but, still, I keep laughing. I only stop when I see the fear on Esther's face.

"What's happening?" Her voice is softer than usual, and in the blotchy moonlight, I see how pale she is. "Are they coming for us?"

For several seconds, I can't think what she means. Then I get it, I shake my head.

"It wasn't a Seeing dream." My voice wobbles.

Esther looks down at me, her brows raised. I don't want to tell her the details. The small vial in my pocket feels like it's burning.

"Are you sure?"

I nod. *I am Untamed.* My lips tremble. That dream, it doesn't mean anything. Doesn't change anything.

She looks at me dubiously. I drop my gaze to the floor of the four-by-four. Heat rushes to my cheeks and my ears. I take several deep breaths. A sheen of sweat bathes my skin; it sticks to me like glue.

"Well, get some sleep then," she says. "I think we're going to have a busy day tomorrow."

I nod, but I can't get rid of the way my skin crawls with invisible beads of water.

***

When someone says tomorrow's going to busy, they're usually right. The moment I wake, there are jobs that need doing.

Esther and I go hunting with Kayden at first light and return with two desert rats and a young drill monkey.

"That'll hardly keep us goin'," Rahn says. His dark glasses are somewhat crooked on his nose, but not enough that they don't protect him. He hasn't worn his wrap-around style ones for a while now—maybe they got left behind or lost somewhere. Or maybe he's more relaxed about it, less worried about losing his sight. I don't think the sun's as strong here.

"I don't see why we even had to hunt." Esther wipes sweat from her brow. "We got food yesterday."

Rahn looks at her like she's stupid, raising one eyebrow, and leans his head toward her a little. "We've no idea how long we've got till the next opportunity to raid a city presents itself. I don't want to be havin' to drive back there. If we're to survive, we've got to be able to be self-sufficient here."

Next, we collect wood to make bows and arrows and spears. There isn't much ammunition left.

There's a surprising amount of wood lying in this part of the desert, considering there are no trees. But I appear to be the only one who finds this strange; after voicing these thoughts to Three, who stares at me like I said the most stupid thing in the world, I keep the musings to myself. But the terrier knows it's strange, I am sure. He doesn't pick any of the sticks up for us to throw. He knows.

I glance around. But I don't know what I'm expecting to see. Spirits? Could they have thrown the wood over the landscape, in a battle of frenzied otherness? Or could the spirits have destroyed the trees that these pieces of wood came from, leaving the haunting reminders behind?

"How much more do we get?" Corin shouts back at Rahn, farther down the slope.

Rahn makes a shrugging motion. "As much as possible."

He ties something together with a long piece of sinew.

Behind him, is one of the little boxes he got from the pharmacist. The pharmacist that had all those beautiful—

I try to blink that thought away, but I'm unsuccessful. The vial in my pocket starts to burn. I swallow hard, and look around, shielding my eyes from the sun. No one is immediately near me. No one's watching me.

Throw the Calmness away now. No one is watching. Do it now and you'll feel better.

My throat dries as I set the broken branches down on the ground. I finger the vial carefully, through my shorts.

"Seven?"

Three's shout makes me jump. He stands farther down the slope now. It takes me a few moments to realize that he's asking if I'm okay, asking why I've stopped. Everyone else is still busy collecting wood.

I let the vial fall back to the bottom of my pocket. "I'm fine," I shout back.

It's too risky to get rid of the augmenter here. I need to wait until I'm *really* on my own.

I scoop up the wood again, doing my best to distract myself. We remain collecting and sorting wood until about midday. The dog lies down near me, his eyes flitting from one pile to the next as I sort the branches by their type.

Another afara. Walnut. Leucaena. Albizia. Two more leucaenas. I throw the next branch behind me. Seize the next; it's one I don't recognize. I frown—my father taught me the names of all the different plants when I was younger. I stare at this one. The wood is a rich dark red color, with fine spikes at one end. I test it in my hands—quite bendy.

I turn and look at the various piles around me. Five different woods, including this strange one. Five different lots of branches in the landscape, but there are no trees. I turn, frowning. I shield my smarting eyes from the sun with my hand as I stare into the horizon. It is flat. Everywhere is flat. There are no tree stumps. Or roots. Or dried, old leaves rotting on the ground. But these branches, a lot of them are still green. Freshly cut. I look at the edge of one branch carefully. It's not splintered, it's been sawed.

I swallow hard.

The terrier jumps up and rushes against my legs. He howls.

That's when I see them. A strong sense of déjà vu hits me, as I see the little figures in the distance, heading toward us at great speed. I turn, look the other way. A strangled cry escapes my lips.

"Rahn!"

In an instant I'm running. I still have a piece of wood—afara—in my hand and I wave it at him frantically. At last he looks up. Corin and Kayden are with him and all three turn toward me.

"It's a trap!" I wave the wood in my hand again. My arm aches. The dog overtakes me as I run. "The wood's a trap!"

Rahn, Corin, and Kayden's heads snap up. By the way tension visibly moves through all of their bodies, and how Corin reaches for a gun, I know they've seen the Enhanced.

"Load the guns!" Rahn shouts, but they're already doing it. "Get to the car!"

I haven't got a gun—only the knife Three gave me—and I turn to find Esther and Three already sprinting toward the vehicle. The terrier races after them.

The knife feels heavy in my hand, but not at all threatening. I drop the afara branch. Ahead, Kayden and Rahn are sprinting. Rahn limps as he clutches one of his boxes under his arm, and Kayden's carrying several bows. I can't see where Corin is. Fear clenches my throat.

I hear the engine of our car and its tires squealing as Esther turns it sharply. I hadn't noticed her get in. But I can see another figure in the front—Three?

I look back around. The desert looks strange. Sort of shimmery and magical. Vast stretches of unmarked sand stretch out before me, right up to our enemies' feet. The Enhanced—there are hundreds of them. A bitter taste comes to my mouth, like cigarette smoke twisted with feces and sweat.

A loud crack hits the earth. I shriek, falling to the ground, hands over my head. I taste dust, something inside me trembles. I cough up phlegm as I jerk my eyes upward. The explosion's not near me. It's over there, the other side of the vehicle. I see Corin running—he's the nearest of us to the explosion. I pick out the gun—no, the grenade launcher pistol—in his hand.

Keep going!

I scramble up, run toward the vehicle. Esther's slowing down. Lactic acids burns my muscles. I can't see the dog. Is he in the car? My breath's in short and rapid bursts. It's too hot. My back is sticky with sweat and my hair keeps falling over my face, prickling the tender skin of my eye sockets, until I can't see.

Ahead, I see Rahn jump into the slowing car, and Corin climbs in. Then the car heads for me. But the Enhanced behind me are closer. They're sprinting straight for me. I pause, and stare at them. My chest tightens. These people aren't *people*. They're machines. No one can run that fast. Or that silently. It's unnatural. Wrong. None of them are sweating, their arms and legs are moving in a mechanical motion. And they all look the same. An identical army.

"Sev!"

I hear Corin's voice and then the car squeals to a stop a few feet from me. Dust clouds over me. The door nearest me flies open and Corin's arms pull me in. I scrape my knee on the doorframe, crashing into his strong torso.

The door slams shut, the engine roars.

"There's nowhere to go!" Esther cries.

I climb up into a seated position, kneeing on Corin and Kayden in the process. The dog barks from the front of the car. Relief floods me.

"What do I do?" Esther's voice is strained. Her knuckles are white as she clutches the wheel. "Rahn?"

Rahn doesn't answer. He's staring straight ahead, at the wall of Enhanced Ones coming straight for us. I squint, but can't see if they're armed.

I turn and look left. Then right. We're surrounded.

"Drive through them!" Three shouts.

"It'll kill them!"

"They deserve to die. Each and every one of them!" Rahn's face is a ruddy red and his hair is soaked.

Esther turns the wheel sharply. I slide into Corin, my elbow jabs his chest. He grunts, pushes me away.

But the circle of Enhanced around us gets tighter and tighter.

"Do it," Rahn barks. "Everyone, seat belts on."

Three straps himself in, and somehow Esther manages it whilst steering wildly. Kayden's used the middle seat belt in the back, and Corin's pulling at the last one. I turn, but, of course, the back of the car's only intended for three people. Not four.

The car slides to the left and I reach for something to hold onto, but the driver's seat doesn't have a handle, and my hand just slides along it. Then an arm snaps around me and Corin pulls me across his lap. He holds onto my body with one arm, and straps the belt around both of us.

I try not to breathe.

His body is hard and feels like stone around me. Strong and cold. Like a cage. I can feel every movement he makes, and the shudders of his chest. His breath is hot on the back of my neck, but not in the unpleasant way that Raleigh's was. No, this is different. This is exhilarating. Scary. This is Corin: the man who hates me.

The car lurches to the right and my head snaps to the side, smashing into the door. I cry out, clasp at the side of my head. Corin pulls me away from the window and I hear shouting. Then we're turning sharply again. The dog howls.

"There's nowhere to go!" Esther cries.

"I said drive through them!" Rahn winds the window down, ready to shoot.

"I can't!"

Corin turns away, his arm moving from me, and he fires another grenade.

It explodes near us, blood and limbs fly through the air.

The car speeds up. Corin's arm snaps back around me, crushes me to him, then Kayden screams in agony. I cower against Corin. The seat belt is a rope around my neck.

There's blood. The blood covers us. Too much blood.

"Keep going!"

The impact of the first wall of Enhanced is enough to slam

my heart into my ribs and send the car off at an angle. For a second, I think we're going to overturn. We don't. Esther screams as she drives toward the next wall of figures.

I try to turn, so I can't see their expressions, but the belt and Corin won't let me. His arm is bloody around me, and something hits my shoulder. I yank my head around. Three lowers his window, shooting through it in an instant.

Sharp pains fall down my arm.

Blood pools on the floor of the vehicle. Something bloody jumps in my face. I cry out, but it's the dog. Someone screams—Rahn or Kayden? I can't tell.

"Keep your foot down!"

"I am!"

Glass smashes behind me, tiny fragments dive into the back of my neck. Rahn curses. More gunshots. But they're not our shots; the Enhanced Ones have weapons. Again. They're cheating.

"There's too many of them."

Something jabs me in the leg. One of Kayden's bows.

"They're everywhere... I can't get through them."

"Keep firing."

"Keep goin'."

Another explosion to my right. I shriek. The air's groggy and red.

"Get down!" Rahn fights against his seat belt as he lunges forward and pushes Three's head down. A bullet whizzes over my brother's head at an angle and hits the windshield. Glass explodes.

"Hold on!"

I scream against Corin as we hit more Enhanced. The impact jolts through me, winding me.

"Left!" Out of half-closed eyes, I see Three lunge for the steering wheel.

Corin's grip on my torso borders on painful and my head feels funny. We're getting faster and faster, faster and faster. So fast until I'm sure we can't go any faster.

The car hits something. I jolt to the left. I smack my head against Kayden's, but he flops forward. He's not moving. His body's like a flimsy doll. I can't see his face, just his long red hair hanging everywhere. But I can see his skin. It's gray—too gray, how can it be that gray so quickly?

I scream, "Kay—"

A bullet slices into my right shoulder. The world explodes with pain.

Chapter Twenty-One

I've never been shot before and the pain is far worse, far more unimaginable than I'd thought possible. My shoulder's on fire, burning savagely. Darkness dances in front of me. I feel sick and light-headed. For minutes, all I can do is collapse into Corin's lap, screaming and screaming as I clutch my shoulder. Everywhere is dyed red.

Corin's arms are around me, holding me as the car lurches at crazy angles. I scream as his hand brushes my shoulder, and my teeth draw blood from my bottom lip.

"That way!" Rahn shouts, but I can't see where he's pointing to. I can hardly see anything. Just the redness and pain.

Corin's arms tighten around me again as we turn sharply.

Then we're driving in a straight line. I can hardly breathe as the pain in my shoulder really sets in. There's too much pain. Too much stuff pouring out my shoulder. Blood. Tissue. Muscle. I try to sit up straighter, but either my own body won't allow me to move, or Corin's cage-like grip is stopping me. I can't tell what's him and what's me.

Then I see Three's dark face peering through the blurriness at me. Something near him shatters but he's still looking at me. No, not at me. At Kayden.

I turn, and try to see Kayden. But Rahn's shaking and shaking him, and I can only hear a faint gurgle from Kayden's throat.

"Keep driving, fast," Corin says to Esther. He moves me slightly, and I lean my head against the window.

Esther's slowing down—I can feel the drag of the engine—and I see her glancing at Kayden in the rear-view mirror. Her eyes bulge and her lips pale.

"Put your foot down! Got to get as far away as possible," Rahn says. His voice is strange, like he can't breathe. "Go west."

The terrier whimpers, moves, and presses himself against my legs. I look down at him: blood-drenched fur.

Corin's grip on me tightens. Rahn retches.

"Is Kayden alive?" Three's voice is quiet.

No one says anything.

I close my eyes, trying to concentrate on the pain in my shoulder. If I concentrate on that, then nothing else can exist. Nothing else *will* exist. It will just be me and my pain. Me and my shattered shoulder. The blood's still pouring down my arm. I can feel it.

The car swerves sharply and my body jolts to the right. My head slams back into the window. I wince, somehow managing to keep my eyes shut. The panel of glass against the back of my head is smooth and cold. I think it's the last panel that's intact. I think—

"Seven?"

It's Three's voice, but I can't look at him. My eyelids are too heavy. And I don't want to see Kayden's body. Why would I want to see that? No, it's nicer here: with my eyes shut, there isn't as much pain. Everything's slipping away. It's nice, yes. I try to reach for it—for anything—but everything, which I really don't know what it is, what anything is, dances before me, teasing me.

"Eriksen, wake her up! She could have a concussion!"

I frown. Doesn't he understand that sleeping is better than being awake? I don't want to see anything.

"Get the medical kit! Rahn! We need—"

"There ain't any."

"*What*?"

Corin shakes me. "Sev, for the Gods' sake, open your eyes." His voice is low, and his breath rubs against my face in an irritating way.

His grip on me tightens and my shoulder's telling me I

should still be screaming, but I'm not. Why would I want to scream? Everything here is calm. It's like I'm Enhanced. I can't feel anything. Beautiful. Everything's under control. Everything is fine. Just the darkness and me and them.

"She's been shot too!" Three's voice bangs through my skull. Why can't he just shut the hell up?

I feel Esther slam on the brakes. My body jerks forward, Corin's arms still around me. The seat belt grabs us and—

I shriek as pain sinks its teeth into my right shoulder again.

"Keep drivin'!"

The engine roars.

My eyes jolt open. Light intrudes. I blink. Feel sick. Going to be sick. Oh Gods.

"Corin, put pressure on her shoulder," Three says.

Blearily, I watch as my brother passes something toward us and Corin reaches for it, holding me back with one hand. I moan.

Corin places a cloth over my shoulder. He presses his palm to it. I shriek. I'm going to faint.

"You've got to stop the bleeding..." At last, Three's words are slipping away. "See if you can tie the...."

Corin tries. He starts to lift my arm. I let out an ear-piercing shriek.

He drops my arm immediately. More pain.

"You have to do it." Three's face looms closer, like the ghoul in a nightmare. "She could die from blood loss otherwise." He's stretching toward us, trying to reach me. Then he's climbing into the back, his knee jabbing at Rahn who makes a hissing sound at him.

There's barely room for four people in the back, let alone five. Even if one of them is dead. Someone grunts. I hear the sharp intake of breath.

"Sev, look out the window!" Corin points across me suddenly.

I turn, trying to see and—

I shriek as Corin and Three tie the cloth tightly around my shoulder.

Then I throw up all over their feet.

One of them swears under his breath. My eyes are closing. All I know is pain and death.

And pain and death feel nice. Good. I'm safe. Corin's arms are around me. My brother's here. Esther's driving; she won't do anything silly, not like Rahn. They'll look after me. And the dog too.

Bright colors... light music... the soft smell of mangoes washes over me. I just want to sleep. Need to sleep....

Someone shakes me. Hard fingers on my back. I cry out, "No!" but I can't hear my voice.

"Seven?"

My eyes flick open. Three's face looms over me, and then he makes a *thank you* sign toward the roof of the car.

We're still driving fast.

"We need... do the unexpected," I mumble as the world spins around me. My voice is weak and cracks in the middle.

Mangoes are flying. Everywhere.

Corin and Rahn exchange a look.

"She's delirious?"

"Where's the medical box?" Three turns around fast, grabbing at the headrest of the passenger chair as the car turns. "Rahn, medical supplies!"

There's a pause, pain flares up in my shoulder. I whimper. Corin holds me tighter.

"I said we ain't got any!"

"*What*?" Corin sounds like he's choking. His lips are by my ear. "You *always* get them. Always. Every raid, you get medicine. Antiseptics, pain relief, tablets—" He's trying to turn around, and my head slams into his. Darkness and white spots flash in front of me.

"Haven't got any—"

"What the hell have you been getting at the pharmacies?"

Everyone's shouting. My head's going to explode.

I stare ahead, determined not to see Kayden's body. Why is it still here? Don't they know we need to send his body off quickly to make sure his spirit gets to the New World without trouble? The longer we wait, the more likely it is that the evil spirits will follow our car. I shudder. The movement hurts my shoulder. I lean back against Corin—

ignoring how tense he is—letting the darkness overwhelm me until everything I know is gone.

***

"I'm pretty certain we've lost them now," Esther says. A good three hours have passed and we haven't seen any more Enhanced Ones since.

Rahn nods. "Okay." He leans forward and I think he's squinting underneath his dark glasses. "There should be a small river over yonder," he says. I see him glance over at Kayden's body, and I know what he is thinking.

The terrain is a lot greener where we are now and it smells fresher, like we're close to a jungle. I look out the window. Corin and I are no longer strapped together by the seat belt, and he's sitting next to the dead man's body. Outside, there are lots of low-creeping plants and even a few trees—naturally placed albizias this time.

Esther continues driving, gulping back tears, and soon enough we reach the side of a river. We get out. I'm wobbly and my shoulder hurts even more with the movement of walking. Three puts his arm around me. We watch as Corin and Rahn lift Kayden's body out of the car.

I try not to look, but it's impossible not to. As Corin and Rahn carry him, I see the bullet that killed him, embedded in the side of his neck. A bloody dark mass of white and red and pink tissues, and darker purple streaky things and almost-black lumps.

I have to look away.

Esther, Three, and I follow Corin and Rahn to the side of the river. The rushing water looks heavenly. Light. Refreshing. Full of hope.

I can't feel my arm at all now. I'm glad.

We watch as the two men take Kayden's shoes off, and then Corin goes back to the car. He returns with one of Kayden's bows and a length of rope.

Rahn ties the bow to the body, and then Corin wades into the shallow part of the river, dragging Kayden's body with him.

Esther's moans fill my ears. I'm not crying. I'm just… there.

Rahn says the Spirit Releasing Words, and after a few moments, Corin lets go of the dead man's hands. The river sweeps Kayden's body away as we watch.

I look around. Five of us are left, whittled down by death. By the Enhanced. I feel sick, and suddenly my hand finds the small bottle of Calmness in my shorts. It's still there. I'd forgotten about it, but I can feel it's intact. How didn't Corin realize it was there? I was sitting on his *lap*.

I swallow hard, don't know where to look.

"Come on," Rahn says to Corin, offering him his hand.

Corin takes his uncle's hand, and climbs out of the river. He then walks off toward the car, presumably to change his shorts.

Rahn looks across at Three and Esther. "Take Seven upstream and clean her wound."

Three pauses for a moment, opening his mouth slowly, stretching his lips. "Do we take the bullet out?" he asks.

Rahn nods. I feel my body get heavier, and my breathing already sounds shallower.

"Use Duct Tape as a bandage," Rahn says, throwing a roll at Three. "It'll stick better. I think there's some brandy left somewhere. Use it as an antiseptic."

"Come on," Esther says, and lightly touches my arm. I flinch, but don't resist as she and Three lead me upstream.

I know it's going to hurt. Badly.

Chapter Twenty-Two

Over the next two weeks or so, my arm becomes a real pain. Three says the bullet didn't do any real damage, skimmed the important stuff and that it's only torn tissue and muscle that needs to repair. Still, every time I move the slightest part of my body, pain shoots through me, wrapping me in its little sticky arms.

The pain keeps me awake several nights running, and multiple times I contemplate taking some of the Calmness— not that I'd be able to open it easily, given one of my arms barely works. But every time I *think* of getting the augmenter out of my pocket, I see my father and sister. I see the looks of betrayal in their eyes. It makes me feel sick. It makes me think I deserved to get shot, that I deserve this pain, because I stole an augmenter, and I'm still hiding it. Maybe Kayden's death is my fault too.

Even after a month, my shoulder is still bad. Just using my fingers on my right hand sends spasms of pain up into my shoulder. I spend most of the time in the car, doing as little physical work as possible. The worst days are when everyone else goes out on raids, leaving me here with the terrier, waiting, wondering, imagining… I grimace. A few times, the anxiety has nearly driven me to take the Calmness. But Rahn and Three and Corin and Esther always come back in time and I don't need the augmenter. I know I should get rid of it, but I can't help thinking there will be a time when I *will* need it. A time when they don't come back….

My shoulder is getting better. Slowly. And I have still got the use of it, even if it doesn't work entirely properly at the moment. At least I still have my arm. At least I still have *my life*.

Everywhere I look, I expect to see Kayden. Even after a month.

It's dark, and we're in the car, supposedly sleeping. Rahn thought it would be safer to sleep here. He's in the driver's seat, snoring lightly. Corin's also in the front. Moonlight silhouettes his profile, and his posture is too tense for him to be sleeping.

To my right, Esther snuggles closer into Three's side and he moves his arm around her, still deep in sleep himself. I look at them both. They look relaxed, almost happy—as if they're not in the middle of nowhere, being hunted down.

I feel groggy, like I'm asleep myself, but I know I'm not. I readjust my position slightly, and it's enough to send a new bolt of pain through my arm, and remind me of the small vial. It's still in my pocket. The same pocket. Still there, undetected. I struggle to swallow, struggle to breathe. They could've found it—any of them could have found it—when I was hurt.

Oh Gods. I have to get rid of it. There's no way I'm taking it, not now they've murdered Kayden.

"Sev," Corin whispers, but doesn't move.

My body jerks.

"Yeah?" My whisper isn't quite as soft as his, more raw and raspy, and next to me, Esther stirs slightly. My heart races.

"Get out of the car. Quietly."

For a second, I don't move. A small lump materializes in my throat. Oh Gods. My legs shake.

Corin's already opened his door, quietly. I open mine, wincing as it squeaks. But Esther doesn't stir again, and Three's out of it. Rahn's still snoring. I shut my door quietly. Corin is already at my side.

He nods at me. Under the night sky, his eyes look darker, and he stares at me in a thoughtful, brooding way. Then his gaze gets darker and my heart lurches. The augmenter. Suddenly it's all I can feel, against my leg at the bottom of the pocket. But he can't know about it. I've been careful.

Very careful.

"Your shoulder," Corin says.

He looks at me expectantly, so I raise that arm slightly, despite the persistent aching.

"No one's checked the wound recently," he says.

I exhale loudly, my stomach feeling all jittery. He doesn't know about the Calmness after all.

"It needs to be checked regularly. No one has done it today."

His observation makes me feel nervous, not because he must have been watching me to know it, but that he'd think of it, and he must have been thinking of it a lot to bring it up. I look up at his face and blink. In his eyes, it can't be *concern*, can it?

Then I remember. His mother lost her arm. It went gangrenous. When I was little, I thought it had just fallen off one day, and I was terrified it would happen to me.

"The tape needs changing too," Corin says. His tone is brisk and efficient; his voice louder and harder than his soft whisper back in the car.

He flicks his head in a *follow me* motion and I follow him wordlessly to the narrow stream. I look up at Corin as we stop, and he glances away quickly. He *must* be thinking of what I did in the pharmacy. I can barely look at him as he takes my arm and unwraps the brandy-soaked scraps of cloth and tape from it.

His touch is gentle but firm, and after tugging harder at the end of the cloth, which had blended into the sticky mess that is my flesh, he looks at me. I can't meet his eyes.

"Sorry." But his voice isn't tender. He throws the bloody strips of cloth on the ground, near the edge of the stream. "It needs washing." He holds onto my elbow as he guides me to the water's edge.

I try not to cry out as he splashes cold water over my shoulder. The wound sizzles, burning. I take a deep breath, grit my teeth, and stare over Corin's shoulder. The sky's darkening, but the space around me isn't dark. I frown, it's like there's another light source other than the moon and the stars. I turn—though Corin still holds onto my arm—and look around. There isn't another light. Behind me, it's even lighter. Yet the sky is still dark.

Evil spirits? It's the first thought that enters my mind, then I look closer at the sky. It's inky black.

"Corin," I say, and I use my good arm to point at the sky. He doesn't answer.

I look back at him. He's not there.

"Corin?" I can still feel his grip on my arm. But he's not here. "Corin?"

I turn. Suddenly, it's daylight. Harsh, artificial daylight. Yet the sky's still dark—swirling purples and inky blacks.

"Corin?" My voice is even smaller. The wind picks up around me, whistling through trees that aren't there. I hear a click behind me. I turn.

A scream escapes my lips. A flash of metal. A gun is in his hand. I try to look around, but can't look away from the Luger. Don't want to look up at him; don't want to see his face. Don't want to see *him*.

"Any final words, Sev?" His voice twists into a gnarled mess.

I'm too petrified to speak. My heart slams against my ribs. My shoulder drips. Cold sweat lines my back, trickling down my spine, pulling at my shirt.

He's standing too close—how did he get here? He disappeared, and yet he's here... and the gun. So close. A lump forms in the back of my throat. I'm going to be sick. My throat is raw. No, *everything* is raw. My mouth, my eyes, my head, my hip, my shoulder….

"No?" Corin raises his dark eyebrows, and a glint of amusement appears in those dark brown spheres. A perfect droplet of sweat glistens from his forehead, then slowly moves down toward his bristly eyebrow where it gets caught. "No last words?"

I can hardly breathe, my chest's frozen. My lungs won't work. The soles of my shoes are too thin. Sharp points dig into my feet. I look up toward the sky; I see the bison. I jump.

What? This is a vision? So this isn't real now. But this could actually happen? The imminent future?

Whenever the bison speaks to you, you pay attention, my father's words, one of the last things I heard him say. *You've been chosen as a Seer for a reason. The future speaks to you. You must not ignore it.*

"I am sorry." Corin takes a step forward, and something under his foot crunches. I can't look away from him, but he's growing dimmer. He's just a shadow. A huge shadow-shape. "This is the only way to preserve our people, to maintain our purity," he says. "You know it really, Sev. Deep down, you know I'm right. I'm always right when it comes to our people—my people."

He's looking straight at me, straight at my pocket where the Calmness is. His stare gets more intense; the glass vial will explode.

He knows. He can't know. But he *knows*.

"How did you think you could hide it from us?" His voice is full of betrayal. "It was inevitable that I'd find out. I always find out in the end. *Of course* I'd find out." His grip on the gun tightens and he raises it until it's in line with my forehead. "I like you, Sev. But there's no choice now. I'm sorry, I really am."

My mouth dries, and I squeeze my eyes shut half a second before Corin pulls the trigger.

Chapter Twenty-Three

I jerk awake gasping for breath, bathed in a cold sweat. It's still dark and I can make out the rough shapes of my companions. They're all still asleep; their breathing's soft and smooth. Even Corin's. I check twice.

I sit up a little straighter, ignoring my throbbing shoulder, and try to quiet my racing heart.

Breathe, I tell myself. I count my breaths. One. Two. Three. Four. Five. Six. Seven. Just breathe.

It was inevitable that I'd find out.

I yank my head toward Corin. He's still out of it. I take another deep breath, and then let the air out slowly. I touch my forehead with my good hand. My fingers feel cold against my hot, sweating skin. It's just my imagination. It's what scares me. A powerful fear in my subconscious. It's not real. He won't find out.

But he will.

I know he will. I'm a Seer, and that's what the Dream Land showed me. It was a warning. They're going to find out. They're going to kill me.

I gulp. What if I change the future? They don't need to know about the Seeing dream or the Calmness—they haven't found it yet, and they can't find it if I throw the augmenter away. I'll dispose of the augmenter, I *will*.

I shut my eyes. Sleep. That's what I need. But the vial under my waistband feels too hot against my cool skin. And its temperature's still rising. The glass is burning me. I need to get the augmenter away from my skin—it was better where it was in the Seeing dream, in my pocket.

I exhale loudly. I *need* to throw the augmenter away, yet I know what will happen if I look at the vial. I can feel the draw of the Calmness already. I can't let that happen.

Think of Finn's body. Kayden's. Think of all the people they've killed.

I do. I let their faces fill my mind, until they're swarming everywhere. But they don't override the burning glass of the augmenter against my hip, or how my heart quickens as I let my mouth salivate.

Ignore it. Dispose of it, when you're stronger.

Yes.

It's safer that way. I nod. It *is* safer. A lot safer. If I ignore it, I can't take it. And then no one will see it. Corin won't see it. I won't be betraying anyone then.

But you've already betrayed them.

***

"Did you actually get any sleep? You look awful." Three corners me as we're refilling the water sacks in the small creek.

There isn't a lot of water flowing now, and we're both stooping low. We're in the exact same place where Corin shot me last night. Only he didn't. It wasn't real. The moment we got up, I looked at Corin somewhat fearfully. I wondered if he knew. But his manner was as condescending as always.

"Seven?" Three comes to a stop in front of me.

"Yeah? Oh. Not a lot of sleep."

Three shakes his head at me in a sad way. "You don't need to worry," he says. "It'll all be fine. There's no need to worry about anything."

If only he knew. And I don't know how he can say that. He must know it's a lie. I'm not a little child; he shouldn't lie to me.

The moment we get back to the vehicle with the water-filled skins, Rahn says we need to leave immediately. It's still early; the sun's been up for half an hour or so.

"Put the rest in the back," Rahn says, after he has taken

one of the pouches from Three and thrown it into the footwell of the front passenger seat.

I go to the boot of the car. It is already open—Esther had been rearranging the food packages only a few minutes ago, trying to keep them away from the fuel cans.

There's a space to the left of the food packages, where the water will fit nicely. I put two of the sacks there—they're not big sacks at all—but there's a box in the way, toward the back. Putting down the third skin on the tailgate, I lean forward and with my good arm, shift the box over. Something jingles inside it, making a tinkling noise. It's that same small wooden box, with ornate wooden carvings, that Rahn's had since we left the village.

I slide the third water sack into the space where the box was, then lean forward to put the box back. My fingers rest on the fine wood—is it mahogany?—and my curiosity surges. What is in it? I run my fingers over the carvings—I still can't tell whether they're of animals, dogs, horses, cattle or spirits—

"What the hell are you doin'?"

I turn sharply, knocking pain through my shoulder, to see Rahn. He's standing behind me and the early sun's glare glints off his dark glasses.

"Th—the water." I point at the sack.

Rahn glares at me. He tilts his head to one side. "*That* is a spirit box. It is not to be opened, tampered with, or examined. At any time," he says, his voice clipping each word short. "Do you understand?"

I nod. "Yes."

Spirit boxes are rare; I didn't even know Rahn had one—though, I'd known he'd had the box, I hadn't realized what it was. Spirit boxes are dangerous. Very dangerous. My mother's sister had one when she was younger. The spirits inside it killed her. Too much dangerous stuff in this world.

"Get inside," Rahn says.

I run and jump into the back seat, ignoring my throbbing shoulder. Three's already there and he regards me with a troubled expression. I look away.

***

"I've never been this far from home before."

Esther's voice breaks into my sleepiness, like a nail tearing at dead skin, digging deeper to find fresher material that it can gouge apart.

"It's beautiful. Absolutely beautiful."

Rubbing my face, I sit up a little straighter, and look out the window. It takes a few seconds for my eyes to focus, and, eventually when they do, I raise my eyebrows slightly. Beautiful? The sunset over the desert, casting warm colors across the sand in a magical light that bakes your sun-kissed skin is beautiful. This isn't. This is colder, and, well, it's green. Very green. There's actually grass everywhere. Trees. Shrubs. It's just all, well, *green*. Like that time I was in the Dream Land. I shudder, trying not to remember it.

On the horizon, I make out a city's outline. The Enhanced aren't far away—they never are. My stomach churns. My skin tingles. I still haven't got rid of the augmenter; it weighs on me like a bad omen.

Rahn presses on the brake and the car slows down. I see him look across at Corin in the passenger seat.

"You think there are any Untamed in the woods?" he asks, jerking his head to the right where a huge forest stretches out.

"Anyone's guess," Corin says. "It might be worth checking it out. It's a good distance away from the Enhanced, but not too far away in terms of getting resources."

"Good. We need to find others soon. Safety is in numbers." Rahn turns the vehicle off the dirt road and onto the grass, then he looks at me in the rear-view mirror. "You had a warnin' about this?"

"No."

The terrier stretches across my feet, and raises his head slightly.

"She'd tell you if she had," Three cuts in. He doesn't try to hide the look of annoyance on his face. "Seven's the most trustworthy person I know. You don't need to ask."

I look out the window, turning my back on all of them. The Calmness— now in my shorts pocket—feels hotter.

"Everyone has secrets," Corin says. "Stuff they want to hide."

I try not to inhale, but I hear the way my breath makes a squealing noise against my front teeth, and flinch. I turn slowly, lifting my head higher. Corin's not looking at me. I take a deep breath. No, he can't know. He just can't. It's that dream I had, it's making me read more into everything. Only it wasn't just a dream. It was a Seeing dream. It was warning me to throw the Calmness away before it's too late. Before they find out. Before they kill me.

But what if they don't return from a raid one day? You'll be left on your own. All alone. You'll need the Calmness then.

Pushing the thought away, I concentrate on the green terrain. I grip the side of the door as Rahn jerks the vehicle onto uneven ground. He drives through the trees, round and round, over the bumpiest and wettest of grounds, for an hour and a half.

"There's no one here," Rahn pronounces some time later.

I raise my eyebrows. If anyone was driving a strange vehicle through my land, I'd make sure they couldn't see me. It's common sense.

"We'll just raid the city over yonder—I think it's New Repliza, there aren't many towns or cities here, but I'm not sure. Then we'll keep goin', south, but skirtin' 'round a little if we need to." He swings the vehicle back onto the original dirt road we were on. Rahn is thinking—the corners of his mouth turn town and he nods to himself as he drives on. "Esther, Three, you'll be with me. We'll get food, fuel, and medicine, so we'll need the vehicle. Corin, you and Seven'll have to be on foot, gettin' clothes. We need more shoes and layers. It's colder here—"

"No." Corin's tone is harsh.

"What do you mean? It is colder, even you must've felt it," Rahn says.

"I mean *no*." Corin stares straight ahead. "I am not going on my own with Seven." He says my name like it's contagious, and it makes me jump. He rarely uses my full name.

For a second, no one says anything. Heat rises to my face.

"Why not?" Rahn's voice is low and gritty. "She may be the weakest of us all, but she's still got to be used in this operation."

"My sister is not some weak little girl," Three says.

"She looks like it," Corin says.

"Hey." Esther leans toward her brother. "Stop it."

Corin turns and looks at me, his eyes are arresting. "I think it's best if you sit out on this one." His stare is hard and harsh, and it's impossible for me not to know what he's thinking. He saw what I was like around the augmenters. He doesn't want me on any raids at all now. Doesn't trust me.

"There are only five of us," Rahn says. "Seven can run fast. Her shoulder's gettin' better. We are usin' her."

Corin folds his arms. "She's *still* injured though. She should stay in the car; I believe she's still trustworthy enough for that." He narrows his eyes. "We shouldn't leave it unguarded."

"The dog will still be in the car," Esther says. "He'll guard it."

"Even so," Corin says. "I don't think Sev should participate in this raid—"

"You're being unfair," I say, my voice breaking. Part of me is surprised. Shouldn't I be glad not to participate? Not to go anywhere near those people? And my shoulder *is* injured. But the thought of yet another day when I'm left in the car on my own waiting for them to come back—waiting whilst the augmenter is in my pocket—sends shivers down my spine. I lean forward, making eye contact with Corin. I *need* to go on this raid with them. "You're so prejudiced against me. Is it because I'm a Seer, and you hate us? Or is it because I'm a weak, little girl in your eyes? Or because you saw what I was like when I was Enhanced and you think that I no longer have the right to be in this group?"

Rahn gives him a sharp look. Corin doesn't say anything.

"Right," Rahn says. "*I* am the leader. You all do as I say. I'm goin' to drop Corin *and* Seven off on the outskirts. They are goin' to get clothes and anythin' else they can. We will drive on and park in a backstreet. We leave the dog in here. I will get medicine, Esther and Three will get food. There is to be no arguin' about this. And," he adds, giving Corin a stern look, "I do not expect there to be any trouble. You two need to learn to get on if we're goin' to survive."

***

A little while later, Rahn drops Corin and me off with our sunglasses on, and we walk deeper into the city. The atmosphere between us hasn't improved, and although I'm sure Corin doesn't know about my augmenter, I can't shake away the feeling of dread that clings to me. Sideways, I glance at him. He's staring straight ahead, looking tense. He's like Rahn: a loaded gun.

We keep walking. The Luger is tucked under my waistband, and Corin has the Glock. There are enough guns for our group now, given Kayden's death. I blink back tears quickly.

"That shop." A few minutes later, Corin nods at a huge department store across the road. It doesn't look like there are any lights on inside.

"It's closed," I say. The door's shut, most likely locked. I don't like the idea of breaking in. No one is about, but I don't want to risk it.

"There'll be a back door," Corin says, already walking toward the shop. It's on the corner of a building, and sure enough, there's an alleyway down one side, with a door at the end.

I follow Corin down the narrow passageway. The walls feel like they're closing in on us as we reach the door.

"Stand back," he says, and I take a step back. He kicks the door in with force and wood splinters. The door hangs off its hinges, swaying slightly. No alarm sounds, but that doesn't make me feel any better.

We step into the doorway and Corin turns back to look at me. He frowns.

"You need to stay with me all the time, where I can see you. No sneaking off. I want you by my side the whole time.

Got it?"

I narrow my eyes at him, but he won't be able to see the movement, as we both have dark glasses on. I nod. "Yes. I've got it."

"Good."

He turns away and ducks under a low doorway. I follow him, stooping under the doorway too. Who actually goes to this shop? The short Enhanced?

We're now in a dark narrow corridor with railings either side. The odd carrier bag is hanging up here and there, and Corin grabs each one we pass, leaving none for me. I push my hair out of my face and force myself to keep up with his fast pace. He opens a door on our left and we step out into a large, bright, airy room.

I know department stores have a wide range of stuff, but this one seems to have more than usual. On one side, there are cooking implements and appliances, and on the other, folding chairs are stacked up to the ceiling. In the middle, there's a display of fabrics and cushions. Near them is a double bed.

"Clothes are that way," Corin points to the right. He steps in front of me and walks past the fabric display. There's a doorway straight ahead, and, through it, I can already see racks of clothes.

I follow him to the doorway—another small one—noting just how broad Corin's shoulders are. He's the broadest man I've ever seen. Once we reach the clothes, he hands me a carrier bag and we begin loading them in. Certainly easier than wearing them. After a few minutes, the pain in my shoulder grows beyond the usual throb. I grit my teeth.

Corin hands me another bag. I start to fill it, beginning with shoes at the bottom, shirts on the top. There aren't many times when raiding shops is *this* easy. I turn to grab another shirt and stop.

Corin stares at me.

He's stopped what he's doing; a girl's flowery blouse hangs limply over his arm. The two bags he's already filled sit on the ground, one leaning against his foot. He's wearing the shoes I got him—well, the ones we both got, back at the other shop. They look worn out now, even muddy in places. The laces are frayed, and the toe of the left one is scuffed.

When I look up, he's still staring at me. But he seems closer now. Much closer.

He moves his hand, as if he's going to touch my face. I freeze. His expression is unreadable—if only I could actually see his eyes. His jaw is tight, square, and firm. His mouth, set in a strong line, shows tension. And he's staring at me.

His nose twitches a little. My heart pounds. He's going to—

He looks quickly down at the clothes, his face reddening.

"What about this blouse?" He holds up the flowery blouse that was draped over his arm. "Do you like it?"

"I—"

A throat clears to my left. Corin looks past me, freezes.

My heart quickens. I turn slowly. We are surrounded.

Chapter Twenty-Four

"Drop the bags, put any weapons on the floor and turn around. Hands in the air."

Corin jumps as the voice booms out behind us. I drop my bag immediately, pull the Luger out of my waistband and turn it on them, just as my father taught me. I hold it there, and look to my left. Then my right.

Oh Gods. There's no way out. They're everywhere.

They deserve to die. I swallow hard. The Enhanced are a disease, taking us over, wiping us all out. Diseases are never good. They don't make us better….

Except the Enhanced lifestyle makes us *feel* better. No pain. No terror. No anger. It wouldn't be so bad to join them….

I bite my bottom lip hard.

Their eyes reflect light in multiple directions. It's disorientating. I shift my weight from foot to foot. These Enhanced are tall, powerfully built, perfect. The image of them all stooping under that low doorway nearly makes me laugh.

"Put the weapons down."

I glance over at Corin; his gun is on them too.

"Back to back," he whispers, already moving. The flowery blouse is over his arm again.

I meet him halfway, and the warmth of his back against mine provides some sort of artificial reassurance as I stare into our fate. I do a quick count. Twenty of them. We don't have enough bullets for all of them. Bullets... the word makes my stomach churn. They're still people. But they murdered Kayden... my hand on the gun tightens.

My mother's one of them now. If she were here, could I kill her? A tremor runs through me.

"Put the weapons down." An Enhanced man steps forward, but I can't see him very well. "We will not ask you again, Untamed Ones."

My hand remains where it is. My Luger's trained on a female.

Pull the trigger!

I hear the shuffle of Corin's clothes as he moves. The blouse falls to the ground, slinking down his leg. For a second I think he's going to pull the trigger on himself— that's what a lot of Untamed do, after all. Then I hear a clatter—he's put the Glock down.

"You too," another one says.

All eyes are on me. Corin should run—they're not looking at him. But he doesn't. Why doesn't he run?

"Put the gun down. Violence is never the answer, you poor Untamed creature. We only want to help. To make you see that life is much more without negative emotions. We want to save you. But violence is never the answer."

My eyes narrow. Try telling that to the one who shot Kayden.

"Sev, put it down." Corin's voice is thick.

"B—but, they're going to get us." I gulp. My ears burn. I try not to look at them, in their clean clothes, well-fed, freshly-showered states.

"Put it down." Corin's voice is a little louder this time.

After a few seconds, I do. A man retrieves our weapons.

"Good." The woman who speaks is wearing a ridiculous shade of orange. She steps nearer. "Take your glasses off."

I bristle, but what difference is it going to make? They know what we are.

Corin backs up against me, and more heat radiates from his body like the desert sun's hot fingers rushing over me.

"No."

The Enhanced share a strange smile. A few of them even nod, looking delighted.

"We know you're Untamed," one of them says. Her voice

is like sugar-coated bubblegum; just the sound makes me feel sick. "Our people never steal. We don't need to. We are the perfect society, stealing has been eradicated in our people." She raises a fragile hand toward us; her silk clothes seem to flow around her arm. "Don't worry, my dears, we know you're scared. But we will help you. We will save you. It is our duty."

She steps forward, until she's only a few inches from us. Her long fingers pluck my glasses from my face. I blink in the harsh light. Her eyes burn mine even more. I feel a strange tickling in the bridge of my nose, like I'm going to sneeze.

Corin doesn't say anything as his glasses are removed. I can tell he's thinking, even though he's behind me. He's just giving off those vibes. Very distinctive, they are.

Thinking, that's what I should be doing. If there's a way out of this, then we need to be able to think. I need to breathe. I take a few deep breaths.

If we want to get out of this…. maybe I should've fought against Corin and Rahn harder when they came to collect me from the compound at New Kimearo. Then I wouldn't be in this situation. I'd have been safe the whole time; I wouldn't have been on the run, constantly scared.

And I wouldn't have the guilt of stealing that augmenter raging inside me like a caged up lion trying to claw its way out.

No. I have to fight. I am a Seer now.

"Ada, call a conversion unit. You take the girl," one of them says. "We'll have the guy."

"No." Corin's hand latches onto my arm. It's my bad arm, and something tears in my shoulder as he pulls me closer to him. I bite back tears. "You can have us if we stay together."

Corin looks across at me briefly, then back at the Enhanced. His eyes are deep. I've never seen his face so pale; his skin is almost white, and it makes the sunburnt patches look like they've been stuck onto his face, like they don't really belong to him.

One of them laughs. "Lovers."

"Brother and sister." Corin coughs.

More of the Enhanced laugh.

"You don't look like you're related," a man says. "You're about as opposite as two people can be."

He's right. Corin's light; I'm dark. Corin's muscular and broadly built; I'm tall and thin.

"I *said* we are brother and sister. Whatever you want with us, we stick together."

The Enhanced woman in the orange dress shakes her head. "I don't think you're in a position to negotiate with us. You—the Untamed—have evaded us for long enough, stopping us from fulfilling our duty. You should be grateful that we're still willing to give you this chance. We could just kill you."

"Violence is never the answer," I echo their words back at them before I even realize what I'm doing.

One of them laughs.

"Seize them."

There's nothing we can do as they close in on us. Hands grab me, and I try to fight them off, but I can't—or maybe I don't want to. I don't even know any more. They yank me forward, by my hair, and I scream. Another Enhanced One grabs my shoulder.

Pain. Everywhere. Just pain. I struggle to breathe, start to fall, but hands force me upward.

"She was shot in that shoulder!" Corin yells. I see him struggling against four Enhanced. He's doing a surprisingly good job. "Don't touch her!"

The Enhanced don't listen to him. Of course they wouldn't.

Corin fights hard, but I barely have the energy. All I can feel is pain down my right side and in my shoulder, kind of like I've been shot again, but with a bullet that numbs everything into a distant blur. Anyway... it's... it's easier to give in... but it's not giving in... it's survival... it's what I want... what I need. And this will be the only way to survive... the Untamed life isn't really living, only the Enhanced truly *live*.

"Let her go!"

Hands pat me down and I squirm automatically so they

don't feel the augmenter in my pocket. Not that I need to hide it from them. They'd be delighted to find it. Maybe if they saw it, they'd be nicer to me.

Don't betray Corin.

He shouts a string of the rudest words I've ever heard, but it doesn't make the slightest difference. The situation we're in has only one outcome.

I gulp, choking. I don't want to remember what it was like to be one of them. I need the negatives to outweigh the positives. The Enhanced pretend they're good, but they still kill. They are monsters. They killed Finn, Kayden, and they tortured and shot me.

Anger flares through me. My arms stiffen. Pain, fully alive now, rips through my shoulder. I crane my neck and get a glimpse of Corin. More people surround him than me, and I can barely see his face. Can't tell which way he's facing.

I swing around, trying to push them off me. Something jabs me in the back.

They're going to convert us. We can't get away. It's like in the desert, nearly two months ago, but, I don't know, is it worse? Can it be worse?

I know what they're going to do. I know what it feels like to be them. And I know how good it was, but also how bad it was. Maybe that's the worst part; I know they'll help me forget the bad stuff they did to me. I would be happy again. I'd be with my mother. I'd have everything. I could forget all the murders I've seen. They'd help me. I'd be safe, for the first time in my life, truly safe.

But you wouldn't be you.

My head feels like it's going to explode. I can hear buzzing and see flashing lights everywhere I look. The roof of my mouth tastes furry, and my knees are weak as numerous hands push me forward.

Is it better to be me or not? Dead or alive?

"Kill us instead!" The words erupt from within me and I gag.

What the hell are you doing?

My ears ring. My head feels too cold—ice cold—and the base of my neck stings. I feel sick. The Enhanced stare at me.

But, I haven't made a difference. They only laugh.

"We don't want to become like you," Corin shouts. "We're entitled to make our own choices."

I freeze. What if they kill him but not me? My stomach gurgles. I taste bile. The light in here's too bright—their shiny eyes swarm around me.

"You don't know what's best for you. How can you choose between two lives, when you've not experienced both?"

"Sev has!" Corin shouts. "And she chose our lifestyle. The *Untamed* lifestyle. Not yours. You need to let us go. *Now*."

"We deserve a choice," I say. He's right. We should each have a choice, the chance to decide....

Laughter rips from them in unison, then they drag me forward. I turn, trying to see Corin, but can't. There are too many of them. They force me toward a different room, away from Corin; my feet stumble over the threshold.

This is right. This is right. Soon you won't know what you were worrying about.

"Sev!"

My heart surges. I whirl around, kicking.

"Cor—"

Something hits me hard against my spine. Pain resounds through me in tiny vibrations, up and down my backbone, into my neck, my head. I lose my balance, fall against two more Enhanced Ones. My left hand ends up on the crotch of one, and I try to push myself away, but my body creases with pain.

Darkness starts to close in above me. I stoop, breathing through my nose—so loudly, I can hear it in my ears like claps of thunder—and turn around. My hands are clenched, ready.

Ready for what? They just want to help. They believe it's the right thing to do. It is the right thing. You know it really.

"Don't worry, my dear." It's one of the Enhanced men— one with long blond hair, dark skin, and multiple piercings. His voice doesn't match his appearance. "This pain is temporary. You'll soon be free of it all. You'll live a pure, loving life of satisfaction. Do not be afraid."

Why would I be afraid?

I manage to get to my feet somehow. "Get away from me." My whole body trembles violently. There is nothing I can do.

"It will be easier for you if you cooperate. I can tell you want to."

"No... no... no, I don't. Get away from me." I gulp. "Where's Corin?"

I try to look at the next Enhanced One, but they all look the same suddenly. I can't distinguish between them. They're like copies, identical, all of them.

"Where's the man I was with?"

"You'll be reunited after the conversion."

The conversion.

I can taste blood in my mouth. My teeth chatter. My tongue feels too big, like it's swollen to three times its size and I'm going to choke on it.

The *conversion*—just the word makes me shudder. I gulp, already feeling liquid pour down my throat as Raleigh's grinning face looms in front of me. My throat restricts and my body convulses.

"Get away from me!"

I back away from the dark-skinned, blond-haired man. Hands seize me from behind.

"Get away from me!"

The cloth is lowered again.

Another wave pours down.

It's not worth it... they'll break you in the end.

"Join us and this will stop."

Save yourself. Give up now.

"I'll never join you voluntarily!"

"It will be easier and less painful for you if you cooperate."

I hear a loud click. A familiar loud click. I freeze. A gun. They paid attention, after all.

Death.

Terror pours through me. I—I didn't mean it! I don't want to die! I'd rather be like them and alive.

Another click.

I don't know how I'm still standing. It's the—they're holding me up. How didn't I notice? They're so close. I can smell them: flowery perfumes, heavy musky scents, spicy aromas. I can see every detail of their faces: the follicles of their skin, the fine powders on their faces, my reflection in their eyes.

Click.

They're going to kill me.

I turn, screaming. Hands fall away, shocked. I lunge forward, grab at the nearest woman, punch her in the face. It's not the best punch I've ever thrown, but not the worst either.

"Restrain her!"

Another click. Oh Gods. Why don't they just do it? Why play with me, making me think I can get away?

Because you don't want to get away.

But I run and I punch another one. Why am I hurting them? It'll do no good; make them sure to kill me.

"Stop it!" I yell the words, both at them and myself.

Another click of the gun.

I turn, searching for the barrel. If I know where it is, I can avoid it. But I can't see it. I look. I keep looking. I strain my eyes. Still can't see it. I search more hands. Ten hands, eleven, twelve. None of them has a gun. One hand is holding a vial of pale orange liquid. I must have imagined the gun clicks.

The vial creeps toward me.

"No!"

Something catches my eye. I blink foggily. And a lot of things happen. A flurry of movement. Something rushes up against me. A man pushes me backward, a wall against my back. I stand with my feet shoulder-width apart, and the Enhanced hold my arms against the wall. Nowhere for me to go.

The orange augmenter winks at me.

She's holding it—the woman in front of me. Dark hair, white skin, shiny eyes. Her face is expressionless.

"Get it away from me," I say, but my voice is weaker.

Tears pour down my face, mingling with blood on my

top lip, but I don't care. My eyes will only focus on the tiny bottle. It doesn't look as beautiful as the Calmness in my pocket. This looks sinister. My heart palpitates. I flush hot, then cold.

But the Enhanced are ignoring me. Of course they are! The steel fingers around my wrists get tighter. The augmenter is too close. Far too close. There's no stopping it. Do I want to stop it?

Remember what it was like! Remember your room, your bed, your wardrobe, your teddy bear....

I scream again and—

Click.

"I *believe*, though of course, I may be wrong, that she asked you to get that thing away from her," a voice says.

I freeze, all the breath knocked from me.

That voice.

I crane my head trying to see past the Enhanced. But I can't see anyone other than them. Light skin and dark skin, and blonde hair and black hair and red hair and white hair and—

The woman holding the augmenter lowers it toward me. It's so close, my eyes can't focus on the vial.

But, that *voice*.

Gods. I'm hallucinating. She can't be here... she's dead. I left her. She'll be dead. Or one of *them*. No, I saw her body. She was lying on the ground. She's dead. I must be hallucinating. It's the shock. The fear. The confusion. The conflict.

I hear the final click as the gun is loaded. I still can't see it. Where is it? Hidden, in the walls?

"Well, you asked for it."

I can't breathe. Her voice is familiar, yet different.

Something moves in front of me. A blur. Fingers fall away from my wrists. Something hot sprays across my abdomen. A gunshot goes off. And another one. Blood splatters everywhere. Two—no three—Enhanced fall. The vial clatters to the ground. Glass smashes. Orange liquid pools in the red.

Marouska steps forward smiling. "Who's next?"

Chapter Twenty-Five

Marouska wastes no time in shooting the others and within seconds the Enhanced are all lying *dead* at our feet.

"Come on," she says. She steps away from the bodies, moving her ample frame rather quickly.

After a few seconds, I get my act together. I follow her, dazed. *Marouska* is here? Marouska, who I left to die back at the village. Marouska, who I saw lying unconscious on the ground back at Nbutai....

I really am hallucinating.

"Your brother's here?" she asks.

"What?" I squint at her, and rub my blood-stained fingers at my forehead. The pain there's sharp and moody.

"Where's Three? D'you know?"

"Uh, no. Corin... Three's not. Corin's here."

Marouska raises one eyebrow, but doesn't say anything. Instead, she moves to the doorway. She's wearing her usual attire: dark rags knotted around her torso, emphasizing her voluptuous curves, and a long skirt torn in several places, with heavy, black boots.

"Where?"

"I—I don't know. They separated us."

"Anyone else?"

"No. I don't know about the others." My words fall out too quickly.

I shake my head, staring at Marouska. She's not the fat woman I remember. Sure, she's still round and has the biggest chest and hips I've ever seen. But her face is scarred and she's *armed.* Her rifle looks a little like an AK47, but not quite. The barrel is too long, and there's something about the shape of it, the welding maybe, that makes me frown.

"*How*?" I stare at her.

Marouska doesn't slow down. "This be no time for stories, Seven. We've got a man to rescue."

"But—"

A scream cuts me off. Corin's scream.

Marouska and I leap forward. I barely notice the pain in my shoulder and back, and, as we're about to step over the threshold, Marouska hands me a knife. It's a big knife.

"Aye, Seven, I'll be doing the shooting," she says, gripping the AK47 look-alike tightly. "This—it's an Enhanced gun. It can't run out of bullets. Don't ask me how it works. I don't know. Just have to keep clicking it. But if any get past me, you stab 'em." She grins rather manically.

I nod and follow her out. We're back out in the big room now, the one where Corin and I got caught. There's no sign of him here, or anyone. Just that flowery blouse on the floor.

"Over there."

Marouska charges toward a closed door. Before I can warn her how many Enhanced Ones will be on the other side, she throws the door open, charges in, and lets out a war cry.

I freeze, blink hard. Definitely not the Marouska we left behind. But if she's survived, Untamed, maybe others have too. Hope surges within me.

"Let him go," Marouska shouts. "I'm armed."

I stumble after her, tripping over the bases of clothes racks, and at last reach the doorway. She's already got all the Enhanced backed up against the wall. I catch a glimpse of Corin in one corner. His face is stricken.

"Put the gun down."

Marouska fires at them, a barrage of bullets leaping to their victims. I have to look away. I don't want to see the limbs flying through the air, or the blood. But I hear their screams. The last gurgles of life.

I concentrate on the knife I'm holding. It's massive and the hilt is made of some sort of metal. Maybe even a precious metal.

"*Marouska*? Sev?"

I look up as Corin approaches. His eyes are still brown. I lean against the doorway, my heart races.

"I would make a formal welcoming gesture in normal circumstances," Marouska says. "But, that would lead to stories, an' like I said to Seven, now ain't the time. So, I suggest we get out of here fast." She hands Corin another knife, then starts to lead the way out.

For several seconds, Corin and I stare at each other. He looks lost and surprised and scared and relieved and amazed.

"Sev, are you okay?" he asks at last. He raises a hand to my face and I freeze as his fingers make contact with my skin. A tiny, electrifying jolt goes through me. "That's a deep cut." He removes his hand. His fingertips have my blood on them.

I exhale and touch my face. It hurts now I know about it.

"Come on," I say, and we follow Marouska out of the department store.

I don't know whether my dizziness is because of the near-death experience, Corin's touch, Marouska's sudden and life-saving arrival or the way the Calmness digs into my leg, laughing at me.

***

I have never seen Rahn look more surprised than when we arrive back at the car with Marouska. His skin turns an eerie white and for several seconds, I think he will faint.

Three and Esther look equally surprised, but they exclaim and laugh and squeal—or at least Esther does, Three's not the type of man to squeal.

Rahn just resembles a statue as Marouska, Corin and I update them. It sounds crazy. Too much of a coincidence, but it's true.

"What the hell?" Rahn finally exclaims. He looks at Corin, then at me. "What were you two doin' in there? How *didn't* you notice you were bein' surrounded?" Beneath his dark glasses, I think I see some movement. His lips twitch.

"Distracted, were you?"

I stare at Rahn. He folds his arms, gives his nephew a sharp look.

"What?" Corin's shoulders jump up. "*Her*?" He jerks his eyes toward me, then back again. "That is a revolting idea."

"*That* is my sister you're talking about, Eriksen," Three says.

"For the Gods' sakes, they're okay!" Marouska says. "There's no point in any of this yelling an' screaming—oh, the little dog's here too, how wonderful!" She crouches and holds her arms out for the little terrier.

But my dog doesn't throw himself at her like he used to, he just comes to an abrupt stop, and bares his teeth slightly.

Marouska laughs. "We've all changed then."

"Right. We need to get in the car and drive as far away as possible," Rahn says. He looks across at Corin, and lowers his voice. "I'll be talkin' to you later."

***

"Aye, it was scary," Marouska says. From the back seat, I watch her unravel one of the large food packages, and begin to divvy it up into six very unequal portions. The vehicle lurches over a bump, and the portions become even more unequal. "I was sure I was dead!"

"What happened back there?" Esther asks. "After we, uh, left?"

Marouska hums to herself as she unwraps another package of food. Some sort of meat, goat maybe. Soon the car smells of it. My mouth waters as I watch her put a scrap of it onto each portion.

"I got shot in the arm, but it was only a laser or something, it healed quickly. Aye, but I was out of it for a while. I guess 'em Enhanced Ones must've thought I was dead; they left me with all the other bodies. When I came 'round, they were gone. Well, I thought I was dead too."

"So, uh, did everyone else die?" Three asks.

Marouska clears her throat. "I saw Yani an' Elf's bodies. An' quite a few of 'em Enhanced Ones' too. Looks like we did good work."

Good. Not a word I'd have used.

"What about the others?" Rahn asks, and I think of my father and Five.

Marouska shrugs. "I didn't see their bodies. They could be dead." She sticks her finger into a lump of fat that fell off the meat and smears it onto some bread. "But it's more likely they're Enhanced now."

A strange tightness holds onto my chest as she says those words. If they're Enhanced, they're alive.

The Enhanced will be the only people who survive, in the long run.

I don't know what expression has fallen over my face, and I look away quickly.

"And how did you get here?" Rahn asks. "We're a long, long way from Nbutai."

"Stole a car. Well, four of 'em altogether." Marouska says the words as if it's the most natural thing for her in the world. "They kept running out of fuel, kept having to ditch em' an' walk. Never realized how difficult it is to drive 'em either."

The vehicle crashes over another bump, and pain bolts through my shoulder.

"I hope that's not my food that's now on the floor," Rahn says.

"No, it's Corin's."

Three smirks. Corin, who's also in the back, but sitting as far away from me as possible, doesn't say or do anything. He's turned his back on everyone, and is staring out the window, probably in a mood.

"Marouska, what happened next?" I lean forward slightly. The terrier lies between my feet, and his ears prick up. Everyone wants to know. But my dog's on guard, tense, I can sense that easily. "How did you find us here? *Why* did you go to New Repliza?"

"Coincidence," she says. "I was looking for the Mariballii tribe."

The Mariballii tribe is something of a legend; few people doubt that a large tribe of Untamed could still exist. I personally don't think so. No one's actually seen them for about fifty years. Same with that other large tribe—the Zharat. They just disappeared. No one's heard of them for years. Either they've perfected the art of hiding, they're dead, or the Enhanced have them.

"But we're not near their grounds," Rahn says. "The Mariballii tribe isn't in this region the last I heard."

"Well," Marouska says. "I travelled east for a few days, but then ran into trouble. The Enhanced caught me. Took all my weapons, they did. But they didn't check my boots. An' I pulled the knife I keep in the left one on 'em." She goes silent for a moment. "The Gods must've been watching over me. I killed a good dozen Enhanced Ones. Aye, an' there were eight chivras too."

"Eight chivras?" Rahn says.

My eyes widen. I look at Esther and Three. They blink in astonishment.

Marouska nods. "Aye. I stormed 'em. To be honest, I thought my time was a'tickin', but it just gave me a concussion. I'm telling you, chivra spirits ain't as evil as we think. An' when they'd gone, I got myself one of 'em Enhanced people's guns—an' I'm telling you this, for a people who don't believe in violence they have a hell of a lot of modified guns in their possession. The one I got from 'em don't even need reloading with bullets. I don't know how it works, but it can't run out."

"It can't run out?" Corin speaks for the first time since getting in the car. He turns and looks toward Marouska.

"Aye."

"Where is it?"

"By my feet," Marouska says. "An', no, you ain't having no look at it. 'Cause I'll never get it back once you've got your hands on it. Here, eat this up." She hands a package of food behind her. It *is* the one that ended up on the floor.

Corin takes the food, looking a bit miffed.

A small part of me is glad Marouska didn't give him the gun. My shoulders tighten. If he has that gun, he might shoot me.

It was inevitable that I'd find out.

No. What the hell am I thinking? I shake my head. Anyway, if Corin was going to shoot me, he has his own gun. Even if it does need manual reloading.

"So there I was, with my gun," Marouska continues, "hunting down 'em Enhanced. Six days like that on the road. Blood on my hands. Hissing all 'round me. Huh. An' then I heard lots of voices an' screams. An', low an' behold, not only did I find the Untamed, but I found you." She turns around to look at me, then twists even further—in a way that doesn't look natural for anyone, least of all her—until her eyes rest on Corin. "Miracle, ain't it? The Gods an' Goddesses an' spirits are watching. Aye, they want us to win this battle."

Untamed

Chapter Twenty-Six

We spend the rest of the day driving along the mud road by a small river, and planning our route ahead. The plan seems to be that we'll drive and keep driving until we find the Mariballii tribe—if they still exist.

Just before dark, we turn off the road and Rahn parks the vehicle in a little copse.

"Should be secluded enough here," he says, as he turns the ignition off. He twists in his seat and looks at us all in the back. "Three, make a fire over yonder. Corin and Esther, see what you can gather and hunt down." He looks down at the terrier. "Seven, you take him out for a walk. Looks like he needs it. Whilst you're out, scout the land. Marouska, we'll sort out what resources we have and what we need to get."

The light's already changing, getting deeper and heavier. We know we've not got long. But, for several seconds, none of us move. We all stare out the windows. There's an acacia tree nearby, and I focus on it, noticing the way its thorny branches cut the sky clean. Behind it, everything looks darker and—

I freeze, eyes wide.

There. Movement. A figure? I blink.

"What's the matter?" Rahn's tone is cynical.

I turn back to the window, my gaze pouring outside to the acacia. There's nothing behind it.

"Thought I saw something," I mumble.

"What?"

Just my mind tricking me, making me think I saw Raleigh.

"Nothing."

Everyone gets out the car, so I force my stiff body to work, groaning a little, and call for the terrier to follow. He does, slowly at first, then more eagerly. His ears are alert and his nose is to the ground as we walk.

I glance about. It's dusk: the evening sky is gentle. The Turning wasn't long ago, but I can't help thinking another will be soon. Strange. I pull my jacket around my body tighter, ignoring my throbbing shoulder — Esther had a look at it when we stopped earlier, and she reckons the wound's healing okay.

I tell the terrier to keep close to my heel. He does. He's a good dog.

We come out on the other side of the trees and the green landscape stretches around us. For a few seconds, I pause, drinking it all in. The grass is knee-high in most places, thin and wispy enough to sway in the slight breeze. To the right, stand more trees, and on the other side, grass spreads out toward the foot of a huge hill. Beyond that, are small mountains with rock formations scattered down their sides. Above, a black stork beats across the cool sky. On the horizon, I can make out several silhouettes. Ostriches, maybe.

The terrier, nose to the ground, trots off and I watch him for a few minutes. Hardly visible in the long grass, he barks every now and again, then reappears by my side. I greet him and fuss over him, telling him what a good boy he is. He looks up at me with his big, droopy eyes and licks my hands. There's something about his eyes, something that makes my heart beat just a little faster. He *does* deserve a name. I know that.

I stare at him, press my lips together. I fought for my name when the Enhanced said I was *Shania*. Names are important, and the terrier needs a name. I fold my arms as I look at him, trying out different sounds on my tongue. But nothing takes. He's always just been our terrier.

"Come on," I say to him and together we run through the long grass. He jumps up at my side, barking loudly.

I run faster and faster. The wind is in my face, exhilarating. I can almost forget the pain in my shoulder.

The glass vial in my shorts pocket pounds against my thigh; it's the reminder that this life is not perfect. It makes me feel strange. Its presence betrays a part of me, and I betray myself because I still have it.

"But I'm Untamed," I shout to the sky. My lungs burn. "I am Untamed."

I *am*. I'm nothing like the Enhanced. They are murderers. I'm not one of them. The spirits chose me for their Seer. I am Untamed.

Yet you won't throw the augmenter away.

The words hit me like a sharp dagger, and heaviness drags me down. I slow until I'm walking again. My breath comes in huge gasps and my chest shudders with every gulp of air. My shoulder's not great either, but I push the pain away as best as I can—I'm used to it now. The dog is a few feet away and I call him back to my heel with a loud whistle. My father taught me how to whistle—he could mimic the birds' tunes too. We walk around for a little longer. The stork is no longer visible in the distance, and the light is fading. The ostriches have gone too.

"Time to go back," I tell the dog.

He whines slightly, but doesn't run off.

We walk back to the trees where we parked the vehicle. I haven't been gone longer than half an hour, but I see that Corin is no longer gathering. He's standing on the outskirts of the trees, looking out over the grassy valley. I shiver slightly, wondering whether he saw me running about. I hope not. I swallow hard. Not that I should care what he thinks of me. I shouldn't let him affect me.

As I get nearer, Corin disappears back into the trees, melting into the landscape. I take a deep breath. It was almost like he was never here, like I imagined it. After all, why would he be out here, watching me, when he was supposed to be hunting and gathering what he could with Esther?

I shake my head at the dog.

"Maybe I'm going mad," I say to the dog. He pants, looking up at me. "Or maybe this is normal for a Seer."

***

That evening, once the small fire has died down, we all sleep in the car. It's cramped inside; Corin's taken his place by the window, but his frame is wider and more muscular than Kayden's. And Three and Esther aren't exactly small either; both are strong and muscular. Then there's me. The skinny, tall seventeen year old with a child's body. I cross my legs, and stick my elbows in, making my frame even narrower. Esther's leaning against me, and I'm sure my side's going to be dead by the morning. I want to move, to stretch, but I can't.

Given my mood today, it is no surprise when I find myself in the Dream Land.

I am lying in a field.

It doesn't feel right. It's a strange transition. My mother told me that usually Seeing dreams start where your real life leaves off. I frown. Maybe this isn't real? But the bison's above.

It's daylight too. *No.* It's brighter than daylight. A lot brighter. The light is white, pure white—the type that blinds you. I squint and shield my eyes as I get up. I look up at the sky. It's white, apart from the bison watching me. *Why a bison?* I study its shape. I think it's a wood bison—the type found in the Taiga land, but I am not sure. I frown. Why is a bison associated with Seers?

Suddenly, the wind picks up; my skin feels raw. I look up at the sky. It's no longer white. It's a swirling mass of pale, pastel colors.

The Turning?

Quickly, I turn and look around. Everything in the land around me is moving. Small rocks—rocks that I hadn't noticed before—moving through the air. Moving at *me.*

I scream and throw myself at the ground. But it's sharp—the ground is made up of thousands of thorns that tear at my skin.

Run, Seven, run whilst you can. The voice booms out from the sky, resounding through the contours of the land and I scream. *Run, Seven, run! He is coming.*

Raleigh? I gulp.

He will always be able to find you... choose your companions carefully, Seven. Some are not worthy... they will lead you down the wrong path... they won't mean to... they cannot help it... keep a clear head... a clear head, Seven. Be yourself, not them...be who you are...let what you are on the inside shine on the outside... don't try to change your fate... we all need you.

I am running. I can't run fast enough. My feet hit the land quicker than I knew they could. But this speed! It's crazy. But it has to be crazy. I have to get away from Raleigh. I have to escape him. Escape him and the Enhanced.

They're coming, Seven. The Enhanced Ones are coming. They'll always be right behind you until you choose a side. A proper side. No dancing in between the Untamed and the Enhanced. Awake now, Seven. For they are coming. Raleigh is coming for you. You. It is you who they want. You. If they have you, they'll have all the Untamed. Run now, tell them all to run, now, whilst you all still have the chance.

Chapter Twenty-Seven

"Rahn!" I shout as I jerk awake. "Rahn, we need to go now." My arms fly out as I try to push Esther's weight off me. "*Rahn!*"

Someone mumbles something, and then Corin and Three both bolt upright, clashing heads. In the near-darkness, I see Corin shove my brother away from him and hear him mutter something under his breath. Rahn turns in the driver's seat, looking at me. The pale moonlight reflects off his dark glasses.

"What have you seen?" he asks, rubbing his neck.

"Seen?" Marouska looks at me.

"She's a Seer," Three says.

"A Seer?" Marouska frowns. I thought she knew. She mustn't have remembered; lots of things happened quickly before and during the attack at Nbutai.

"Are you okay?" Esther's looking at me.

I nod. "We need to go now. Raleigh's coming for me."

I look around, trying to peer out of the window. I feel strange. Jittery. The bison's words still pound my head: *They're coming, Seven. The Enhanced Ones are coming. They'll always be right behind you until you choose a side. A proper side. No dancing in between the Untamed and the Enhanced.*

I swallow hard. I've chosen a side. I'm Untamed. I'll always be Untamed now. I have to be.

But Rahn's survival lesson echoes in my mind, and it makes me feel sick: *Never let yourself be Enhanced. Once it's done, there's no going back.*

The lesson's right. I'm not the same. The augmenter is in

my pocket.

And the bison knows what I've been thinking, about how the Enhanced will be the only people who survive. All this time I've been insisting to myself that I am Untamed, yet what if I can never truly be Untamed again?

Once it's done, there's no going back.

I shake my head. But the bison said I need to choose a side. I focus on that. That means it's still my choice. I can still be Untamed.

But now Raleigh's coming for me. I gulp. The bison said if they have me, they'll have all the Untamed. Oh Gods. My heart hammers against my ribs. I hug my arms around my body, ignoring my shoulder. I never used to be bothered about the dark before, but now it causes unease in me; it watches me squirm whilst knowing all the things that are out there, just waiting for the first mistake.

"Raleigh?" Corin says, his voice deep. His shoulders tense up. "We should've killed him when we had the chance. No matter how many bullets it took."

Rahn clears his throat, looks at me. "You're sure about this? We need to go *now*?"

I nod.

Raleigh, and the Enhanced, is always going to be after me until I choose a side. Why me? What's so special about me? Why am *I* the key to all the Untamed?

"Right," Rahn says. A few seconds later, he turns the ignition. "Where do we go then, Seven?"

I freeze. "I—I don't know. Just that we need to keep moving. Raleigh's after *me*. Not you, not at the moment... it's me who he wants—" I gulp back tears. "I'm putting you all in danger. You should leave me."

As soon as I say those words, I wince. I don't want them to leave me on my own. The Enhanced would get me... I gulp. The augmenter feels heavier in my pocket. What if I choose the Enhanced *because* I am on my own?

If they have you, they'll have all the Untamed.

There's a long silence. My heart palpitates. Rahn's actually considering it.

"We're not leaving you behind," Three says. "I'll always

be with you."

"We all will," Rahn says. But his voice sounds strained, like he's got a lump of soup stuck to the roof of his mouth, and he's trying to swallow it down. "We are a group."

Esther nods. Marouska doesn't say anything. Neither does Corin. He just gets a cigarette. Rahn doesn't even say anything as Corin lights up, in the car.

Three leans forward, across Esther and takes my hand in his. "Don't worry, Seven. Raleigh will never get to you again, that is a promise."

"No. He won't," Corin says. And there's something about the determination in his voice that rings in my ears for hours after he's said the words.

***

We drive on through the night. Just as it's getting light, we stop so Three can take over the driving.

"I don't mind driving," I say.

But Rahn won't listen. Neither will anyone else.

Three drives more carefully than Rahn does and we crash over fewer potholes and take fewer turns at sharp, crazy angles. It could almost be considered a relaxing drive if I wasn't terrified that Raleigh was going to jump out from behind every tree.

"Oh, the Gods!" In the mirror, Three's eyebrows shoot up. "There's a car."

My heart slams into my chest. All of us turn, peering. My shoulder stings. He's right. There *is* a car. We haven't passed a single car on the roads in all our journeying. Yet now there's a car. The bison's words echo through me again, and I shudder.

"Is it followin' us?"

Three looks in the mirror again. "Don't know. It's speeding up."

"It's them," I whisper.

Rahn shakes his head. He's now sitting in the back, on the opposite side from me, with Corin and Esther squashed between us. "We don't know it's them."

But we don't know that it isn't.

"Speed up," Rahn tells Three, then adds under his breath something about how he wishes he were driving.

Three puts his foot down. I grip the door handle as though it is life support. My fingers tingle. Only my window and the windshield still have the glass intact and the friction slows us down. The wind is cold, adding an ominous atmosphere. The engine roars around us, fills my ears.

"It's okay," Esther says, but her voice doesn't reassure me. Beneath her soft tones, she wobbles.

"It's getting closer," Three says.

Corin leans forward to where the rifle is on the floor. Due to its size it's usually not the most popular gun and Three—or Kayden, when he was alive—normally uses it, but here it's Corin's first choice. "We're going to have to shoot it. Everyone, get under cover. Sev, hold the dog. Three, put your foot down!"

Esther leans forward, trying to press herself into the seat. I do the same, hauling the dog into the space between my feet. He's shaking, and his big, droopy eyes catch hold of me. Esther squeezes my hand. She's murmuring something under her breath, over and over again.

"Marouska, get down!" Rahn shouts as Corin takes his first shot.

There's a *clank* as he hits something. Maybe the metalwork of the car. He fires several more shots, and the sounds make me hunker up and my shoulder sears in memory. Then we hear the clank as the rifle runs out of ammunition. The other magazines are in the back, wrapped up with the other supplies.

"Marouska, give me your gun."

"No, I'll use it." Marouska turns in her seat. She's not stooping low at all, and there's no glass in her window. Wind howls through our car's frame.

"I've got a better aim," Corin says. "Give me that gun."

Something hits my door. I let out an instinctive scream before I can stop myself. Esther tries to pull me toward her but the dog leaps up in her face. Then he's on Rahn's lap, howling into his ear.

"Everyone okay?" Three yells from the front.

I see Corin twist around. The dog howls again.

"Marouska, give me your gun. *Now*." There's a pause. "*I've* got the better shot!"

But it's too late. I look up to see Marouska leaning out the window, firing the AK47 look-alike. The sight would be comical, were it not a life and death situation.

I frown; Marouska's changed. A lot. Not physically— she's still the round woman I remember, but she dresses in warrior attire now. And she's tougher, stronger and more confident. Fiery. Back at the village, it took Keelie a good few months to teach Marouska how to get a decent shot, and that was on a stationary target. Yet here she is, shooting at the Enhanced from the window of a *moving* car, and not missing. She's hanging out the window, yet her weight isn't overbalancing her. Incredible. Whoever says people can't change is wrong. People can change for the good—and for the bad—adapting to their environment.

Another bullet hits the metalwork of our car. Esther and I scream. We cling to each other. Then we wait for the next impact, the next bullet, the next death.

"They're not keeping up with us now," pants Three, a few minutes later.

"I hit their fuel tank!" Marouska turns, grinning from ear to ear.

"Just keep drivin'," Rahn says. "Do not slow down at all. How fast are we goin'?"

"One twenty-nine."

"Not fast enough. We need to lose them. Lose them for good."

***

When we eventually stop off for the evening, it's because the engine's overheating and warning lights have come on. We've only got about three miles' worth of fuel left too, and Rahn's reluctant to use that except in the most dire of emergencies. We're well south of New Repliza now, in what Three says must be the outskirts of the Steele Forest.

The sky hasn't begun to darken properly yet. We still have enough light to build a fire, sort through our resources, and maybe even catch a few animals and skin them before nightfall. Three and I are leaning against a huge tree trunk. The bark is rough against my skin. The dog is jumping up at him, but he's ignoring him. I look at my brother carefully. His eyebrows are knitted together: he's deep in concentration.

"Where's Esther?" he asks after a few moments. He unfolds his arms and looks around.

"With Marouska," I reply. "Sorting the food."

Three frowns. "Marouska's changed."

I agree, and neither of us says any more.

"There's a lake over yonder." Rahn reappears through the trees. He and Corin were scouting the land, but Corin's not with him now. "That path there, leads straight up to it. Quite a big one. Clear water, too."

Three nods. "Any edible stuff out there?"

Rahn shrugs. "Some. But most of the ground plants are foreign to me."

"Where's Corin?" I ask.

"Checkin' out the land past the lake," Rahn says. He turns and looks back at the car. Esther and Marouska are still busy. "I suggest we all sleep in the car tonight. We don't know how safe this land is."

Three and I agree, though I know Rahn isn't really bothered about either of our opinions. He doesn't look either of us in the eye, and angles his body away from us, as usual. To others, it might look like he was fine talking to us, but I know the signs to look for. They're always there. Corin's mostly the same now too, ever since I was Enhanced, then became a Seer.

A few minutes later, Corin returns. He limps slightly.

"No sign of a city," he says, "Or any Enhanced. Though, there's a small mountain over to the right—about two hours' walk. We'd be able to see farther from the top of there."

Rahn nods, then he turns to me. "Go run up that mountain and take a look. The sooner we locate an Enhanced city or town, the better—"

"Unless we just stay here," Corin says. He folds his bulky arms over his chest and leans against the trunk of a larch. "It feels safe here, secluded. We could probably live self-sufficiently."

Rahn shakes his head. "We wouldn't survive for long. We don't know the land. We have to find an Enhanced town." Again, he looks at me. "The mountain. Are you goin'?"

After a few seconds, I nod.

"Good. Three, go and ask Marouska to sort a food pack for Seven."

"She can't go now," Corin blurts out. "It's getting dark."

I look up at the sky. It's still light, but I've heard the night falls quicker the farther south you are.

"And we don't know this land," Corin repeats Rahn's own words back to him. "Or its animals."

"She can take the dog with her," Rahn says. He looks at me. "Be as quick as you can."

Corin takes a step closer to Rahn and stares down at the leader. "I said *no*."

There's a long, long pause. Rahn gives Corin a sharp look. "Am I mistaken? Am I no longer the leader of this group? Do we now follow the orders from a man who only has twenty years' experience in this world, and who makes decisions based on his own personal feelings, and not the welfare of the whole group?"

Corin doesn't say anything, but doesn't drop his glare either. Three and I exchange a look.

"Well then," Rahn says.

Corin shakes his head. "It's too dangerous for her to go on her own."

"Eriksen's right, for once."

"She'll have a gun, and she's got a knife," Rahn says. "She can take the dog. He needs a good run and he'll protect her. If trouble comes, I think she can defend herself, despite her size."

Three looks at me. "Or you could climb a tree."

Still, Corin shakes his head. "She waits until morning—"

"We need to know *now*."

"Just what is the urgency with this?" Corin snaps and

clenches his fists. "The Enhanced haven't followed us. We actually lost them. We've found a place that's untouched by human foot. A *safe* place. Security, and all that, at last. And you don't want to stay here? You want to go back to living on the edge, next to the Enhanced? Yet, the other day, you said we need to be self-sufficient! Now you want the Enhanced? We don't need them—"

"We do!" Rahn shouts. "How else are we goin' to get fuel?"

"If we stay here, we don't need a car." Corin's eyes narrow.

"And if we have no car, and they come for us, what are we goin' to do?" Rahn shifts his weight until his feet are shoulder-width apart. He folds his arms over his chest. The shirt he's wearing today is Corin's and it's way too big for him—whereas it would stretch tightly over Corin's muscles, the fabric hangs from Rahn's frame. "There." Rahn sounds triumphant. "My point exactly. As soon as Three's got the food pack from Marouska, Seven will go and scout the land—"

"By the time she reaches the top, it'll be dark," Corin says. "She won't see a thing. We'll be no better off. And she could get hurt. I bet there are cats about. Is it really worth her getting hurt when she won't even be able to see any Enhanced cities anyway?"

"Yeah, because the Enhanced don't have electricity, do they? They don't have any use for artificial lightin'." Rahn snorts. "Shut up, Corin. You're showin' your naiveté. At this rate, I'll be passin' the leadership on to Three."

Corin gives him a dangerous look and exhales loudly. "She shouldn't go on her own. You wouldn't send Esther on her own."

Rahn turns toward him with such speed that I'm certain he's going to strike out. But, after a few seconds, he still hasn't.

Rahn raises his eyebrows above his dark glasses. "I don't know why you're so protective over Seven. After all, it can't be for the obvious reason, can it? Because what were your exact words? Hmm. Let me see if I can remember? Yes, that it would be *revoltin'*?" He pauses and I can already feel my cheeks reddening. Three tenses, then steps closer to me. Rahn holds a finger up to Corin. "But you've obviously got some reason why you don't want me sendin' her off on her own. So I won't. But I want that mountain's view checked *tonight*. So you'll go with her. And no funny business, Corin. I know what you're like with girls."

"*I'll* go with Seven," Three says.

I don't miss the relief that washes over Corin's face.

"No." Rahn holds his hands up, palms facing outward. "Corin is obviously concerned. He should go." And the way he says it, we all know it isn't a recommendation: it's a command.

Three's eyes darken. "Eriksen, you so much as touch her, you're dead. Don't think I don't mean it."

"*Her*?" Corin snorts, looking down his nose at me with an air of contempt and disdain. "As if." He turns and looks back at Rahn. "Fine. I'll go with her. But only because you're insisting—"

Rahn takes a step forward. "*I'm* insistin'? You were the one who was so adamant she mustn't go on her own in the first place."

Corin's eyes narrows. "You're insisting that *I* go with her. Her brother's offered. But seeing as you don't want him to go for whatever reason, I *obviously* have no choice. So let's get it over and done with. I'm going now. I'm not waiting for food, it's getting dark already. Give me your knife."

After an exchange of glares, Rahn hands his nephew the knife from his belt. It's almost as big as the one in my belt. Then Corin storms off, still limping. Rahn gives me a sharp look, and I follow Corin, despite the uneasy feelings within me that tell me this is a very bad idea.

***

We walk in silence for a good hour. Maybe more. In the end, the dog stayed with Esther, so it's just the two of us. Corin leads the way, and I stick close behind him. Under the broken canopy, it's hot and there's only a slight wind.

Insects buzz around me.

I want to ask Corin what happened to his leg; I'm pretty sure he wasn't limping yesterday. But I don't feel brave enough to speak now.

The land begins to decrease in angle. I walk with my knees bent, arms out, ready to stop myself from falling. A few minutes later, over the far edge of the steep land, I can see the glistening surface of the lake Rahn was talking about. It looks beautiful and I have no choice but to look at it... like I had no choice but to steal the Calmness.

Just thinking about it makes the tiny bottle under my waistband feel bigger and more obvious. A part of me can't believe it's still there, that the others haven't found it yet. That I *still* haven't thrown it away. But I will, I tell myself. Of course I will. I nod. I've gone this long without it; I *definitely* do not need it. And I won't need it. There's no way I'm joining the people who stole my mother, killed Finn and Kayden, and tortured me. Good people don't do that.

But it's comforting to know you still have the augmenter with you, isn't it? Comforting to still have the option, just in case....

"This way," Corin says. He stops in front of me and holds back the long branches of an unfamiliar tree, revealing a pathway of sorts. "You go first."

I freeze and look at him, trying to work out his agenda. A lump forms in my throat. Suddenly, I can't stop my hands from shaking. The Seeing dream burns through me. Is this where he confronts me? I gulp. I look at the land. The pathway looks wet, muddy in places. Easy to slip. He could push me, and it's steep. I'd go crashing down the mountainside.

"Why?"

Corin looks somewhat amused—or maybe it's the angle of the light on his face, I don't know.

"So I can stop you from falling. It gets steep up there. Well, I'd *try* to stop you falling. I tripped earlier. Look, I'm just doing the gentlemanly thing here," he says. "Three would kill me if you got hurt. But if you want to fall, then you better not kill yourself as you'll need to explain it to him."

I squeeze past him. There isn't much room and I end up pressing closer to his body than intended. Then I've passed him. I start up the path. His footsteps behind me are heavy, but his intakes of breath are heavier. I walk a little faster. My shoulder's not hurting as much now.

The ground gets even steeper, trickier. Tree roots stick up underfoot, and several times I nearly fall. But I don't—Corin doesn't have to catch me.

My shoes squelch on a waterlogged patch. I swipe at my bare lower arms as I march on. The air's humid and sticky, and I can feel sweat forming in several places on my body. I speed up.

"I'm sorry," Corin says suddenly. His voice is odd, like he's choking. Like it's a confession. Or an apology that comes before the crime.

I freeze, and turn back to look at him. He too stops, inches away from me, looking down at me. Huge leaves shadow his face, and the light's beginning to seep away. His skin looks flushed, and a rash creeps around the side of his neck.

"What for?" My voice is weak. I try not to shake.

Corin pauses for a few seconds, pressing his lips into a thin line. His eyes do that weird flitting thing, like he can't decide where to look. He clears his throat, and I see him swallow.

"I don't think it would be revolting," he says. His shoulders rise and fall a little. "I just had to get Rahn off my back. He thinks because you're the only girl of my sort of age left, who I'm not related to, that we're going to run off into the woods and have sex at every moment." He takes a deep breath.

I try to look away from him, but there's something about the warm depths of his eyes that capture mine, making it impossible.

"I told him before that—that he's wrong, but he doesn't believe me. Back at New Repliza, when we got caught, at that department store, he thinks it's because we were… you know… mind you, he speaks from experience… he's probably banging Marouska right now."

A dark shadow falls over his face for a few seconds as the

wind moves the foliage above us. But then it's gone before I can really notice it. Or maybe I imagined it.

Some birds call above us. I jump. My skin prickles.

"So, yeah," Corin says. "Sorry for saying that about you. But I'm *not* interested in you. Anyway, your brother would kill me if I were." He laughs slightly.

A moment passes. Neither of us moves. My breathing is a rushing in my ears. Then I turn and continue walking quickly. I keep going, concentrating on the rhythm of my steps. I can hear him behind me, keeping up with my pace. But I don't *want* to hear him behind me. I want to be on my own. More than anything else, I want to be on my own now, and I don't even know why.

Chapter Twenty-Eight

I awake early the next morning to Esther throwing up into a carrier bag. She's in the back seat with me, but by the other window. Corin and Three, in between us, jerk awake, nearly clashing heads again.

Marouska bends over in her seat, searching for something on the floor as Esther coughs and retches. Rahn turns to look at her, wrinkling his nose. His glasses do a jiggly dance.

"Ugh! Get out!" Corin pushes at Esther as the putrid smell fills the car.

Water comes to my eyes. My own throat starts to convulse.

Breathe, Seven, breathe.

Three leans across, pushing the door open and ushers Esther out. He follows, climbing over Corin, much to Corin's annoyance. The wind rips through the car, whistling. Rahn and Three patched up the windows last night, before we slept in here, but most of the curtains have fallen down since.

"Anyone else need a bag?" Marouska asks from the front seat.

Rahn grunts. "Last thing we need is a stomach bug. Let's hope she's just got food poisonin'."

I swallow hard. "We've all eaten the same food."

"Well maybe her hands weren't clean then," Rahn says. I can hear him tapping his nails on the wheel.

Outside, Esther retches again. Three turns her away from the car, and, next to me, Corin grimaces.

I sit up straighter, forcing myself to look the other way.

My stomach gurgles. "I don't feel that well either."

Marouska thrusts a paper bag in my face and Corin tells me to get out of the car. I obey; my legs feel weak. I lean against the closed door, inhaling deeply.

Three appears next to me. "You as well?"

I close my eyes for a brief second. It's probably just the effect of Esther being sick. "Is there any bottled water?"

Three shakes his head. "Corin had the last of it. And we haven't got any water purification tablets left."

"There's the stream up yonder that feeds into the lake. You'll have to drink it untreated," Rahn shouts from inside the car.

"But that could've caused it in the first place." Three frowns. "Why the hell haven't we got any water? That's, like, *essential*."

"Well, don't drink anythin' then."

"We have to rehydrate." Corin steps out the car, and holds a hand tentatively against his own stomach. Color drains from his face.

"All right?" Rahn's voice sounds odd.

Corin nods, then grabs my empty paper bag.

***

"You're lucky you've not got this," Esther nods at Rahn, then Marouska.

We're all sitting outside, on the ground. Esther still looks queasy and Corin's not looking that brilliant either.

Rahn drums his knuckles against the hardened ground. He frowns. "There's still time."

"We're going to have get more supplies as soon as we can. We need purifiers, baking soda for emergency rehydration— yeah, I checked, there's none left—and anti-nausea tablets," Three says.

Last night, Corin and I eventually reached the top of the mountain and saw lights on the horizon. It looked like a big city, about two or three days' hike away, on foot. My guess is as soon as we're all well enough, we'll be raiding that city.

"Are you sure we haven't got any medical kits left?"

"We've got none." Three shrugs. "I checked. Rahn, you mustn't have got as many as you said you did. It's easy to get mixed up, confused."

My head spins as I blink up at the sky. It's hard to see the sky—broken fragments through the trees. I'm not sure I like being in the forest, being cut off from the sky. For the majority of my life—or, at least, everything that I can clearly and consciously remember—I've been in the desert, where nothing separated me from the sky. The trees were sparse and mostly skeletal. The vegetation stayed on the ground, where it should be, creeping along the sandy mountainsides. Here, anything—or anyone—could be creeping up on us and we'd have no idea until it was too late. At least in the desert you got warning. It feels like we're hiding, just waiting to be caught.

I count to ten, letting the air fill my lungs. I swallow cautiously. My throat burns as bile rises. I turn and fumble with the bag.

"Classy," Corin mutters. I catch him wrinkling his nose as I struggle to breathe.

"I'm not the only one." My teeth taste disgusting. "Is there any mouthwash?"

Corin shakes his head.

"Anything else?"

"No."

I wipe my sleeve across my mouth, swallowing frantically. But the taste won't go away. It's all around my teeth, my tongue, my lips, just like it was back at the Enhanced Ones' compound. Just like... I shudder.

"Great. We're doomed."

"A bit pessimistic there, Sev."

I snort. The augmenter in my pocket burns. I've moved it to the inside pocket of my jacket now, so it's less obvious to them—there's no bulky shape against my thigh now—but more obvious to me. With every breath I take, I can feel it.

I sigh. "The Enhanced don't get ill." They're the *Chosen*—but the word still doesn't sound right. I look at Corin. "Illness could wipe us out so easily—"

"Yeah, because it's really worth it, converting yourself so

you don't get ill." Corin glares at me, fire in his eyes. "Get some backbone, Seven. Or join them and leave us the hell alone."

***

"You and Eriksen have got to get on better," Three tells me a few hours later.

He looks a bit better now—in fact we all do. What's it been? Forty-five minutes since anyone's been sick?

"Seven? You hear me?"

I nod. "Fine."

I stretch my legs out, groaning inwardly. The ground beneath me is damp, but I don't have the energy to move back to the car. And, besides, everyone else is there. I just want to be on my own, away from them all. Even Three, at times.

"Good. Because as soon as we're divided, that's when we'll be weak and—"

"We're already weak," I point out.

"It's probably only a six hour thing," Three says. He's sitting opposite me, his legs drawn up to his chest.

"There's still time for Marouska and Rahn."

Three shrugs. "Maybe they're immune? But, you're avoiding the point here."

"What?" I squint at him, feeling jittery inside. Behind him, the trees wobble.

"You and Eriksen have got to get along."

I frown at him. "I just said I would, didn't I?"

"But that doesn't mean you *will*."

I turn to Three, my face burning.

"And this act you're putting on doesn't mean you like him either."

Three's eyes narrow as he frowns. "What?"

My eyes narrow. "Am I the only one who remembers that Corin and Rahn are responsible for our mother's current situation?"

Just thinking about her makes me feel bad. I haven't done anything to rescue her. I've just left her with Raleigh, where she has clean water, food, shelter, safety...and I've been traveling with the two men responsible for her situation. I've let them get away with it. I haven't even been thinking of her much recently—what kind of person does that make me? My eyes smart as I stab a finger into the soft, earthy ground.

"Seven, you—you can't say that!"

"I just did."

Three leans forward. "You weren't there—"

"Neither were you!" I shout. My fists shake. "Do you not even think about her?" In the car, about a hundred yards away, I see Esther's pale face turn toward us.

Three bows his head. "She chose them." His voice is quiet, subdued.

I bite my bottom lip. "You and I both know that's a lie." I fix my eyes on an acacia ahead of us. It's a small one, and some big cat has scratched deep claw marks down the base of its trunk, scarring the bark. "They know what happened to our mother. Exactly what happened. I *know* they're not telling the truth."

Three shakes his head, lets out a long, long breath.

"Well," he says at last. "Seeing as we're not doing much else today, you can help me rig up some more radios. I was going to ask Corin and Esther to help, but their fingers are like walruses. And, besides, you think they're—what? The devil's spawn?"

Chapter Twenty-Nine

"Don't worry," Three says as he hugs me tightly. "We won't be gone that long, I promise."

I nod into his chest, trying to remain calm, but I'm close to tears. Just the thought of him—of them all—undertaking this journey to the Enhanced makes me want to build a cage around them all. What if they never come back? Rahn reckons the city Corin and I saw must be New Sié. A massive Enhanced city. They'll have scanners there, and all sorts of other technologies to detect any Untamed who sneak in. I gulp. What if I never see my brother again?

Three leans away from me slightly, but still watches me intently. "Don't cry, Seven. You'll not even notice I'm gone." He smiles, but now I can see how nervous he is, the look in his eyes says it all. "Don't worry."

I nod, my lips trembling as I breathe in the musty smell of his jacket.

"Three, come on," Rahn says.

He and Corin already have their backpacks on; Corin reckons it will take them at least a day to walk to the city—I think that's far too ambitious. They're taking nearly all the supplies we've got left, tightly packed into their bags. Esther walks over and joins them. She swings a large pack onto her back. It feels like they're all going off, and leaving me all on my own, even though Marouska's staying here too.

I want to go with them more than anything—after all, I *am* the fastest runner. But Corin insisted I should stay here. He got his way this time.

"Remember, Marouska, you two must stay together all

the time," Rahn says. "I don't want us comin' back to find only one of you still alive." He glances over at me, and I get the feeling that, nonetheless, he wouldn't mind if I disappeared. "You've got enough food to last you if you ration it, and you'll only need to go and collect water daily, but that ain't far. Just stay here. There's no need to go off huntin' or gatherin'. And I want you both sleepin' in the car."

Marouska salutes him. "Yes, Comrade."

Rahn nods and looks at his traveling companions before nodding again. "We'll see you in about three days," he says. He nods at both of us. "Four or five, at the most. We will be back."

Three hugs me again. "Look after yourself," he whispers into my ear.

Then he walks away. He exchanges a few words with Esther and Rahn. Corin has already turned away. He's been mostly silent all morning.

"Bye, Seven." Esther waves at me and I smile back. But it is a bittersweet kind of smile that leaves my lips aching.

Then the four of them walk away, each resembling a packhorse. The dog, by my feet, barks at them and Three turns back, taking one last look at us for a second. Then their figures disappear into the thick mass of trees.

"Good luck!" says Marouska, and after a few seconds, I echo her words. But the four of them don't hear, or, if they do, they don't respond.

***

I spend the rest of the morning helping Marouska collect water and sort through the food packages. There aren't many left.

"All right, Seven?" she asks. She's tied her long, graying hair into a high bun on the top of her head, and several wispy strands hang down, swaying in the slight breeze. It's colder today, and the air's more humid.

I nod, and unwrap a new parcel. It contains thin strips of fatty meat, and I wrap it back up carefully.

"They'll be fine, y'know," she says. "Aye, they're always fine."

I look up at Marouska and I can see in the way she holds her head at a slight angle that she doesn't want to accept reality. But accepting reality is something you have to do, if you want to have the tiniest chances of surviving and beating your enemies. But, after all, the Enhanced *are* the perfect beings; is it reasonable, or just delusional, for us to believe we can actually survive in a world dominated by them and their robotic, mechanical version of humanity? What if becoming Enhanced really is the next stage of evolution, and we're resisting the next stage? What if it comes down to dying or becoming Enhanced? Would it be so bad if that were the choice? We'd be safe if we were Enhanced, we'd have food, shelter and water. We'd be safe. A lot safer than we are now.

I think back to my room at the Enhanced compound. I think of my teddy bear, John. How I left him behind, where he's safe. I think of the cake. My mouth waters. My stomach groans. I touch the augmenter in my pocket....

But we wouldn't be ourselves if we were Enhanced. We'd be going against everything we fought for. And we'd be joining them, the murderers. And if the Enhanced have me, they'll have all the Untamed. That's what the bison told me. I grimace.

By the time evening draws in, we've sorted through all our food, spare clothes and the few weapons the raid party left behind, and have cleaned the car's interior. Surprisingly, Marouska is still in possession of the AK47 look-alike gun.

"Aye, Seven, these tires ain't in too good a shape." Marouska kicks at one, which doesn't help the situation. "An' look, we've lost a hubcap."

We're going to lose another one, if you carry on doing that.

I watch her walk around the car, tutting and shaking her head as she goes. My seat on the mossy ground is damp, despite no rain, and the gnarled bark of the tree trunk digs into my back.

"Should've got a better model than this," she says and I snort. "It's surprising this vehicle's made it this far before it died."

"It overheated," I say. "And we've practically no fuel left." I fold my arms across my chest. "It's a perfectly good car. Any other car would be in the same situation."

She tuts under her breath. "The bonnet's starting to rust through. I'm surprised we ain't had no oil leak yet."

I shake my head and get up. "It's not easy to steal a car," I mutter, thinking of Kayden. Really, this is *his* car. He got the Land Rover Discovery. "There isn't a catalog we can order from."

Marouska looks up at me, her pale gray eyes getting bigger and bigger. But she doesn't say anything. She just looks at me. After a minute or so, I have to look away.

I go back to my seat on the ground, and, breathing deeply, I try to remain calm. But I can't.

Because everything is going to go wrong. I can feel it. My Seer powers? Or just common sense? But, either way, I know it: Three, Esther, Corin and Rahn are going to be killed. I'm never going to see them again.

Going to New Sié is a suicidal mission. They'll have scanners in the city for sure, and our people will set them off.

I rub at my forehead. Why didn't I stop them? I didn't even try. I didn't say a word. I could've made something up about a Seeing dream. They would've listened. They would've stayed. I wouldn't be on my own now. They wouldn't be dead.

But you're not on your own. Marouska's here too.

My legs shake and I clamp them together. But they don't stop shaking. The vial of Calmness in my pocket shakes with them. I can see its rough shape through the khaki fabric of my shorts. It's so obvious. Why did I even put it back there?

A jolt runs through my body, and I look up at Marouska. Her back is turned. She can't see it. It's fine. I breathe deeply. One. Two. Three. Four. Five. Six. Seven. It's perfectly fine. I won't need the augmenter, because I'm not on my own.

You'll never see them again. They're probably already dead.

Tightness pours through my body. They'll be, what, nearly there by now? Anything could've happened. A car could've come along; the Enhanced would've found them, converted them.

No. Rahn and Corin and Esther and Three would've shot themselves.

I try to blink away that thought, but can't. The image won't leave me alone, drills itself into my head, over and over again.

I clench my fists. I take big breaths. I look up at the sky, then at the trees. But the trees are whispering about their deaths. I feel sick, like I can't swallow enough air. But I can. One. Two. Three. Four. Five. Six. Seven. Of course I can, I'm still alive.

I haven't just walked off to my death. I'm still here. I can survive. And I'm with Marouska, I'm not on my own. This is nothing like when they left me in the car alone for a couple of hours at a time after I was shot, whilst they went off raiding. I'm not even on my own. I'm being pathetic. I need to get a grip.

A jungle bird screeches overhead and I jump. The trees are all closing in on me. The sky's falling on me.

Oh, Gods and Goddesses! Help me!

My good hand's on the vial in my pocket. My fingers clasp around it.

Don't do it, Seven.

Do it, drink it. It'll make you feel better.

It'll make you a traitor.

It'll calm you, you can think straighter then.

It'll change you....

I can hardly breathe.

What if I never see them again? What if that *was* the last time I ever saw my brother, the last surviving Untamed person of my family? I can feel my blood pressure rising. My heart pounds, racing ahead of me until I know I'm going to fall. I can hardly breathe. Rushing noises fill my ears, and my throat's too dry. The roof of my mouth feels like the cracked surface of cold lava and my teeth taste *dirty*.

I gag as I pull the augmenter from my pocket. My fingers clench the vial closer to me.

No. Don't do it. You're stronger than this.

It's true. I've had the augmenter for *weeks*. I've had it with me, and I haven't taken any of it. When I got shot, I could handle the physical pain. When they left me alone whilst they went raiding, I coped. I didn't actually take any.

But today's not like *those* days. And I don't know if I can handle this. This uncertainty. Three and Corin, Esther and Rahn could be gone for up to *five days*. Longer, if they get into trouble.

Forever, if they're caught. I gulp.

I stare at the augmenter. The bridge of my nose feels prickly, the kind of prickliness that leads to tears. I unscrew the cap.

Don't do it. Put it away now.

Drink it. It'll make you calmer, then you can work out how to help your brother. How to help all of them.

You don't need it. You don't want to be an Enhanced One again. You're an Untamed Seer. You don't need it. You haven't needed any yet, and you don't need any now.

Look at you! You're too worked up to be of any use at the moment. Everything will work out better if you drink it. You'll be calmer. You can plan a rescue mission for Three if you drink it. You can help everyone.

I raise the vial to my lips. The glass rim tastes cold against my tongue. I salivate; my fingers shake as I tip the end up slightly.

No. Don't.

I take a deep breath. Memories of safety flood back. The security of the Enhanced Ones' compound, the food, my teddy bear....

The Calmness comes in a slow trickle at first.

But the tap's been turned on. I'm actually doing it. A part of me can't believe it. But I am. I'm drinking it. I'm embracing it again. And this time, it's my choice. I'm not being held down against the desert floor. I'm not being strapped to a bed, force-fed. I'm not being drowned.

It's *my* choice.

I gulp the Calmness back like it's water, like my very life depends on it. It's beautiful. So beautiful—

It was inevitable that I'd find out.

I gulp, choking and wrench the vial from my lips. Half the

Calmness is gone. I can taste it in the crevices of my teeth, under my tongue, on my chapped lips. A sort of sweetness that melts away, leaving a strong aftertaste.

I breathe deeply. My hands stop shaking.

There's still half left.

Ration it. Rahn said to ration everything. Oh Gods. He's right, that's what I need to do. With inner strength I didn't know I possessed, I screw the lid back on and pocket the vial.

But, oh, Gods....

The augmenter's kicking in. I can feel it diving through my veins, spreading its goodness in a tiny web that's so intricate and complicated it can't be removed.

I take a deep breath and half-close my eyes. I run a hand through my hair. It's tangled, but that doesn't bother me. Nothing can bother me now. Everything is so beautiful. There isn't anything that can worry me. I feel weightless, free.

Safe. For the first time in weeks, I feel safe. Like at the compound. With Raleigh—no, that's not... I blink. My face relaxes. My head clears. The jittery feelings in my chest evaporate. Weight lifts from my shoulders.

I feel like a naughty child who's stolen some baked sweets from a forbidden jar. I feel giddy with it, delirious, happy.

I smile. If I go back to the Enhanced, I can be like this all the time. I'll be with my mother. Maybe my father and Five too? We can look for Three and the others then. The realization drops on me like the daintiest of feathers and I smile broadly.

I'm not on the run any more. I can go back now. I know how to get to New Sié. Three spent ages last night planning the route with Rahn and Corin and Esther. I overheard everything. I could trail them at a safe distance. I could watch out for them. We can all join the Enhanced.

We'd be together, safe, *and* we'd be on the winning side of the war. I want to leap up and run around, do something crazy and stupid. Why isn't this obvious to them, to everyone? Why do the Untamed even exist? *Why* are we resisting? Why was I? Because I thought I wouldn't be myself.

But I am. This is me. I can still think. I am still me. This is who I am.

This is who I am, and now I can survive. No one can hurt me now.

"Shania?"

I jump and turn. The trees spin.

Oh Gods.

But it's okay, a voice in my head tells me.... *she'll understand... it doesn't matter....*

But the look of betrayal and hatred Marouska gives me says that it *does* matter. That it matters very much.

Chapter Thirty

For what seems like an hour, neither Marouska nor I say anything, and the dog just whines from inside the car. Marouska watches me, her eyes big and sad and grayer than usual, with her lips scrunched up. She's breathing slowly and deeply through her nose. With every breath she takes, I hear a wheezy sound, like the soft howl of a distant wind.

I lean back against the tree trunk, letting the rough nodules of bark dig into my back, but it doesn't hurt. I stare back at her. Should I just run off now? Head straight for New Sié? It's late, and if I go now I'll be traveling at night. Not the safest of times.

"What've you done?" Marouska asks at last. Her voice is faint.

I don't say anything. I just sit here. I can feel the vial in my pocket. It digs into my skin, harder and harder. But if feels nice, safe.

"Seven? What was it?"

She pauses, and reaches out, as if to touch me, then changes her mind. Why's she even sitting here with me? She should be running away. She knows what I am. I can't hide it. I thought I could. I persuaded myself I was still Untamed. But Rahn's survival lesson is right.

Never let yourself be Enhanced. Once it's done, there's no going back.

Because the Enhanced life is safer.

"Which augmenter was it?"

I look up at her. "Calmness."

"You got any left?"

"No," I lie. I don't know why I lie. I just do.

She nods slowly. Then she grabs my hand, tugs at it. She leaps backward, wrenching me forward. Her fingers dig into my bad shoulder. I stumble as she drags me along. And suddenly, I see the sky. How beautiful it is. Mesmerizing. Stunning. I can't see enough of it, but I need to!

I trip over a tree root as we reach the back of the car.

"Sit there," Marouska says, and pushes me at the ground.

I watch as she opens the boot of the car. Her large figure hides what she's doing. My breathing is deep and slow; its rhythmic quality makes me want to fall asleep, but I can't. I have to see the beauty of the world. I take another deep gulp of air, and look at the sky. It's a peachy color, with streaks of the setting sun and mauve filtering through it. It's so beautiful. Why wouldn't Marouska want to appreciate this?

I look back at Marouska and gulp. What's she doing? My eyes widen. We—we keep weapons there, and Rahn and the others didn't take *all* of them when they left. She's going to... would she? Would she really? What would Rahn say when he returned? Corin? Esther? My *brother*?

No. She wouldn't. But she has justifiable grounds. She killed all those Enhanced Ones back at that department store. She could kill me. It's what she needs to do, to save herself.

But I can save her. I start to reach for the augmenter.

"Drink this." Marouska's harsh voice interrupts the beauty of the world, and she shoves a wooden cup toward me.

I take hold of it. My hands feel too heavy.

"Drink it, now." She's watching me, hands on her hips. That disapproving look still hasn't left her face.

Raising the cup to my mouth, I sniff the orange liquid. It's the most disgusting thing I've ever smelt. Poison?

"What is it?"

"Just drink it," she snaps. "Then run over there." She jerks her head to the left, to a thicket of trees.

I sniff the liquid again, my nostrils curl. This is bad. I shouldn't drink this. Every rational part of my brain is telling me this. Don't drink it. I don't want this serene feeling to go, and I know it will if I drink it.

But you've done something terrible.

No, I've chosen my own pathway. No one forced me. For the first time in my life, I've chosen who I want to be. No one can tell me what to do any more. I'm being strong. Everyone's always telling me to be strong, to stand up for myself.

Now, I am. This is me.

"Drink it, Seven."

I stare at the orange liquid. I feel more relaxed now than I have in weeks. I don't want it to end. The vial in my pocket feels heavy.

It was inevitable that I'd find out.

Marouska knocks the cup against my mouth. The edge of it hits my teeth, but the foul-tasting liquid goes everywhere—all down me—and I end up taking a gulp of it. Droplets trickle down my throat. I drop the cup as the world around me spins. My throat burns.

Marouska grabs my shoulders, pulls me to the left. I fall, scraping my knees on the roots, and wince. But Marouska doesn't let go of me, she's still pulling. I try to scrabble to my feet, but I can't. I cough and splutter.

"Come on," she hisses. "I said get over there!"

I throw up all over her feet.

***

"I'm really sorry." I gulp and look up at Marouska in between splashing water over my face, hoping she doesn't realize just how high-pitched my voice is.

Marouska makes a *hmmf* noise and hands me a cloth. She turns away, so I can't see her disproving look as I clean myself up.

After a few minutes, I follow her back to the car. She sorts through some stuff in the boot, and I climb straight into the back of the car and lie down. The world around me spins. The beautiful colors have gone. Now, it's all grays and blacks and navys. Now it is full of darkness, with only pinpricks of light.

My eyes will be Untamed again very soon—that's what Marouska says that liquid did. It destroys the eye-mirrors. I don't know how she knew about it. I take a deep breath, and groan. Then I swing myself up into a sitting position and lean forward, pulling down the fold-up mirror over the passenger's seat. For several seconds, I stare at my reflection.

I'm not the girl that I was. My eyes, although they are still the same deep brown in color, hold fading ghosts of silver. My face is lined and my dark skin has several cuts and scrapes on it. My hair looks limp and the tangles are disgusting.

I groan again, and lean back onto the seat, blinking rapidly. Tears come to my eyes. Why does it have to be this way? Why can't I be Untamed *and* safe? Why's it have to be one or the other, because once the need for self-preservation kicks in it can only go one way. We all know that. If we're not safe, we're going to be dead. I could die tomorrow.

Or I could leave, find the Enhanced, and join them. I'd be with my mother again. I'd survive. I'd have a home, safety, security, food. No more starving. No more raiding for resources. No more getting caught.

It's so obvious, it hurts.

Marouska opens the driver's door and gets in. I sniff and turn away as she looks at me in the mirror. Her unblemished Untamed face meets mine for a second.

"I won't tell 'em," she says. Her voice is strange, kind of soft, but kind of hard at the same time.

I look up at her. "Why?"

She pauses. In the mirror, I see the corners of her mouth lift up. "It can be our little secret," she says. There's a long pause, and she doesn't say anything else.

"Thank you." I manage to choke the words out.

"But that liquid doesn't destroy the effect of the augmenter," she warns. "Just changes your eyes."

I lie back into the seat, curling myself up into a tight ball despite my protesting shoulder. I don't feel calm at all.

The augmenter is still in my pocket. Marouska didn't search me—stupid, if you ask me. But I'm glad. It's security. The option is still there. Thinking about the sweetness of the

Calmness, how it purified me, makes my mouth salivate.

I scratch my arms, desperately. I bite my tongue, then my bottom lip, until I feel pain. If Marouska catches me taking it again, she'd kill me. We won't have *our little secret* any longer.

No, I must be careful. I need to plan my actions. It's the only way out of here, alive. I was right before. Becoming Enhanced must be part of evolution's plan. Living in fear without the basic necessities can't be the desired path for humanity.

Willing myself to fall asleep, I block out the light. But I can't sleep. Everything's too noisy, the sounds of the jungle, the whispering wind, Marouska's breathing. Everything's keeping me awake. My throat feels raw. I want to cry, but I don't want to draw any more attention to myself.

At last, when I fall asleep, the events of the evening replay in my mind, like I have no control over them: the vial, my lips, the taste, the—

I bolt upright with such vigor that something in my shoulder tears.

Marouska turns to me in a flash. "What is it? Have you seen something?" she asks. The side of her neck twitches.

I pause, then shake my head. The movement makes the pain in my shoulder flare up. "J-just a bad dream," I say. But she's not convinced, and I can't lie to myself.

Marouska called me *Shania*.

She called me my *Enhanced* name when I'd taken the augmenter. And I'm pretty sure I haven't told anyone what the Enhanced Ones named me.

I shake my head. How could she know? Did Raleigh call me by that name at Nbutai, when she was in hearing distance? I blink again. I look at Marouska. She faces the front again now, but I know she's awake.

Shania...but Marouska wouldn't call me that. I must have imagined it. Yeah. I nod. Of course, I am thinking like an Enhanced One—I'm part of the Enhanced now, of course I'd hear that name. Marouska wouldn't call me that... she hates the Enhanced just as much as the rest of them do... she killed the Enhanced who held Corin and me hostage. I see her and myself, from an omniscient point of view, as she makes me throw up the augmenter.

I must've imagined the Shania thing. Marouska hates the Enhanced.

But I don't.

Chapter Thirty-One

The next morning my stomach churns with every breath I take. I can barely eat the small amount of food Marouska's prepared for me. Every bite of the meat pie curls up against the roof of my mouth, clinging there like a limpet until I force my swollen tongue to push the wad to the back of my mouth where, with great difficulty, I manage to swallow it down.

I take a deep breath. It's too risky to take some of the augmenter again, I know that, I'm not stupid. I have to be stealthy. I mustn't make Marouska suspicious. I have to remain alive until I can join the Enhanced.

In the early hours of the morning, I considered leaving as soon as the sun rose. But so much could go wrong. A cat could get me. Or I could meet Rahn and the others on their way back. They'd stop me. They might kill me—would I be able to lie convincingly to them, make out that I was checking to see if they were all right?

No, as soon as Rahn and the others are back, and we're on the next raid—with all of us taking part—I'm going to leave. It's the best way. Sure, I'll have to wait a bit—and it's not ideal—but sometimes you have to sacrifice personal conveniences for safety.

I just can't live like this for much longer.

I need my mother.

"We're going up the mountain," Marouska says after we've finished breakfast. "Aye, I want to get some more of 'em yellow roots. They give soup a good flavor."

I look at her for a few seconds. "But Rahn said we're to

stay here." My voice wobbles. I know I'm not in a position to decide what we don't do.

Marouska shrugs. "I need to replenish my stock," is all she says, and then she walks off. She can move surprisingly fast for a woman of her size.

Hastily, I follow, calling the terrier to my heel. He rubs against my legs and barks playfully. He still loves me, despite what I did. I can barely look at him, though; I won't be able to take him with me when I leave for the Enhanced city.

Marouska sets a hard pace—maybe I'm struggling because I'm not exactly in the best shape, or maybe she wants to test me—but I manage to keep up. We reach the lake, but instead of going uphill, the way Corin and I went, Marouska surges straight ahead.

"Rahn said he saw some of 'em roots up ahead, by a twisty tree," she explains, and flicks her arm to the front.

I nod, and continue walking behind her. It's getting hotter now, and I can feel perspiration forming on the back of my neck, down my spine and under my arms. Soon, it'll be scorching out here. Yet, it's not the dry desert kind of heat I grew up in. It's a more humid heat that clogs up your throat; a sticky kind of hotness that latches onto your skin and never lets go. And the air, itself, is thick with mosquitoes that squeak and buzz and hum in your ears. The overall combination does nothing for my nerves.

A few minutes later, Marouska finds the roots she's after, and I sit down on the mossy ground whilst she digs them up.

"They'll be okay, y'know." Marouska looks across at me. She's crouched like a ground squirrel, in such a position that emphasizes how large she really is. Giant thighs. Giant breasts. "They'll all come back," she says. "You'll see."

I nod and look back down the jungle-side. My heart pounds, my skin tingles. I press my hands against my stomach, feeling sick. Only a few more days, I remind myself. They'll be back soon. We'll be on the move again. It won't be long until we need to raid again.

"You'll see him again." Marouska gets up and shoulders

her bag with the roots. "I've got this wee feeling in my gut. You an' Corin, you—"

"What?" I turn wearily to her as I stand up. My ankles are still crossed, and my arms hang by my side.

Marouska doesn't say anything more, but her gaze darts from side to side.

We take a different route back to the car—Marouska wants to scout out the northern side of the lake a little more—and, this time, I am in the lead. We head out farther into the denser parts of the woodland, sticking to a path that looks like medium-sized mammals made it. It's strange, we haven't seen many animals here... yet, the paths are worn down.

The sun gets hotter and hotter as we walk. After an hour or so, the air feels heavier, thicker, like it's trying to drag something down. Or hide a secret.

I pause for a second and listen, letting my senses scout the land. My chest catches slightly, and that's when I know something isn't right. The terrier growls, then runs back the way we've come.

I hold my arm up to halt Marouska. I hear her stop behind me. I listen hard. All I can hear is the heavy buzz of the jungle's life. Mosquitoes. Birds. Rustling leaves. The rushing sounds in my own ears.

Cautiously, I take a step forward. Marouska doesn't follow me. I take another step ahead. The path goes around a corner, and the mass of trees and vines hide what's around there.

Slowly, I get my knife out of my belt and hold it as strongly as I can in my good hand. But my grip isn't the best, and my hand shakes. I know now is not a good time to let nerves get the better of me.

With the knife in front of my body, blade out, I walk as quietly as I can toward the path's corner. I wish I had a gun, but we left the two we have in the car. It didn't occur to me take them, probably because of the Calmness in my system. My legs tremble. I can't hear Marouska's footsteps following, but I daren't look back to check on her; I have to remain alert and face the danger.

Listening carefully again, I pause. No sounds jump out at me as being unusual or dangerous. But I am not fooled. There could be a big cat—a leopard maybe—on the other side. I place my left foot in front of my right, and lunge forward with speed—my father always said a speedy confrontation was better than a slow one.

I pounce forward. My knife flashes in the stripy sunlight. I skid to a stop. I look around. No leopard. No wild pig.

Then I see it. A strange, strangled sound escapes me.

I see the body lying at the side of the path.

"Seven?" Marouska appears behind me.

I step back so she can see it. She walks past me, looks at it.

I have to look away. But the image is scarred on my mind. Tiny fingers with dried bloodstains on them. The small, fragile body. Wide eyes that stare at me, full of fear and hurt and pain.

I'm going to be sick.

That body, that could've been Three. It could've been Esther. It could've been Corin. It could've been Rahn. It could've been *anyone*.

It could be me, when they find out....

"He's been dead for a few days," Marouska says. "Something's been eating his flesh on this side. A cat maybe."

My head whirls. An Untamed child... an Untamed child *this* close to where we're staying... or maybe it could be an Enhanced child? Do the eye-mirrors fade after death? My skin scrawls.

I look around, trying to look anywhere, but at the body. The knife is still in my hand, ready, and I'm glad. Anything could be out here, waiting for us.

"What killed him?" I ask at last.

I hear Marouska's footsteps as she steps closer to the body. Then I hear a sound that I'm sure can only be her rolling the dead body over.

"A bullet. In the back." Her voice isn't husky at all. She sounds normal... *normal*... how can she *not* be affected? Even *I'm* affected by it and there is half a vial of Calmness in my system.

A twig cracks above, in the jungle's canopy, and my body snaps toward it. I raise my knife in a flash, but it's just a bird.

"The Enhanced?" My voice cracks.

"Most likely."

The Enhanced have to be responsible for this, don't they? Or could it be the Untamed? They kill as well.

I take another deep breath, letting the air fill my lungs to their capacity, before I look back in Marouska's direction. "We need to send the body off," I say.

"It'll be too late," she says. "It's been days."

"We should still bless his body and say the Spirit Releasing Words in case his soul's trapped." My voice is dry and cracks as I speak.

Marouska nods, but she doesn't make any indication that she is going to do it, so, after having stern words with myself, I step forward until I'm right next to the body. Until his curled, bloody fingers are inches from my left foot. I push my knife back into my belt. I take a deep breath, and try not to cry as I make the signs of all the Journeying Gods and Goddesses over his fragile body.

"Travel safely to the New World," I murmur, and a tear falls from the tip of my nose, onto his tiny body. I glance into his unseeing eyes again—

I have to look away as I finish the Spirit Releasing Words.

I walk back down the path, so Marouska is between the child's body and me. I look around.

"We shouldn't be staying here. The Enhanced could be nearby," I say.

"But other Untamed could be here," Marouska replies. She's looking at the tiny body, hands on hips, shaking her head. "They could help us. Anyway, we have to wait for Rahn to return."

"No, we need to go," I say. We can't stay here. I need to get away; I need to be with the Enhanced Ones.

She looks back up at me, and I see movement in her eyes. I freeze. What if she's realized my plan?

"No, we wait for Rahn and the others. If we leave, we'll never see 'em again."

I gulp. I'd never see Three again, once I leave. He'd be

on his own, still on the run, still in danger. He wouldn't be safe. Could I live with that? But I'd be with my mother. That would make up for it and we could persuade him to join us later on, once he sees we're both still the same people. The Untamed are just scared of the Enhanced because they don't understand them.

"Fine," I say. "But we're not staying here any longer than we need to. What if this is a regular place the Enhanced scout out? They could be coming here now." I try to sound scared, not happy.

There's a long pause, during which Marouska turns back to me slowly. She shakes her head.

"I don't think so—"

"Why?" I throw my hands up in the air. "There's a dead child; even if that child belonged to the Enhanced, and was killed by us, it still means there are Enhanced Ones about. Don't you—"

"That bullet wound in his back wouldn't have killed him immediately. It's off-center," she says. "I think there was a struggle, quite a way from here. The child was hurt, but escaped. He died running away."

I shake my head, my lips pressed together so hard the skin on my bottom lip nearly splits. "We don't know that. We need to leave as soon as possible."

Chapter Thirty-Two

That evening, nothing feels right. I curl up in my seat in the car, my chin resting on my knees and stare at the bowl of soup Marouska gave me a few hours ago. It tasted funny despite her reassurance that it was perfectly normal. I couldn't eat more than a spoonful.

As I stroke the terrier—we found him back at the car when we returned—I think of my brother and the others. They must have reached the Enhanced city by now. So long as nothing went wrong. I push away the thoughts and concentrate on Three's smiling face. I think of how reassuring he is, and how his presence calms me.

Maybe they've already done the raid and got everything we need, and are on their way back. They could be walking through the grassy lands, or reaching the mountain...no they can't be that close already

My eyelids feel heavy and I lean back against the seat. It is leather, but it hurts my spine. I sigh loudly. Marouska, in the driver's seat, does not move.

I close my eyes. That's when I see them.

Well. No. I don't see *them*. I see Corin. He's standing in a room. An unfamiliar room. He's walking toward a table, and has a bag slung over his back.

The room's lighting is strange and eerie; it makes Corin's hair look almost blond and his face less lined, less sunburnt. The tiled floor looks expensive, and there are tapestries along the walls. The room gets longer with every new tapestry I notice.

I look closer, and suddenly, it's like I'm zooming in. The

colors are rich and bright, luxurious, even. They each show a scene. One depicts a young girl—only a few years older than me—with an infant clinging to her. Her arms wrap around the child in a protective stance.

I move on to the next one. A large wooden table, big enough to seat two hundred men. The table is laden with plates and dishes of what I'm sure is the finest food. Only, amongst the dishes, there is a man lying on the table. He is pale-skinned and has red hair. *Kayden.*

I back away slowly. My mouth feels dry. Suddenly, I realize that *I* am in the room. I am in the room with Corin.

I turn to him. "Corin," I shout.

But he's not looking at me. He stands with his back to me. His clothes aren't the tattered, worn out shreds he left in. They are expensive garments. A nicely tailored, crisp white shirt with a wide collar. But the collar's low enough so I can see the taut muscles in his neck, and just a teasing glimpse of his chest. His slacks are black with pristine lines down the front of each leg. I look up. His hair is shorter than it was when he left. But it is him.

"Corin?"

I run around him, trying to see his face, but he turns away just as I'm in front of him. I keep moving. So does he. I go faster and faster. But he anticipates every move. I twist back on myself, changing direction, but he does it just that half a second before me again.

"Corin! What—why are you doing this?"

I stop, and pant heavily, my hands on my knees. And that's when I realize my shoulder isn't hurting. I bring my left hand up to it, and push up the sleeve of the long shirt I'm wearing. I swallow hard. The skin beneath it is unblemished. It's perfect.

The Dream Land?

My heart is pounding. Oh Gods, is this a warning? Are they in trouble? Do they need my help? I run to a window that wasn't there a few seconds ago and peer out toward the sky. It's a nice pale blue and is unmarked. There's no bison.

I run to the other side of the room and a window appears there. I open it, lean out. There's no bison. I look down, and nearly scream. Tiny dots below me—

I feel his hands on my hips. I freeze. How did he get here? He pulls me back, and folds me within his embrace.

"You don't want to fall, Shania," he whispers into my ear. I smell strong liquor and feel his hot breath on the back of my neck in the most unpleasant of ways.

I freeze.

"Get away from her."

Raleigh turns—I'm still in his arms—to face Corin. I can't breathe. I try to move away from Raleigh, but can't. His arms are too strong—of course he'd be strong. He's the impossible man.

"Leave her alone." Corin raises the sword that appears in his hands. His face is full of a power I didn't know he had. "I said, leave her alone. I mean *now*."

"You think you can beat me, *boy*?" Raleigh's laughter sends shivers down my spine.

Corin lunges toward us.

And, suddenly, I'm flying across the room, but not toward Corin. My body catapults itself in the opposite direction, arms flailing. I land on the cold, tiled floor. I get up, and I turn, and I jump and—

I can't move.

I am suspended in the air. Or, at least, that's what it feels like. My body is weightless, but I can't move. Just trying to move my fingers feels like my arms are breaking. Oh Gods! Help me!

But they can't. I can't. All I can do is watch Corin and Raleigh fight.

In the time I was flying, Corin's already taken a blow to his shoulder. A red streak stretches across his shirt in the most precise of angles. He falters and grimaces, pulling a hand to his side.

That's when Raleigh stabs him. Stabs him with the longest knife I've ever seen.

I shriek as Corin collapses to his knees, his body crumpling. But he doesn't cry out or scream. He doesn't make a sound.

Raleigh's advancing on him. He raises the extraordinarily

long knife above his own head, and I have no choice but to watch as it's plunged into Corin's chest.

I try to move, but can't.

"Corin!" I scream and sob and sob.

Corin sinks closer to the ground, until he is lying in a pool of his own blood. I watch the redness soak into his shirt, until I'm sure it can't take any more.

"Do you see, boy?" Raleigh smiles and his pure white teeth glisten. "You cannot beat me. The Untamed cannot beat the Chosen Ones."

Then Raleigh disappears. And I am left, suspended in the air, to watch Corin taking his last breaths of life.

Chapter Thirty-Three

"It was just a dream."

I say the words aloud to make them more true, to satisfy the doubt in my mind. But it doesn't. It doesn't change a thing. I should be relieved it wasn't a vision, but I don't feel relieved. My head pounds, my sight blurs, my skin tingles.

I'm still sitting, shaking in the back of the car. Darkness is all around me, trying to soak up my fears and pain, but even the night cannot help me now. Only one thing can.

No. Can't risk it.

I look toward Marouska's sleeping body. She made that drink for me. She knows how to do it. Those yellow roots we collected, were they involved? Marouska said they were for soup, but that might've been a cover-up. I swallow hard. Could I make it? I could convert myself and hide the outward signs quite easily. But how can I find out the recipe?

Marouska breathes heavily in her sleep, stirs a little. But she'll sleep through anything this night; I don't know how I know. I just do.

But I can't ask her for the recipe. She's suspicious enough of me already. And guessing would be too risky. If it fails— which it most likely will—she'll kill me. Or the others will when they get back.

I pause. Is there a way to consume the augmenter without getting the mirrors? I press my lips together. Could I sniff it? Inhale it? Or would that give the mirrors too? I can't risk it to find out.

I take a deep breath. I just have to wait. Soon, I'll be able to get away. I rub at my arms. The skin has goose-fleshed and the bumps feel horrible. I am jittery inside again. Uncomfortable. My stomach turns.

It's because of the dream.

A bad dream. That was all. It wasn't a vision. It wasn't my Seeing powers. The bison wasn't there. It was just a bad dream. Another nightmare, like the one of my father and Five.

My father used to say dreams personify our worst fears; we remember them so we can learn a way to overcome them.

I can still see Corin's bloodied body. With a painful jolt, I realize he was lying in the same position as the dead Untamed child was. I swallow hard. I just saw Corin die. One of my worst fears?

No! I want to scream. His death is *not* one of my worst fears. He means nothing more to me than Rahn does. And Corin's not interested in me. I know that. So why am I dreaming about him? Why does the concept of his death scare me so much?

I blink away hot, angry tears and sniff loudly. I'm not interested in Corin. He's arrogant. He thinks he knows best. He's prejudiced toward my family because my mother's a Seer, because Two was a Seer, because I'm a Seer. He hates me. He's disappointed in me. Why would I ever be interested in him?

I bite the inside of my cheek, until I draw blood.

No. Corin's death isn't my worst fear.

Being left alone with Raleigh is. Yet, it's his people I'm going to join.

***

When morning eventually dawns, I get up early, and, leaving a note for Marouska—I peeled the paper off a can and used mud for ink—I head out into the jungle. I take my knife and the Luger with me. Also attached to my belt is a small package of food.

I start up the small mountain—the one Corin and I first went up. From the top, I can look to see if they're in sight. If they're not, then I'll have to leave. I can't keep waiting until they come back, if they never return. I'll just have to tell Marouska that I'm worried about the others, that I'm going to see if I can find them. It will bide me some good points in her book. Hopefully, she won't suspect why I'm really going. She won't, not if I play my cards right.

My legs move, almost in a mechanical manner, directing me. I have no choice. Something's compelling me to go there. So I do.

It's hard going, but it's cooler than the average temperature, and the air is refreshing against my skin. I've tied my greasy hair up into a high knot, and I can almost forget about my disheveled, dirty appearance as I lose myself to the mountain.

I listen to its sounds, smell its earthly aromas, take in its bountiful supply of beauty. Soon, I am at the top. There are a few stubby trees, and a fallen trunk. I sit on it and watch over the valley below.

The trees look tiny. Like they're not real. Like nothing's real in this world. There's no guarantee of anything. I take a deep breath, and breathe in the jungle air. My knife rests on the trunk next to me. The gun is back in my belt. My pockets are empty, except for the augmenter. It would be the perfect time to get rid of it. If that was what I was going to do. There's no one else here. And I *know* that the right thing would be to dispose of it, to remain Untamed. The bison told me that. Still, the need for self-preservation is strong.

I pull the vial out my pocket; my fingers almost cling to the glass. I stare at it: my connection to the Enhanced. Throw it away, or drink it. Either way, it's just one sudden movement of my arm.

My lips feel strange.

Make up your mind. Take it or throw it.

Something stops me from doing either action. I don't know why. It's silly. I already know I'm going to join the Enhanced—I've already decided that—so I don't know why I'm pretending to hover in between.

***

Over the course of the day, Marouska doesn't come up to find me. She must realize I need to be alone. Maybe she's wondering what I'm doing. Maybe she's not.

Around midday, I eat my food. What's left of the meat pie is starting to go stale; it does little to revive me. The meat tastes a bit funny too now, though Marouska insisted last night that it was okay. I need water. But I left that behind. I can't bring myself to move from this spot to go and find some just yet. I don't even know why I'm not on the move. New Sié looks so close, in the daylight. I could be on my way now, quite easily. I'd be there in a matter of days. Probably sooner—I'm the fastest runner the Untamed have.

For a few minutes, I entertain the idea of leaving now. I see myself just walking away, dancing in the city, and drinking augmenters. I breathe in deeply, letting my mind wander. But I don't move. I just sit here, alone, with only the jungle's sounds for company. It really is beautiful. Amazing. Wonderful.

In all the time I'm up here, I see no animals. Nothing. Other than mosquitoes. I sit still, blending into the background, yet no animals come through. No birds. No rodents. Nothing. Even in the sparsest parts of the desert, I'd have seen some sort of life, but here there's nothing.

It's like the life's just gone out of this place. Zapped away. Drained. It's the fear, that's what it is. Everything in the wild is scared—the people: the Untamed. Everyone lives in fear. It doesn't have to be like this. I know that now, and the knowledge frees me.

A few hours later, I stretch my legs out and groan as they click and crack. They feel dead. I wait for the blood to return to them. It does, and my legs tingle.

A little while later still, I hear the first sounds of proper life since climbing the mountain: the faint hum of human voices.

I get up and walk over to the edge of the mountain, peering around the trunk of a young larch. I see them, far, far below. They're walking on an open pathway. Four of them. My heart lifts. Something strange fills my body. How didn't I see them earlier? And how can I hear them, from here?

They're laden down, huge bags humped up on their backs. For several minutes, I admire them, relief pouring through me. Corin. Three. Esther. Rahn. They're back. They survived.

I watch them for a good fifteen minutes, mapping their progress along the track. I look at them, then toward the part of the woodland where the car and Marouska are. They'll be there in less than half an hour. Then it dawns on me that I won't be there in time. Even if I set off now, and run at my top speed, I'd probably make it back a few minutes after them. That's if I hadn't killed myself falling down the mountain.

After a few seconds, I shrug. I'll stay up here then. Rahn will be angry. But his anger won't really make a difference to me—that's what being up here all day has made me realize. Nothing can *really* affect me any more. Not now, since I'll be leaving anyway.

So, I sit back down on the fallen tree.

***

Time passes slowly when you know you're going to be in trouble, even if you're not that bothered about it. Several times, I have to stop my legs from shaking as I sit on the tree trunk. My nerves are on edge, but I remind myself that soon—very soon—I'll never feel like this again. It gets me through it, for now anyway.

I look ahead at what I can see of the valley. There's no movement. Everything's still. Waiting for me to go back down.

I don't feel like going down. I don't know if I'll ever feel like going back down. I wonder whether Marouska has gone back on *our little secret* and told them about the augmenter. This very second Rahn could be banishing me from the group. Would that be a bad thing?

Evening draws in. Heat melts away. The mosquitoes' constant buzzing gets louder and louder. I bat more and more of them away from me. My stomach rumbles loudly, but I ignore it. I brought no more food with me.

Then I hear a sound, like the pushing back of foliage. And footsteps. A twig snaps and I stand up, legs braced. The sounds come from the woodland path leading up here. I pause, then grab my knife. Something is coming up here. Something is coming toward me. An animal? A leopard? Or Rahn, ready to disown me, to kill me?

My mouth gets drier as the sounds get closer.

I can hear humming. A human noise.

My hand shakes as I hold the knife. I remember about the Luger in my belt, and pull it out. But I'm holding it with my weaker hand and my shoulder burns. The weapons should be the other way around; I'd get a better shot with my left hand. But I don't know if there's time to switch them. Whoever is coming is big. The footsteps are heavy. I swallow and flex my left arm slightly. The knife's sharp blade glistens.

I see the figure.

Corin.

He pushes his way into the secluded area and his eyes rest on me. He folds his massive arms slightly, making his body look even denser, even more powerful. The patches of skin that were burnt raw before, are now browning and beginning to peel. But his dark hair—a lot darker than it was in my dream—and clothes are scruffy, not neat and tailored.

"What're you doing?" He doesn't look away from the weapons in my hands.

I lower them, scowling. "I—I was sitting here."

Corin crosses the glen, stopping a foot or so away from me. His eyes narrow. "You were supposed to stay with Marouska." When I don't say anything, he continues. "She says you might be angry with me."

I blink, remembering my dream in vivid detail, then how annoyed I'd been that the powers that be thought I cared about him more than anything in the world. Had it been that easy for Marouska to read me, especially when I thought she was asleep?

"*Are* you angry with me?" He looks surprised.

I shrug and the motion sends a dull ache through my bad

shoulder. Oh well. I can get that fixed soon. Corin's eyes flicker to it, then back at my face.

"Look, Sev, just because I don't want to be with you it doesn't mean you've got to behave like a spoiled kid, does it?"

"If you think you're the reason I'm up here, then you're even more obnoxious and arrogant than I thought." I put the weapons back in my belt. His expression doesn't change. "I'm a Seer, Corin. Seers need solitude sometimes."

Well, everyone needs to be on their own at times. It's just human nature.

Corin nods slightly. "Okay, but Rahn wants you back now. We're leaving again."

I look up at him. He's not that much taller than me. "He sent you to get me?"

"He said if you weren't back before nightfall we'd go without you."

Yes, do that. Then I can leave for New Sié without any objection.

"And Three isn't trying to find me?"

The corners of Corin's mouth twitch and he brushes at his dark hair with a grubby hand. "He went off in the wrong direction. I knew where you'd be."

I grind my teeth. The *arrogant*—

"But I got you this." He produces a small bottle from his pocket.

My eyes widen. A neon blue liquid. My heart races. I freeze. My back stiffens. My ears burn.

Corin frowns, glances at me. "It's the one you like best, isn't it?"

I take the bottle slowly, turning it around in my fingers. It's not labeled at all. I can barely breathe. What will it do? The possibilities are endless. But... *Corin?* I look back up at him, his face blurring before my eyes.

"I couldn't take the whole bottle," he says. "But I found this small one, and transferred some. It was the best I could do... you do still want mouthwash?"

The wind whistles through the trees.

"Yes." My voice is weak as I meet his eyes. "Thank—"

My gaze jerks behind him. Movement. In the foliage. An animal. Soft eyes. A large muzzle. Velvet fur.

A big cat. I know that look; it's been watching us. I freeze. How the hell didn't we notice it?

"You need to come back now, Sev," Corin says. "Rahn's serious. He will move on without you. Marouska told him about that child's body. It's not safe here." He takes a step backward, but doesn't turn away.

The cat takes a step forward, lowers itself into a pouncing position. A leopard. I can see it clearly. It reminds me of a carcass Kayden brought back a few years ago.

The mouthwash drops from my fingers.

"Don't move." I pull my gun from my belt. The Luger flashes in the streaky light.

"Sev? What are—"

The cat springs forward, eyes on Corin.

Chapter Thirty-Four

The moment the cat moves, so do I. I flick the safety off the Luger, lunge to the right, pull the trigger.

The cat pounces toward Corin, but the bullet—although not hitting it—sends it off path, slightly. But it's enough.

Corin swears loudly. Then he reaches for his Glock. The cat jumps forward, his head following me, but then darts toward Corin. Skids, changes its mind, turns, bounding away, tail weaving through the air. I line my shot up with its retreating body. I fire again as the leopard turns.

This time, I don't miss.

The leopard falls onto its side, dead.

Corin turns and looks at me. His face is white, save for the sunburn—though even that's faded.

"They still like me then," he says, his voice wavering.

"What?"

"Cats. Always attracted to me."

"Oh." The wildcat, when we were younger. I shake my head, breathing hard.

A few seconds later, Corin walks to the cat's body. I stay where I am, I don't want to move.

"You got it in the heart," he calls back. "A heart-kill."

I take a few steps forward. I feel strange. Dizzy. Corin meets me halfway.

"Sev?" He swallows, and his Adam's apple bobs up, then down. "You can put the gun down now."

I stare at the semi-automatic pistol for a few seconds. I saved Corin's life. He could have been dead now.

I flick the safety on, then put the gun back in my belt. My

fingers shake.

"Hey," Corin says, and he touches my good shoulder. His touch is tender and full of—full of something I don't know. Something new. "Uh, thanks, Sev."

I make the mistake of looking into his eyes and the smallest of shivers runs down my spine. We're standing so close to each other. So close I could—

Corin leans forward. His hand moves from my shoulder to my jaw. His touch is soft, and I think of the leopard's fur as he tilts my face up slightly. I'm looking into his eyes already, but the change in angle makes it more intense. My heart speeds up. He closes his eyes.

He kisses me, his lips warm and soft despite the sunburn. It's short, over even before I can comprehend what's happened. I watch him as he lets go of my face, stepping away. His hands shake and, stupidly, all I can think of are his words from the last time we were on the mountain: *I'm not interested in you.*

I don't say anything. He doesn't add anything. We stare at the cat's body. It's big. Impressive. My heart pounds. I can still feel the adrenaline pumping through my veins. I glance sideways at Corin, feeling my face burn.

"If the Enhanced get me, they'll have all of us. All the Untamed," I blurt out, surprising myself. My spine clicks. "I think I'm the key to it all." I freeze. Why the hell am I saying this? I'm leaving him—them all—soon.

Corin meets my eyes. His are unreadable, and there's something within them, something of real depth that I can't identify.

"I'll protect you."

His words float above us, then he pulls me to him. I half expect another kiss, but this time his arms awkwardly hold my shaking body against his. He feels sturdy, safe, and strong. His arms are like a cage around me.

"We need to get back." His voice is hard. "Come on."

"I—the mouthwash—" I start to turn back, but he shakes his head, stopping me with a hand on my shoulder.

"It smashed. I'll get you more. Come on."

I let him lead me back down the mountain, my hand

encased in his.

***

A few minutes before we get back to the car, Corin lets go of my hand. Esther sees us first. She waves at me. She looks the same as she did when she left, except she's more tanned. Healthier, especially after that stomach virus.

"Oh, Seven! We were worried! Three, she's here!" She grins as my brother appears.

Three's eyes link with mine, and his figure sags with relief.

Corin walks off, maybe to find Rahn.

"Where have you been?" Three demands as he jogs over.

After a few seconds, I say I was meditating. Three questions me no more.

"Rahn says we're to leave as soon as possible," Esther says. She's patting something onto her arm—a thick paste of baking soda mixed with a little water. It helps mosquito bites and bee stings. "Marouska told us about the child. Oh Seven, that must've been horrible."

I nod. My fingers clutch at my belt. "How did the raid go?"

Three nods. "Not too bad. Got fuel. And a few other things."

"But," Esther says, "we got into a bit of trouble with the Enhanced. Corin shot two. Then one got his hands all over me, and knocked Three unconscious."

I glance toward Three, his face is expressionless. He doesn't look like he's badly hurt. He's standing tall. And, as I'm looking at him, I realize my brother really does look his age. He's twelve years older than me, yet normally I think of him as Corin's age. But, now, I realize that's wrong. Three's experienced in a way Corin's not. Yet Three was the one knocked unconscious.

"And," Esther's voice gets higher and her words faster, "they're really strong. Stronger than normal. We saw this poster of their rules, and it said only the Supreme Enhanced are entitled to use violence, so long as it's for the good of humankind." She makes a face. "I bet all of them will be promoted to the Supreme level soon, given their mantra about equality. Yeah, and we saw a warehouse that was *full* of augmenters. It was amazing. I had no idea they had so many. All different colors...."

***

That evening, I fall asleep to the rumbling of the car engine and the motion of the moving vehicle. I'm no longer next to the window as Three wanted to be there; he felt sick. I'm squashed in between my brother and Esther. Rahn hasn't said anything to me about going off to the mountain alone, but I'm pretty sure Corin's spoken to him. Though whether Rahn knows about the leopard, I don't know. The kiss, definitely not.

When I awake in the morning, the car's still moving. Three's now driving, and, in the rear-view mirror, I see him yawn. Corin sits on my right, and Rahn's by the other window, Esther and I are in between the two men. Marouska's still in the front passenger seat. I make eye contact with Corin; he gives a strange smile. I try not to burst.

We're now in a rather flat land. Fields stretch out as far as I can see to the right, and straight ahead is the glistening plane of a lake.

"No Seeing dreams?" Corin taps me lightly on the arm. It is my bad one, but it doesn't hurt so much now.

"No."

Corin, Three and I seem to be the only ones awake; we keep our voices low.

"We're going east?" Corin sounds surprised, and I see him look up at the compass, which has been stuck onto the ceiling in between the two front seats.

Three grunts. "Rahn told me to keep driving east."

"So we're just going east?" I frown. New Sié isn't in the east.

Next to me, Corin shifts slightly, taking over more of my seat. Just that movement makes me feel like I've been hit. My

243

breath quickens.

I'm going to have to leave Corin behind, he'd never come with me.

Oh Gods. How didn't I think of it before?

I swallow hard. I need to get it into proportion. It was just a kiss. It doesn't mean anything. I can't base my survival on it. I need to go to an Enhanced town. I have to. Even if it means Corin won't go with me. Yet just the thought makes me shudder. I'd be betraying him, when he realized. It would be the thing he'd remember most prominently about me. And he said he'd protect me when I told him what the bison said, about me being the key…oh Gods.

"Just east," Three says.

"We should have a proper plan." Corin frowns, and I try not to look at him. "Wandering around aimlessly isn't going to help our survival. We could walk right into a nest of the delightful vultures."

Three makes a nonchalant sound. "Well, obviously I'm using my own judgment as well. I'm not stupid." He sounds annoyed. "If I'd just gone east all the time, we'd have cruised right into another Enhanced city."

Corin nods grimly. He looks past me, toward Esther and Rahn. "We shouldn't be on the road all the time. We're asking to be caught. We should be finding our own base, settling there. Increasing our resources and chance of survival. Or trying to find a tribe, the Mariballii or the Zharat."

"But Rahn says we need the Enhanced to survive," I say. We use their fuel, their clothes, their medication, their food. We may as well be them.

"We're only dependent on them if we let ourselves be," Corin says. "We need to be strong without them. We don't need them. We should've already found somewhere for us to stay permanently, as far away from them as possible. I don't know what Rahn's playing at. It's like he wants us to get killed, sometimes. Or converted."

Chapter Thirty-Five

"I'm catching some radio waves." Three's mouth sets into a thin line, and Rahn slows the car, so the engine quiets a little.

I lean forward, my eyes on Three. He's against the window, on the other side of me. Marouska makes a huffing noise. I'm trapped between Esther and Corin.

"About bloody time," Rahn says.

The foxhole radio in Three's hands—a careful construction of wire and bits of metal—hums. Three's got the earpiece clamped to the side of his face, and his nostrils flare.

"What is it?" Corin asks after a particularly loud crack emits from the radio.

Three waves a hand at him.

"Is it an Untamed channel?" Rahn's voice is low.

Three turns his back on us all, hunching over the contraption. "No."

I sit up straighter.

Rahn glares at me in the rear-view mirror. A few seconds later, the vehicle stops and he turns the engine off. The silence is bigger now, and I strain my ears. After a few seconds, I hear murmured broken voices.

"Give it here." Rahn stretches a hand behind him, more aimed at me than my brother. But his hand remains empty.

"Aye, let him listen," Marouska says.

Esther leans closer to me. We all listen.

I make out the words "Big" and "Rock", but that's it. Corin's breathing begins to get louder. Rahn frowns at him.

Three lifts the gadget higher, until it's level with his head. He frowns.

"Signal's going."

There's a raspy noise from the radio and the sound of metal scraping on metal. The faint whirring tails off. My brother curses under his breath, and Rahn drums his knuckles on the steering wheel. Next to me, Esther crosses one leg over the other, and Corin leans back against the leather seat.

I remain where I am. Rigid, in between the two siblings, sitting bolt upright. My eyes are on Marouska. I frown. Something's not... I bite my lip. She wouldn't tell them now, about the augmenter, would she?

I try to shrug away the feeling—I don't even know where the thought came from, it was just there like an ambushing insect—but it clings to me. Like the Calmness. It's in the inside pocket of my jacket. I can feel it against the side of my right breast, inches from my mother's pendant. I stiffen.

"Well." Three sighs, and the radio drops into his lap. "Some broadcast about music." He looks across at me for a second and my skin tingles. "I don't think we should stay stationary though. I'll keep trying."

Rahn makes a snorting noise. "And I thought you were finally goin' to prove useful. Thought you might tell us the Enhanced Ones' next steps, what their plans are, but no—"

"Rahn." Esther leans forward, tapping him on the shoulder. "Three's doing his best."

"You couldn't do any better," Corin mutters, but his voice has an almost sarcastic tone to it that I don't understand. "Do as Three says. Start the engine. Sometimes we need to listen when a Sarr speaks. Properly listen and not twist their words, like what really happened with Katya—"

"Shut up," Rahn says.

My body jerks. "What did you say?" My neck cricks as I turn on Corin.

His eyes are shut, but I can see movement beneath his lids. "Nothing."

"My sister said *what did you say?*"

My heart pounds.

"Nothin'," Rahn says. "Corin's just stressed. We all are. We need to stick together. We'll carry on drivin'. Three, keep at it with your metal shards and wires and *stuff.*"

It takes a good few hours for the atmosphere to diffuse.

"It was proof," I whisper to Three when we stop for a few minutes later that afternoon. We're outside and the temperature's dropped alarmingly. "They practically admitted it. They know what really happened to our mother." I swallow the gritty air — we're not as much in the wilds now, closer to civilization.

"We *know* what happened." Dark shadows haunt Three's face. "She chose them."

I touch his arm. I think of my mother. All the stuff she stood for. Sure, she's on the surviving side now, but I still know she wouldn't have chosen it voluntarily. Not like I will….

"You can't still believe that," I say.

My brother turns toward where Rahn and Corin are standing. Corin's stooping slightly, his head lowered to Rahn's height, and I can see their lips moving, though I can't hear the words.

"I'll believe it if it keeps us alive."

"So you do suspect them then."

"This conversation never happened," Three says as he walks away, toward where Esther and Marouska are playing with the dog.

Nope, I grimace. None of this is happening. But something will.

***

We stop near the third lake we see on the following day, and Esther and Three take the terrier for a walk. I watch them as they walk across the plains, their figures silhouetted in the evening light. The day's gone quickly. I turn back and look at the little camp we've set up. We're about thirty miles from a small Enhanced town: New Salvus.

My new home? Corin and Rahn are in deep discussion about whether we should raid it. I want to go over and encourage them, but it might make them suspicious—I never liked raids before. And if I do go and join in Corin and Rahn's discussion, I might lose my nerve about leaving. Could I really leave them all behind? Could I leave Three behind?

Could you leave Corin behind?

Marouska's inside the car, sorting out the remaining food. Apparently, we have a lot left, but I'm not sure I believe that when our meals are getting smaller.

The lake we're at now is huge. We've parked not far away from the water's edge, but there are trees dotted about, and lines of shrubbery provide some seclusion. I stare at that water. It looks so bright, pure, appealing. Yet deadly. Like it has fingers that will grab me, never letting me go, as soon as I touch its unrippled surface.

But I *do* need to wash.

I walk back to the car, grab a spare set of clothes, some soap, a flannel and a cloth to dry myself with, and head toward the most secluded part of the lake I can get to.

It takes me about fifteen minutes to find a place I'm satisfied with. Trees provide privacy, but when I'm there, and the concept of undressing is real, the place doesn't seem nowhere as near as isolated.

I look at the lake's untouched surface. I can do this. And I am going to go through with this.

I put my clothes down on the grass, folded up, and take one last look around. Corin, Rahn and the car are in the distance, hardly visible. The chances of them coming here are slim. I hope. Three and Esther have gone in the opposite direction, and Marouska had been making it clear how much her legs ached the whole journey. She's not going to make the trek.

Anyway, I'm not going to be long. They'll probably not even notice I've gone anywhere. Corin and Rahn might think I've decided to catch up with Esther and Three.

I strip my clothes off, and fold them up next to my clean ones, careful not to let the augmenter shatter. I put my mother's pendant on top of the pile of clean clothes. It feels wrong taking it off, like I'm losing a part of myself that I'll never get back.

Next, I break off a small chunk from the soap bar, then, taking one last look around—and covering up as much of myself as I can with my arms—I skip the few feet down to the water's edge.

I gasp as cold water splashes over my ankles, and try not to scream as I run deeper and deeper. Gravel underfoot moves in torrents, and small, sharp pieces scratch at my feet.

The water slams against me.

My body's crushed deeper into the platform.

My throat constricts. I taste bile. I turn, trying to pull away. More water hits me.

Mumbled voices over me. A laugh?

Too much water.

I push off from the gravel, forcing my head above water again. For several seconds, I drink in the air.

"I will not drown." As I say the words aloud, I shudder. "I won't. I can do this. I will do this. Raleigh is not here."

I scrub myself down with the soap and the flannel—a cleanish piece of old cloth. My teeth chatter, and the water seems to be getting *colder*. I look back toward the shore. My clothes are still there, and I can't see anyone else.

I dunk my head under the water for a few seconds, then work the remaining soap into it. It's a pity I didn't bring any shampoo with me. I lather the soap up and then rinse it out. I swim out farther, to a part of the lake where the water isn't soapy—it's organic soap made from a root Marouska found—and revel in it. A willow's branches dance in the water up ahead and I swim toward them, then under the hanging branches. I smile as I resurface, shaking my wet hair out. Droplets fly everywhere. *This* is freedom. Even if it is cold.

A few minutes later, I climb out of the lake—the sides aren't too steep—and start toward my clothes. Then I stop. Ice shards run through me. I run.

I reach my clothes and push them aside, my eyes searching hungrily. The fabric falls away, soaked under my fingers. I push my shirt out of the way, revealing the mud and the bank. Frowning, I search through the garments again, my hair dripping over them.

My mother's pendant is not there.

I pull back the clean oversized T-shirt, not even caring that I'm getting loads of water all over the fresh, dry clothes. I look on the ground either side, then at the long khaki shorts. I shake them all out. I pick up the clean underwear, and shake it, in case it's somehow caught amongst the garments. It isn't. It's still not there.

I pause, look again. And again. The sinking feeling in my heart makes me feel sick. After a few moments, I dry myself, pull on the clean clothes. But they don't do anything to fill the ragged, gaping hole within me.

I'm breathing fast as I search the grassy land around me. There's nothing there but my old clothes. I check for the vial of Calmness in the shorts. It's still there. I move the vial to a pocket in my clean khaki shorts.

The pendant—my mother's Seer pendant—has gone.

Chapter Thirty-Six

When I get back to the car, I feel like I'm dying. I didn't think I'd been gone long, but Esther and Three are already back, and everyone's standing around.

"It—it's gone," I cry. "My... my mother's pendant... it's gone!" I skid to a stop, panting, next to Esther and Three.

Esther frowns at me. "What? Are you sure?"

I nod. I've never felt so empty.

"We need to find it," Three says, his voice deep. He glances over at me, then at Rahn who's just come over to us with Corin. "We all need to look for it. She could get trapped in the Dream Land without it—her pendant's gone, Rahn."

Rahn frowns. "You've lost it?"

"We need to find it," Corin echoes my brother, folding his arms as he stares at Rahn sullenly.

Rahn looks at me. "When and where did you last have it?"

I tell them about my swim in the lake, and how the pendant disappeared. I struggle to get the words out fast enough.

"So there are other people about?" Three frowns. "If it's been stolen—"

"There are no other people here," Rahn says. "We'd have seen tracks."

"But we *have* only just got here," Corin says. He moves closer to me and lightly touches my back. I think it's an automatic reaction on his part, because when Three glares at him, Corin doesn't seem to notice. "There could be others watching us."

Untamed

The thought of someone watching me swimming naked doesn't make me feel any better. My hands shake, and I feel faint. It's just the worry, I tell myself. I'll get the pendant back. I have to get it back.

"We'll divide up and look," Three says taking charge. I see him glance toward Rahn for confirmation of the plan, and our leader nods. "Right, Seven, show me where you were swimming. Esther, you check the car, and update Marouska. She might have seen it. You two," he addresses Corin and Rahn, "look everywhere else."

Corin snorts something about *everywhere else* and Rahn frowns.

"Come on, Seven."

I show Three where I swam, but sure enough, the pendant hasn't miraculously materialized.

"Do you think it's really been stolen?" I ask, looking up toward the sky. It's going to be dark within a few hours. I can't sleep without its protection. I gather up my wet hair and tie it back. Not that it does much good now—my shirt is already soaked from it.

Three shakes his head. "I hope not," he says, eyes dark, "because that means it was an intentional action to put you in danger. I also don't like the idea of someone watching my sister undressing and bathing either."

***

By the time evening's drawn in, the pendant still hasn't turned up. Esther and Marouska are trying to stop me from hyperventilating.

"It'll be okay," Marouska says. But what does she know? She's not the one in danger.

Esther looks at me sympathetically. "Corin and Rahn are still out looking. They could've found it by now, and be on the way back with it." She glances over to where Three is lighting a fire.

I know she's only saying it to reassure me. They won't have found it. No. Somebody stole it from me. Somebody wants me trapped in the Dream Land. And that someone has to be one of us.

Three? No. He wouldn't. He's my brother. Esther? I shake my head. She's my friend. Corin? No. He wouldn't. Rahn? As much as I don't like the man, I know he puts the welfare of the whole of his group first and foremost, and he wouldn't do that. Not even to me.

That only leaves Marouska. I look across at her. She smiles back at me as she pulls the bones out of some meat. I don't know what to think. She saw me take the augmenter. She probably hates me, hates how weak I am. Could this be some sort of revenge? A way for her to get rid of me without getting blood on her hands?

I try to breathe, willing the memory of the Calmness to take over my mind, and, minutes later, it's all I can think about. I want to be free of all these worries, all this danger. Would it be so bad to take some now, in this situation? I'm going to get trapped in the Dream Land tonight—or if not tonight, tomorrow night—anyway. Would it be so bad just to have an evening where I didn't feel anxious, worried, nervous?

The vial's in my pocket. I only have to reach for it.

No. I can't. I won't. Not in front of them. Too risky.

I clutch my hands to me. My cold fingers shake. Echoes of pain run through my knuckles. My throat feels raw and my eyes sting. I slap my hands onto my knees, trying to still them, but it's impossible.

It *is* too risky, isn't it?

Far too risky, Seven, don't do it. Remember what happened before. Marouska found out. She won't cover for you again. Everyone will know.

You're going to leave anyway. Do it. It won't matter. And you'll feel better.

I jump to my feet.

"Seven?" Esther also stands up.

"Uh, I want to check the lake again," I mumble. My hands feel clammy, and they're still shaking.

Esther nods. "I'll come with you."

"No," I say, and then soften my tone. "I'll be really quick. There's no point. I'll be back in a minute."

Then I'm running as fast as I can, away from them all. I don't even make it as far as the lake. It's too far away, anyway—a ridiculous goal. I dive for the thick cover of the nearest trees, and crumple to the woodland floor, tears streaking my face.

I pull the vial from my pocket, my fingernails ripping the fabric. I crawl forward, and lean against an acacia trunk. I hold onto the vial as I cry. The blue liquid winks at me. My heart leaps. My breath catches in my throat as I unscrew the lid.

The liquid is just as sweet and delicious as I remembered. It courses through me, driving away the evil, protecting me, helping me.

That's when I know it: I can never truly be Untamed again. I have to go back to the Enhanced Ones. I can't keep stalling. It's lesson four after all: *Never let yourself be Enhanced. Once it's done, there's no going back.* It's true. I *can't* go back to being Untamed. Everyone knows no one will ever be the same after tasting the augmenters. I belong with the Enhanced now. Trying to pretend I don't is futile. When I've tasted the sweetness of sugar, how can I go back to living on salt?

I breathe deeply, and gulp some more of the augmenter. I need to leave now, even without my pendant. The Enhanced will help me; they must know other ways to stop me becoming trapped in the Dream Land. I'll tell them—I'll tell Three and Corin and Esther and Rahn and Marouska that I need to go. I can't wait until another raid, I *have* to go now. I can't live like this any longer, in this perpetual state of danger. Sometimes we need to sacrifice something for safety. Rahn's said it enough times: *sacrifice yourself.*

If I go, it will help them all. I can't hide what I am any more—the eye-mirrors will prove it. I can't keep lying to them. They're free to live as they want. The Enhanced want me. Raleigh wants me. As soon as I'm gone, the Untamed will have better chances of survival.

Except if the Enhanced have you, they'll have all the Untamed.

My throat tightens. Light swirls in front of me, tiny crystals forming into a solid shape, like Three's old kaleidoscope. I blink, adrenaline racing around my body—

"Mum?"

Her face, inches from mine. Long black lashes grace her cheek as she blinks hurt from her eyes.

"Mum?" My voice gets louder, and the sweetness from the Calmness clings to my teeth like a limp bit of stale food I can't swallow, no matter how hard I try.

I reach toward her. My fingers shake. She shimmers.

"What have you done?" Her eyes bore into mine, like daggers, and my skin flushes. Razors dive across my neck, channeling into my throat, gauging out the flesh until I'm raw. "Seven, my child, look at what you've done. After everything I told you. Do my words mean nothing?"

"But, you—"

"I—"

She's gone.

What have you done?

I look down at the vial in my hand. The dregs are still left, and they swirl as I tip the glass vial from side to side.

"I'm joining, you, Mum," I whisper.

But I can't think properly. I scratch the side of my face, hoping my nails have drawn blood. I grab at the back of my neck. I can feel my heart rate rising. This isn't right. I *should* feel calm now.

There's still some of the augmenter left. The pale blue liquid smiles, shimmers. I raise it to my mouth, again. My breath comes in huge bleeding gulps.

"Sev? What the hell are you doing? *No!*"

Startled, I look up to see Corin. My grip on the tiny glass bottle slackens. He lunges toward me. I scrabble backward, but the tree's in the way, there's nowhere to go. Then he's on me. The back of my head whacks against the tree trunk. One of his hands forces my shoulder back as the other seizes the glass vial.

"No!" I cry. "No! Please!" My fingers clench around the augmenter.

Corin snarls something at me, but doesn't let go. His knee crashes into mine and I try to throw his weight off me, but I can't. He's just there, inches from me. His eyes are—

Movement. In his eyes. Reflection. Mirror. My mirror eyes, reflected in his dark pupils.

He swears at me.

I freeze. He pulls the vial from me, throws it out of sight. The sound of glass smashing fills my ears.

For a few seconds, I can't move. I can't look at anything else but his eyes. They are full of hatred, so dark, so dangerous. They're so close to mine, inches away as he leans over me. One of his hands is still on my shoulder, and our bodies touch in several places.

Then he stands up. The look of scorn on his face is enough to make me wish I hadn't been born. Or that I hadn't been caught.

It was inevitable that I'd find out.

"Anyway," Corin says, his tone full of disgust, "I came to give you this. Not that you deserve it."

He pulls something out of his pocket and hands it to me. My mother's pendant.

"Don't thank me," he says. Then he walks away.

Chapter Thirty-Seven

"You were spying on my sister?" Three growls. Esther's hand is on his shoulder, and it's probably the only thing stopping my brother from ripping Corin to pieces. "You watched my sister, then you stole her pendant. Then you tried to be the knight in shining armor, giving it back to her."

"I didn't steal it from her," Corin says tight-lipped.

The six of us are sitting around the fire Three built. None of them look at me, and no one is sitting close to me. Marouska hasn't offered me any of her potion to hide the eye-mirrors, but I can't exactly bring that up without them all finding out about before. I gulp.

My mother's words ring in my ears: *What have you done? Seven, my child, look at what you've done. After everything I told you. Do my words mean nothing?*

"But you were still spying on her?"

Corin freezes for a second, mouth open, then exchanges a glance with Rahn. "No," Corin says a few minutes later. "I wasn't. I'm not interested in her. I've already said what I think of her—"

"Yes, we all know what you think, and you need to get off your mountain," Three says. Esther's hand slips from his shoulder, and he steps closer to Corin. "My sister is not a little girl. She's a woman. You'd do well to remember that, and give her respect, else I'll—"

"Else you'll what?" Corin asks, his arms folded. He raises his eyebrows and smirks. "Exactly. It's all just—"

Three punches him in the face.

"Three!"

Rahn lunges forward and tackles Three to the ground. Esther races to Corin, who clamps his hands over his bloody nose. He curses and gives me and Three dirty looks.

"Does no one care that she is Enhanced?" Corin shouts, throwing his arms in the air. He turns on Three. "Your sister's one of them. Yet you're punching *me*? Can you really not see Seven for what she is? Look at her! Look at her *eyes*."

"It's not her fault," Three says, but doesn't look at me.

"Not her fault?" Corin shouts, then laughs sarcastically. "So someone forced her to drink that, did they? It wasn't of her own free will?" He laughs louder and the shadows that the flames cast over his face make him look even more dangerous.

"Everyone knows it's hard for the Enhanced to stop using augmenters," Esther says, but she's not looking at me either. "That's why our numbers are falling... and it wasn't Seven's fault the first time, she didn't choose it the first time, they captured her—"

Corin snorts loudly. "Maybe I should've left her there then. She's one of them. Not one of us. No Untamed are going to be interested in her. Least of all me."

"Corin!" Esther exclaims. "That's completely unfair. She's only drank some *once*! What the hell's wrong with you?"

I try to cover my face with my hands, but they're shaking and the tears won't stop. I can still feel their hands on me, when they searched me, expecting to find more augmenters.

Corin snorts. "Wrong with *me*? Why, *nothing*! I'm not the one with mirror eyes. I'm not the one going against all that we fight for."

Rahn shakes his head. "Corin, that's enough."

Corin looks like he's going to say something else, but, in the end, doesn't.

Marouska gets up slowly. "We should talk about this tomorrow. Sleep on it," she says. "It'll look better in the morning." She walks over toward the car, and Rahn and then Esther follow her.

Corin still hasn't moved, other than shifting his weight for a few minutes to get a cigarette and lighter out his pocket.

"Seven?" Three prompts. He raises his eyebrows as he

looks at me. But his voice hasn't got the usual warmth in it.

"In a minute," I say. "I'll be there in a minute."

After shooting deadly looks at Corin, Three leaves.

"Corin," I say.

He lights a cigarette carefully, and inhales from it deeply.

"Corin?"

When he doesn't reply, I get up and walk over to him. I tap him on the shoulder. He jumps at my touch. But he doesn't pull away. He turns to look at me, his whole body seething with anger. I nearly take a step back. But I don't. Close up, his bloodied nose looks even worse.

"I didn't take your pendant," he says, his voice flat. "And I *wasn't* spying on you."

He looks me dead in the eyes, and I see the revulsion cross over his face. I don't want Corin to abandon me.

I start to turn away. "Sorry."

"It was Rahn," Corin says. He gets up and faces me, full on. There's something about his stance that makes me think of a warrior.

I freeze. Alarm filters through me. "*Rahn* was spying on me?"

"No. Well, no," Corin mutters, shaking his head. He smells of cigarette smoke. "He wasn't—look, I just found the necklace—your pendant—in his jacket. I don't know why he took it. Probably an accident." He moves to turn away, but I stop him with a hand on his shoulder.

"Thank you," I say, my voice quiet. I bow my head slightly.

He shrugs. "You're pathetic, Sev. You're addicted to that stuff. You're trying to hide it from us, pretend that you're going to be different to all the others we've rescued before, but at the first sign of danger, worry—whatever it is—you just can't help yourself. It's controlling you, And you're letting it. I've seen how you've been struggling, and I thought that you were winning. But you're not." He shakes his head. "The Enhanced are winning. I said I'd protect you from them, but I can't protect you from yourself as well." He shakes his head at me slowly, and then turns away.

I gulp once or twice, and then, with a huge sob, I let the

tears fall, trickling down my smoldering skin.

***

Rahn took my pendant.

From the back seat, I watch him. Why would he want me trapped in the Dream Land? Does he really want me dead? Or did he do it because he knew I had an augmenter and I'd try to convert myself—and that would give him proof of who I am—and a valid reason to throw me out of his group?

I've got the pendant back on now, but no one—least of all Rahn—has commented on it. I cry silently, and turn away so no one can see me. They won't let me stay with them now. Just the thought of not seeing them—any of them—again makes my heart feel like it's breaking. Even if it was what I wanted before. Even if I will be with the Enhanced.

No one speaks for the next hour or so, except for Rahn and Marouska, in the front. They make small talk about the dog having fleas and their favorite type of food.

We stop for the night by a small stream. Rahn, Corin and Three put up a sort of tent for themselves—surprisingly, Rahn says he will share the same tent as the other two—leaving Esther, Marouska and me in the car. Neither of them talk to me.

They're angry, betrayed by me. Taking that Calmness, it wasn't worth it. It would never be worth it.

I catch Esther looking at me out of the corner of my eye, but as soon as I make eye contact, she turns away from me.

That night, I am almost fearful of sleeping. Surely I'll be called into the Dream Land. But I'm not. In the small time that I actually manage to sleep, I'm not taken anywhere. Staring out at the dusky sky, in the early hours of the morning, I know I've ruined everything. Of course I'm not going to be summoned into the Dream Land... why would they warn me of the Enhanced coming after us, when to everyone else I look just like one of those robots? I've betrayed everyone.

I shut my eyes, and wonder if the mirrors have completely gone. I hope they have, I really do. I don't want the others to have a physical reminder of what I've done. But they'll remember it. There's no way any of us can forget this.

***

The next time we stop is just after midday; Three reckoned the car was overheating again, so Rahn ordered us to stop. We're sitting outside—although no one's immediately next to me—and Marouska and Three are sorting out some food.

"Too many flies here," Corin says, batting away some mosquitoes.

"Well move then," Rahn snaps. He's not in a good mood today, that's obvious.

To my surprise, Corin moves and sits fairly near me, the nearest out of all the others. I feel a spark of hope.

"Your eyes are back to normal," is all that he says as he stretches out on the grass.

I don't know what to think. I should be pleased he even spoke to me, and that he's sitting reasonably close to me. But I'm not. I glance over at Corin as subtly as I can. What is he doing? Why sit by me when he definitely hates me?

You're pathetic, Sev. You're addicted to that stuff.

I choke back tears.

A few moments later, Marouska hands out wooden bowls of soup. I smile at her as she gives me mine, but she doesn't return the gesture. I try not to let it upset me and look down at my soup. I have a different flavor to everyone else, if the color's anything to go by. I take a sip of the soup. It's hot and spicy, a strange aftertaste. I have a bigger mouthful of it. I can't place the flavor, but I'm not sure I like it. No. I definitely don't.

I look across at the slight hills ahead of us. They're the yellowest hills I've ever seen, and I can't work out what's growing on them. To the right, is an oddly shaped tor. It's perfectly square, leading high up into the sky, and then it just stops, as if one of the Gods has cut the top off.

I look around at the rest of my group. Esther and Three are over to the left, and Marouska and Rahn are nearest to the car. We're all kind of sitting in pairs.

I look across at Corin, and he nods at me. Maybe he's realized it too, and now he's embarrassed that he's sitting with me. I can smell the smoke that clings to him, even from here. He turns his head and looks toward where Esther and Three sit together. They're both laughing; I feel uncomfortable watching, like an unwanted observer. My brother and Esther are sitting close together—really close—and the way they're looking at each other—

"Something's going on between them." Corin doesn't sound happy. "She's been acting strangely recently. Very strangely." He looks at me. "Warn your brother away from her. Or I will."

When I don't say anything, or do anything, he says my name very loudly.

"What, *now*?" I stir my soup.

"Yes. Or I'll do it."

There's something about his voice that says it would definitely be better if I did it, not him. So, I get up and walk toward my brother and Esther. My hands shake and I clench them together in front of my churning stomach.

My brother looks up at me, shading his face with one hand. His posture is relaxed and he looks comfortable. He nods at me. "Seven."

"Corin isn't happy with how close you're sitting to Esther." It sounds pathetic.

Esther sighs. "It's none of his business."

"Nice of you to be his messenger," Three says. "Doing whatever Eriksen wants."

I hang around for a few more seconds, but he doesn't say anything more, and Esther won't even look at me. As I walk back to my place, Corin picks up my bowl of soup and dips his spoon in.

"Didn't think you'd actually do it," he says as I sit back down.

Corin grins, struggling not to laugh at me. He takes a big mouthful of my soup and—

"Bloody hell!" He spits it out, all over the grass. He jumps up, throwing his spoon at me and I somehow manage to catch it, though I get covered in soup. But Corin's already sprinted over toward Marouska. "What did you put in her soup?" he demands, still spitting.

Marouska frowns at him. "How dare you question my cooking."

Now everyone's looking at Corin.

"Corin, sit down," Rahn says, standing up in front of his nephew.

Corin doesn't move. His gaze is locked onto Marouska. "You put something in her soup. You tried to poison her."

There's an intake of breath from Esther and Three.

"What?" My brother stands up. He frowns, turning slowly, then he's looking at me. "Seven?"

"Uh, I'm okay."

I didn't have much of it, if there was any poison in it. Anyway, Corin's over-reacting. The soup didn't taste *bad* to me. Just different, spicy. And I don't like spices.

Rahn throws his hands up in the air. "This is ridiculous. Marouska wouldn't do that." He pushes his dark glasses higher up the bridge of his nose.

"So why is Sev's food a different color to the rest of ours?" Corin folds his arms.

"Because I didn't have enough vegetables to make her afang soup too," Marouska says. She stares at Corin with a defiant expression. "She's got ogbono."

"So you made her an entirely new flavor?" he prompts, and Marouska nods. He glares at her. "Doesn't taste like ogbono," he says.

Rahn claps his hands. "Everyone just sit down and eat, for the Gods' sake."

"No. She's tried to poison Sev. I'm telling you, that's not obgono! So why would she lie?"

Rahn scowls at Corin. "And why are you so bothered?" His glare flicks to me and I feel even more uneasy. "Unless somethin' *is* goin' on between you and the Enhanced girl?"

Corin shakes his head, just as Three shouts, "She is not *the Enhanced girl*."

"But she is though." Rahn looks at me. "I was right. You're a lost cause, Seven. Sure, you could go for years without an augmenter, but all you need is one moment of weakness, and you're livin' their life, not ours. You may as well go and join them now, Seven, you ain't any use to us. And they'd be delighted to have you, a Seer." He's changing the topic and his words reel off as if he's been practicing them. He probably has been getting his speech ready ever since I took that augmenter.

"No. Seven is stronger than that," Three says.

"It wasn't her fault," Esther says.

"We need her," Corin says. "She's a Seer. She's powerful. We need her. We are not giving up on her. We needed Katya too, *remember*." He narrows his eyes at Rahn and the tension in the air between the two men doubles instantly.

"What?"

Three and I stand up in unison.

"You *did* set her up," I say slowly, focusing my eyes on Rahn. I look toward Corin for confirmation—or maybe I'm including him in my accusation, I don't know—but he doesn't look at me.

"You slimy—"

"She chose to go," Rahn shouts at me, his voice breaking. Sweat drips in huge glistening beads from his forehead, onto the rims of his sunglasses. "She did!"

"She *did* go willingly," Corin says. He holds his hands up in a surrender mode, looking across at his uncle. Then he slams a hand to his thigh. "Tell them what happened, Rahn. What *really* happened. Not this pathetic story that makes you feel better."

My throat tightens. Three's expression gets darker and Esther turns toward Rahn, shaking. The leader doesn't say anything.

"What happened?" I can barely stop myself from screaming the words at him.

Rahn opens and closes his mouth three times. "I—I—"

Corin snaps his fingers, pointing at the older man. "It was his stupidity that got us into the situation. The three of us—me, Rahn and Katya—got caught." His eyes briefly meet mine, then he looks away, at Three. "We were caught. Katya had this plan. She said she'd seen it in the Dream Land a few days ago. But only two of us could escape. She'd thought it would be that day when it all happened, and she insisted it had to be her who stayed. She sacrificed herself—"

"Like I said, she willingly joined the Enhanced," Rahn interrupts. "She went willingly!"

Corin coughs, looking at me and my skin goes cold. "To save us! A *sacrifice*. It's a completely different thing. And you—" He turns on Rahn, like a gust of wind. "You insisted we spun this stupid story about how she just went, how she wanted to be one of them. And I can't believe I went along with your story." Corin takes a step toward me. "I'm sorry, Sev. And Three. Katya was a good woman. She was. It's him." He points at Rahn. "*He's* the poison."

"This does not change the fact that Seven's a liability." Rahn's face is bright red. "She's addicted to augmenters, for the Gods' sakes."

He's right. I am a liability. What will happen the next time they allow me on a raid and I come across some augmenters? I know the answer. I gulp.

"Don't change the subject," Corin warns Rahn. "This is about you and your lies, your prejudice."

Rahn stabs his finger in the air, toward me. "But Seven has to go. She's practically an Enhanced." He looks toward Marouska, for back up, but Marouska shakes her head.

"We are not giving up on her," Corin says. He swallows— apparently with some difficultly. "Sev is one of us, not one of them—no matter how much they try to convert her. She's still with us, isn't she? She hasn't gone back to the Enhanced *because* she is an Untamed—her soul is Untamed. She never will be part of the Enhanced. I won't let her be."

For a second, he seems surprised by what he's said; he holds his head carefully. Then he nods. Corin meets my eyes. I look away quickly.

"No." Rahn's voice booms out. The volume is terrifying. "I will *not* have her in my group."

I raise my brows, taking a step backward, as though some invisible force pushed me. Fear—real fear—courses through my veins. If I go, I won't see them again. I—I don't want to join the Enhanced. Not on my own. No, not at all. Right?

That's right, isn't it?

"You can't kick her out!"

"I will do what I want. This is my group. I am the leader." Rahn folds his arms and the sun glints off his dark glasses as he turns back to me. "We'll drive you to the nearest Enhanced town. Don't worry, I don't expect you to walk."

I need to sit down. But I can't move. My body's locked in place.

Corin shakes his head, taking more steps toward Rahn, until the two men are as close as possible, without either of them touching the other.

"You cannot do that to her!" Corin shouts.

Rahn stamps his foot. "She's too much of a liability, she can't control herself. And you," he turns to Corin, "I'd expected better from a son of my brother. He'd be disappointed in you, lettin' your feelings for one individual put the whole group in danger."

"We're not in danger," Esther cries. "You can't kick her out."

"I can, and I will. She should've been banished from the Untamed the moment she took that damn augmenter." A vein in Rahn's neck pulses. He turns on me. "You may be a Seer, and you may be valuable. But you're weak and easily tempted. You're a liability. And you're a traitor."

"She's one of us," Esther says. "Rahn, you can't. She's a Seer, the spirits still trust her—"

"They won't now."

"You still can't throw her out."

"I can—"

"If she goes, I go too," Three says. He steps over to stand next to me. Relief washes over me.

"Me too." Esther copies Three's movement. "You'll lose me as well."

"And you, old man, you don't even need to ask where I stand," Corin spits the words at Rahn, like they're bullets. Then he steps away, and joins Esther, Three and myself.

I am shaking. Mutiny, over *me*.

Now Rahn looks toward Marouska. She takes her time in replying. I'm sure she's going to choose Rahn over me. She's watching him intently, nodding, not even glancing at me.

"I will go with Seven," she says. "It is my duty to protect her."

Corin looks at her, and he tenses. *"Your duty?"*

"Your duty should be toward your leader." Rahn fumes. I've never seen him so angry, so—

"You're unfit to be a leader," Corin shouts, stabbing his finger in Rahn's direction. He turns and looks at me, and for a second, I pause. The message on Corin's face is clear, and I don't know why he's asking me, but I nod. "I'm taking charge."

For a second, Rahn looks stunned. Then his hand slips to his side, and in a flash, he aims his gun at us.

"Rahn, put it down," Three says, holding his hands up.

Rahn doesn't move. He stands like a statue, one arm raised, with the gun. His dark glasses add ominosity.

"Lower the gun *now*," Corin says, his voice the most authoritative I've ever heard it.

Still, Rahn doesn't move.

After a few seconds, Corin takes out his own gun. The Glock.

Oh Gods.

"You'd really kill me for the sake of that girl?"

"I'd kill you to save my group." Corin doesn't move. His gun is aimed at Rahn.

"Your group?"

"My group," Corin repeats, stony-faced. He's standing strong, his feet shoulder-width apart, legs braced.

Esther takes a step forward. "Put the gun down, Rahn." She takes another step and—

Rahn's arm jerks as he pulls the trigger.

I scream, lunge forward. My body collides with Corin's as he throws himself toward me. I hit the ground, his weight falls onto me.

"Rahn, put it down!" That's Three's voice.

I hear the click as another gun is loaded—Three's. I try to move, but Corin's holding me down. I taste rust and blood. Then Corin's pulling me up. His nails graze my shoulder.

"You've lost it," Rahn cries, his hand with the gun

shaking. Now it's on me.

I should be shaking. My heart should be racing. My head should be pounding. But, instead, I feel like I can see and breathe and think clearly for the first time in a long, long time.

"You've all lost it!" he screams. "It's her! She's doin' this to us! She's one of them! But she's not like me... she's worse..." He breaks off, crying. "She's worse... we need to kill her before she joins them."

I hear the click of his gun as he loads it again. But I can't look at his weapon. I stare at him.

She's not like me.

A jolt runs through me. I feel sick, cold and detached. How didn't I notice? How didn't *we* notice before?

Oh Gods.

Rahn's Enhanced.

Chapter Thirty-Eight

The gun's still on me, I'm looking straight at its barrel. Rahn's watching me, tears streaking his face.

I look at him, try to look past his glasses, but no, it's too difficult. They're too black. Too heavy.

"Take your glasses off," I say. He doesn't do anything. "Rahn, take your glasses off."

"You have no authority, whatsoever, to be doin' this."

"Sev, what are you doing?" Corin grabs me by my bad shoulder, jerking me back.

I wince and dark spots cloud my vision for a few seconds. But I get free from Corin, and then I'm facing Rahn.

"Take them off!"

Rahn faces me, moving like a cat. His gun is still between us. I'm still not shaking.

"Seven, what the hell are you playing at?" Three shouts. I hear his footsteps behind us. Then Esther's.

"He's Enhanced!" I shout. I lunge forward, knock the glasses from his head, dodging the gun.

But it's too late for him to do anything. We've all seen. Huh. *Sensitive eyes.*

For a second, I feel strangely betrayed, looking at our Untamed leader who's really Enhanced, when before, I was too. Deception, it's all around us.

"I'm nothin' like you!" Rahn says. "I'm the leader here. I'm the *Untamed* leader!" He's trying to cover his eyes, but the mirrors are too bright, too obvious.

"You're Enhanced?" Corin says. His voice sounds weaker now.

"Then kill us both!" Rahn grins manically. He turns toward me, his other hand outstretched, like he's begging me. "We can't change what we are... come on, Seven, you understand that... it's better that we're both dead..."

Corin steps in front of me. I think he's forgotten about Rahn's gun. I bite my tongue as I take my own Luger out of my belt.

"How long?" Corin barks at him.

Rahn doesn't say anything.

"I said *how long*?"

Rahn's body's trembling and I wonder if he's about to have a heart attack.

"The medicines you've been getting," Esther says in a small voice. "They're augmenters... when we needed medicine, you didn't have any... only them."

Corin swears loudly. Then he punches Rahn. There's a loud grunt. Ice fills my veins.

Three races past me, and I think he's going to pull Corin off Rahn, but he grabs Rahn's gun. Then my brother hits Rahn.

"You—*you* lying, deceitful traitor. You were going to exile Seven for making one mistake with the augmenters, when you've been using them for years."

"Years?" Corin's shoulders shake. "*Years*? How long? Five? Ten? Twenty? More?"

"Oh, it's been a long time, hasn't it Rahn?" Three says, and suddenly, I notice the knife in his other hand. And how close the tip of the blade is to Rahn's neck. "That box. The spirit box, or whatever he calls it... Esther, go and get it. It's in the car. I'm almost certain what we'll find in there."

Esther runs to the car. Marouska and I watch her retrieve the box. I pull my jacket closer around my body, locking the cold air out. But I'm already cold.

Marouska glances over at me; she's silent. The expression on her face is unreadable, blank, vacant.

Esther puts the box on the ground. It is the same small box, with the ornate carvings all over it, that I'd nearly opened before, when Rahn had gone mad at me about it.

"Open it," Corin orders.

Esther tries. "It's locked."

I hand her the knife from my belt and she pries it open, using the blade as a lever.

"No! No! Please no!" Rahn wails. I glance back at him. He's on the ground now. Helpless. Corin and Three hold several weapons over him.

The lid of the box opens with a huge crack. We all see them. Hundreds of tiny vials, packed in tightly. Hundreds of them. Deep blues... bright reds... pure golds... dark green hues... sparkling yellows... beautiful pinks....

"Sev!"

Corin's arms snap around me before I even realize I'm walking toward the augmenters. He pulls me back, and Esther smashes the vials. Corin forces me to turn. I sag against him, my heart pounding.

"Get down," Three yells, and I look up to see him struggling with Rahn.

"You can't do this!" Rahn cries. His mirror eyes lock onto mine and I go cold. "Look at her! She's desperate for them, I'm not! You can't kill me, and not her! You can't have a separate rule for her and—"

"She hasn't been Enhanced for thirty years solid! She's stronger than you. Don't even compare yourself to her." Corin's whole body burns against me.

"You're lettin' your feelings for her cloud your mind—"

"No." Corin holds onto me tighter. So tight that our bodies are pressed together all the way down. "I'm protecting her from you. She's innocent. You're not. You're really not."

Rahn tries to get to his feet, but Three presses the barrel of a gun into his neck.

"You have to kill her. She's not one of the Untamed. She's too powerful, I've known for ages. She's goin' to go to the Enhanced in the end."

I gulp. Was that why he stole my mother's pendant from me?

Rahn screams. "She'll be one of their Seers, and then we've got no hope! Kill her now, before she kills all of us!"

Corin does not say anything. He just nods at Three.

I have to look away. I fix my eyes on the sky as I hear the gunshot, so loud, so close. The dog barks. I blink back tears. I don't know when I'm going to be able to look back at the scene in front of me. If I'm ever able to.

I gulp, staring at a purple patch in the sky. It's bright. Reassuring.

Then I *really* look at the sky. It's a swirling mass of purples, with black shapes that move and jump. The wind picks up, howling and screaming.

My mouth goes dry. The hairs on the back of my neck stand up. Feeling floods my body.

How didn't I notice? How didn't *anyone* notice?

"It's the Turning!"

Corin twists around, forcing me with him. I feel him take a sharp breath and then he's reaching across for Esther.

"Everyone, join hands! Three! Marouska!" But Corin's words are stolen from his mouth as he shouts them.

I see Three's figure approaching us. A tree flies past him. Something screeches next to my ear. I scream.

"We need to get under cover," I yell, holding onto Corin's arm. I look around, but I can't see anything. Only Corin and Esther.

"Three," I yell. "Three!"

Marouska's figure appears out of nowhere, and then the air's getting darker and thicker. Stickier. I can't feel anything, only Corin's fingers on my arm.

Something flies toward me. White and gold. I try to move, but Corin's in the way. The white and gold thing hits me. Corin's not there. I'm falling. Something hard presses against my back.

Then the world goes dark and all I can hear is screaming.

Chapter Thirty-Nine

The spirit stares at me. I can't look away. It's the most hideous thing I've ever seen. Its body is skeletal, but instead of being solid, it's wispy and floats above me. Long tendrils connect its horrible frame to my own body.

I'm lying down, pressed into the grass.

It's getting lighter all around me. Although I can't move my head, out of the corner of my eye, I see another body. Someone else is lying near me. A spirit feeds from them too. I strain my eyes trying to see. Trying to work out who it is, but I can't see much. I think I can see pale skin, dark hair. But that's it. Just a blur of an image. Corin? Esther?

The spirit feeds from me.

My father warned me this would happen if we were outside during the Turning. The spirits are angry. Have we angered them? It turns its head toward me. Gaunt eye sockets stare down at me, and its mouth—if that's what it is—curls at the edges.

Sleep, says a voice. It's a luring voice, a voice that wants to be listened to... a voice that wants to be obeyed. *Close your eyes... sleep, Seventh One, sleep.... we'll help you.... once we're strong enough... sleep for now, my lovely Seventh One....*

You're special, you're the seventh child of the light—so easily identifiable to us, but also to them. Be careful, Seventh One, for we'll help you. But others will want you. Others will destroy you. For there is no mistaking that you are the one. Your parents knew... they made it easy... easy for us to know... easy for others to know... be careful, Seventh One. Stay Untamed and be careful.

Now, sleep, Seventh One, sleep....

So I do. I close my eyes. I don't want to stare at the spirit any longer. I smile. And I sleep.

***

The bison gallops across the sky. I am running. Running after it. The bison, I can't look away. It's so beautiful, and I, the Seventh One, know why it's there; it makes sense.

When I was little, my father told me stories of bison and buffalo.

A bison represents stability and strength, consistency and gratitude, prosperity and provision, blessing and abundance.

I can still remember his voice as he looked out toward the setting sun and the streaks of the world's colors across the sky. We were sitting by Isra's Rock, near Nbutai. He'd been telling me what the bison stood for—because he must have known I was a Seer, the Seventh One. All the things the bison stands for—stability and strength, consistency and gratitude, prosperity and provision, blessing and abundance—are what Seers need, what we are, and what we can give.

I'm a Seer.

I clap a hand to my mouth, almost in disbelief. My father knew. He said he didn't, but it can't be a conincidence. My mother, she must have told him. She must have known, because she left her pendent with Esther for me. And I am a Seer.

I need to be strong. I need to be grateful for my life, for the opportunity. I need to be prosperous, I need to help others, provide a safe world for them. I've been blessed with this gift, and only when it's used correctly, as it was meant to be, will the Untamed life be abundant once more.

East, we're going east. The tor is ahead. The oddly shaped tor. They're behind us. Deafening footsteps.

The spirits are still with us, but I can't tell whose side they're on. They're just running with us. Flying at us. Screaming before we do.

"Sev!" Corin shouts. He throws his Glock at me, and, somehow, I catch it.

I skid, my feet hitting mud, and I slide forward as I turn. I pull the trigger on the nearest Enhanced. He falls immediately.

My lungs burn as I run. Three's up ahead. More Enhanced are on him. I hear gunshots far too close. And then I'm falling.

A hand seizes me—Corin's. He pulls me to my feet, wiping at the bloody side of his face.

"They're everywhere," he pants. "We can't do this. We can't outrun them. They're made for running."

They're made for running.

Chapter Forty

I jerk awake, no longer in the Dream Land. The spirit has stopped feeding from me, just hovers in my peripheral vision. For a few seconds, I don't do anything. Just listen to the pounding of the land. Footsteps. Hundreds, maybe thousands. They're not walking. They're *sprinting.*

I jump up and nearly run into a lingering spirit. This one's golden and recoils from me. The sky's still purple, but it's softer.

"Three, Corin!" I yell and I'm running toward the nearest body.

It's Esther. She opens her eyes.

"Get up! The Enhanced are coming!"

I don't need to look out toward the horizon and the approaching army to know who they are.

Esther stares at me for a few moments, then stands. She's crying, her arms and legs trembling. She looks like a scared little girl caught up in events that are way too grown up and powerful for her.

"Seven?"

I see Three getting to his feet.

"Are you still okay, still Untamed?"

"Yes." My heart races. I am, aren't I?

Be careful, Seventh One. Stay Untamed and be careful.

"Just give us a warning if you're going to go all Enhanced on us."

"Corin! Marouska!" I can see them. "Get up!"

The pounding of feet gets nearer. I turn, can't see the dog.

"We need to run now! They're closing in on us!"

Oh, the Gods. These Enhanced can run fast.

"Which way?" Esther asks. The five of us are on our feet now. Just behind Esther, I can see what I think is Rahn's body.

I turn and look around the horizon. I freeze. My blood boils. They're coming for us. The Enhanced are here; the majority of them are behind us. An army marching in when the spirits were feeding from us.

I check my belt for weapons, but there's nothing there now. I curse, then check the others: they've still got their guns.

"That way." I point toward the oddly shaped tor. "And don't stop, don't slow down. Get your weapons out now, and shoot them. Go!"

For a second, a part of me is surprised that I'm commanding them—and that I'm commanding them to shoot the Enhanced. To hurt them.

You were going to join them. You still might.
No.

Then we're running. Three pulls Esther ahead of Corin and me, and Marouska is at the back with her strange gun. Corin grabs my hand, and I turn as we run, looking at him. Our eyes meet for a second. We keep running.

The first gunshots go off.

Corin twists around and fires at an Enhanced man.

My lungs are going to burst. Not enough oxygen. Can't think.

Breathe. In. Out. In. Out.

They're too close. I can't move properly. I'm losing speed. How can they run so fast?

I look ahead. The desolate horizon is moving, jolting up and down with every step. The land is desert again now; I can't remember when we left the trees behind.

I wrench my head around, checking for Marouska. She's still right behind us. For her size, she can run fast. Very fast.

"Sev!" Corin yanks me to the left, pulling me out of the pathway of a bullet.

I scream. His grip on my hand tightens. I surge forward with new speed. My hand flails at my waist, automatically going for my Luger. But it's still not there—where the hell have my weapons gone?

East, we're going east. The tor is ahead. The oddly shaped tor. They're behind us. Deafening footsteps.

The spirits are still with us, but I can't tell whose side they're on. They're just running with us. Flying at us. Screaming before we do.

"Sev!" Corin shouts. He throws his Glock at me, and, somehow, I catch it.

I skid, my feet hitting mud, and slide forward as I turn. I pull the trigger on the nearest Enhanced. He falls. And I get the strangest sense of déjà vu.

"Eriksen!"

I look up to see Corin swerve.

There are too many. Everywhere, all around us. Hundreds of them. Thousands, I don't know. All I know is that we're outnumbered. Way outnumbered. Oh Gods. How can we—?

It would be easier if you joined them.

No.

Pain sears through me. My mother's words blur through my head. *What have you done? Seven, my child, look at what you've done! After everything I told you! Do my words mean nothing?*

I can't join them again. We can't. We mustn't.

But there are too many here. We can't win. We can't. It's impossible. We're going to die.

My mouth dries. We all have guns. It could be over in seconds. All of us. We'd be safe then. In a twisted, ironic, sick sense of the word. And the Enhanced wouldn't get me, so they wouldn't get all the Untamed. Yet.

I stare at my gun. The light glints off it. We *could* do it. All of us.

It would be the easy way out.

My lungs burn as I run. Three's ahead. More of the Enhanced are on him. I hear gunshots far too close. And then I'm falling.

A hand seizes me—Corin's. He pulls me to my feet, wiping at the bloody side of his face.

"They're everywhere," he pants. "We can't do this! We can't outrun them! They're made for running."

They're made for running.

My head pounds. This happened before. I know it did. That… that was a Seeing dream. I freeze, and then I'm moving again. Corin's right. They *are* made for running. These people are designed to run.

Lesson one: You can never outrun the Enhanced. They are better, faster and stronger than you.

We're not going to be able to get away. They're made for running. To them, nothing else matters. Running is their goal; running is all they need to do. Running is what they do.

"Sev?" Corin yells as a spirit whizzes past his ear. "We can't outrun them!"

I look at him as best as I can as we sprint, then I'm slowing down.

"Stop running. That'll confuse them," I shout. It's a long shot, I'm aware of that. In fact, it's ridiculous. But we're going to die anyway. And we may as well die when we're not sweating and out of breath. "And *then* we shoot them."

"They'll kill us immediately!" Corin shouts back, his voice buckling under the wind.

He's getting farther and farther ahead now. Part of me knows I should be keeping up with him, not letting the Enhanced catch up with me. Sure, these perfect beings look like they're made for running, but they have weapons, they'll be the Supreme Enhanced—surely they won't have maxed out on speed augmenters, to the extent that they can't do anything else until they wear off? But right now, the running *is* controlling them. And that's what I'm hoping for.

"What the hell are you doing? We can't give in!"

"I—" A spirit rushes against me, and I look ahead... the spirits… them feeding from us... *we'll help you… once we're strong enough*… and I get it. I realize why the spirits are here, why another Turning came around so soon. This is their land too.

"Stop!" I shout. "Three! Esther! Marouska! Stop running!" I shout even louder, hoping I'm right. Because if I'm not, I've just assigned us all to our deaths.

They stop running. The five of us group together, back to back, so we've got eyes on all directions. Our guns are ready.

The nearest Enhanced Ones run straight past us.

They're skidding, but they can't stop quickly enough. Arms flail about, legs are kicking, but they can't stop quickly. A strangled laugh escapes my lips. They've got too much speed that needs using up.

"What the hell are we doing?" Three hisses. "They're going to kill us!"

"These Enhanced are made for running," I say. It's almost funny. "Not fighting."

"We can't win like this," Three says.

The Enhanced are still running past us, but more are coming. We're right in the center of their group. They're confused.

"We need to run! Not fight them ourselves!"

"We're not the ones who'll be fighting them," I say. I pause and look up at the sky. "*Spirits*!"

Chapter Forty-One

A chivra flies past me. It's a mass of red and black smoke. I can't focus on it properly.

For several seconds, I can't believe that this is real life. After everything I did, everything that I'd planned, the spirits are obeying *me*.

"Sev!" Corin grabs me and pulls me toward, him. His hand in mine is warm, and reassuring. I lean into him, inhaling his warm, smoky scent.

More spirits are moving. Hardly able to stand up, we cower against each other. The wind picks up again. My hair whips forward, out of the band.

"What are they doing?" Esther cries.

I look toward the spirits in front of me, and then to the left; we're in the middle of the growing circle of spirits. They're blocking the Enhanced Ones from us.

My ears fill with screams. The sky's painted red. I look up and—

"Get down!" I yell, twisting around and pushing Marouska and Three out of the way of a flying uprooted tree.

Esther screams as a bloody limb hits her.

It's getting colder. The wind's so icy we're all shivering.

"They're trying to freeze them to death," Corin says.

I turn to look at him, and tiny ice crystals grace his stubble. He smiles at me; his hand in mine is still warm and reassuring.

Then a chivra flies toward us. Red. Black. Mist. It doesn't stop.

Marouska screams and the four of us push her out the way of its path. I hear something tear, and a sharp sound, but can't place it.

"What the hell is it doing?" Three pants. "They're after us too!" He raises his gun, and I see him take aim, but he doesn't fire.

"No! Must be a mistake!" I whirl around; my elbow hits Esther and she whimpers. But I can't see the chivra any more.

"Marouska, are you okay?" Corin's voice is hoarse. He's still squeezing my hand.

Marouska mumbles an affirmative reply. I turn back to the spirits. It's cold.

Corin's grip on my hand tightens. "They're getting through," he says, his voice small. "Some of the Enhanced are getting through the spirits."

He's right. Hazy figures. The Enhanced, walking through the spirits. Mist flies, turning into shards of glass that cut the Enhanced... but they're still coming.

"We need to run," Three says.

"Sev?" Corin asks. His eyes are wide.

I watch the Enhanced Ones break through the spirit wall. "I—I, uh—"

I can't talk. The words just fall away.

He is coming for me.

I take a step backward, crashing into Three and Esther.

"Are we supposed to be running?"

"Why aren't they fighting back?"

I can't answer their questions. I can't think clearly enough to form a reasonably articulate reply. I can't do anything.

Corin pulls me closer to him, then pushes me behind him. I hear him swear, and I know he's seen Raleigh too.

I look down, and alarm springs through me. "Where's the dog?"

I frown. I can't remember when I last saw him. My mind's fuzzy. Was he with us when Rahn was—

Esther screams. In a second, I'm facing her.

Enhanced Ones surround her. They all scream at her, red-faced.

One steps forward, and Marouska fires at her with her special gun and the woman falls. She shoots at another—a tattooed man—but there are more. They're coming for us from two sides. In a second, my gun's in my hands. I take aim.

"Run!" Corin yells. He wrenches me along with him. I stumble, trip, and he yanks me up.

"What's happening?" Esther screams. "Cori—" Her scream's cut short.

I whirl around. So does Corin. But I can't see her. The spirits are still fighting. But something's not right. The Enhanced, they're closing in. Raleigh is in the lead. I see him, and his teeth sparkle.

I freeze.

"We need to keep going."

I hear Marouska shouting, but I can't make sense of it. Something wet splatters over my shoulder, blood.

A spirit's body explodes overhead and for a second, we're all plunged into darkness. I can't feel Corin's hand in mine. It's not there. He's not there.

I turn, and the darkness lifts and—

An unfamiliar Enhanced man stands in front of me. The smells of strong alcohol and mint wash over me—mixed with danger and pain. He's taller than should be possible—must be an augmenter's work—so tall that I only come up to his elbow.

"Shania." His teeth are pure white, perfect. Predatory. His hands take hold of me by the waist, pulling me forward. "Come on."

I scream, trying to turn away. "Corin! Three! Esther!"

The Enhanced man laughs and I can't take another breath. But I remember the Glock in my hand. Before I have a chance to think, I fire it at him. He crumbles forward, clutching his leg. I see the agony on his face, in the way it contorts, and all I can smell is blood. It's everywhere. I'm drenched in it.

I run from his body as fast as I can.

Spirits still fly around. One rushes at me. I duck and scream.

Something hits me in the side and for a few seconds, I'm so winded I can't move. But I have to. I force myself to run. I have to get away. I have to find the others, if they're still—I snap my head back the other way; the pain jolting through my neck distracts me nicely from the end of that last thought.

I hear barking. Loud barking. Canine barking.

"Dog!" I yell, trying to see through the thick white mist and masses of spirits that swirl around. "Dog!"

He barks again. There's a flash of brown in the distance and I run as fast as I can, pain jolting through me with every step.

"Shania."

I scream and duck as a hand appears out of nowhere reaching for me. My feet hit a lone limb on the ground. I skid, stumble.

An Enhanced man looms up in front of me, a knife in his hand. I freeze, my eyes lingering on his face. That tattoo, I saw it only moments ago, out of the corner of my eye... Marouska shot him. He was dead.

But he's *here*.

I dive to the side, just as his knife comes down. I twist around, spraining my wrist as I fire at him. His screams deafen me as he dies for the second time... or maybe a lot of them have that tattoo. What am I even thinking? Of course it had to be a different man. Unless he was super-Enhanced.

"Dog! Where are you?"

I keep running, but I'm limping now.

Everywhere I look, I see blood, detached limbs, bodies, spirits flying about. Enhanced figures are coming toward me, through the hazy mist and I turn and run the opposite way. A chivra and another spirit—a black one—skids past me. Icy crystals graze my skin and I scream as something else hits me.

I twist around, trying to go to my left, and duck under a flying bullet. I turn and see Three running toward me. His arm is bloody and he's screaming at someone behind him. I raise my gun, trying to train it on the Enhanced, but I'm shaking too much and there's too much movement.

The dog bounds into view. Gun barrels flash.

"No!" I lunge forward. Dust kicks up in my face. I slam into a figure, see mirror eyes and yelp.

Fingers grab at me. I squeeze the trigger. Someone shrieks. Blood. I turn, the dog's running away.

"Go!" I yell. "Go!"

And—and it happens.

The Enhanced man grins as my brother's body drops to the ground. He reminds me of Finn, the way he falls. Not graceful. Three's head rolls to the side, his eyes facing away from me. A line of blood forms across his forehead. His lips quiver as he drags oxygen into his lungs.

"No... no... Three!" I'm running. My feet crush the sand, compacting it into irregular tiles. "*Three!*"

His head turns toward me. His left cheek is gone. It's just a mess of blood and muscle and tissue and teeth.

I'm going to hurl. I turn, lights blinding me. An Enhanced woman roars past me. She's got a gun. Her gun is aimed at my brother's limp form.

I raise my own, pull the trigger. My bullet gets the woman after hers plunges into my brother's abdomen.

Dust and blood and mud cling to my face. I can taste it everywhere.

Then Marouska's in front of me. Her eyes are wild and her skin is a funny color. She grabs me by the shoulder with surprising strength, and throws me a few feet to my right.

"That way, Seven!" she shouts, and she's turning to me, pointing behind me. She lunges forward, retrieving a fallen knife. "He's waiting for you up there."

All I can hear is solid firing as a band of Enhanced descend on us. Marouska prods me, telling me to go. She's pointing. Shouting at me. The Enhanced get closer. The gaps between them are disappearing.

"Give me your gun!" Marouska yells, and I do.

She turns and shoots at the Enhanced with her the strange AK47 look-alike. Mine's in her right hand, by her side. She's not using it.

"Run, Seven! You're a powerful Seer, you have to survive this with the right people!" she screams, her eyes flitting from side to side. "Go, he's waiting!"

So, I do. I run. I don't want to leave Three, but I run. My lungs scream and I don't know how I manage to take each breath. My fingers are sore and blood drips down my arm, and the throbbing in my shoulder... have I been hit? Three was hit... my brother's—

I can't think the word.

I look ahead. The air is thick and coarse; shards of broken spirits are falling around me. Bright lights everywhere. Oh Gods. Where I am going? To Corin. Yes. That's what Marouska said.

I peer ahead, squinting. But I can't see far. I could be about to walk off a cliff. But Marouska told me to go this way.

Focus, Seven, keep going. Corin's waiting for you.

I'm running fast, arms and legs pumping. I clamp my good hand over my bad shoulder. It comes away sticky and wet. Red. Oh Gods. I need to stop, but I can't....

I see him. He rises out of the ground like a ghost.

I stop as fast as I can. Mud sprays up over me. My legs aren't quick enough. I can't stop in time.

Raleigh lunges forward, grabbing me by the wrist as I try to change direction. I see the flash of a gun as he holds it near my head.

"So glad you could make it, Shania. It would've been a shame if one of my men had hurt you before our meeting. I trust you got the message okay?"

He's waiting for you up there.

Marouska? No. I feel sick, it can't be. But she took my gun from me. She left me unarmed. Sent me up here, unarmed.

Marouska? Oh Gods. The Enhanced must have forced her to do it. Marouska sent me to *Raleigh*.

He smiles. "Yes, my friend delivered the message then. Good."

Friend?

"Clever, wasn't it? Getting my good friend to pose as that batty old woman and rescue you."

What? I twist my head, stare at him.

"I mean, I could've just kept you back at New Repliza,

when my men caught you. But that wouldn't have been any fun at all. And I would've just got two of you. You and that boyfriend of yours." He smiles softly. "But I wanted you to choose us. Bev—or Marouska as you know her—that's where she came in. Feeding you small amounts of augmenters, hiding your eye-mirrors so even you didn't know, you just felt the need to be with us. You feel the right thing."

My stomach hardens. Marouska wasn't Marouska? My eyes widen. No…how didn't we…we all said it! How different Marouska was when she joined back up with us. Yet none of us thought….

"And you've come to me voluntarily, *and* my men will be getting your brother, your boyfriend, and that woman too. Perfect. We'll have four of the most powerful, disciplined Untamed creatures. I'd say it was definitely worth the wait, wouldn't you?"

I don't speak. Just his words, *your brother*, rip through me. Three's dead. Raleigh doesn't know.

Raleigh laughs. "I won't let you get away again. You're too powerful, too recognizable to others." It's the same words he said when he first met me. "This time, you're ours…look, Shania, there's a gun inches from your neck." He sounds suddenly annoyed. "I suggest you stop struggling."

"I'd rather be dead." I twist around, trying to get a grip on him. But I can't. He's too quick. He anticipates my every move. And his pistol flashes.

His laugh is so deep it might be seductive on another man. "I don't think that's going to happen," he whispers, his lips by my ear. "I know what you are, how valuable you are. I know, Shania. It's frightening, isn't it? Being valuable with the possibility of falling into the *wrong* hands. Well, I'm rescuing you now." His hand on my waist squeezes. "I'm just like you. We need to be on the same side. We'll be unstoppable together."

"Kill me now," I tell him. "Do it. Do it now." Somehow, I manage to keep my words steady and powerful, full of authority.

I feel the cold metal of the gun press against my hot skin.

"Oh, I've got a much better alternative to just killing you. That would be boring. And such a waste, when I could have you."

His lips press against my neck. I shudder.

"And I won't let you fly away from me again. I'll keep you by my side. My butterfly in her cage. We'll be together forever, just you and me. We'll win the war easily. Think about it, it'll be quicker, less lives lost."

For a second, I don't say anything. Then I step forward and turn to face him as much as he'll allow me to. I see every pore in his dark skin. I see the way his mirrors draw a sort of unity between the whiteness of his perfect teeth and his eyes... the doors to his heavily guarded soul.

Coldness rolls through my body. I need to stay calm, but being calm in this situation? Gods, help me! I don't have a gun. I don't have anything. I don't even have my knife.

"We'll be unstoppable together, Shania. I'll protect you— you know I will. We'll be the most powerful couple ever. We'll win. Two of the greatest, most powerful Seers together. We can end this war right now, save thousands of lives. We'll save everyone together. You just have to trust me, Shania. Let me convert you right here, right now."

My heart pounds in a dangerous, frightening way. If the Enhanced have me, they'll have all the Untamed. I'd thought I wanted to be an Enhanced One before, but Corin's right. Their way of life is pathetic. Joining the murderers out of fear is wrong. I'd rather be able to feel every raw, harsh emotion and be in complete control than a cold automaton, devoid of humanity.

I *am* Untamed. I am not going down easily. I will fight for us. I will. I have to.

"No." My voice is the firmest I think it's ever been. I glare at Raleigh.

For a few seconds, all I can hear is the battle going on around us. I know it'll be a miracle if Corin and Esther are still alive.

"Well then," Raleigh says. "It's you against me. The strong against the strongest. But Seer strength's only part of it. Physical strength...well, we don't even need to contest that, do we? I'm male, and I'm a Chosen One. You're female, and you're a poor Untamed weak little creature. No more elaboration's needed here, is it? I'm going to enjoy this."

He shoves me and I lose my balance. My bad shoulder hits the ground first and I shriek. His weight hits me seconds later. I twist away from under him, screaming for help. Pain rips through my injured shoulder. For several seconds, I can't see a thing. But I know no one's coming—

Then the pain in my head, it's—oh Gods. I can't do anything... can't... help... ice, everywhere. Bullets. Sharpness... in my head, my body, my soul... tiny shards of deadly ice drive into my brain, tearing up my body, cutting through my flesh...

Something's coming. Something bigger than Raleigh. I can't breathe. It's not just him. The color's fading. I don't understand.

"You're making this too easy, Shania," Raleigh laughs. "Maybe I was wrong... maybe you're not as powerful a Seer as I thought you were... definitely... you're making this too easy... it's not even scratching the surface of my powers, but this, this is brilliant. You can't do a thing, can you? Utterly helpless. My helpless little butterfly."

I can't move at all. Can't do a thing. Too much pain. Too much darkness.

"My beautiful little butterfly."

I can't do anything.

"My precious, beautiful little—"

"*Get off her.*"

Chapter Forty-Two

Darkness descends as the voice shouts again, and I turn, try to get up — try to reach him — but everything's gone. Gone. I gasp, can't understand. But Raleigh's gone. Everything's gone. I'm gone. And the world is... the world is gone.

I'm here. Yet I'm not.

Your mother's gone.

The voice is in my head, but it's not. It's everywhere. I scream, and I'm standing in the darkness. The lifeless darkness. I'm standing with him. The figure, but I don't know who he is. A dark cloak, thin, bony arms that stick out and elbows that glow. I can't see his face — something tells me I mustn't see his face.

I don't know what to do. Too much darkness. I can't see anything. Yet I can see him.

Something smells wrong. Too —

Listen.

I listen.

There are voices around me. Now I know they're there, I hear them, louder. But they're not right. The wrong language. I can't understand them. Yet I know what they are. Little whisperings of truth, of memory, of....

This can't be real. This has to be a dream, a nightmare. There's no bison. No one to help me. Just the hooded man. And darkness.

I'm dead. This is what death is. This is the New World.

That familiar voice — the last thing I heard — he didn't save me. He went. Walked away. Left me. And now I'm dead.

Dead.

Something cold slaps across my face—bony fingers.

I scream, look for Raleigh. But the hooded man jumps toward me again. I smell something on him, something dark... the worst thing ever... my insides heave and my eyes burn as I stare up at him. Can't breathe, can't speak, can only listen to the words—his words—as they wrap around me, strangling me over and over again with new slaps.

"Death knows all. Death sees all, and Death is drawn to you. The stench of a traitor—new or old—clings to your skeleton, with little shards of glass that will never let go, scratching and digging deeper. You are marked for what you are. The mask of betrayal hangs over your aura, like gold cobwebs, rusting. Your body will rot under Death's command, long before your soul is allowed an escape from the decaying flesh of your ribs."

He pauses for a moment, then the air's cold. I still don't know where I am. Not on the hill, not near the battlefield. There's no one else here, and I don't understand. I look up at the sky. Still darkness. No bison there to guide me.

The hooded man's robes billow out. I think he's smiling, though I can't see his face. Something tugs within me, something that says I should know who this man is—that everyone should know....

"Death knows who you are, Seven Sarr. Death will be watching you. Soon, I promise, soon it will be your time. The day of your death is marked to end the suffering, but it is not today. A traitor's soul is never free. A traitor's soul is Death's soul. Remember that. Death will collect what belongs to Death. Death will not forget."

My spine clicks. My arms and legs jerk out as I fall, as the darkness wraps round me, like an old, rugged blanket.

I'm still falling, falling... and... and I smell things: blood, smoke, fear. I see things; the sky, the man with the—

"You're making this too easy, Shania," Raleigh laughs. My breath catches in my throat. He—no. This—what? I don't understand. He already said that. "Maybe I was wrong... maybe you're not as powerful a Seer as I thought you were... definitely... you're making this too easy... it's not even scratching the surface of my powers, but this, this is brilliant. You can't do a thing, can you? Utterly helpless. My helpless little butterfly."

I can't move at all. Can't do a thing. Too much pain. And I look up, ready for the heavy darkness again, expecting it. But the lingering darkness lifts.

I don't understand. This already happened. Raleigh said those words. Those same words. But the darkness fell, after them, claiming me. And now?

The day of your death is marked to end the suffering, but it is not today. A traitor's soul is never free. A traitor's soul is Death's soul. Remember that. And Death will collect what belongs to Death. Death will not forget.

"My beautiful little butterfly."

I can't do anything.

But it is not today. I will not die today.

"My precious, beautiful little—"

"Get off her."

Chapter Forty-Three

"Get off her. I will not ask you again."

Oh Gods. This is real, this time? I'm not sure. Can't be sure of anything. I can still see Death's hooded figure every time I blink.

A traitor's soul is Death's soul.

My body feels too heavy. My head pounds, but Corin *is* here. He's really here. He pulls Raleigh off me. Corin's got a knife and—

I look away, but I hear it all. I hear the sound of the knife as it plunges into Raleigh's chest. It makes a squelching noise like feet stuck in mud. I hear Raleigh's sharp intake of breath, the choking sounds he makes and the thud as his body falls. The gasp of his last breath seems to echo.

"Sev?" Corin's frantic by my side, trying to pull me up. I let him, leaning heavily on him. I can hardly move, hardly... my head... so painful.... full of Death... I see the flash of Raleigh's pistol, now in Corin's hand. "What's he done? *Seven*?"

I clutch at my head, my breath coming in rapid, short bursts. "I don't know," I say in a small voice that doesn't sound anything like my own. But I don't know who I'm talking about any more. Raleigh... or Death?

That's when it hits me. I saw Death. Actually saw him. He spoke to me. But no one sees Death… no one even talks about Death... and I saw him.

Corin's arms are around me, holding me against him. There's no space between us. He looks down at me, his eyes so alive that I tremble.

I am a traitor.

Death knows I'm a traitor. I don't know what to do, who I am, who I should be. No, of course I know. I am Untamed. That is me. That is who I am.

I want to tell Corin everything I saw. But no one talks about Death because no one sees Death—no one's *supposed* to. I don't know what it would do. Telling Corin. He might not believe me.

Death knows who you are, Seven Sarr. And Death will be watching you.

Or what if Death takes Corin away because I've told him? Oh Gods. What if none of that was real? All in my head? No one talks about Death... because he doesn't exist?

I take a deep breath that shakes my body. I look up at Corin, at those eyes. I have to save him. I can't tell him. I can't tell him, in case it was real, in case Death is watching, and in case Death doesn't want Corin to know.

Corin draws me closer still. I try to forget.

"I love you," he says, as though it is the simplest thing in the world. The way he says it fills my chest with warmth, makes my head spin, my arms shake. Everything else is gone. Just like that.

I can't breathe. All I can do is stare up into those eyes. Those warm chocolate brown eyes. His body is a cage around mine, and I've never felt so safe. Then his lips brush mine, tenderly, as though he's scared that I might break. I can't move. I freeze.

He pulls away, but his arms are still around me.

"Come on," he says, steering me forward.

Somehow, I manage to walk, although his arm around me feels like it's a lifeline—without it I'll crumple into the nothingness that had me before. The darkness.

"Who else is...?" I trial off, my voice cracking again.

Corin steadies the gun in his hand. He hasn't got his knife now—it must still be in Raleigh's chest.

"I saw Three earlier, he was carrying Esther—"

"No... he... he got shot..." I shake my head. I can't think about it. I know Death was here.

Corin's eyes darken. "I had to find you. I haven't seen

Marouska."

"She's not on our side," I gulp. "It's not her."

"What?" Corin's voice is thick. "She's a traitor?"

I am a traitor.

No, I *was* a traitor. But I didn't hurt anyone. No one suffered because of me. I'm not a traitor. Death was just messing with me, messing with my head.

I force myself to think of Marouska. The imposter. "It wasn't her. It was all Raleigh's set up. She was some Enhanced woman he made look like her."

"But, her eyes?"

Oh Gods. Why hadn't I realized this before? She knew how to make liquid that hides the eye-mirrors. I look up at Corin.

"The drink..." I take a deep breath. "She—Corin, I drank some Calmness when you and Rahn, Esther and Three were out raiding." The words come flooding out. "I'm sorry. Marouska—whoever she was—gave me a drink. Some concoction that got rid of the mirrors. She said it would be our secret. I—I think she's been making that drink to hide her eyes here, I'm sure. She's been making it all the time... But, Corin, I—I was going to leave you all. I was going to join them. I was going to be a traitor too."

Corin swears loudly. "I—"

"I'm not now though. It's wrong, I'm so, so, so sorry."

Screaming fills our ears. He tenses, and our pace quickens considerably. But he's still holding onto me, and that makes all the difference.

"We need to get out of here," he says. "I don't know if it's worth looking for Esther and...."

"Of course it's worth it!"

Corin looks at me for a long second. "I'll get you to safety first."

I shake my head, and gasp as pain pours through my neck. "No," I stammer. I don't deserve safety. "No, you're not leaving me on my own. I'm just as strong as you. I'm not weak."

"You're valuable, Sev. They can't get hold of you again. I won't put you in danger, we can't risk it."

"We're sticking together," I say firmly, squeezing his hand. I owe it to him, to them all, all the Untamed.

Spirits fly past us, coldness washes over me.

And I see her.

My Seer pendant burns.

I look up at Corin. He's seen her too. We start running, faster and faster. Corin pulls me along. Faster and faster and—

My mother stands in front of us. It's her. I'd recognize her anywhere. Sweat glistens on her forehead, in tiny beads. It really is her this time. This isn't a vision. This is *her*.

She points a gun at us.

The whole world stops.

I see the way the slight wind catches the stray tendrils of her dark hair, lifting them away from her face. I notice just how similar we look: we have the same full lips, the same well-proportioned faces with noses that are just a tad too long. But her face is lined; grooves dig their way around her face. I'm surprised she's kept them, now she's Enhanced. I thought she'd look different. Younger, with skin that was as smooth as an unrippled surface of a lake. But it's not, she's not. And now I'm looking, I recognize the small scars on the side of her neck, and the one on her right shoulder. She looks the same.

I take a deep breath, feeling myself going to pieces inside. Biting my lip, I look up at her directly. My throat tightens. Her eyes.

"You shouldn't have sacrificed yourself. It should've been Rahn." My voice catches in my throat and a strangled noise escapes.

She smiles and her beauty nearly breaks me.

"It was essential I joined them," my mother says. "I saw this. I saw an Enhanced One would stop you. I knew I had to sacrifice myself in that raid because I realized it was *imperative* that it was me who tried to stop you."

"You're going to stop us..." Corin trails off. His gun's on my mother, and his hand's shaking. I want to reach over, to push the barrel away, but I can't make my arms move. They're static, by my side.

My mother trembles. "I'm trying... I have more self-control... but I'll lapse any second. You need to kill me before I kill you...there's no one else here to stop you, so kill me and go."

Corin drags me back as her gun swings low.

"Kill me before they make me kill you!"

"No!" I try to get out of Corin's grip. "Mum!"

I trip against a loose stone and Corin pushes me behind him.

"Do it now, Corin! Please, do it now! I can't be one of you again! But I can save you from being one of me. Shoot me now, please—and get out of here!"

I understand it now, more than ever before: the choice of life between being Untamed and being Enhanced. My mother sacrificed herself, becoming Enhanced to ensure that Corin and I remained Untamed. Even if I hadn't realized myself that actually *living* was preferable to being in an induced state of false security, then I definitely did now. My mother had thrown her life away to ensure I knew this. And it *is* obvious. We have to be raw humans—embracing the positives and the negatives—to really live, to really be ourselves, who we are, not who they want us to be. Someone has to fight for humanity if we're to survive.

The only way to save ourselves is to be Untamed.

Corin pulls the trigger. My mother screams. I hear the soft thud as her body falls to the ground, almost in slow motion; hear her gasps and moans.

I can't move. I should be running toward her... I should be... she's my mother! But—

I shriek, blinded by tears. My legs turn to jelly, I start to fall, but Corin's there and—

"Get away from me." I try to push him, but he's too strong. I can barely stand. "You—you killed my mother... you've really killed her. You—you shot her." I turn frantically, looking for the looming figure of Death. But I can't see him—of course not! I've never seen him before when I've witnessed deaths. I turn on Corin again, anger fueling me. "We could've saved her! You saved me! Why didn't you try? No! Don't touch me!"

"I shot her in the thigh," he says. "Not life-threatening." He steps back suddenly, tucking his gun into the back of his waistband. I watch him do it, annoyed at his expertise. He's a hunter. He's killed my *mother*.

I shake my head, tasting bile and dirt against the back of my front teeth. I start to gag as Corin repeats his words over and over again. I look back at my mother. Her body stirs.

Corin clenches his fists together slowly, and I see the whiteness of his scarred knuckles. I start to move toward my mother, but then he's stepping closer to me. His hands reach toward my face, until his thumbs are lightly tracing my jaw, and his forefingers are on my temples. I freeze; the red-hot poker of anger is zapped away instantly. It's replaced by a slowly growing ball of warmth, comfort, that grows from the center of my chest. He flexes his fingers slowly, then he's leaning closer

He trembles as our lips touch. My eyes are wide, but his are shut. His eyelids flutter as he kisses me deeply, holding my head in an embrace of security and something more. I move my head to the right slightly, freeing my nose from his. I feel him pause, then lean back a bit, looking down at me. His warm chocolate eyes have never looked softer.

"It will be okay," he says, leaning his forehead against mine. He's shaking. "It will be. It will."

My heart pounds and we stay like that for a few minutes. Then, I pull away from him. His hands drop to my arms.

"Corin, we... this is a battlefield. We shouldn't be kissing here."

Not to mention that my mother could gain consciousness at any point.

My mother.

But... she's one of them. She said it herself, there's no way she can be one of us again. I feel sick. She's with the Enhanced. And she's an Enhanced One so we can still be Untamed.

"We need to go." I swallow hard, feeling as if—just by saying the words—I'm condemning her to the Enhanced life, betraying her. But I'm a Seer too, and if feels horribly *right* to leave her. I know there's no other way. More Enhanced Ones could come at any second.

"We might be the only ones left," Corin says.

"We might be," I echo. What else can I say? Disagreeing plants hope—false hope.

There's a long pause, in which neither of us say anything. Then Corin's hand tightens around my arm. He pulls me forward, and for a second I think he's going to get my mother's gun. But we run past her.

We run toward the spirits that were behind us. Beyond them, the air is thinner, clearer, and I can see the oddly shaped tor. But it's not a tor. I realize that now. It's a temple. A spirit temple. A place of safety, if the spirits will allow us in there.

We run. There are no Enhanced following us. No one chases us at all. We've left the battle behind, just like that. We slow to a walk. He doesn't let go of me, and I'm glad.

Corin looks at me. "So that soup the Marouska-imposter gave you before, it *was* poisoned: she's been giving you augmenters along with that drink to hide the mirrors… she was trying to keep you addicted."

I think of what Raleigh said earlier. And yes, it *does* make sense. Marouska said she wouldn't tell anyone about the augmenter. Because she wanted to trick me into trusting her, when she was just using me. I'm close to tears.

"They want me on their side. I'm the Seventh One." Corin doesn't question me. "Raleigh's a Seer too, a powerful one… he said they'd win with me and him… Marouska—the imposter—was trying to align me with the Enhanced, so the Untamed would be wiped out." I sniff.

Corin nods like it all makes sense. "That rifle she had, it didn't kill them. It stunned them. I'm certain of it now."

I look up into his dark eyes and nod. That tattooed Enhanced man I'd seen, it had been the same man.

"Do you think they're still alive?" I'm nearly crying as I mentally trace the lines of his face. "Esther? Or… or…?"

Or are we the last Untamed left in the world?

At last, Corin shrugs.

"We are alive," he says. "So it's possible. Anything is possible." But his eyes are dark, and the depths are so deep, and they speak more about the inevitability of the situation than he does. "But at least we've got each other. And we're not afraid of them any more. We know it's us against them. It always has been. They can't hurt us any more. They've already stripped us back to the bare rawness that we are. They can't damage us any more than they already have. We're stronger for it."

He holds me tightly. I rest my head against his chest— breathe in his musky scent, the faint shadows of cigarette smoke, and the rusty smell of blood along with my tears.

"We've got each other. We'll always have each other. I mean it, Sev. I'm always going to be here, with you."

Fragmented
Book 2 in the Untamed Series
By Madeline Dyer

After the terrible battle against the Enhanced Ones, Seven and Corin find themselves on the run. With the Enhanced closing in on them, Seven knows they can't survive on their own. So, when the opportunity to seek refuge with the Zharat, one of the last surviving Untamed tribes, arises, it seems like the perfect solution. After all, these people can offer them safety, medicine and food.

But the Zharat's lifestyle is a far cry from what Seven's used to. With their customs dictating that she must marry into their tribe, and her relationship with Corin breaking down, Seven knows she's got to do something before it's too late, if she wants to be with Corin. But that's easier said than done in a tribe where you're the outsider, and going against their rules automatically results in death.

And, with the Enhanced still out there, nowhere is truly safe for the Untamed. Least of all for the most powerful Seer in the world, and Seven soon discovers the true extent that people will go to in order to ensure that she's on their side in the War of Humanity.

Battling against the emerging web of lies, manipulation and danger, Seven must remember who she was meant to be. Her life has never been more at stake. Nor has humanity itself.

FRAGMENTED
Book Two in the Untamed Series
by Madeline Dyer

Chapter One

I awake to the feeling of feathers running along my shoulder blades. I take a few seconds to open my eyes, and when I do, the light is pure white around me. I blink several times, then roll over, careful not to disturb Corin's sleeping body next to me.

I sit up and look down at him. He's a big man, broad-shouldered, tall, and he takes up most of the mattress we are sharing. His eyes are shut, his eyelids smooth, his expression peaceful as his chest rises and falls with the security that the Untamed have only dreamt of for years. For several moments, all I can do is stare at him, drink in his appearance. He looks so relaxed, so peaceful, lost in sleep, that it's almost possible to forget what has happened... all the blood, the loss, the death....

Something cold washes over me, and I sit up straighter, looking around. I shiver. The temple is cold, but the air is clear. I can't see the spirits, but I know they're here.

I shut my eyes for a second. I try not to hear the echoing cries and screams and last gulps of breath. But I can't. It's all around me. The memories are too clear. I look down at Corin. I don't know how we managed to sleep. I can't even remember getting here, after—

The spirits are moving. I can't see them, but I can sense them. Coldness and icy particles. A flurry of movement against my bare arm. I rub at my eyes and lean back slightly. My mother's Seer pendant around my neck feels heavier, and more bulky than usual, but it's a reassuring presence. For a few seconds, all I can see in front of me is my mother.

The memory of how she looked yesterday. How reflective her eyes were.

How Corin shot her in the leg.

"Sev?"

I jump slightly at Corin's voice. He's awake, and he's looking at me.

"Are you okay?" He sits up, and draws me in closer to him.

I lean into his body, savoring his smell and the feeling of being close. I swallow hard, my fingers only shake a little. Am I okay? I bite my lip. Nothing's *okay* any more.

"I'm not sure," I say at last.

Corin nods. He understands. Of course he does. Because we're the only two left.

The sounds of last night's pain gets louder, echoing around us. I see a flash of gold—a chivra spirit—fly past us, and hear a soft whooshing sound. Then something cracks and cackles behind us.

The stone walls around us are tall and sturdy, secure, with no windows; it should be dark, yet it is light in here. As though the sun is hidden amongst the spirit-laden air.

It's getting colder. Much colder. Too cold. The wind's picking up. Howling. Something splashes over me and I taste rust. Corin flinches as something I can't see hits him. He holds me close to him, frowning deeply.

"What are they doing?" His voice is a low whisper, and his arm around my shoulder tightens, pulling me closer to the safety of his body.

I take a deep breath. Eviction. They want us gone. The message is clear. "We need to go."

"Have you seen it?" His dark eyes are intense with emotion.

I shake my head. I'm a Seer, but the Dream Land hasn't suggested that we go. I just know it. It's obvious. Obvious in the way the spirits are calling silently to us, crying for their own losses, and tightening the air around us.

Corin nods. "Okay." He gets up.

I, too, stand, and he holds me for a brief second. His touch is warm and it sends sparks through me. A new sensation.

I look up into his worn face. His warm brown eyes stare back at me. I don't know what exactly I mean to him—until recently, we'd never got on, but last night he'd said he *loved* me—but I know what he's thinking.

"We need to see if they're still out there," he says. He frowns, starts to choke. "We need to see… if she's… alive…"

I nod. I can barely think about it... the death... how the Enhanced One came for us... how, at the moment, Corin and I are the only survivors....

Only survivors. The words sound strange, unfamiliar, not right. There were four of us who fought the army of Enhanced, once Marouska revealed herself to be Raleigh's puppet. Now we're just two. I gulp. Three's dead—I saw him get shot. We need to bury his body. But Esther could be alive.

We have to find them.

We look toward the door. It is a small gap in the stone wall. Corin goes first, but he holds onto my hand tightly. So tight, I can almost feel his heart beating. With every step, the journey toward the door gets easier, and we walk faster; the spirits are pushing us.

As we walk, my eyes fall on the gun in his belt. There's a knife in my belt—one we found at the temple last night. We reach the door. Corin steps out, then pulls me with him into the outside world.

Sheets of rain smack into the bare skin on my face and shoulders, stinging me. The wind howls, grabbing me with icy fingers. Corin's grip on my hand gets tighter. He pulls me forward, then stumbles before regaining his balance. We stop once we're a good ten feet from the spirit temple and look around.

The air is hazy. But the landscape is clear. If I only look at the sky, I can pretend it isn't the remains of a battleground. It's quite easy really. Just looking at the soft blue hues that mist into one another, and the gentle orange and peach streaks that leap across the horizon... it's beautiful. But the land beneath it isn't.

"They've all gone—the live ones. It's just their bodies, left behind," Corin says after a few moments. He squeezes my hand.

I nod. I know he's talking about the Enhanced. Now I have to look. I have to see the bodies strewn across the landscape as though an unseen power picked them up and threw them down with such force that could break their lives. I look toward the hill, for my mother's body—can't see her.

I turn back to the other bodies—there are so many of them. It looks like a graveyard. A graveyard that goes on and on and on. Logic tells me that they suffered more than us; there are hundreds and hundreds of bodies, the majority of which have to be Enhanced.

And two of us Untamed, I know, survived. I squeeze Corin's hand. We did well. But not well enough. I focus my eyes onto a lump on the ground about three hundred feet away. That could be Three's body. I gulp. My brother. Dead. It doesn't feel right. It will never feel *right*.

I look up at Corin. His expression is unreadable.

"Do you think it's safe down there?" he asks, his voice husky. "To look through the bodies?"

I stare at the fallen soldiers. This shouldn't have been the answer. This shouldn't be what the world's come to when the majority of people want to use chemical augmenters to alter and control their own feelings, appearance and lives, and force the use of the augmenters onto everyone else. We shouldn't be fighting to keep our own lives pure.

Pure. I am not pure.

I gulp slightly at the memory. It's in the past. I have to focus on that. Corin says it wasn't my fault. But the memory—the feeling—of me unscrewing the lid of the vial and tipping the sweet, delicious augmenter into my mouth is beautifully strong....

But it's not right. I have to stay Untamed. I know that now.

"I don't know." At last, I look up at Corin. I'm tall for an Untamed girl, but he is taller. He is built like a true warrior: tall, and strong, and broad. Powerful. "The Enhanced have gone. I don't want to stay here long." I pause, trying to steady my breathing. "We should look quickly, then leave."

He nods, his eyes sombre. We start out for the scattered remains of humans, hand in hand. This is what our life is now: looking through bodies for our friends, and always being on the run, trying to find the safe place for the surviving Untamed, a place that doesn't exist. I don't even know where we're going to go next.

The ground is wet, and slightly squelchy underfoot. We go to each body together. If we can't see the victim's face—but the build and coloring of the body matches either Three or Esther—then one of us nudges the body over, until we can.

We keep doing this, over and over again. Five minutes. Ten. Twenty. And we'll keep doing it until we've found who we're looking for, or until we've turned over and looked at every body.

It's rhythmic, really. We're in a routine. Walking forward. Turning the body. Checking the face. Looking for the next body. Walking forward. Turning the body. Checking the face. Looking for the next body....

I haven't actually thought about what we're going to do when we find them, dead. When we're confronted with their bodies. I don't think Corin has either. It's not something that either of us want to think about. But we are, subconsciously. I imagine myself crying, falling down, fainting even? But it's not happening now, and it doesn't have to happen... I don't want to find Three or Esther's bodies.

After rolling over a particularly mutilated body with my foot—getting my only pair of shoes covered in congealed blood and guts—Corin nods toward a body. His face is ashen, and I follow his gaze.

I freeze. Cold air wraps around me as I stare at the body. It's *Corin*.

It looks exactly like him. He's lying at an angle, his dark hair semi-obscuring the deep gash across his forehead. The red on his white, gaunt skin is blinding. I feel heat rising in my throat, and, after looking at the dead Corin's open eyes—the mirrors are still bouncing light—I have to look away. A part of me is relieved. But only a small part. I squeeze Corin's fingers tighter.

"How?"

"They've cloned us all," Corin says. He pinches the bridge of his nose. "I suppose we leave DNA in the Enhanced towns when we're raiding. Or it's their appearance-altering augmenters...oh, Gods. This is messed up. Clones." He shakes his head and the early morning sun glistens in the flecks in his dark eyes. He looks down at the body. The body that's modeled on *him*. "They've made us into their soldiers... made us attack *us*."

For several minutes I can't say anything. I don't know what to say.

"Come on," Corin pulls me forward. "It's just another Enhanced."

But it's not. It's him. That Enhanced is—or rather was—identical to him... and if I lose Corin... I don't know what I'd do... the reality of our situation is terrifying. I don't want to be on my own.

"If we find them, we'll have to check their eyes... that they're not actually the Enhanced copies of them." Corin's hand shakes as he speaks, and I hold onto him tighter, as though my life depends on it.

We carry on checking the bodies. Corin never lets go of my hand. I am glad.

"Oh Gods." The words escape from my mouth before I can stop them. My eyes are already trying to examine the body, even from our distance away... short, cropped, dark hair... a muscular build, just like Corin's.

"Sev?"

Corin's hand tenses, all the muscles in his fingers going rigid against mine.

Then we're running.

It could just be a clone. It could just be a clone. It could just be a clone.

The mantra's shouting itself over and over again in my head.

But the more I look at the body, the more I am sure. My spine's tingling, my heart's pounding. I can hardly breathe.

The young woman's lying on her side, her back to us. Dirt and grime and dried blood cover her pale skin. Her arm twitches.

Esther.

It's Esther. She's alive. She's still alive. Hope erupts from within me. If she is then surely—

No. I saw my brother get shot. He's dead. We're not going to find him alive. We'll be lucky to find his body.

"Esther..." Corin says. His voice is strange, too quiet.

Then he throws himself down at his sister's side. I step around him, and look down at her. Dark eyes, like warm chocolate, just like Corin's, watch me. There's still life in them—Untamed life—but she's weak. Her face is divided in two by a long, bloody gash. Her skin's too pale, I realise with a jolt. Far too pale and—

A bullet is in her shoulder.

I can see it. A harsh glimpse of metal amongst the torn muscle, bloodied tissues and shredded skin. I feel bile rising in my throat. I bite my lip, and look around her. There are other bodies not far off; I don't recognize them.

Esther makes a gurgling sound, and rolls over onto her back with a blood-curdling scream. She looks at us, and I can't help but observe her. I watch her absorb Corin's appearance, noting the obvious relief on her face, and the way her shoulders sag slightly. Then her dark eyes move a fraction until she's looking at me.

"No." I look at her, shake my head. "No... no, Esther, *no.*"

Her eyes are on me, and she nods, and I know she knows what I'm thinking. And she knows that I know what she's going to say. But she can't say those words, she mustn't. I clench my fists, feel the blood vessels over the back of my hand bump up.

I don't want her to speak. Esther *can't* say the words.

Blood drips down the side of her face. Corin tears part of his shirt off, tries to dab all the redness away.

Her lips start moving, and her eyes are still on me. "Seven, please, he's alive—"

I shake my head. He can't be. Half of his face was shot off, and another bullet went into his abdomen. There's no way he could have survived that.

"He *is* alive. He was still breathing. I saw him, but—"

My spine clicks. Something strange happens to my legs and I fall as she speaks.

"They've taken him. The Enhanced Ones have taken Three."

ACKNOWLEDGEMENTS

There are a number of people who I wish to thank for their help, support and encouragement with this book. Without you all, I couldn't have done it.

Firstly, to my parents, and my brother, Sam: you have been wonderful, and given the best support and help I could've asked for. And thank you so much for answering my questions, no matter how many times I asked them, or how annoying I became. Thank you for believing in me.

I'd also like to thank the rest of my family and my friends. Your enthusiasm has been great and very uplifting!

Alison Heller Auerbach and Ela Summer, thank you so much for the many read-throughs, the detailed feedback and plot critiques. Equally, E. L. Mitchell and Ava Jae, thanks for answering my many questions at such short notice, and I am grateful for all the advice you have given me. To my lovely beta-readers—Josie Noonan, Anna Harms, Tim Bedford, Emmy Kuipers and Graeme Ing—your comments and suggestions were brilliant, and greatly appreciated.

Now onto my excellent editor, Deelylah Mullin: I'm so glad I got to work with you. Thank you so much for all your ideas, and your extraordinarily quick replies to my (many) emails. You've made the whole editing process a delight, and I'd love to work with you again.

To everyone at Prizm Books/Torquere Press who assisted in editing, proofreading, marketing, and design: thank you so much for believing in this book, and making it all possible.

And finally, to everyone else who has offered me support, encouragement, feedback and enthusiasm: thank you.

ABOUT MADELINE DYER

Madeline Dyer is a fantasy and science fiction writer, whose fiction has been published by several small presses. Having always had a love for mythology and fantasy, it seemed only natural that Madeline would write speculative fiction due to the endless possibilities and freedom this genre offers. A number of her short stories appear in print and ebook anthologies, as well as online. *Untamed* is her debut novel.

Madeline can be found online:
http://www.MadelineDyer.co.uk/
https://www.facebook.com/MadelineDyerAuthor/
https://www.twitter.com/MadelineDyerUK/
https://www.goodreads.com/author/show/7244204.Madeline_Dyer/
https://www.pinterest.com/MadelineDyerUK/

Untamed

Lightning Source UK Ltd.
Milton Keynes UK
UKOW06f2036210916

283538UK00009B/151/P